THE COSMIC
SEEDERS

DAVID L. PRITCHARD

 FriesenPress

Suite 300 - 990 Fort St
Victoria, BC, V8V 3K2
Canada

www.friesenpress.com

ISBN
978-1-5255-0486-0 (Hardcover)
978-1-5255-0487-7 (Paperback)
978-1-5255-0488-4 (eBook)

1. FICTION, SCIENCE FICTION, ALIEN CONTACT

Distributed to the trade by The Ingram Book Company

Dedication

th all due respect to reporters of UFO sightings, abductions by
s, and intellectual literature devoted to beings from outer space,
ink it would be best for us, as Earthlings, to enter the exploratory
se of space travel, willingly, and open minded, holding hands
e children being children, skipping together, towards a new play-
und. Confronted with weaponry puts any being into a prepared
vival mode, if not us, then them. Could we handle it? Are we
lomatic enough to endure it? I shudder at the alternative.

These puzzles have plagued my mind and provided the impetus
r this book. My wife, bless her Earthbound heart, provided the
neline, and the wall, from which I have bounced my off-the-wall
leas. **To Paula, I dedicate this book.** To our children, and their
children, I hope there is some truth in the essence of my story line:
- that extra-terrestrials do exist, on a more equal plane then they've
been portrayed, or dare I say, purported to be! Let's meet them and
greet them as a 'supreme' being intended - like Adam met Eve in the
Garden of Eden, in naked innocence of purpose; simple, and open-
minded. I hope for the happy outcome.

Acknowledgements

I am grateful to my family and friends, who have endured some trying times in helping to push my ideas out of my head and onto paper.

A special thank you to Dr. Ken Roberts for my second breath of life.

I thank FriesenPress for their assistance and their encouragement.

Why?

Did I reject his "gift"?
A gift of life so blessed;
"He bled to return from the dead!"
This lore of old
Is worth retelling;
Its value greater than gold.
Now, I stand and search
The Sky
To find the place
That answers
"Why?"
But,
Will I?

- by David L. Pritchard

THE PEACEKEEPER BESTOWED

Chapter 1

John lay prone on the forest floor to allow the grass to conceal him from the two stags. He focused the lance's sights on the closer one – a good twelve-point elk, and at least eight hundred pounds. His Smythen Laser Lance had a smart-sight, which displayed a tiny metallic disc icon in the viewer whenever it was locked-on target.

Resting his right cheek against his lance John thought, "Here, disc. Nice disc. Come to Papa."

Perspiration from a pore rolled irritatingly down his cheek. That warm, blood-filled cheek seemed like bait for a very persistent and pesky mosquito. Still he concentrated.

The backside of his red hunter's vest provided the mat for another predatory contest. A deadly brown spider illegally imported to North America from Australia dropped from an overhanging branch in pursuit of a very fat, very juicy, moth larva, which was slowly making its way across John's lumbar region. Damn it, extremely poisonous John thought. The spider stalked the larva. Still, he concentrated.

The larva ambled aimlessly across John's vest oblivious of the spider's focused and constant repositioning movements. No one noticed the head cocking motions of a raven roosting overhead.

An 800-pound stag; a warm-blooded cheek; a fat, juicy, moth larva; and a spider; all on nature's menu for some fine dining. Nature's food chain in action.

Canada's Tobatarioque Recdomes built way back in 2215 by Manitoba, Ontario, and Quebec were world-renowned tourist traps for sports enthusiasts and vacationers. Environmental maintenance rules were printed in the brochure upon entering these Recdomes. Fifteen-year imprisonment terms were imposed on convicted violators of the Recdome's environmental protection laws. Serving as a constant reminder was the presence of enforcement officers. This system John appreciated and was now basking in its efforts.

It was a tranquil scene in mid-October of 3349 A.D. An early morning haze hung over the meadows, while a thicker mist intermittingly covered the forest floor. Nearby the river flowed with a noisy rippling and gurgling, that covered the movements of clumsy hunters and unwary elk alike.

It was: - a cool morning but not cold, damp yet not wet. Hunting weather was easy to focus on prey. Another bead of perspiration followed the first one down John's cheek.

The two stags, wiggling their ears and noses, ambled to the water's edge to drink just 35 yards from John's scope.

The Lance's sights locked on John's target metallic disc on the stag's neck, that showed the Recdome's fulfillment of the Ministry of Natural Resources Regulations.

"Showtime," he thought, squeezing the trigger.

Suddenly, a laser-like energy bolt sizzled through 35 yards of forest mist to smash into the metallic 'locator' disc on the stag's lowered neck. The mosquito's proboscis plunged into John's sweaty skin. The spider's fangs pierced the larva's furry coat. And a black-feathered death swooped and scooped spider and larva together in a hardened beak. The stag's forelegs buckled dropping it face first into the water. John smacked his left cheek spattering blood and mosquito alike. The raven landed on a branch and gulped down a protein lunch.

No sooner had the bolt hit the disc then John was sprinting the distance between them to touch the Lance's butt to the elk's disc negating the knockout effects of the energy bolt. The other stag bolted safely away.

John sprinted fifteen seconds for cover behind some trees. He just made it. The stag had recovered in nine of those seconds and ferociously charged at John who was now behind two birch tree trunks. One second later and John's flesh might be peeling like the bark on the birch trees. The stag's sharply pointed antlers were its weapons and very threatening. John showed respect by slowly backing away.

Careful to keep the trees between him and 800 pounds of vengeful fury John matched pant for pant, while watching the elk for any signs of injury. Finding none he backed away for camp just as his ear's com-link signaled an urgent message. He sprinted on to camp.

Chapter 2

Venezuela's Angel Falls has 979 meters of an uninterrupted fall, and is picturesque for most grounded shutterbugs. It usually doesn't top the list for many mountain climbers. Janet Marshall and her two student assistants had thought the retrieval of a rare species of the Figwort family (Scrophulariaceae) would be a pleasant way to spend the weekend; while her husband John, spent a relaxing vacation hunting in a Canadian Recdome.

Hammering in the last of the pitons, two above and one below, the cave's mouth with the safety line off to one side, she slapped a carabiner on the ring slipping the safety line through and tugged twice.

"I have it," Ellis said into his helmet's microphone tugging more to check its tautness, than for acknowledgement.

As out of place like a black eye, the opening in the rock face was large enough to house Janet with her climbing and specimen collecting-gear for a yet-unnamed, rare hybrid of Slipperwort and Foxglove. Sunlight, at its best angle, only lit the first third of the cave allowing perfect environmental conditions for both of its main tenants - the plant which she traveled thousands of miles for, and a mutant, poisonous spider! She photographed the interior and took readings on her biometer; Rh 68%, 309.95°K, (36.8°C), gases showed normal, Vol. 96.8m^3, 87lumens and two life signs.

She picked the closest plant, and, then carefully examined each plant by moving it around in her gloved hands. Swiftly and deftly she set about her task with the utmost concentration. Only the fact that her direction of sight was toward the rear of the cave enabled her to catch a glimpse of a telltale set of eight eyes staring at her from the shadows.

Janet hated spiders. The shadow moved.

Simultaneously Janet shrieked, then jumped out of the mouth of the cave. The rope first stretched and strained at the sudden force exerted by her weight pulling taut on the pitons just above the cave. As if expecting trouble, luckily Janet had hammered a double anchor of pitons. The second one held but the first one pulled out of the rock face knocking her helmet from her head on its way to the precipice's bottom almost 3,000 feet below. Her safety belt broke her fall like a hangman's noose, literally snatching her from a smashing death.

In the excitement, she lost track of the shadowy object. She let out a blood-curdling scream for help from her assistants, the nearest being twenty feet above the cave. She tried desperately to angle her body perpendicularly to the rope to give maximum distance between her and her fast climbing arachnid stalker. She quickly took a carabiner ring to slip it on the rope, and let it slide down to the collection bag, hopefully knocking the spider's hold on the rope.

"Ah-h, success!"

She watched the spider fall towards the bag and seemingly bounce to one side of it. The cacophony of jungle noise subsided, as if in recognition of her triumph. She thought, "There will be no tasting of my blood today, my arachnid friend."

Ellis, the closer assistant, spoke to her from three feet above her asking, "Janet, what the hell happened?"

"I had cut my last plant sample to examine for parasites when I caught a 'glow' of eyes looking back at me from a shadowy shape at the back of the cave. The hair at the back of my neck seemed to stand on end. Then I saw it move. So, I jumped. When I looked around to see if it followed, I saw it climbing up the rope which was holding the collection bag."

"So, what was it?" Ellis pressed.

"Ell, I'm not sure; however, I don't want you to think it's my phobia of spiders that's clouding my judgment, but I think it was a Bird Spider or large Huntsman Spider."

"What!? A *Theraphosa blondi,* up here?" he asked, disbelievingly, pointing at the cave. "Must be a mutant. So, what did you do to it?"

"I took out a carabiner, put it on the collection bag rope, and let it fall along the rope to the bag, to knock the spider from the rope. And … it did!" she said with a triumphant lilt in her voice and a toothy grin.

"Remember what John said the last time we went climbing?" Ellis asked.

The jungle noise below had gone deafeningly silent, as if punctuating Ellis' question.

"Yeah, something about, 'spiders would make the best mountain climbers' because they constantly anchor themselves to the surface that they're traveling on." Realizing what she had said, she looked back at the collection bag and saw a set of legs just appearing over the rim of its girth.

They reacted simultaneously. She screamed and flinched away.

Ellis dropped below Janet; she disconnected the rope from her waist, but held on to it. As if previously choreographed, their movements were well timed. Ellis reached the bottom of the bag, and connected a safety line to the reinforced hole at its bottom. Janet held the top rope until the last possible second. The spider climbed the rope. At a precise moment, Janet tossed the rope away from herself and Ellis, while he cut the rope at the top of the bag, allowing rope and spider to fall to the jungle floor below. Janet breathed a loud sigh of relief.

"Jan, you said that was a Bird Spider?"

"Yeah, and if I'm not mistaken, it was a female. Do you think it had…"? They both looked slowly upwards to the mouth of the cave and saw little black legs appearing over the edge and shouted in unison, "Baby spiders? Spiderlings."

Ellis scrambled back up his rope as fast as he could toward the mouth of the cave, keeping his eye on two of the baby spiders. With one deft movement of his left hand, he removed a specimen container from the assortment of lids he had attached to his belt and clamped it over the two spiders climbing up the rock face near him. Triumphantly he crowed to Janet, "I trapped two of them!" The other spiders escaped in various directions. A frustrated grimace soon crept across Ellis' face. He realized he had yet to put the lid on the container.

Janet grinned and started for the top of the cliff. Ellis played out some rope, and tied it off while holding the jar against the rock face with his leg. In this position, he removed a sample lid from his belt to place it on the jar. Plants and spiders out of their normal habitats. How and why, he wondered?

While engrossed in his work he felt a tickling sensation up the backs of his legs and passed it off as flies or mosquitoes pestering him.

While he was safely storing the jar in his collection sack, he noticed two sets of legs passing under the hems of his shorts. By the time, he reacted to brush away what was happening, he felt spider fangs piercing the skin of his scrotum. Pain free but cursing aloud, he used his hand to cover his genitals and squeezed hard. A mix of red and tawny-colored soupy fluid, oozed out from under his hems to flow down his legs.

"Shit!" was all he said, and climbed to the top of the precipice.

Looking at him as he was approaching the edge of the plateau, Diego had to ask, "*Señor Ellis, se-e-nor, ha-ha-hah!* "Señor Ellis, what happened? You look like you shit yourself, se-e-eñor! Ha-ha-ha," Diego mocked.

Ellis quipped back while glancing at Jan, "It seems I was bagged too." Catching a knowing look on Janet, Ellis leaned toward her as she whispered in his ear, "I'll rip the rest of your balls off later." They both chuckled.

Jan and Ellis put their hands to their right ears in response to the internal vibration from their com-links and started for camp immediately.

Chapter 3

John was approaching the Recdome's gatehouse and swore under his breath when he saw the checkout queue. This called for some special action.

"Pardon me folks, but would you let me go to the front of the line? I seem to be bleeding a little."

They turned to look at John, and saw a birch bark branch protruding from an ugly abdominal wound, spewing blood. He was doing a poor job of trying to hide it.

"Oh, how awful!" the closest person shrieked. "Let him through!" she exclaimed.

John feigned his best wounded act, and was kindly assisted by two of the burliest men in the lineup.

"You're not doctors, are you?" he asked, weakly eyeing the weary looking hunters.

"Nope. But we can remove that toothpick from your gut, mister. Say the word, ya'ear." he drawled, returning the cigar to his beard-covered dental gap.

"I'm always accused of being a hypochondriac, who just fakes illness. I do look wounded, don't I?"

"Mister, if yuh ain't wounded, then me 'n' my buddy ain't survivalists. An' we bin survivalists for a mighty long time. And we know wounded," he said, spitting again.

"If yuh want, mister, why, me 'n' Bert here could get yuh pas' checkout real fast!"

"Oh, I don't want to be any more trouble to you both. Just leave me in the office. I'm sure they will recognize the priority of my situation. But, thank you both, very much." John replied, hurriedly. "Pleased to have made your acquaintance, Bert." John extended his hand in gratitude, while grasping for support on their shoulders. "Uh, you too mister..."

"Fred. Fred Thompson," he said, completing John's extended handshaking introduction query, while supporting John's other shoulder.

By way of distraction, he said, "By the way, I noticed you dropped your personal credit cards just outside the gatehouse doors." John said, while struggling to stand against the wall.

They looked back at the doorway and saw their cards on the path where John was pointing. "Well, here's your lance, mister. If yuh ever get down to Texas, yuh might want to look us up. We run the Rockin' Rhino Horn exotic animal enclosure near old Dallas."

"Yeah, we'll show yuh some southern hospitality, if yuh don't lose yer appetite for it after that wound there is taken care of, mister ...?"

"Marshall. John Marshall. Yeah, I'll do just that and thanks for your help," he smiled. When they discovered they had leaves in their hands everyone would yell at them to get to the back of the line. John's wound disappeared immediately.

John stepped up to the self-serve identification booth and pressed the button labeled "Card Declined" in favor of the "Retinal Scan" which was usually reserved for emergency personnel. The scanner crossed right to left and back again across his right eye. The computer voice stated matter-of-factly, "One moment." Then it said, "Mr. John Marshall, enter the security room on your left."

When he entered the room, he placed his lance in a special metal container against the wall, which automatically locked it in place with internal metal clamps. Then he removed the "disarm" disc from the butt end. When he placed the disc on the counter, an attendant said from behind the doorway off to the left, "Hi, Mr. Marshall. I'm just finishing up your trophy. There we go." She wheeled out the copy of the Elk's Head trophy on a cart.

An arched eyebrow betrayed John's masculinity while his eyes narrowed in on a very attractive, very short uniform, struggling to cover a beautiful young lady. He made a mental note to buy Jan a special gift for those 'intimate moments' that seemed to be getting rarer as time went on. At the right height for John's taste in women, she captivated him with her sea blue-green eyes, and gracious personality.

Repeating herself, she teased, "Would you like to take it with you, Mr. Marshall, or shall I have it delivered?"

The background sound of Muzak, other people talking, and the attendant trying to remove the Genetic Restructuring and Identification Disc (G.R.I.D.) from his hand, brought him out of his trance-like stupor as he stammered a reply.

"Delivered, uh, oh yeah. Please deliver it...uh, you have my address on record, uh, don't you...Miss..?"

"Sure." Pointing to her nameplate pinned to her uniform's left lapel, "Bustee! Truly Bustee!" she charmingly filled in for him.

"Yes, of course! I, uh, had my mind on other things," he quickly replied, clearing his throat, while handing her the G.R.I.D.

The sheen of her raven-like hair showed when parted over her shoulder, as she placed the plate in the return basket under the counter. John saw the prefix of her genetic code near the nape of her neck. She was a Bione. Standing erect again she smiled, eyes sparkled, and stated inquisitively, "See you again, Mister Marshall?"

"Sure."

She was a biologically engineered, reconstructed clone nicknamed a Bione, which came from the idea that anyone authorized could buy one. All genders could experience all human emotions, concerns, injuries, *etc.* but not reproduce. They could show tenderness, sensitivity, sensuousness, and sexual ardor. And they never forget.

John snapped back to reality. "Uh, yes, excuse me, but are there any C.C.S. links here, Miss Truly?" he asked, looking around the room sheepishly.

"Yes, sir, through those doors in the main lobby of the Gatehouse Inn. Did you wish to settle your account here or there, sir?" she asked almost teasingly.

Wanting to contact S.E.T.I.A. as soon as possible, John replied, "In there, thank you."

"Very good, sir. Hope you enjoyed your stay and you'll return soon!"

"I'll do that, Truly, and could you put my trophy in storage for me?" John asked again, smiling purposefully. He glanced back to see her climbing a ladder. John walked through the doorway and into the main lobby as Truly nodded her acquiescence.

He inserted his card into a C.C.S. link and the screen blinked reading, "Pick up handset," with options available to him.

Putting the cordless handset to his ear, John obeyed the instructions to state his name for voice recognition purposes. An electronic field engulfed him making him impervious to any type of 'eaves-dropping.'

"Good morning, Mr. Marshall. Patrick's Col. Harding wants to see you by 1500 GMT! An air car will be here to pick you up and ask you how your ear is. Thank you, sir." Click.

The handset went dead and John placed it in its cradle. He thought to himself, Patrick Air Force Base in Florida by 1500 Greenwich Mean Time to see Colonel Harding? SETIA's #2 man, h-m-m-m, I wonder what it's about?

Chapter 4

Jan, Ellis, and Diego were following the river bank towards camp when they could hear a mechanical whistling or whirring sound. Sensing the possibility of danger Ellis, a Bione and a S.E.T.I.A. agent, ensured that Jan was led to safety into some nearby foliage. A military Hummingbird hovered overhead while two others silently circled the area. They were the problem solvers.

"Mrs. John Marshall?" the external speaker system announced. Again, it blared, "Janet Marshall?"

Janet, and her two assistants revealed themselves from the foliage even though the Hummingbirds had them on surveillance cameras. Touching down on the plateau's surface, the engines silenced leaving a sudden calm. Two military officers stepped out from a side hatchway and removed their sun shielding helmets from their heads. They walked toward Jan, Ellis, and Diego.

"Mrs. Marshall? How's your ear feeling?"

Recognizing the cryptic question, Ellis turned to Diego, "Why don't you finish taking these things back to camp? I think we're going to be busy for a while and make sure you bill us for another 5,000 credits to keep for yourself."

"Si, Señor Ellis. No problem. Shall I wait for you in my village?"

"Yes, we'll contact you later. But don't decline other assignments while waiting for us, okay Diego? And Diego, it's true, you are the best guide."

"Gracias, Señor, gracias," Diego replied, with a broad smile of appreciation forming on his face.

Ellis stood by and watched Diego depart toward his village. He knew Diego was being watched and would soon be joined on his return. Ellis waved one last goodbye, reseated his sunhat on his head after wiping his brow and turned toward Jan and the two military officers who were waiting patiently.

He walked toward them while observing them carefully for Jan's safety. She would never know that John had requisitioned him as her permanent bodyguard, and of late he'd had to do some silly stuff to keep up the pre-text of incompetence that only a student working with her would display. He read the word Patrick on their baseball caps and noted the rank of captain on their epaulets and the metal letters SETIA. Ellis suspected something askew.

Ellis saw their eyes looking at his wet and messy groin area and realized he must look a sight. Smiling he tried to take control of the situation, "Believe me gentlemen, it's not what you think. So, what or, who sent you?"

"Directive from C.O.W.A., Sir," one replied, quickly. Ellis mentally noted his military behaviour. Ellis also noted the Council of World Affairs shoulder-insignias and expected the worst.

"Sir, Ma'am, we've been directed to bring you back to Patrick Air Force base in Florida, WFIN," the taller captain said.

"To see whom?" asked Jan adding, "and force won't be necessary!" while glancing at their side arms.

The other captain stated, "Sir, Ma'am, we're in an HB4M Hummingbird Helicopter and are authorized to fly full throttle on our return. Our escorts are HB5M Attack Heloships to resolve any problem situations which might arise. We can only assume sir, that with the capabilities of these two ships we shouldn't have to worry about most unexpected contingencies on our return. Therefore, both of you are what we call HP Packages meaning high priority."

"Well, we hope that won't be necessary, Captain," interjected Jan, "so we better get going."

"Colonel Harding will brief you upon our arrival. Also, I'm authorized to tell you that your husband should be en route at the same time as us, Mrs. Marshall."

"Sir, would you like to clean up a little while en route to Patrick? If so, we could fill a water bottle and ..."

"That won't be necessary, Lennox," Ellis replied, cutting him off.

"Sir?" the captain responded, slowly reaching for his side arm. As he did so, Ellis placed himself between Lennox and Janet, and saw that the other pilot standing just behind Lennox already had his sidearm drawn and poked it into Lennox's back interrupting and halting his motion. With his free hand he removed Lennox's sidearm from his hand.

"What's this about, Ellis?' Jan whispered.

"Procedures, Jan. Those Hummingbirds are only used for one of two purposes. To either wipe out enemy locations or equipment, which are otherwise impossible to reach without detection, or to be a part of a non-operation," Ellis explained.

"A non-operation?" queried Jan.

"Ma'am, Sir, if you would just board the craft there I'll be in to join you shortly," directed the one captain.

They turned and walked to the craft and Ellis' keen hearing heard a 'thup' and figured that Lennox had been killed. They walked toward the craft as Ellis answered her question while climbing in.

"It goes something like this, "All covert operations may be questioned by the General Council or by a member, if he discovers some information or whatever; it really doesn't matter how the information came to light, but rather that it was just exposed and ..." They were inside the craft and Ellis covered Jan's mouth tightly from behind, whispering in her ear, "Ssshhhh, we'll talk later with John," as he pointed to various surveillance devices.

Just then the other captain appeared in the hatchway giving them both a penetrating stare as they looked at the devices then silently got into his seat and prepared to get under way.

"Were you two close?" asked Ellis.

"Brother-in-law!" he snapped, "make sure your belts are fastened. We're going to do Mach 2 to 'The Keys', after which I'll feel safer and slow down so you can clean up before we land."

Jan gave Ellis an inquisitive look and he returned it with a 'later, not now' expression on his face.

Chapter 5

John waited outside the main entrance/exit to the Recdome preferring to wait on the bench by the parking lot where he could expect his vehicle to arrive with a valet. No one had owned a vehicle since 2175 A.D.

John's air car came from one of the rental companies that most federal government departments routinely used for diplomats. Having the latest in aerodynamic design, with its sleek, swept-back lines, and shiny black coloring, seemed interrupted by a simple card slot into which a customer would insert his 'Personal Credits' plastic card. John did so, and the smoked glass screen flashed "ENTRY/ CIRCLE CHECK". John pressed CIRCLE CHECK and stood back.

The on-board computer's feminine voice had a complete audio, interactive, discussion session with the potential driver, while he watched the vehicle turn clockwise in front of him. The internal lighting illuminated the part under discussion. John went one step further, and requested the Vehicle Computer Analyzer, (VCA), to display "WIRING" and "UNDERBODY". First, he pressed the icon for wiring and the car's exterior skin became transparent, showing the wiring, illuminated, under the surface and into the deeper interior. The voice prompted, "Do you wish a connection, or a circuit isolated and displayed?"

John responded, "When was the car last used, and where?"

"108.5 hours ago, from Toronto, Canada to Syracuse, New York, United States of America for a 'return' pleasure trip. Duration was 78 hours of total usage," was the reply.

"Has this car had any maintenance work done to it that required alteration of any sort to the original wiring specifications?" he pressed.

"Yes. Replacement of the power cell." The VCA displayed it.

"Magnify the circuitry and ignition connections, please." As it slowly showed the power plant circuitry and connections John noted a small metallic disc on the firewall mixed in with the ignition connections. Pausing the display, John requested further magnification of the disc. When magnified, he read the lettering on the disc, "COWA-ESD 14." John knew the vehicle was 'bugged' and requested the purpose of the disc from the computer.

It replied, "Unknown."

"If the disc is removed, will the circuitry be compromised?"

"Yes. The remaining wiring will be intact, but the disc provides part of the analytic programming."

"Can the disc be replaced with another of similar metal but not the same type of disc?"

"The disc cannot be touched without the expressed written authorization, personal witnessing of removal, and installation, and permanent recording of the event by COWA, or authorized agent.

John went to the side of the car again and touched the prompt signal, 'ENTRY.' The outline of a door formed, separated from the car, and rose upwards. He entered and sat into a body-molding gelseat, which formed around him as he sat down. Body restraint belts were fastened, after which the door lowered and sealed with a hiss and a slight 'ppuupp' sound. The car hummed to 'life' providing complete interior climate control and atmosphere for his riding pleasure as requested. A head apparatus secured his head for driving as there was no steering wheel; steering was mentally attained or automatic, while exterior sensors maintained complete collision avoidance.

From the drop-down personal comforts screen, John selected temperature, air pressure, humidity, and classical music like Bach and R. Wagner's most popular works. Also selected was a video disc on the <u>History of Man's Quest for the Stars</u>, and a variety of action-adventure movies. Finally, he touched the screen for fastest routing, having an arrival time of 1445 hrs. GMT on the date required.

After seeing to his riding comfort, the computer prompted for 'PAYMENT'. He inserted his plastic card into the slot in the dash and the computer read his S.E.T.I.A. priority. The computer requested his destination. He said, "Patrick Air Force Base, Florida, U.S. of A." The computer replied with 'Total Travel Time of 32.66 hrs." and automatically selected AIR RIDE, PRIORITY CLEARANCE. Spitting the plastic card out the screen showed TRAVEL COST: 9500 Credits withdrawn on the SPECIAL SERVICES ACCOUNT.

The computer voice announced, "At present Mr. Marshall, there are forty-five thousand vehicles using the routing chosen and this is the lightest traveled." Simultaneously the air compressor, which was mounted in the front engine compartment, powered up, turned the car 180°, speeding it away to head for the Border Crossing at Sault Ste. Marie.

"Enjoy your trip, Sir", said the computer's voice.

The Wasp selected a 'Priority Vehicles Only' air tube and John felt his ears pop when he entered. With the tube's hatch closed and sealed, John looked at the dash display screen showing the car on "Air Drive" doing a speed of 368 km/h and just relaxed and smiled. He should be there on time and comfortable.

Quickly John plugged in his idea of arrival time, 1445 hrs. that very afternoon and again the computer spat his credit card out, as if in a huff. Travel time had been cut to 3.26 hrs. and the tube was cleared and pressurized.

Chapter 6

When people reflect on their lives they usually do so during times of solitude or periods of monotonous inactivity, such as a long non-participating drive or flight. Under clear skies and warm sunshine Janet now had *that* type of time for just pondering.

Janet looked back in history to the twentieth and twenty-first centuries and tried to imagine what she had seen on the holo-discs in its context of the period. Famine, droughts, disease, natural disasters and wars had a culling effect of the human population. Progress in technology and science went in leaps and bounds, far surpassing sociological advancement. The world's human population soon surpassed the optimum level.

Still space exploration could not be rushed.

She reflected on the advancements in the medical field and the needs of people for treatments of ailments, which could only arise out of an over-populated world. Catchwords and phrases such as global warming, DNA tracking and identification, environmental pollution, recycle-reuse-recover, and cloning were tossed around without having the appropriate impact on the population that it should have had.

The devastating earthquakes to the North American continent had a severe effect on the Great Lakes system destroying Niagara Falls forever but creating another lake now known as the Lake of the Great Divide.

But it was the methodical, step by step process that the involved nations of Earth and the North American Space Agency (NASA) took to put mankind in a better position to explore space, which had focused Janet's 'reflective' concentration. As she reviewed what the history discs had presented to her, she tried to put into perspective the great developments in the fields of some of the life sciences such as anthropology, biology, medicine, psychiatry, psychology, and sociology. The equipment used to perform experiments and provide living quarters for the scientists involved, necessitated an unprecedented co-operative involvement on the part of many countries.

Still, space exploration couldn't, shouldn't, and wouldn't be rushed. Delayed by economics and political setbacks the settlement known simply as "The Martian Station", outlined in old NASA scheduling, soon became a reality under "The Council". The Council of World Affairs was formed after events involving the United Nations made the UN appear to the world to be the weak "peacekeeping busybody" their critics had made them out to be. Furthermore, the stronger UN members who could provide the muscle soon became shunned as greedy, power-peddling, hegemonic cultural bullies.

In 2285, a motion from the UN membership 'to disband the UN's charter in total', and then reform as the Council of World Affairs, soon became the single most important event in the history of mankind. Only later in the 24th century would the world benefit. Unfortunately, a world war, WWIII, which ushered in the 23rd Century, occurred before this benefit would be fully appreciated.

Looking at Ellis, she thought of the first human clones and how they were used for medical purposes providing 'the medical necessities' such as blood, and body parts used for vital surgical procedures and during post-disaster situations such as cave-ins, wars, earthquakes, and so on. She shuddered like someone had walked on her grave.

Earth's over-population and hegemonic cultural tactics 'excused' authorization for things, which would not normally happen: - DNA mapping of the human genome; its info storage, and retrieval; personal identification, at first of certain criminal elements, and lately, of every living thing from all five kingdoms.

"Excuse me, ma'am, but would you both prepare yourselves for landing in six minutes?" interjected the hummingbird's pilot.

"Wha,' oh, yes of course," Jan replied, straightening herself from her reverie. Remembering Ellis' predicament she asked, "Do you happen to have a Type B first aid kit here, captain?"

Before answering he gave Ellis an obvious racist glare and then said, "Yeah, it's in the cabinet under his seat."

"Let's get something straight, Captain," Ellis demanded. "If you've got something against biones or me in particular I really wish you'd out with it because I don't particularly like you either."

"Ellis!" Jan snapped.

He shook his head ever so slightly but his look at her commanded 'silence, and to follow his lead.'

"Listen, if it weren't for biones like you my brother-in-law would be alive," the pilot snapped back.

Jan reached under Ellis' seat and pulled out the metal box with the Red Cross logo and large B in reflective tape below it. Ellis was already pulling his shorts down.

Wondering if he had read him right Ellis reassuringly said to him, "You mean you don't know about us?"

"Know what?" the pilot said, cutting him off.

"That he isn't dead. Just stopped!" Jan interjected.

"What the hell are you talking about? I shot him point blank and he was propelled backwards almost four feet and at least two feet off the ground you mush head."

"Maybe you should contact our escorts when you get a chance and you might be surprised," Ellis said.

"Not if I find out that he's a bione," the pilot sneered.

"Why? What do you have against biones?" asked Ellis. "Other than the obvious that we aren't 100% human."

"Simple, whenever something goes wrong with one of you, it's always at a time when it's difficult to turn you off, like in combat. Or during sex?"

"Is that it or is there more like you just don't possess the ability to recognize us on sight for instance?" Ellis needled. "Or maybe you're just plain afraid of us." Ellis saw that he was becoming agitated and pressed further. "That's it, isn't it? You're afraid of us because you don't know how to recognize us or better yet, control us. So, what was it with you? A violent situation or one of intimacy like sex?"

"Ellis, back off, will you? And hold still, while I try to put you back together," Jan snapped at him while trying to hold his scrotum with one hand and 'glue' it into place with the other. Aqueous spider silk was fast acting so, comical as it looked with Ellis' shorts down and his genitals exposed, the serious side of surgery always occupied Jan's mind first.

Ellis glanced at the pilot's fingers to check for signs of a relationship ring; none.

"...with a pleasure ..."

"You bloody obnoxious ... if I wasn't flying this bucket ..."

"Ellis!"

"...doll in a sex dome. The only thing that could possibly get you this ticked off Captain, is that you must have shut her down somehow or other. A word maybe? That's it, isn't it? You shut down a pleasure doll during a moment of intimacy and it triggered a previous traumatic event. Right, Captain?"

"Look, I don't know how you ..."

"Captain, let's get one thing straight."

Jan was listening to the dialogue with eager anticipation of its outcome. She knew Ellis was in his element.

"Neither one of your events is your fault. Your brother-in-law was shut down. Stopped! And whatever happened back at the dome was mere coincidence. You probably don't even recall the words you spoke to the doll and she probably just slumped where she was, assuming it was a she. Right?"

"You friggen piss-ass %@##!"

Sensing a potential out-of-hand situation on the part of the captain, Jan squeezed Ellis' scrotum getting his attention, "Ellis, back off, will you?"

"Captain I want you to watch this, if you can, okay?"

"Watch what?" he replied, glancing over at Ellis.

Ellis looked at Jan and said, "Shut me down Jan, will you?"

"What?! Are you crazy?"

"She's going to kill me captain, right before your eyes. If you just remain calm she's going to shoot me with your sidearm if you wouldn't mind?" Ellis said, extending his hand to receive the sidearm.

"If this was under any other circumstance mister?"

"Don't worry captain, you must know we must be special otherwise you wouldn't be picking us up like this," Ellis said soothingly.

After handing Ellis his sidearm the captain kept his back-up weapon handy.

Turning to Jan, Ellis said, "Aim for the heart, Jan. It's alright, don't worry." Ellis' eyes were looking at her intently and she understood his unsaid message.

She picked up the gun, set it for maximum, aimed and fired.

"Good God! What's the matter with you two? Are you both crazy?" The captain vented the hummingbird's interior because of the stench of burnt flesh.

"Shit, now how the hell are we going to explain the blood on us and your dead friend here?" the captain asked incredulously, as he watched the blood spilling out of Ellis' chest where his heart had just been.

Jan kept stitching Ellis' scrotum together until she was finished behaving as if she had just shot her patient with another anesthetic and no more.

"How can you keep sewing his fucking balls on as if nothing's happened?"

"Because nothing has captain, other than the fact that you've just extended my mending session because you must have missed a briefing session on biones. You see captain, Ellis' point here, is that you've experienced a lot of grief and displayed bigotry, because you missed a critical information session in the past. What he wanted to show you was that he can't be killed in the sense that you or I can be killed; he was just shut down so that he can no longer operate. What is supposed to happen is that Ellis gets returned to Bionic Reclaiming, BR. However, since we seem to be equipped with a "Combat Level" kit I can give him a heart with this pacemaker and bypass pump," Jan said, holding a beigey-pink fluid-filled bag labelled AH90.

Examining the bag closer, she noted the separate pocket containing the 90-Day batteries was empty causing her to go ballistic. "Where the hell are the god-damned batteries, Captain?" she asked, screeching at him and practically slamming the bag in his face.

Yelling his reply, "Look lady, I just fly this bucket wherever, and whenever, I'm told. The bloody ground crew is supposed to check it and re-stock it, but for what it's worth to you those cannons use the same batteries for back up power. Just pop open the rear door of their electronic guidance and aiming device. It's labelled EGAD."

"How friggen appropriate!" Opening the starboard cannon's door, she saw two batteries and a button labelled Power Test. She pushed it and took some solace in seeing the L. E. D. flash "100%". She pulled one for the surgical procedure, and took the other as back up.

She looked back at the captain furtively and left the door open. Damn, she thought, she could explain their absence, and grinned ever so slightly. She quickly returned her attention to Ellis, and removed the Steri-gun, and surgical iodine from the kit.

Placing the batteries on sterile gauze pads she loaded, aimed the gun and fired, simultaneously sweeping Ellis' chest with the beam.

She splashed his chest with iodine, thinking to herself like boiling water during birth, useless but something to do!

"Captain, for the next twenty minutes see if you can fly this thing level and steady." She worked steadily but fast, severing tissue and bone around the heart for accessibility; repairing burnt and damaged tissue; and finally, inserting the pacemaker and mini-pump.

The pilot took the opportunity to advise Patrick of the delay and increase the fresh air supply.

She thought damn you, Ellis. Why do you always have to be so damn melodramatic with COWA's military enlisted? Always the teacher.

Between Jan's surgical expertise and flying the Hummingbird, the pilot had plenty to occupy his attention. She worked fast and efficiently, not wasting time or movement. She knew each second his neural system went without nourishment beyond thirty minutes, could risk his performance upon waking: *ergo* he would have to go to BR. Up to that point she had full authority in decision making.

The Atlantic was calm today giving rise to a 'steady' weather situation. Taking advantage of this the captain put the hummingbird on auto-pilot and notified his escorts. He checked his watch and advised her on each five-minute interval. Christ's sake how do they function? Maybe I better do some reading when I get back.

"Fifteen minutes, ma'am," the captain said, finally showing some respect.

"Captain, in a couple more minutes I'm going to 'kick-start' Ellis."

"Don't worry doc; I'll not be adversarial."

"That will be the least of our worries, captain. We better hope your equipment is up to scratch when the power sensor indicated 100% availability. Can this thing fly on auto-pilot for a while, when I rouse him?"

He said, "Yes, it is already."

Closing his chest she liberally spread a salve on what was the fissure and watched it 'til it 'took'. She tried to pull the two sides apart and was satisfied the closure was secure. She thought, if only our ancestors knew of aqueous spider silk. Socially unaccepted in its making, but fully embraced after its surgical discovery and subsequent improvement.

"The ship is on AP and it's just gone twenty minutes." Then smiling at her as he unbelted himself, he said, "You've got some technique, Jan. May I call you Jan?"

"Thanks." Pointing to where she wanted him, she said, "When I 'start' him he's very strong and he's going to grab his chest and gulp air as if drowning. I just don't want him ripping the fissure open, understand?" She grabbed the starter from the kit bag, and placed it on his chest. "Ready?"

"Ready," he said, taking Ellis' arms and holding them down.

Jan pushed the button. The pilot was astonished by Ellis' strength as he recovered. Ellis practically threw him like a ten-pound bag of potatoes against the side hatchway causing the pilot to hit the handle with his arm as he fell. At the same time, Jan was yelling at Ellis for calm explaining everything was okay.

Ellis was coming back to life and was gasping for air. In all this commotion Ellis sat up in time to see the side hatchway opening and starting to pull the pilot out, without realizing it was he who accidentally threw him against the doorway. He quickly shoved Jan aside and grabbed the pilot's ankle, just as he was falling out the hatchway.

Unceremoniously Ellis lifted the pilot straight up and pulled him back inside to let him fall into a seat, while he closed the hatch. Just before it slammed shut Ellis noted the astonished look on the face of one of the escort pilots. Jokingly he flexed his left bicep muscle and smiled. Expecting to be pounced on by both Jan and the pilot, Ellis turned around sheepishly to get his penance but at the sight greeting him he started to laugh.

The pilot was upside down in the passenger seat behind his, while Jan was very unladylike shoved headfirst into the pilot's foot control well with her nose pressed up against the glass. Righting the pilot they both helped Jan back to her seat to regain her composure.

With both of his passengers back in their seats everything seemed to calm down until they looked at Ellis and saw him for the first time. Jan had forgotten to wash him off and zip up his shorts. The tension of the situation released itself in gales of laughter.

Checking his instruments the pilot looked at his passengers and said, "Two minutes to Patrick AFB and the 'old' man."

"You wouldn't happen to know where I could lay my hands on a clean pair of pants or shorts would you, Captain?" Ellis asked while they were all still chuckling.

"You know Ellis, I guess you're all right for a bag of bones." They all laughed again.

Jan sensed the pilot would catch up on his 'info' sessions.

Chapter 7

Patrick Air Force Base located on the Atlantic Ocean side of Florida was important enough for the Council of World Affairs to consider it for a base of operations for SETIA. And apparently, William Jefferson Harding Jr. was important enough for the Joint Chiefs of Staff of the U. S. to consider him for the promotion to Colonel and take command of 'Patrick'.

If the Search for Extra Terrestrial Intelligence Agency, SETIA, was <u>not</u> involved in this transfer, then there wouldn't be any involvement from the Joint Chiefs of Staff. SETIA needed someone who could look you straight in the face and tell you the absolute truth, and nothing but the truth, but you still wouldn't believe him.

Ditto with the base. On the outside, it looked 'normal', even with the three Hummingbirds parked there. After all, they were just parked like they weren't staying long anyway; but long enough to refuel after dropping off 'a package'. And just to keep up appearances, the 'package' was greeted by a maintenance crew sergeant who gave instructions as if he were talking to everyday visitors. SETIA was an expensive, politically festering 'boil' that some members of COWA wanted done away with, but still was necessary for the protection of the planet.

This was the reason why the Security Council ordered one of its departments to keep SETIA locations and operatives under constant surveillance. Their agents were mostly biones whose senses were extremely keen like those of the grubby, greasy-looking ground crewman preparing one of the escort Hummingbirds for refueling.

"Sergeant Chong, is it?" Ellis asked, reading the surname sewn into the right chest area of his orange coveralls.

"Yes sir, Ed Chong at your service. Tires, lube, refueling, and complete circle check walk-about, at no extra charge for vehicles with that logo, indicating the Air Force Wings. What can I do for you, sir?"

"I'm impressed," said Ellis, smiling at Jan and the pilot standing beside him. "My new friend here, Captain Dan Rennick, said you might be able to fix me up with some suitable clothing before we see the Colonel."

Reading Lennox's name patch the sergeant exchanged looks with the Captain and said, "Oh sure. See Sergeant Peters over in Stores, door number '4' over there," Ed said, pointing to the building over his left shoulder. "He'll fix you up, and tell him I sent you. That will clear the air for you. By the way, if you want to take a shower they're off to the left inside the door," he said, glancing down at Ellis' shorts. "I'll have a car ready to take you over to Admin when you're finished, okay?"

"How considerate. Thank you, sergeant," said Ellis, winking at Jan and nodding his head to follow along.

Chapter 8

The 1500 hrs.-GMT rendezvous was thirty minutes hence and John's car was 40 minutes away. Unfortunately, the causeway to the Base road was not automated. John grabbed the opportunity in the form of two A.P.'s in a Base vehicle at the side of the road. Pulling up behind them he parked, got out, and walked up to them.

"Gentlemen," he said, startling them into a sitting salute position causing them to spill their ketchup-coated french fries on their uniforms, "Colonel Harding is expecting me and I was wondering if I might impose on you to, uh, run interference for me, so to speak?"

"General Marshall, Sir," the closest one stammered after glancing at the brass name bar. "Tommy, hand me a magnetic 'Visitor' sign, will you?"

Airman Tom Nguru opened a compartment door on the dash and pulled out a rolled-up piece of vinyl and handed it to Sergeant. Hesser

"Sir, if you put this on the driver's side door of your car and follow us, we'll whiz you right over to the colonel without having to stop."

"I'm on your six, Sergeant, and thanks."

"Happy to help, Sir," the sergeant replied almost mesmerized.

The 'general' turned and walked to his car and placed the magnetic vinyl sign on his door, removed his hunter's vest, chuckled, then got back in.

With sirens wailing and red/blue beacons flashing, the Air Police vehicle screeched away from the side of the road with the 'general' hot on his tail listening to Tennyson's *CHARGE OF THE LIGHT BRIGADE* from the classical music selections available to him in the car. By the time, he pulled in to the administration building's parking lot, he was just finishing R. Wagner's *RIDE OF THE VALKYRIES*, presenting a stirring scene to those standing outside the main entrance.

Both Jan and the Colonel were chuckling to themselves.

"Sir, the General is here," the Sergeant said with a snappy salute.

"Thank you, Sergeant. You're dismissed," Colonel Harding said, returning the salute.

John got out of the car and walked toward them. As the AP's were departing, Jan reached to take her husband's right arm while arching her eyebrow. She quietly announced, "The General is here, Colonel."

Harding looking at John by way of explanation harrumphed, and mumbled something like, "Shit disturber!"

Ellis quietly laughed as he walked in behind them when the door was opened.

Under the Council of World Affairs, Patrick Air Force Base operated with a double mandate. The first was to provide the host country with proficient and specialized air services support as required by the military policy of the host country's Department of National Defence. The second was to fulfil the mandate set out by the Security Wing of COWA, with due regard to its specialized requirement in SETIA. This was covert.

This was the reason why John and Janet Marshall and Ellis were here to see Colonel Harding. This was also the reason why Colonel Harding closed his office door and locked it from inside. Upon pushing a button on the underside of his desk, the office was lowered two concrete-enclosed stories. When the office stopped, he unlocked the door gesturing that his guests follow him; follow him through the hub bub of computerized monitoring equipment and personnel, into another office. They entered this office and he locked the door after them.

Taking his place behind the desk he motioned for them to take a seat and asked in his friendliest base voice, "May I get something to drink for anyone?"

"Not pink lemonade but anything else which is cold," they replied in unison which brought a bit of a laugh from everyone including WJ as he was known down here. WJ walked towards the wall on his right and waved his hand like a hand-held Japanese fan. A large walk-in, fully automatic, pantry was revealed. Lighting illuminated the darkened areas progressively as he moved about in the pantry.

"Very nice WJ but your culinary reputation didn't come that way," Jan chided teasingly.

"You've probably noticed that small amber flashing light behind my desk," WJ commented as he pressed the button to dispense a four cup-carry tray. Putting the ginger ales and one pink lemonade in the cup holes, he returned to his desk to serve and sit. "Well that's because one of you is a bione and under any other circumstance I would have to run a security check before I continued with this pre-liminary briefing. And since I personally know Ellis here and watched some 'general hospital' while you two were enroute," looking at Ellis and Jan, "we can dispense with the tedious security formalities and get down to some serious chit-chat. Mind if I smoke?" he asked, pulling out a pipe.

"Oh, no, go right ahead." John reached for two of the drinks and gave one to Jan on his right, while Ellis walked back to the desk from admiring some military curios and mementos on the opposite wall to the pantry.

John assumed a relaxed but sprawled posture in the body-hug-ging sofa with Jan beside him, who had snuggled into his enveloping right arm. Ellis now sat in a cross-legged relaxed manner in the side sofa chair to the Marshalls' left and, like the Marshalls, faced WJ.

Except for a striking pen holder set and a three-page document, the top sheet of which having only the words '●TOP SECRET●' stamped across it, his glass-covered ebony desk was clear.

"That wouldn't be a representation of the 1876 Battle at Little Big Horn would it WJ?" John asked, indicating the pen set with the index finger of his left hand which was holding his drink.

After lighting the contraband real tobacco in the briar's bowl and puffing at it, WJ looked up and said, "It would and it is." WJ removed his glasses almost like a teacher who was about to give a student a personal lesson. "It's Custer himself," he began in a craggy, but deeply bass voice, "and it constantly reminds me to never judge people by what they look like. Custer's big mistake was assuming his enemy would back down under superior firepower. His second was failing to recognize that time was on his enemy's side. Patience, my boy, 'patience 101', a course we would all do well to excel in," WJ said in thought, while looking at his pen set which was now being turned in his big hands before John's watchful eyes.

Turning to Jan he replied with pride to her earlier comment, "Someday, you two must come to my place as our guests, whereby I can demonstrate why I have the base's reputation as best artistic cook; a reputation, I might add, a certain Flight Sergeant over in maintenance is continually trying to sully."

Waving his pipe in his right hand in emphasis for parts of his conversation, he continued." Jan, on a more serious note, would you like to finish what you started with Ellis? If so, the surgical theatre is available to you," he said, trailing his offer, while awaiting a reply.

Jan looked at Ellis and said, "Certainly. That's very thoughtful of you, Colonel. Do you have replacement organs here already?" she asked, elated at the prospect of making Ellis whole again.

Looking at his watch, he replied, "I didn't mean to be presumptuous but they're enroute from Barcelona by a Woulf Executive SS-Jet, which left approximately twelve minutes ago. So, it should be here in about a quarter hour, which should give you time to set up."

Jan made a mental note that the conversation inside the hummingbird while enroute to Patrick was monitored. She figured that Ellis also knew.

"Jan, what are the risks involved if I refuse this surgery?" asked Ellis.

Both Jan and John looked at Ellis for some revealing clue in his facial expression as they were totally caught off guard by the candor regarding his "life". Ellis' eyes remained fixed on the pen set.

It was WJ who voiced what they were thinking. "Ellis, first, it was SETIA who requisitioned you and even SETIA must abide by COWA's policy on human reconstructs, Bione – Ħ classification. Therefore, you must remain with the Marshalls until recall; secondly, I believe you have a 90-day mechanical heart that needs replacing. If it isn't replaced by the eighty-ninth day, then you must be nearby a reconstruct plant or, God forbid, a reclamation center.

I shudder at the thought of your expiry time in the presence of an unsuspecting public. Why? What were you thinking?" WJ asked Ellis.

"Since we've obviously been called here for some other purpose beyond which meets the eye, I just thought that it might be a good idea for Jan to check her theories regarding her plant specimens and open heart surgery in a microgravity situation. This means that I am presenting myself as the experimental specimen and relieving SETIA of any legal obligations towards my survival by refusing surgery now."

"Ellis! Both Jan and I consider you a friend, not a body on loan," interjected John gruffly.

"Jan, John, I was just trying to help by answering the question which I'm sure you would never ask me. I know how you think of me in our existing relationship. And it's because of this relationship, that only you could detect any psychological changes to my personality because of the surgical procedure which uses this new form of curare from the hybrid plant samples." Ellis was staring at the figurine pen set on the desk avoiding eye contact with anyone. "I really didn't have anything else in mind."

John was watching Ellis carefully and caught a very familiar facial expression, which triggered a memory flashback of Lorne Saunders.

Ellis was a 'biological reconstruct' of John's late best friend Lorne Saunders who was killed in a freak accident during a space walk for an external maintenance maneuver around the international space station. Apparently, a single undetected asteroid, moving at 65,000 mph, blew the head section of Lorne's spacesuit clean away from the body, taking everything inside the helmet with it. The body section pin-wheeled towards Earth burning up in the atmosphere.

A piece of the helmet was found two years later at the bottom of an impact depression on the moon during a routine geological exploration tour given by COWA's Lunar University for Astro-Physics and Astronomical Sciences. They thought they had found evidence of an A. L. F. visit until NASA had it analyzed. It was only then that they could piece together the film footage with the missing helmet section and reach a conclusion.

Apparently, the helmet followed the trajectory of the asteroid, bouncing off the Earth's atmosphere onto an intersect course with the moon, and collided several hours later.

There was no evidence of any tissue, except two hairs, which Lorne always stuck in the seam of the padding, directly above the centre point of his skull, for good luck. This section was all that remained. When John finally got to see it in his hand he looked at it with the same facial expression that Ellis had now. John wasn't sorry he named Ellis after the initials of his friend, and right now he felt for him.

Showing concern, John asked, "El, you feel okay?"

"Huh? Oh, yeah, sorry John. I guess I was just daydreaming there a bit. 'Cause I'm a 'reconstruct', and let's call it what it is" said Ellis, waving his left hand as if trying to calm someone with this motion, "I could quite possibly have a slight personality change with the transplant of this replacement heart. Since tissue matching doesn't have to be so exact as it is for 'intacts' because of the fluid in my circulatory system, there remains the possibility of a personality alteration as the circulating fluid adjusts to assimilate the new heart. The testes are irrelevant in the case of a bione. So, however small the personality changes, Jan should be able to detect them."

"He's right John, and furthermore, if that dossier on WJ's desk contains anything that might take us off Earth then we should know about it, now. Down here." Jan said, accenting her demand by gesticulating downwards.

"Well, Colonel?" John said leaving the decision to him. "Do you have the room down here for the surgery, post operative care, and psychological testing?"

"The theater is being prepped as we speak. The psychological testing can take place one level below and with as much time and equipment you need for the next - here's the bad news - seventy-two hours; after which, you are all Mars bound. And that brings me to this little item." WJ picked up a dossier on his desk and turned it over.

Jan and John looked at each other and swallowed hard thinking the worst.

"Is something wrong with Uncle George, Colonel?" asked Jan, concerned for her uncle's safety on Ganymede.

"No, my dear. He's quite well and, from the importance of this document, I would also say he's quite busy. Are you all ready?

Once I break the seal we have only twenty minutes to read the document and I can only record the sounds we make and the audio portion of this communiqué."

Looking at each other in anticipation they responded, "Ready, go ahead Colonel, read it," they said collectively.

As he ran the metal opener down the right side of the communiqué, he said, "Recorders 'On'."

Within the room, computer-controlled sensors began recording sounds, visual activity, all movements, physiological responses, atmospheric changes, literally everything, except the visual aspects of the document on the Colonel's desk. In fact, the video recorders could only pick up his hand and arm movements as if he was reading some sort of document; a document, only while its seal was in place, but now undetectable. Scanning devices such as x-ray, infrared and ultra-violet lighting revealed nothing; microwave sensors revealed a power source in the shape of three pages but that was the extent of their capability.

Aloud, WJ read quickly including, marks of punctuation, word and phrase locations, describing any diagrams, boldness of type, *etc.* leaving nothing to guess at, visually, if a reproduction was required; and it was, in this case. It read: -

S E T I A
October 12, 3349
Chairman Samuel Davis
Search for **E**xtra-**T**errestrial **I**ntelligence **A**gency
c/o 100 Galileo Ave., Pod 2-0, #100
Columbus Square, New Washington,
Pioneer Colony 1-1A
Mars, P4SS-Pc1
Colonel William J. Harding
COWA – SETIA BASE 2
Earth, P3SS-N.A.
Patrick Air Force Base
Cape Kennedy, Florida, 32920
U. S. of A.

P.S. Caution -
Before reading any further, request Janet and John touch the SETIA symbols with their left index fingertips, John the right symbol and Janet the left!!

They did so and their internal ear pagers shut down.

WJ read aloud....

Dear Bill,

"It was the best of times; it was the worst of times." It seems Charles Dickens best sums up the predicament we find ourselves in now.

As you recall from our last communication I didn't want to interrupt Janet and John's well-earned vacations, however, I think that will no longer be the case. It appears the dolphin wants to walk on land. Soon. So, please prepare instructors by January 14, 3350.

Ellis, this portion of my letter you <u>must</u> commit to memory – [long peptides of DNA strands] The time may come for you to use this portion of genetic coding, and per your requisition information, it will be effortless for you to enact. You will understand later.

John, do you recall the barbecue chicken we had at your parents' last garden party two months after your military graduation? Well, it appears that caterpillars do undergo metamorphoses into wonderful adults, no matter where they come from.

Janet, Christopher Columbus was right when he said, "I've discovered a new world!"

WJ, George says, "Hi" and would just love to take you up on that student exchange program he mentioned in St. Maarten while on vacation with you.

Bill, I think that concludes my letter for now but I'm sure we will be talking to the parent corporation within the next couple of years. I'll keep in touch via the usual message systems, and until then, all my best to Lynda, and you; take care.

Regards,

Sam.

P.P.S. Bill, when you finish reading this letter, place it on your desk, front side down and press the metallic closure together. **Do not attempt to re-open or stop what follows!**

COWA, Form 2349/10/12-PAFB-1

WJ placed the letter on his desk, closed and front side down. He sat back to watch the letter as he puffed away at his pipe. The three pages slowly dissolved leaving only two cubic centimeters of pink ash.

Janet, John, and Ellis looked at each other incredulously and remained silent. It was WJ who broke the silence.

"Recorders off. Would anyone care to have their drink refilled before we thoroughly analyze his message?"

"If I may be so bold, Colonel, I would like to offer my interpretation if we are in an isolated room," Ellis said.

"We are and be my guest, because that genetic coding was beyond me, and it would certainly save us some time."

"Well, Colonel, right now, I'm afraid I can't offer an explanation specifically for that. However, I believe Samuel is saying that he expects all three of us on Mars for a mission briefing by January 14, 3350 which is top secret and: -

1. an urgent need may arise for Jan's genetic gardening talents which she started on Mars but will be needed elsewhere; to what extent she'll be told later; and,

2. both John and Jan are going to do the 'Christopher Columbus thing' but how and when is not yet known; and,

3. an A.L.F., and he stresses possible, wishes to meet, greet, and intermingle with us, again how much is not disclosed; furthermore, he advises to keep an open mind!

4. And as far as the genetic code is concerned, I would guess that it has something to do with a gene, its existence and reason for alerting me to it was not disclosed; and,

5. I think the Marshalls might not like this item, but he says the importance of this mission is of a level where prior approval of their clones replacing them on Earth has already been granted.

I think that about says it all, Sir, except I would like to add my personal comment that I had absolutely no idea of the letter's contents when I asked Jan about the risk of refusing surgery. I apologize for making anyone suspect otherwise."

"Well, on that note I think we better get on with the transplant operation unless there are any questions?"

"Thousands, but I just know you are going to reply with, 'Sam would be the best person to ask' to all of them; so, I will ask one. May we see our clones?"

"John, I know you and Jan trust us so, I'm going to make this brief – no."

Jan gave John that "well-you-might-have-known" look, softened with a teasing smile.

Turning to the Colonel she asked, "WJ, could you check on the status of Ellis' new heart?"

"I'll do better than that, Jan." WJ pressed a finger on a communication icon in the glass-covered portion of his desk to the left of him and a transparent screen came down from the ceiling displaying the pilot of the plane. "There, you can talk to him yourself. He's a practicing Neural-Cardio Surgeon who also happens to be a fan of yours, young lady. And his co-pilot is a circulatory systems specialist and anesthesiologist who said he used to play ball with you and your friends at the ball park when you were kids."

The pilot spoke first.

"Dr. Rafael Degado here. I guess I better get the statistics out of the way first by pressing this button here."

A voice recording came on giving a position check, direction of travel, airspeed, wind direction, and E.T.A. of 12 minutes confirming the information on the screen which was courtesy of COWA's

Atmospheric Vehicle Tracking and Monitoring System, AVTAMS. It also showed the relative positions of their Executive Jet, EJSS-4COWA, and the two escort fighters.

Because of all the satellites orbiting the Earth, there was a danger of collision, or 'absent-mindedness' in monitoring the effectiveness of a given satellite's orbit. Therefore, just prior to 'orbital decay' the responsible company or parties would be notified that at such and such a time their satellite would be "shot, disintegrated, and allowed to burn up in the atmosphere, and they assumed the costs. But AVTAMS also monitored covertly, all air traffic for SETIA.

"Well, Doctor, or should I say, Pioneer Professor Janet Marshall, we finally meet. I am indeed looking forward to this meeting and the opportunity of exchanging ideas. I know we are rushed for time, but we can talk during the surgical operation. I've brought, I'm told, a mutual friend who has volunteered his time to assist us. Also, I've left instructions with WJ's staff on what equipment we'll need in the theater. Enough from me, we'll talk more, later; over."

"Raphael it's my pleasure. Did you bring the donor's Coded Implant Disc? Over."

"Yes, it's in the Organ Tissue Port-a-pak. Here's Pietro. Over."

Raphael's Spanish accent gave the conversation the rich feeling of co-operative, international intensity, that the moment deserved. Jan reveled in it.

When Jan saw who, Pietro was she let out a little squeal of delight at seeing one of her childhood's best friends.

"Pietro? Pietro Andreacchi, is that really you behind that beard?" Turning to John she whispered that he was almost bald as a kid and he used to call me 'raffe referring to my giraffe-like legs.

John smiled impishly, while his blue eyes silently expressed his devilment causing her to lovingly poke him in the side.

"Hi, 'Raffe. Long time since we kicked ball around. Hey, 'Raffe, hows about you 'n' me and my competition there get together for a little kickball after? Hey, what do you say, huh?"

"Hey Pandy, like, uh, what's with the thick Anglo-Italian accent?"

"Nostalgia. A little nostalgia, princess. I miss you both. Hey, Johnny boy, you treating my best friend good, eh?"

Without giving him a chance to answer, Pietro said, "Look, we'll see you both before you can finish reading the menu. Out."

"Pandy? Ha, ha. Pandy?" John chortled, teasing her about her friend's nickname she had for him. "Let me guess, you condensed his first and last name 'because you couldn't pronounce it as a kid, right? Or, he used to give you bear hugs or maybe his favorite toy was a stuffed Panda Bear? Ha, ha, ha, I love it!"

Chapter 9

Pietro, although he was never romantically involved with Janet, used to behave like her big brother and protect her from all the neighborhood's lechers. Raised in tenements along the Humber River valley just north of the megalopolis of Greater Toronto, she learned a street level form of self-defence and survival. She had to fight harder and dirtier to prove her abilities. With this same feistiness, and recognizing the opportunity, she approached education and won scholastic award after award. Of course, an I. Q. of 178, a genetic mystery to her parents, certainly helped her school studies to be conquered a little easier. "...but what the hay?" as Pietro used to say with a little chuckle.

"You bugger, you," Jan laughed quietly and spoke softly, close to his face. "I'll get even later" she threatened him and poked John gently again, hitting his well sought-after, ticklish spot.

John behaved like the gentleman she adored; without jealousy or envy, but lovingly and enjoying the company of her friends as much as she. They shared this intimacy in their looks of softness, the gentleness of touch, and the tenderness of a long-awaited kiss.

"Well, unh, yes, ah, Ellis, unh, are you finished? Ahem, we might as well continue," WJ said, getting up from his desk and shutting off the screen.

Ellis had pulled a little portable electronic diary from his back-pack and was just finishing entering the genetic code when he looked over at WJ and followed his line of sight to the Marshalls.

"Wha-t? Unh, oh yeah," and cleared his throat while getting up from his seat.

"It's okay you two. We're quite ready also. Let's get down to the operating theater and get Ellis fixed up, so to speak," Jan said smiling at them.

"Do you want to assist, honey?" she asked John.

John had already stood up from his seat and couldn't resist the by-play of the moment as he replied, "I'd love to play nurse for Ellis, wouldn't I Ellis?"

"Jan, just make sure he counts everything or I'm liable to get heartburn every time I pass by a junk yard," Ellis retorted, quickly returning the humor.

Chapter 10

"I was looking through some medical history holograms recently, Rafael, and I think that some surgical procedures basically haven't changed much down through the centuries, like open heart surgery."

"That's probably because you're not doing the stitching and by that, I mean the hands-on, day by day work that's required on the part of the surgical team as well as the patient John. I'll tell you right now that our cardio-surgical predecessors who pioneered this type of surgery back in the twentieth century, as well as their patients, would just be in awe of what we do now. Furthermore what we can do now we have them to thank, patient and practitioner alike."

Dr. Degado kept scrubbing with John, who was enjoying the banter. When they were finished scrubbing they placed their hands up to their elbows into the UV light for the required five second 'purple icing' scrub step and then walked through the electronically-triggered air lock outer doors of the theater. The banter continued.

"In fact, just prior to your marriage to Jan, did you know that she'd been doing some pioneering work in this field and she's going to try it finally on her first patient, that being Ellis?"

Pssshshsh pop. The air pressure changed and the outer doors sealed. The atmosphere was contained and the amber light beside the inner door changed green. The inner door opened. Rafael was impressed. While talking, they entered the operating theater and a nurse greeted them with gowns and surgical gloves. Rafael's personally designed head set was placed on him and eyepiece aligned. He was now able to see the minutest of heart muscle fiber if the need arose.

"Yes. She was discussing it during one of our brief moments together. She said something along the lines of using a derivative mixture of curare, cocaine, and digitalis together in certain amounts so it can be substituted as an anesthetizing agent during certain surgical procedures such as what we are about to do now. That is, provided the circulatory system is that of a bione and not just blood like a human's. But I don't see how, since I haven't been keeping up to date," said John.

Interrupting what he thought would be an excuse, Raphael said, "Oh, I understand," gesturing with arm and head movements. "Not enough time in a day to pursue your work, attend meetings, travel time, and keep the home fires burning and so on, right? Don't misunderstand me. I am not demeaning the importance of your career but when you work with people everyday who are grasping at anything that offers them a glimmer of hope to give them a further chance at life, then one begins to appreciate the meaningful things in life, like quality time with family. That's the very essence of medicine."

A fluid-filled, aquarium-like apparatus on a cart, with tubes and wires emanating from a heart organ contained therein, was prominently placed near the operating table. It was accompanied with a second container simply marked, 'Male Gonads'. Janis and Roberts Surgical Technologies was the name of the company that literally put surgery to bed; hence the name of the table became known as "JR.'s Living Bed, nick-named junior's living bed. This was shortened later to 'Junior'.

The table's features housed such computerization for things as patient-shape contouring, blood pressure and cardiac monitoring. Also, it checked blood, and body temperature controls, and had cranial sensors. There was special circuitry which allowed a surgeon to look in a body non-invasively. As a surgeon worked he could have a dialog with the table's computer, *e.g.* "Junior this bione must have a new heart inserted, connected and started and then the area closed. Can you assist, please?"

"Yes, doctor, do you have this other person here as a spectator or an assistant?"

"Strictly a spectator. His name is John."

"Then I will look after the patient's vitals for you, monitor your equipment, and ensure your surgical procedure goes without any obstacle. Doctor I noticed you don't have the usual thread for stitching. Are you using something new?"

"Yes I am. Aqueous spider silk which Janet Marshall developed. Will that be a problem?"

"No doctor I just need to make the necessary environmental adjustments so that it cures and seals properly. Doctor, his gurney has informed me that his scrotum area needs a little finesse in repair as well. Are we handling that procedure also?"

"Yes, junior. Are we prepared now? Can we start?"

"Yes."

The surgeon could discuss his procedure *in vivo* and the best recommendation of surgery adopted. Procedures were recorded and could be reviewed later for teaching purposes.

Probably the most outstanding feature was the table's ability to predict and project failure, thereby alerting the surgeon to take preventative or compensatory action. A fail- safe alarm and monitoring system prevented manual over-riding of mutual decisions between doctor and table. Patient deaths during surgery dropped to 'nano' percentage points. Moreover, potential carelessness, ineptness, or 'fluke' accidents were virtually eliminated. Negligent and malpractice law suits finally became a thing of the past.

What "junior" did not have was yet to be discovered.

Approaching the table, while they were scanning Ellis, Pietro was first to comment. "Looks like I lose; they did find the way after all, ha, ha."

Lightly chiding them, Jan said, "We were just about to dig in without you."

When Rafael had approached the table, he switched gears from friendly conversation to medical seriousness.

"So, Ellis are you ready for this procedure?"

"I think so. Where's John?"

"Right here, buddy," he replied, coming at Ellis over his right shoulder and beside Pietro.

"John, I know I'm in good hands, but if there is a personality change in me, will you follow my instructions to the letter which Jan has in her possession?" Ellis asked urgently, with an undertone of desperation.

"Hey, don't sweat it, buddy. Consider it done, O.K.?"

"Thanks."

Chapter 11

Ellis' G.R.I.D., half a centimeter in diameter and one-millimeter-thick, was glued into his right *temporal fossa*. To the covering skin area an electrode was placed and held magnetically. The monitor screens came on and charted his cranial neural activity. Janet isolated the readings of his *deep* and *superficial cardiac plexi* nerves and then highlighted them on the monitor's screen located in the wall to the right of the table. Other screens displayed his vital signs: - blood pressure, respiratory rate, heart rate, and electrolytes; pain threshold's current level; bionic blood chemistry; emotional status or 'E' Factor with respect to his original 'E' Factor when he was activated. This was the screen that Jan was concerned with the most and right now it was displaying a constant reading of 23 ± 0.5; normal for a bione, which was usually ten points above a normal human, per Rosen-Heitel's theory of 2105 A.D.

"Ellis, I'm going to operate with local anesthetic only but if things get out of hand I want you to tell us immediately. Don't try to be a hero because we might need to do this procedure in space. I've set your pain threshold to your present neural output as an additional indicator and it will sound an alarm if it rises by five points per second. At that point, Pietro will put you under and we'll continue the surgery from there. Do you understand?" Jan asked.

Ellis nodded his acquiescence.

Prior to John and Raphael's entrance Jan had explained the surgical procedure to the 'table' and was immediately met with resistance until she identified her 'Pioneer' status of her Doctoral degrees. Further, Dr. Rafael Degado was technically the principal surgeon although it was Jan's procedure that was being tried. Therefore, Junior and Dr. Degado had a running dialogue of disagreement but would allow the procedure to go ahead as is, since it was being pioneered by a licensed professional.

A depilatory gel pad was fitted to Ellis' chest and lifted off, taking with it all the hair and dead skin cells from the surface layer of his skin. Next, surgical iodine was applied to his flesh where the pad had been, after which Jan applied her test local anesthetic. To check its efficiency and depth, Dr. Degado used a laser probe with the guidance of 'Junior's' 3D-Imaging. It displayed zero sensation as far as the anterior surface of the sternum. The procedure was begun as Rafael made the first incision lengthwise along the midline of the sternum from the midpoint of the union between the *manubrium* and the 2nd *piece* to a point one centimeter past the *Aponeurosis of Transversalis*.

"Doctor, you are doing well. I find no fault in your procedure," said Junior.

At each step through the procedure 3D-Imaging suggested surgical methodology which was quickly refined to conform with the goals of Jan's theory. "Jan, your thoughts of outer space procedures look very promising. You are on the right path. This procedure of yours Mrs. Marshall should be used in your lectures or passed on within this clinic."

Her local anesthesia enabled Ellis to remain completely conscious, and the monitor screen for his pain threshold never fluctuated more than two points. First the 90-day artificial heart was removed and then his own. Each incision was preceded with an application of anesthetic, a protective pad put in place, and then the laser knife used; all the while the table made a running commentary of events.

When it was all over, no more than one unit of 'bionic' blood was needed. Dr. Degado closed Ellis' chest by applying a coat of transparent surgical glue, cementing bone in place, and flesh together, each to its own, as required. The Port-a-Pak now contained the damaged heart, and the artificial one was bagged and discarded.

Rafael looked up at Jan, winked, and quipped, "Well, do we give him his nuts back or shoot some craps?"

John added, "Talk about odds in favor of the house," patting Ellis gently on his right thigh. "Don't worry, old buddy; Johnny boy here will make sure you get a fair shake."

Jan chuckled a bit, but didn't lose her concentration.

When finished, Pietro disconnected Ellis. All that remained was his recovery, which wouldn't take longer than 4 to 8 hours. Timing was everything, as their 'launch window' was in 67½ hours. With so many vehicles in the atmosphere, launch windows now became more important than ever.

"So, how do you feel now Ellis? And please don't say like a new man."

"Jan, you're not going to believe this, but I feel awfully thirsty," Ellis replied. John moistened Ellis' lips with some water.

The surgical team had a stress relieving laugh as equipment was cleared, sterilized, and stored. Total time for the procedure was under four hours. Ellis could walk out of the theater now but, as they were preparing for a space launch, complete cohesion of his wounds was required. Therefore, Ellis was wheeled on 'Junior' into a recovery room where Jan could conduct further tests on his psychological profile. This would be compared with his original profile at the time of requisition. Until Jan was satisfied, Rafael and Pietro remained at Patrick Air Force Base.

Chapter 12

WJ knew that the Marshall's were going to be sent on a one-way mission; why else would SETIA authorize the creation of their clones? Knowing this, he decided to give them a 'business breather' and took them to meet an undercover operative Supreme Court Judge, Justice Edmund Daniel Davies known as 'Bud' to his circle of friends. From the Florida, Supreme Court, it was Bud who had direct ties with COWA. He was the most difficult to persuade, but was also the most influential on matters of social reform.

They met at the Dolphin display and put on a most believable performance for anyone who was watching.

"Bud! Fancy meeting you here. What's the auspicious occasion?" asked WJ.

"Well I'll be damned! If it isn't my old Air Force Instructor, WJ Harding!" Quietly Bud whispered, "talk later?"

Both men shook hands and performed some sort of over hand-under-hand-body-turning maneuver reminiscent of some secret boys' club. Bill winked.

Bud was the same height and coloring as John, showing the care and the time required for personal physical body matters; overall, a handsome 47-year old male and the youngest of the state's 7 Supreme Court Justices.

"Bud was one of my finest pupils, John, and stood number one in his flight," said Colonel Harding.

"Man, those were the days; Harding's Hawks working out in Wojo's Dojo as we used to say."

"Wojo's Dojo?" John queried, arching an eyebrow at WJ, as both he and Jan did a bit of a mock laugh at Harding.

"Yeah, I guess I was a bad guy back then," Harding reminisced wistfully as a grin crept across his face.

"I guess that's the best thing about our damn jobs, WJ., the memories. They seem to be the 'glue' that pulls us back to reality," added John.

"Ever since the inception of the Council of World Affairs back in the late twenty-first century, this world has never functioned better on the things that matter, such as disaster relief, social unrest and upheaval, riots, military uprisings, terrorism, environmental matters, freight and passenger transportation, *etc.* But most of all, it has galvanized the world to focus on progress in medicine and space travel. We seemed to have been concentrating on ourselves as a planetary race of individual beings rather than our planetary collectiveness. And I guess that brings us to this meeting.

Sam is going to meet you on Mars to brief you, but before you go, he's asked me to create your clones on your behalves. What you must do now is seriously consider that you will not come back. It is strictly one way!"

Pausing for effect to see if they had wrapped their minds around this concept. Bud and WJ looked the Marshalls square in their faces.

"Obviously, Sam has his reasons for asking us to go on this mission and, knowing SETIA, there must be a back up plan in case we refuse, so, I won't ask 'why us?' but, I will ask, what role does Ellis play regarding us?" asked John, suspecting something sinister stewing here.

John had hardly finished asking his question when Jan's facial expression displayed realization of apparent betrayal or manipulation.

"John I think Ellis will be with us ..."

"... for your own protection," WJ interjected. "He has better control over his emotions and, with your co-operation, will analyze information much quicker. Beyond that, Sam must tell you but, what is more important right now, is that you understand the message that was sent from Sam is carried out.

As we talk, preparations are under way on the moon to transport you to New Washington Square on Mars to see Chairman Sam Davis for your detailed briefing. Between here and Mars you will be under military escort. There is a faction within COWA that will stop at nothing to discredit SETIA and the entire space program.

"Then we must be operating at a high level of security, right? Like three or even two, WJ?" asked Janet.

"Zero, zero!" replied WJ with a dead pan face.

"What?" John asked incredulously. "We've never had a double zero operation, WJ! Sam know about this?"

"His directive."

The Marshalls looked at each other searching for reassurance, understanding. "Do you mean?"

"Kill first, ask questions later!" WJ said, cutting John off for emphasis. "That includes Sam, Ellis, anyone, everyone on Mars, *etc.* as may be necessary." Holding his hands up to stop them from interrupting, WJ continued, "And by killing, Sam means expunging; complete erasure of any organic evidence at the molecular level. Everything!"

"Bud, we know there is or, there must be an A.L.F. per Sam's message. Is there something we're not being told which is giving rise to this level of security?" John asked.

"There probably is, but even I don't know the answer to that question. You must ask Sam. That's all I can tell you at present and if I get anything more before launch time I'll let you know. Bud quickly shook their hands and just as quickly disappeared into the crowd.

WJ asked, "Ready to go?"

Looking at each other the Marshalls nodded yes.

"Good. Because you have an eighty million-plus kilometer journey ahead of you to meet Sam for your mission's briefing. So, let's get down to the launch pads where Ellis will meet you and get you outfitted. By the way, this is strictly a 'no-flag' journey at least to Sam. Any questions?"

Shaking their heads simultaneously the Marshalls replied, "No, none" and started walking with WJ back to their cars and the awaiting military police. While walking, the full gravity of the situation was taking over them. Jan's hand slipped into, and held her husband's. As they walked she leaned her head against his shoulder. They passed a young mother who was sitting on a bench breast feeding her infant, which brought quiet tears to Jan's eyes. John gripped her hand a little tighter sensing her emotional need.

They thought to themselves, why would a double zero level of security be discussed in this park? The young mother was smiling now at her infant removing the toy mic from its mouth.

Chapter 13

"T- minus 22 seconds and counting ..."

The Marshalls and Ellis were strapped into their seats and were observing all the pre-launch activity while listening to the launch control center continue with their countdown.

"Shuttle bus flight SBF 223-CM confirms ignition; all systems are green for go. Confirm gantry and umbilical disconnect."

"She's a bird Houston and all yours; launch control out."

"Roger that launch control; we have your 'bird'; MET is three minutes and twelve seconds".

MET time (Mission Elapsed Time) was still being used since its initial usage in the twentieth century. After all, it is not like every major city has an impulse launch pad.

The call letters signified the 'bird' was one of NASA's reusable shuttles; flight number two, on its twenty third launch for COWA with a military designation, CM. Basically, it was a 'bus' enroute to an orbiting space station where its passengers could board another ship for a farther destination; in this case the COWA military base on the moon.

"Houston to SBF 223-CM."

"Bus 223; go Houston."

"Be advised we show you are right on the money for "station" rendezvous in 12 minutes, 42 seconds. Do you copy?"

"That's a copy Houston; we have ditto dials."

"Marty, look at this."

Marty, a flight systems manager, looked at Carla's screen and checked the IRW, which was flashing "UI". He looked at Carla and said, "Tell 'im. It could be something!"

Pressing her throat 'mic' she said, "Sir, it's Carla. I have an Unidentifiable Image on my Image Recognizer Window."

"Thanks 'Tracking'. Did you tag it?"

"Yes sir. Number 2."

"Good. Display 15 on main screen, please."

Carla's computer screen was displayed up on the large screen for everybody to see.

The shift supervisor announced that the item tagged #2 was the UI. The other personnel in the room focused their computers on #2 image on the IRW.

"Records, any ideas?"

As soon as the large screen displayed the tagged UI, Jimmy was already flipping through thousands of computer files cross-referencing with COWA's International Records.

"Nuttin', Sir! I went back ten years and done a cross reference t'rough COWA. There's nuttin' there."

"'Did', Jimmy, 'did'."

"Sir?"

"You 'did' a cross reference; not 'done', but did."

"Yes Sir. That's what I said. I done a COWA cross reference for 10 years back an' there's nuttin'."

Rolling his eyes upward, Ben said, "Archives, do you have anything?"

"Ten-four, Sir. Personal screen?"

"Thanks, Ilana. Please do."

Just as Ben was looking at the feed from Ilana's computer on his screen, the speakers blared, "Houston do you copy a UI, five o'clock starboard, approximately 22 miles?"

"We copy shuttle. Any ideas, Major?"

"Sir, if memory serves me correctly it resembles a twenty-first century Whippet." Even as the word 'Whippet' was heard by everybody, counter measures were being scrambled.

"Major Lau, are your microwave shields on?"

"That's a copy, Houston."

"Good, stand by. Put 'Tracking' on screen, please."

The screen displayed a few smaller screens and windows, each projecting different informational aspects of the central window, which showed the visual of the Shuttle and the UI while in motion. Since the Shuttle was in the atmosphere, there was the possibility of the 'UI' becoming an 'obstruction'.

Checking the screens, Ben found that the 'UI' was 1.) displaying no I.D. at all; 2.) had an armed warhead 3.) was on an intercept trajectory and closing fast 4.) identified as a Whippet, supposedly taken out of service back in 3268, 81 years ago, and 5) not responding to vocal communication attempts.

"Tracking?"

"The UI is targeted, Sir! Co-ordinates have been sent, received, and automatic tracking has started by 'AVTAMS', Sir."

"Top marks, tracking. Major Lau, any change?"

"Negative, Sir."

"Standing by for the trigger code, Sir."

"Damn," Ben said under his breath. "Bloody thing is supposed to be for satellites in decaying orbits only."

In the middle of his console Ben unlocked and lifted backwards a clear transparent plastic box on its hinge. Simultaneously a klaxon alarm sounded for five seconds while a taped public address statement announced, "The Control Center is for Security Level 2 clearance only. All others will leave the area. You have ten seconds...nine...eight."

Reporters, shuttle, and equipment monitors, weather monitors, statistics, and other non-essential personnel were escorted to the exits, while other COWA military guards ensured only white and yellow I. D. badges remained in the room.

"...three...two...one."

The doors closed and sealed, leaving the Captain of the Guard in the Control Center with Level 2 Cleared personnel. He recorded this information on a pocket-sized computer. With his hand resting on his holstered side-arm, he stood next to Ben Eisen, the Director of Houston Control. A tacit, facial message of preparedness was exchanged.

"Tracking, set key for code."

"Key is locked in and 'set for code', Sir!"

Ben removed what looked like a red luggage label, and after breaking the foil seal, he pulled out a bright yellow tag with black lettering on it and read it aloud.

"Fox trot, Lincoln, Tango, Bravo, Bravo, 2, 9er, 6." As he said the code, it was repeated by 'tracking' and keyed into her and Ben's consoles. Then all eyes watched the main screen.

Ben pushed the button.

In the interim the Whippet had managed only to close within 17 miles of the Shuttle, two miles beyond its targeting capability range of fifteen miles. The screen displayed both vehicles so precisely that one could see the 'COWA' logo on the six engines of the Shuttle ... and, now, the little cracks currently forming all over the skin of the Whippet. And then, it just seemed to disintegrate into dust; no explosion, no noise, no 'mess.' From the ground, it would appear like a fireworks sparkler trailing the Shuttle had finished burning. Easily explainable.

On a closed transmission came, "Confirm disintegration, Houston!" Major Lau said with relief. "No side affects to the Shuttle."

"Control copies, Shuttle."

Knowing better, Ben whispered to himself, "Bull! Story and film at eleven is more like it." Turning to his computer he isolated the event from "continuity" for a follow up investigation later and cursed again.

The Captain of the Guard whispered, "Sucks to be you, Ben. See you at the roast," and went to re-admit the other personnel while the main screen continued to display only Shuttle information. If nothing else, at least the others didn't get to witness the awesome quiet destructiveness, even though they knew of it.

"Houston to Shuttle 223."

"Go ahead, Houston."

"Satellite tracking shows you are 6 minutes and 19 seconds to rendezvous."

"Copy 6 minutes 19 seconds, Houston. Any news from 'eyeball-1'?"

"Shuttle 223, we've been told off-the-record that COWA's Space Station would have appreciated a phone-first type of visit so they wouldn't have to scramble to tidy up before your arrival."

"Roger that, Houston. Just put their number in 'memory' will you? Next time we'll give 'em a wake-up call, heh, heh."

"Houston, we are 'set' for docking."

"We copy 'set' for docking, Shuttle. 'Eyeball'-1 has left the porch light on for you. The Commander is out walking the dog. Houston out and God speed!"

Ellis, and the Marshalls were intent in observing the 'action' going on outside the shuttle by watching the main viewing screen inside the passenger compartment.

"The Commander is out walking the dog?" Jan echoed inquisitively. Seeing that Ellis was about to respond she held her hand up to silence him and said, "No, wait. Don't tell me. The station Commander is out doing a spacewalk inspection of the station's exterior and he's using an apparatus nicknamed 'DOG', right?"

"Right, Jan. Only the 'leash' this time is a safety line connecting him to the station while he maneuvers the 'Damage Outside Gatherer' to enable a routine maintenance check. Solar flares, believe it or not, cause a lot of ion damage which require constant maintenance attention, otherwise they could lose electrical power, communications, and radioactivity shielding capability.

Knowing they would be disembarking very shortly, Jan gripped John's arm affectionately causing Ellis to politely turn his attention elsewhere. She took the opportunity to ask, "You O.K., honey? I think Ellis is recalling Lorne's dreadful incident from three years past."

"He does seem to be unusually concerned about safety issues, now that you mention it. Maybe he did undergo a slight personality change from his surgery, as he said he might do. Hopefully, it's not a disadvantage or that it won't become a problem. We need him."

"I'll keep an eye on him and keep you updated."

"Thanks, Jan; and uh, just looking at the screen, I guess it does bring back that moment," John said sadly, nodding his head towards the screen which was displaying the station's external check activity. For all his bravado and devil-may-care attitude, John had a strong emotional side to him. With all the checks and double checks, systems and back-up systems, programs and built-in redundancies that COWA, NASA, and the International Space Programs have in place for astronauts, they still step into space like a little boy for the first time allowed to play outside, while overly cautious parents are watchful of his every move. Safety, and the survival of every being and ship that goes into space, encompass every operation or event - or it just doesn't proceed.

Yet accidents do happen. They must be analyzed for cause, prevention, and resolution: - later, for its implementation. Against the black backdrop of space, the Marshalls could see the construction of an ion-magnetic shield surrounding the Space Station, which appeared like a faint glowing shape of a watermelon's green outer skin. They knew the monitoring system inside the station was on high alert for any particle larger than the size of a pinhead but, what they didn't know they wouldn't find out about until they reached Mars.

Turning to the Marshalls, Ellis said, "I know there are some people who live year to year just to see what the automobile industry has produced for use on the inter-urban roadways but don't you two get excited with anticipation to see the changes made to the space station whenever you return?"

Looking at each other questioningly, they turned back to Ellis and burst out, "Excited about work? Hell, no!" and they chuckled.

Just then the 'pilot' flashed the passenger compartment sign, "Docking, Remain Fastened in Your Seats". A few seconds later it flashed, "Docked - Pressures Equalizing."

"C'mon El, let's take one giant step to work," John said, as he pushed off in the direction of the hatchway, while still chuckling. Jan quickly followed with Ellis close behind, who was smiling almost knowingly to himself. As they entered the IVS, Inter-Vehicle Station compartment, the exterior vehicle side closed and sealed behind them. While awaiting the station side to open they checked that they had their personal belongings with them.

They heard the faint hiss and collapsed like limp, upright marionettes encased in pressure suits. Ellis smiled, reached behind them into a small storage compartment and pulled out two belts, which looked like they had small carry pouches on them. He noticed the COWA logo. Reaching into the pouches he pulled out two tiny disks and touched them to the 'pineal gland area' at the nape of their necks. Returning the disks to their respective pouches he depressed their 'Activate' buttons and put on his best greeting smile as he hooked his thumbs through his 'belt'.

Reviving immediately, they asked, "What happened? We must have passed out due to lack of ..."

"Ellis, what's going on?" Jan asked admonishingly while pointing at the atmospheric gas mixture indicator's L.E.D. which read 5.000 mmHg.

"Oh, just one of the newer innovations," he said smiling and after quickly and smoothly connecting them to lifelines he threw them

David L. Pritchard

out the doorway *sans* spacesuits. After putting one on himself he pushed off gently from the open hatchway as a scuba diver pushes off from the bottom of the ocean to glide effortlessly to the surface just under his air bubbles.

Worried about the belt's effectiveness they signed by hand their concerns to Ellis.

He signed back for them to relax and pointed behind them to the Station's Commander who was fast approaching. When he reached them the 'dog' approached inside their belt's protective fields without compromising their integrity. Now John was interested and looked at Ellis who was almost laughing with bemusement. The Commander checked his readings, then signed "thumbs up" and to return to the Station. Pulling hand over hand they pulled themselves back in, this time to stay.

Pressurization procedures were greatly reduced in time by using the 'belt' because of its ability to densely pack and contain a 'personal atmosphere' at a pressure of 0.95atms. The second feature of the 'belt' was to protect its wearer from UV, IR, Microwaves, X-rays, and Gamma rays but this ability was limited to only forty-five minutes yielding an effective usage time of thirty minutes. The 'belt', classified as top secret, was called the Saunders Life Preserver, named in honor of John's late best friend.

When the Commander reached his quarters, he turned to them and gesticulated to enter while holding his other index finger to his lips for silence. His quarters, by far the largest as personal quarters go, comfortably enclosed his guests and he sealed the hatch and pressurized the interior so no one could just 'barge' in.

In a deep base voice the Commander began, "First I would like to welcome you to COWA's International Space Station, which some of us have dubbed as Earth's CISS n' Spy. Your pilot has left to return to Earth," he said, looking out his window. Continuing, "And I'm expecting an incoming SETIA ship from the Moon which we will all board for the eight to nine-week journey to Mars. Now, excuse my manners, but I think I better introduce myself. My name is Commander Lau, Benjamin Lau and I have a level three clearance with SETIA."

"Can we trust you?"

"I certainly hope so, Ellis. Now you probably have ..."

"... More questions than there are answers," John interrupted. "What the hell is going on, Commander? And I'm not referring to that welcoming exercise that occurred before our arrival. I mean how we were conducted into the space station, like the belt and your secretive mannerisms; shall I go on?"

Motioning for calm, Ben said, "As you recall the Council of World Affairs was formed way back in the late 21st Century to benefit all countries; the Earth in particular for Space Travel. After all, our planet is the provider of food, shelter, and an invigorating, interactive, random variation of life forms.

It was only after the global destruction from the third World War did we come to appreciate that simple concept. That resulted in the world having too many people, with too few living, who support space travel; and too many social, and environmental problems. Again, the world became a powder keg with a short burning fuse.

Hence, COWA came into its own.

And hence, the production of new twists to the age-old problems of jealousy, greed, and power struggles. The reason we are in my quarters is because that 'twist' I mentioned has caught up with us but, we don't know to what extent. The 'we' being SETIA specifically. And that means Lassiter, Davies, Harding, Davis, and ourselves. We should be the only personnel to trust. At least, I do."

It was John who spoke for the Marshalls at times like this when trust was at stake. And when he spoke, he always expressed the merged thoughts of himself and his wife, Janet. And always with a stern sincerity.

"Now, look Lau ..." he stammered.

"Jo-h-h-n ...?" Jan said smiling while pressing his arm.

Ben, watching the Marshalls, was already chuckling by the time she looked over at him.

"That's quite all right Mrs. Marshall. Alliteration is one of the fascinating aspects that I love most about the English language."

Hearing this dialogue made John realize how he had started his question, which brought a broad friendly smile to his face.

Recovering his composure, he started again. "Ben, what's going on? I suspect you have already been informed ..."

"Sorry John," Ben interrupted, "But I'm going to be quite blunt with all of you. First, we will not succeed if we lose sight of the fact that a faction within COWA does not want us to succeed. Secondly, they will stop at nothing to achieve results. Thirdly, the reason for this mission must have been revealed to you covertly during your briefing with Col. Harding. And finally, you are going to have to expect the unexpected from here forwards. You can only trust Ellis to get you back safely."

Ellis wasn't saying anything, because he wanted to see who all the players were and their roles. If he revealed his thoughts ahead of time, John may react differently. He knew John and Janet were of prime importance. Why else was he created and assigned to them?

"Why only Ellis?"

"I believe he can explain that to you better than I."

Ellis started, "John, remember the briefing we had with the Colonel when I was given a genetic code to memorize? Well, at the appropriate time I'm to inject myself with that protein in a bione blood base to prevent any alteration to my structure."

"Ellis, there's no such code in existence, at least I don't know of one," said Jan.

"Jan, there isn't one, for human beings. And, no laboratory on Earth would get away with creating one for biones. Otherwise, we could become a super race of beings - no germ or disease or surgical procedure could touch us. But we are not on Earth; we're in space, on a special mission. And if my suspicions are correct about this mission we may just need to do that, for everyone's protection."

"Ellis, that would mean that you are not only here for our protection ..."

"... but you're on a collision course with death," Jan said, finishing John's assertion. "That code he was given is part of an immune-deficiency gene that was present until the mid twenty-first century. In humans, our systems would weaken and be unable to fight such minor things as flu, but this one goes beyond that.

Since Ellis is a bione, a human re-construct with requisitioned alterations, he's capable of things that go beyond the abilities of normal people. He can also recognize on sight another bione, a quality I wished I possessed," Jan finished.

"But I am a human re-construct nonetheless, complete with a built-in obsolescence; I know when I will die! I just don't know how. At least, I don't have the complete picture, yet."

"Well, Ellis, I can't help you there, but you may find out during the mission. And I know you didn't mean anything personal by what you said, because you realize your creation was for human protection and preservation," said Ben, recognizing an emotional attachment growing between Ellis and the Marshalls. Much like the one between he and Julie, who was at the other end of the station monitoring technical data and viewing an inbound COWA military transporter.

The screen displayed the spotlighted ship in the center of the large screen. A computer window to the left side showed: -

Distance _____ 0.800 kms.

Velocity _____ 0.00056 kms/sec. ↓

Abort _____ ± 0.300 kms

Pos. L. T. _____ $0{\downarrow}0{\uparrow}0{\rightarrow}0{\leftarrow}$ 0C / +0

while another window showed other surrounding activity.

The docking "Laser Positioning Docking Target" flashed zeroes indicating the ship was not in range for an automatic docking alignment. The arrows indicated how much *yaw, pitch, and roll* was required and in which direction. Positive readings on the last indicator showed distance to the station. This enabled the ship to align its hatch with the station's hatch, ensuring proper pressurization and seal. The procedure was one that most pilots could accomplish manually, but regulations demanded automated control with manual readiness as back up.

"Commander?"

"Lau here, go ahead, Julie."

The intercom announced that the arrival of the military transport could be seen through the Commander's port viewer. In twelve minutes, sunrise would cast the docking procedure in a vivid bright light. A stirring moment for any observer.

Chapter 14

"Twenty-three minutes until docking, Commander.

Sir, that's the good news. The bad news is that we have a short period of sunlight due to a solar eclipse and we expect some troublesome activity."

"Thanks Julie. Put the station on 'Alert Status' and send the usual signal to Houston.

Turning to his guests Ben said dryly, "Never figured out why we have to notify Houston. They know immediately when any change in status occurs. Safety precaution I guess. Anyway, I digress."

Suddenly everything was bathed in a yellow pulsating light. The Commander pressed a button at the bottom of his personal viewer to receive the feed from Julie's monitoring station.

John looked at Jan and Ellis, and then disbelievingly said to Ben, "COWA's Space Station under attack?"

The screen did not display anything other than the impending arrival of the military transporter.

John continued, "If this group is so bent on our failure, then why attack us here, in full view of the world? Will the solar eclipse provide such a plausible excuse for an event of sabotage?"

"John, maybe we should look at this from a sales point of view. President Kennedy sold the Americans a belief in their ability to be first to land on the moon. When Astronaut Armstrong proved this to the world this other group needed to squash the very spirit of further exploration. If we are destroyed in front of the world's eyes now, then, they could win over the tax paying public and stop the space race. These people provided intellectual voice for political protests within the involved countries. Demonstrations were at first peaceful, but soon gained in momentum, and violence.

That's when the second group revealed themselves. By fuelling the protests with wild allegations of government agencies devising plots to make the public believe in discoveries of alien life forms; they deflected any credibility in the continuance of the space program.

The Roswell, New Mexico, incident of the 20th Century couldn't hold a candle to the April 2824 incident in the Antarctic where global warming finally revealed a downed and damaged UFO encased in ice...complete with a frozen crew of seven ALFs.

Dating techniques pegged it at 5 years before the discovery of that Martian meteorite."

Jan, John, and Ellis exchanged looks of doubt at each other.

Gesturing for calm with his hands, Ben went on, "What I mean is this. When scientists discovered the meteorite, the surrounding ground was tested as well. When this was matched up with findings from the UFO site, NASA scientists proposed a few theories: - 1. it was a simple random meteorite landing; 2. somehow it was 'drawn' to this location, as evidenced by the presence of some markings in the ground. This was later reworked and speculated as theory three; 3. the meteorite landed by a 'controlled landing' *as in* being drawn in by some machine or apparatus which was obliterated, *or* it was sent to Earth *as in* being 'shot' from some extra-terrestrial source which still obliterated it, and whatever else was there at the site of impact."

"Excuse me? Obliterated?"

"Semantics, John. If vaporized, or vanished without a trace, sounds better, use it. But they mean the same thing ... disappeared! In any case, the ship came 5 years before the landing of the meteorite. The ship was found just a few miles from the meteorite site, but the meteorite was discovered in the twenty-seventh century.

Now, here's the clincher. On Mt. Kirkpatrick, there was a dinosaur discovery in May of 1994. When COWA's scientists went over this region, their findings revealed definite proof that, the UFO was here to do exactly what COWA's scientists were doing."

Lau paused. Their military transporter was arriving.

Chapter 15

"Don't pause now," said John, even though everyone's eyes were watching the transporter's arrival through Lau's window portal.

"Keep going."

"It was reasoned thusly. The discovered UFO apparently was sent here to determine the whereabouts of a previous extra-terrestrial landing in the same area.

When Neil Armstrong landed on the Moon he left boot prints in the lunar dust, which don't move as there is no lunar wind. If the Lunar Landing Module had taken off with the crew when they left, we would have seen evidence of it. Evidence was in the form of rays emanating from a central depression from rocket exhaust spewing out the rear end of the Eagle. But since it was still in place with its landing pads down, the pads left prints.

Now, if a non-rocket drive was used on take off, then those landing pad prints would still be there. And that's what was found in the ground 500 feet from the meteor landing site, approximately three feet below the surface, along with this."

Commander Lau handed him a photograph of what could be an energy-discharging weapon much like the laser lance John used in the Rec-dome.

"Dating techniques have placed this landing during the Jurassic period; 178,567,654 years ago. In June, to be precise."

"Did they say what day? John asked, with a bit of disbelieving sarcasm.

"June 6, 178million, 567thousand, 654 BC." Looking at their looks of incredulity, Lau shrugged his shoulders and said, "We speculated that something happened inside their ship to their chronometer, locking it on a date which was roughly translated to be June 6."

"178million B.C." John finished for Ben, who was wearing a sheepish grin from being exposed. "Seems to be a memorable date in history." John said again, dryly.

Ben continued, "They were hunters out hunting. Their planet sent a scientific team to find them and discover why they hadn't returned home. When they had landed here they found out the 'where' and 'when'. We can only guess the 'why'. Sort of opening a Mesozoic missing persons' file, ahem."

Ben studied his guests while they looked at the photograph. John thought that the end of the 'dinosaur' age caused by a meteor impacting the area in the Gulf of Mexico, or so say some schools of thought, opened a whole new can of worms. He shuddered.

Ben continued, "Even with this strong ALF evidence the space program has had to fight continuously for its existence. It's been plagued with fatal accidents, technical setbacks, financial subsidy roller coasting, etc.

Ever since the two recreational areas were built on the Moon, the space program has received the benefits from private funding. COWA's Lunar schools of space science studies is tangible evidence today of that fact.

Even the sabotage which the programs experienced during the latest World Wars were clumsy, discrediting efforts. However, when COSSIOS (the Committee of Scientific Studies of Inner and Outer Space) created SETIA with a new mandate, which went beyond the previous centuries' mandates, there seemed to be a renewed effort of sabotage, replete with new resources."

David L. Pritchard

"Tell me something, Ben. Is the point you're trying to make that the sabotage brains originate from inside SETIA or COSSIOS or even COWA? 'Cause if it is, then what has been done about it? Sabotage certainly hasn't been anything that just started up last night, for instance." John was getting a little testy because of some underlying implications that were being made. "If I was a delusional sort of person who believed in conspiracy theories, I might just suspect that this sabotage that's been dogging the space program, and now us, has been allowed to continue, to justify the existence of, say Ellis here, or the development of new weaponry. Hell, financial subsidies would grow if accompanying benefits could be realized as a return for the public's money."

"John, what are you saying? Uncle George is in SETIA! Surely you don't suspect him, or me for that matter, do you?" Jan was getting quite angry, but controlled.

"Honey, someone of an administrative nature ..."

Interrupting John, Lau said, "John, let's continue this at another time."

"I think I know where you're going with this, and I think this should be talked about later," Ellis said suggestively, while putting his hands reassuringly on the shoulders of his two pals. If John didn't trust Ellis 100%, this would be the time to show at least some resistance; but he seemed to sense that Ellis had recognized something, which might well bear heeding him. So, he didn't resist.

"John, until we find out, and by 'we', I mean everyone in SETIA, the licensing body COSSIOS, and the political body of COWA, I'm afraid we are all under suspicion; including Sam. That's his orders!" Lau exclaimed.

"What about 'outsiders'?"

"They're under suspicion first, John. But it's easier to investigate us first. Sort of like, clean up your own backyard before cleaning others. Get rid of clutter."

76

They could all see the COWA transporter docking against the station. The white hull provided the perfect background for the COWA flag. They watched intently, almost transfixed.

The old American constitution embodied the concept of freedom within the heart of COWA. A concept which some people used selectively, but it was this concept that united the American people and gave them strength in the face of adversity - even if the adversity came from within.

This concept was reworked when the Council of World Affairs came into being and was embodied into a slogan on its flag. Contests were held in schools worldwide and the combined thoughts of the winners yielded a flag that John and Jan were going to be proud to bear on their mission.

"Tell me one more piece of information, Ben?" John asked, while watching the transporter's docking procedure.

"If I can."

"Has SETIA discovered the whereabouts of the ALF's origin, or any other follow up information for that matter?"

"I'll be absolutely honest with you, John. I do not know. I think the best, and only, person to answer that question would be Sam himself."

Turning back to the window portal, Ben said, "The transporter has come fully prepped for the two-month journey to Mars so, if there is nothing else remaining, then I think we should get under way."

"We'll be right along, Ben" Jan assured him and Ellis as they left together. Resting her head on her husband's shoulder she quietly asked him if he remembered how the ambassadorial flag of Earth came to be the flag of COWA. Being a history buff, John said that he had and that he had reviewed some historical files during his drive to see Colonel Harding.

The C.O.W.A. flag embodied all of Earth's tribulations and symbolized the uniting of its nations for a single future in peace and harmony. Thus, this was reflected in the flag's creation: -

- a white background with Earth's Eastern hemisphere on one side of the flag and the Western hemisphere on the other side; and,

- with the flagpole to our left, the top left corner of the flag has a yellow triangular patch inscribed with the words ONE WORLD in blue lettering; the bottom left corner has a black triangular patch inscribed with the words ONE HOPE in white lettering; the top right corner has a red triangular patch inscribed with the words ONE RACE in green lettering; and the bottom right corner has a magenta patch inscribed with the words ONE FUTURE in gold lettering; and,

- across the face of each hemisphere is the black lettering "C O W A", below which appear the words "Council of World Affairs".

Chapter 16

"John, have you given some thought that this mission might not give us the opportunity of ever seeing our home again as we now know it?"

"We face that possibility with each mission, Jan. Why has this one given you such profound feelings of permanent detachment?"

When she didn't answer right away he turned to hold her in his arms and looked in her eyes. She betrayed herself with a slight tear forming in her right eye.

Suddenly realizing something else might be the matter, he asked, "Are you pregnant?" lowering his gaze to her waist area.

"No, and that's our problem. If we do get pregnant now, what's to become of the baby?" she asked, sobbing and laughing at the same time.

"I'm sorry I haven't been giving you much attention lately, but what would it matter if the baby was born in space?"

"I just thought it might have been better for the baby if it was born on Earth, to sort of give it roots so to speak. That's all. I'm not against pregnancy, if that's what you think."

"Well, sweetheart, it seems we've got at least ten weeks ahead of us and I'm sure there should be plenty of time for intimacy. It was something I was daydreaming about while enroute to see Harding."

Taking her in his arms John gave her a long passionate kiss.

When they broke, they started towards the hatchways' inter-tube and she playfully asked, "Why didn't you tell me?" poking him in the side causing him to jump.

"That, my dear Janet, is going to be answered during the next few million miles."

Getting ahead of him, she flirted with, "Don't be so sure of yourself, mister," light-heartedly laughing as she broke from him.

Zero gravity conditions made lovemaking and games of 'catch me' that much more interesting and challenging. After all, they were still wearing their Saunders Life Preservers.

Chapter 17

"Julie, let me know when you are ready to come through and show Eduardo 'In Command' on the Log," said Ben when he had gone through to the Transporter with Ellis.

"If Raminder has finished that experiment assignment NASA requested, you can show him on COWA's time, and there won't be any bitchin' about costs regarding time-sharing. And he's Eduardo's gofer until the new team complement has arrived, okay?"

"Roger, Colonel. Give me five minutes. I've put the tracker on 'auto'."

"Roger, Julie. Any 'blips' yet?"

"Negative, Sir. But I have a theory."

"Good, tell us when you're on the transporter. We can use a good story."

Julie handed over command of the station's Command console to Major Eduardo Iglessis, one of NASA's astronauts who was sent up to CISS for a six-month tour of "Planet Watch" and any "other duties as assigned." Usually, a full station complement consisted of eight to twelve personnel depending on what was required of them. With every complement of personnel, one was a bione, a COWA regulation. Julie was a bione; Ben's bione. The mission they were going on would reveal to what extent.

Julie relinquished the console to Eduardo but not before she keyed in a SETIA code sequence that might come in use later. After showing him the three 'blips' on the screen, she warned him to expect trouble and that a crew complement was enroute from COWA's pad on Cape Canaveral with an E.T.A. of forty-two minutes.

"And Ed, keep the station on 'Standby Alert' until the Commander tells you otherwise."

"The relief Commander, or Ben?"

"Ben. See you."

"Bon voyage, Julie, and call me from Mars, will you?"

"Heh, heh. Yeah sure, collect. Bye." She then left for the inter-tube.

Chapter 18

In the absence of gravity and starlight, the black void of space has a profound impact on the senses. The three ships were in the umbra of Earth's shadow making them difficult to see visually. They were suicidal, they were all rigged to self-destruct whether they were successful or not. They were built for speed and 'invisibility'; a mirrored exterior reflected visible light; an inner shell circulated a coolant through it, distorting the heat signature. That was the plan; so far, it was successful.

Oh, they were envied.

They waited in the Earth's umbra, undetectable; almost invisible, camouflaged against their starry background. They had the advantages of surprise, speed, singleness of focus, and someone on the inside. The four 'S' test for successful predation. Two important factors remained; target acquisition and target distance. Timing meant everything. The target had to be: 1) detected; 2) within a non-escape range; 3) locked on; 4) fired upon, and the target 5) have its destruction confirmed, all within seven seconds.

Seven seconds was the amount of time the COWA military transporter needed to detect and react to the presence of an enemy. Less than 7 seconds and even a totally bionic crew on board would not be able to react. If the enemy had already discharged its weapon(s?) the prey had less than one second to complete an evasive maneuver. All things being equal, that is.

"Sir, my scanners indicate we should not be having any mobile energy readings coming through the blackened areas of the Earth's shadow."

Ellis checked and said, "Commander, I think our saboteurs have found us despite any preprogramming their ships had."

Chapter 19

"Sir, there's a closed com-link for you on 'H-one'."

"Thanks, Belida. You might as well break for lunch and if you happen to pass that new take-out joint on Main and Fifth, could you pick me up a 'corn beef on light rye with mayo' and their special salad?"

"Mayo? Off your diet already, sir?"

"You get to count to fifty this time when I do sit-ups. That should compensate."

"Y-y-y-yes, s-s-sir." Belida said, setting him up for her best stammering count. She clicked off the intercom, pulled her shield down over her computer work area making it completely invisible and left the outer office. "S-s-see you sh-sh-shortly." and closed the door.

Smiling, Bud rolled his eyes upward and sat down to take his call. He pressed an illuminated area on his desk and a transparent three-dimensional display appeared before him. The Director of the Central Intelligence Agency was casually dressed standing before an outdoor barbecue. This was simply a transparent clear plate with a surrounding IR heat source. He flipped a couple of the soya patties on the plate and Bud could almost smell the 'meaty' aroma. Bud made a mental note that the H-Link made Ira look ten pounds heavier, so Ira must think the same of him.

"Bud, how are you?"

"Ira, you look like you're on a well-deserved day off, so why are you making a clandestine call to me through my office?"

"Clandestine? Bud, I'm hurt."

"Oh, cut the crap, Ira. You're on a secure line without having being switched by my secretary and you're not Sam, or the Chief Justice. So, clandestine fits you to a 'tee', along with sneaky, surreptitious, slimy, slippery."

"Words of praise my friend. Thanks. I'll get to the point. You will have registered mail to pick up shortly. Say, how's the wife? You both, still coming over for a wild weekend?"

"If I can settle some pressing matters by Friday afternoon, then we should be there by late Friday night, otherwise it will be Saturday. Just make sure our sleeping quarters are in order, okay Ira?"

"No problem, Bud. Betty and I will see you and Darlene, when you get here. Take care."

"See you then, Ira," Bud said, closing off the com-link. Muttering to himself, "Blood sucking son of a bitch!" Bud knew what 'registered mail' meant. 'Technical difficulties' he would support, but nothing beyond that. How long could this 'shit' go on? When and how, would it all end?

When would Ira conclude that my usefulness was over? Indeed, when would *my* turn come to fulfil the adage, 'there's no honor among thieves'?" Justice Davies was always a cool, calm, deliberate man, but he knew he was in over his head. His temples perspired.

Thinking out loud, "Every time I've had the chance to crawl out of this cesspool of lies, deceit, and corruption, up pops that slime ball. Damn him!"

He pressed his com-link again, "Council of World Affairs. How may I direct your communication?"

"Angélique Marshall, please." Bud just took the first step towards ending his nightmare.

Chapter 20

Julie had entered the military transporter and was strapping herself into her seat restraints when the public-address system announced departure readiness.

"Mooring umbilicus secured, sir. All passengers are fastened in."

Checking his display board, all systems showed normal and engine condition was nominal. Cabin pressures stabilized.

"Thank you, helm. Back us out, Robert, five meters per minute increasing to ten per cent mix until we reach trajectory insertion point."

"Acknowledged, Captain."

"Welcome aboard, ladies and gentlemen. I am Captain Dilpreet Noor. Please call me David or Captain Noor. We will reach the Mars Insertion Trajectory in twenty minutes.

We are in one of five of COWA's latest Solar System Cruisers, the Duglass Aerostar 1211. So, as of right now this ship will maintain an 'alert' defence condition until we reach Mars."

While Captain Noor was stating the Aerostar's defence status, the 'Ferris Wheel' at the centre of the ship took on a faint blue glow and the men in the six observation domes seemed to disappear into the background of stars. The 'Ferris Wheel' was computer guided with armed 'cannons'.

It was designed jointly by sisters Georgina and Elizabeth Ferris in the late twenty-seventh century. It easily recuperated its massive research costs when it destroyed three would-be asteroids, each of which could have effectively wiped out life on Earth. It was twenty years later, in 2791, that COWA developed smaller sizes for their military transporters going to and from Mars.

Captain Noor continued, "And, effective immediately, all personnel are to wear Saunders life preservers. We are expecting trouble any time now, that is all we know. Captain, out."

The Captain then turned to his guest on the bridge, "Well, Benjamin, it is indeed a pleasure. One I'm sure we will enjoy more when we discover what we are facing and can deal with it."

In his deep resonant voice, Commander Lau imparted self-confidence as he spoke. "David, can we bring Julie up here? I think she has an interesting tale to tell us."

"Certainly." Pressing a button on his console, David spoke, "Julie, would you come forward to the bridge, please?" Smiling at each other, they waited for Julie's arrival.

Disconnecting herself from her restraints she hand-over-hand gripped her way forward to the hatch connecting the passenger compartment to the bridge. She entered the bridge and closed the hatch behind her.

"Captain Noor, I would like you to meet Julie, who was basically my right arm on the Station. She was saying to me that she has a theory about the 'trouble' we are expecting."

"That's right, Captain. Station sensors detected an anomaly in the Earth's shadow. If there was to be any trouble, whatever it was, would await its opportunity within the shadows then strike sometime during our nine-week journey to Mars. But the part of this I have a theory about sir, is this ambush will occur within the first five million miles. I believe whatever is going to come after us must be fast, undetectable and on a one-way trip."

"Why the first five million miles, Julie?" asked the Captain.

"Optimum strike efficiency, sir." Looking at Ben and the Captain she could see they wanted a more detailed explanation.

"Sirs, the way I figure it. The faction that wishes to thwart anything to do with space exploration, or research, will have its own substantial financial resources. If we can accept this first premise as a 'given', then the rest of my explanation will be more plausible." She looked at them expecting an expression of acceptance.

They returned her look, but it was her 'boss' who spoke, looking at her, while addressing the Captain. "You know, David, if we do accept that premise we must look for the answer to the question of whom", Benjamin commented.

"Ben, we already know there is a major faction that wishes to thwart all outer space activity, so really, each event of sabotage must be chased down to reveal the culprits. It would be nice to expose the leaders. But it is impossible to expunge their ideal. So, what you were going to say here Julie, is that whoever is behind your prediction of a possible event of sabotage, should either be financially well off to avoid exposure or have connections within COWA and maybe SETIA itself."

"That's what I'm thinking, sir."

"Ben, I think it's time we hear Julie's idea, but let me get the Marshalls up here first."

"I agree and bring Ellis here too, David." The captain nodded his acquiescence, and made the announcement request. Commander Lau made introductions, while they were strapping in.

Captain Noor began, "John, I've called you forward because we feel that you should listen to Julie's idea with us."

Turning to his helmsman, Captain Noor said, "Robert, previous order stands, and place a DISC in our parking space. Advise the station using old Morse code and have it activated."

"Morse code? Aye, aye, sir." Robert turned back to his console and punched up the Morse code program to search for the information he needed to carry out the captain's order.

"Julie's idea regarding what, Captain?" asked John.

"John," Julie began, "just before we left the station I told Commander Lau that sensors had detected an anomaly but the signal could not be locked in. So, I followed procedure and notified Commander Lau. Sir, I believe there was something out there lurking in the Earth's shadow but because I couldn't lock it in I can't prove it. Since I didn't have authorization to swing Solar II into a visual angle, and Solar I was diametrically out of the picture, I formulated a theory." Reluctant to continue, Julie paused for their readiness to hear the rest.

"Go on, Julie," David said.

"I believe that we will be attacked within the first five million miles of our journey to Mars. The reason I'm suggesting this distance is because whoever is out to sabotage this mission is going to want to hit us, hit us hard, and won't care about their survival or return to Earth."

John seemed to sense where she going with her idea and offered, "Captain, why don't I use my code to set up Solar II for a 'visual' and then ..."

"No," Ellis interrupted, "Sorry, John. If Julie's correct with her speculation, whoever is out there will have all sorts of monitoring and tracking devices. We shouldn't jeopardize our location. I believe the Captain can confirm that."

"John, I think Ellis is referring to the DISC that I wanted left in our 'parking spot' at the station. It should buy us some travel time and distance as it will produce both a visual field and a sensory detectable field of our ship moored at the station. Furthermore, tape playbacks will produce realistic conversation between the station and the Digital-Imaging-Synchronic Chronogram. Sort of a Saunders Life Preserver in reverse."

"That's all sci-fi stuff. How is that poss...? Unless ... In the absence of an atmosphere, ions will gravitate to a body of greater mass or charge. Right?"

"Exactly," the Captain agreed and turned in his swivel seat to Julie. "So, why don't you speculate about some logistics, lieutenant. I want details."

"Captain, was your flight plan based on a cruising speed of 35,000 mph?"

"Yes, so COWA could calculate fuel consumption and release the amount of fuel required."

"Do you have to adhere to that consumption rate under regulations?"

"Captain's discretion Julie, why?"

"Just trying to calculate in some variables, Sir."

"Julie," Jan said, to get her attention, "Let me add to that, Captain. Since we are on board this ship I believe the Captain has been given some extraordinary leeway with supplies," Janet interjected.

"Jan's right in this case Julie, so consider your fuel as unlimited, okay? You've also got to know that the safe delivery of the Marshalls and Ellis to Mars **is** our mission."

"In that case I must figure that whoever might be out there waiting for us also knows our mission. This is my list of logistics," she said, giving him a hand-held computer.

The Captain read her notes: -

- two, most likely three ships; launched from portable, or concealed pads such as a Super Aircraft Carrier like the CNS Lexus Floating Airfield, or from somewhere in the Sahara Desert, where a launch could go unnoticed;

- ships which are stripped from experimental, storage, recreational facilities and with pared down life support, sufficient fuel for a suicidal one-way trip;

- equipped with state-of-the-art armament;

- ground-supported with computerized monitoring, tracking, detection, guidance, and decoding, via on-board sensors and tight band broadcasting relay devices;

- ship cloaking or concealing devices;

- sacrificed defensive devices such as shields in the hopes that they could get in close enough to be targeted and the resulting explosion could either wipe us out or be a decoy long enough for the other two to move in for the kill;

- might be armed with a weapon multiplier, meaning one ship would be missing equipment that the others would have, resulting in a dependency on weapon readiness, and firing; can be watched out for when enemy ships are in formation;

- firepower - more than required to simply vaporize us; would have sufficient to vaporize themselves with no trace of evidence;

- finally, maneuverability and detectability; the former having a high level but very short range in distance; the latter would demonstrate non-detectability under UV, IR, Micro-wave, or simple visual conditions;

- qualitatively - probably sponsored by a minimal number of wealthy backers or have people on the 'inside' of SETIA, COWA, or both.

"Sir, I sent your request to the Station as ordered, but I have an incoming Priority One from COWA."

"Receive it, Robert, but do NOT acknowledge it. Understood?"

"Aye, Sir."

With quarters cramped on the Bridge due to the presence of guest personnel, it made moving around difficult but not impossible. However, the possibility of an accidental switch tripping also increased.

"John, Ellis, I know both of you took courses in Aerospace Tactics and Safe Practices. And it seems that Julie is suggesting we will be fighting some unseen, undetectable, pesky 'insects'. So, let's hear some ideas."

As the Captain finished talking, the computer console announced, "Locating buoy, deployed." Janet moved away from the console quickly feeling guilty.

Robert was already dimming the bridge console and highlighting the maneuvering and sensor scanning sections.

"What happened, helm?" the Captain pressed for an answer.

"Captain, I think I accidentally hit a switch when I turned to and fro watching the dialog action. Sorry for the inconvenience." Jan said apologetically.

"Don't apologize. I wasn't sure where to start with this sabotage problem but now I am. Helm, what's our position in relation to the station and the Martian injection point?"

"Sir, we're five miles away from the station and two miles from the M-I point."

"Good, give us a 100% burn, forward thrusters for thirty seconds and don't alter course."

"Acknowledged." Robert dialed the fuel mix and set the timer digits in the computer. His computer responded by showing that the course trajectory with these figures was directly back to the Moon. Uncovering the ignition button, he pressed it with his right index finger and turned to face the Captain, "Sir, that will take us back to the Moon."

"Acknowledged, Robert."

"Effectively backing the car into the garage, so to speak," Ellis quipped. "Close the garage door by keeping the Moon in front of us, and whoever is out there will think we are wherever the buoy is and home in on it until they get within five miles. Clever, Captain, as the burn occurs the station is shielding us."

"Exactly. Monitor our speculation, Helm."

"Aye, Sir."

"Now, if we are successful, then this should buy us some 'escape' time, provided we don't have to fire the engines again until the other side of the Moon." The Transporter's status remained on 'alert'.

"So, we're on the run going backwards, hopefully facing the enemy. Therefore, I need to make use of all your talents - hmm, where to put you?"

"Okay Julie, I need you and Ellis on the bridge. John, I would like you to assist back at the 'wheel'. And Jan, I expect there might be casualties so, could you go astern and set up a 'sick bay'? Any problems with any of that, people?"

"None." they responded in unison.

"Good! Let's get ready to kick ass. And John, let my men have some fun too because if you people weren't on board, this mission would be just another nine-week bus ride to Mars."

"Boring, huh?" quipped John. "Just like our vacations" he added, and the Marshalls and Ellis chuckled as they assumed their stations.

As they left, the Captain turned to Ellis and Julie and said, "Now, let's talk tactics; what's what, and where, on the Bridge. Oh and Julie, the portable pad in the form of a floating airfield - wouldn't work, uh, uh. Too many witnesses, too many people involved. A concealed polar or Sahara Desert launch pad; now that's been a topic of discussion since the twentieth century! But whose? Who would be the backers? And once we find out that answer, then what do we do? And would we want to know? Something like facing the ET who was witness to the formation of our planet and more importantly, the life on it."

"The one with the answers to questions like who we are? Why we are what we are? Where are we going? Our reason for existing? Just to name a few," offered Ellis.

"Exactly, Ellis! And the big one: - what's to become of us, i.e. we humans?" the Captain said, finishing Ellis' assumptions.

"You know, we're thinking like a team," the Captain said, and began showing them the use of the computers.

"Maybe not. What makes you think there was a witness to our creation, Captain? What makes you think it was a sentient being?" Ellis admonished, good-naturedly.

"A hunch - just a good old-fashioned, seat-of-the-pants hunch," the Captain shot back.

Chapter 21

The American President's birthday gala was scheduled for November 12th, more than a month before the COWA convention. The guest list was a veritable who's who in politics, and diplomatic circles: - business tycoons from all over; COWA members and their immediate entourage of security and aides; various military leaders; royalty; religious leaders; entertainers with renown stardom; and friends and family. Of course, it was the "usual group" the leader of one of the most powerful and influential countries of the world would have invited to a 50th birthday celebration. A 'run-of-the-mill security headache for the Secret Service boys', as Darlene Davies was so fond of saying.

A lot of back-slapping, morale-boosting, and 'clique' type of grouping and conversations would take place; fuelled by 'secrets' digging, chasing career progress, research disclosures, and of course, good old gossip and rumor-mongering. There would also be the usual lying compliments about personal things, like golf game expertise, sport achievements of note, aging and appearance. The socialites' sundae sauce specialty! A diplomat's knife hidden-in-the-cake, smuggled past the guard of an untrained set of ears to a wagging tongue. Pity a debutante at this soirée!

There would be no need for other entertainment, yet some music would supply a certain ambience. So, a nice middle-of-the-road twenty-piece orchestra would play 'appropriate' music for the happy occasion. Gossip mags and rags like the 'Ptolemy Gazette' and other leading magazines could report for months.

The New White House gala would be reported as the sort of event anyone in the public would give their eye teeth for to be in attendance, to be seen hobnobbing with the world's movers and shakers. It was also the 'perfect' cat-and-mouse arena for the C.I.A., N.S.A., the President's Secret Service, various diplomatic bodyguards and spies, and COWA's Secret Police, the C.S.P.

"Howard and Angélique Marshall, how are you? Haven't seen you two since John married our daughter," said Mrs. Lassiter.

"Doing great, but I am looking for Bud since he asked for me," responded Angélique.

Because the event was personal, the V.I.P.'s of note were the birthday boy, President Anderson of the United States, and Queen Shaneen Weinstein of Saudi Arabia, the current Chairperson of COWA. The honor of announcing the two highest VIPs to the gala went to the Master of Ceremonies, the Vice-President of the United States, James Edwin Thomsen III, the former Governor of Georgia.

Dressed in formal wear, which was tailored to enhance his squared jaw-line and swarthy complexion, it hung on his 6'6" 'Ranger' frame as if he were modeling it. As a retired two-star general from the army his booming baritone voice had no trouble being heard by the President's guests, a stature complimented by his gift of thinking on his feet, made his delivery entertaining, respectful, and light-hearted.

Standing to the right of the main entrance to the International Dining Room, Jet, as his closest friends called him, announced, "May I have your attention, please." Pausing to allow the commotion to settle down, he then raised the wireless mike to speak again, "Honored guests, it is my privilege to introduce the Chair of the Council of World Affairs and her husband, the Queen and Prince Consort of Jordan, Shaneen and Tibor Weinstein." (*The International Anthem Approved by C.O.W.A. was struck up by the orchestra*)

Wearing her formal sash of office, its shimmering spectral color-blend against the background of her full length, golden-gilded, white brocade gown was very moving as evidenced by the guests' complete attention and wave of murmuring awe.

COWA stirred the same feelings of patriotic pride in people that 'Old Glory' did when she was sent up a pole, only this was pride in the planet Earth. Smiling a perfect set of white teeth in acknowledgement, the Queen of Jordan awaited her Prince Consort while he checked his Regal Sword with the U.S. Marine 'Guard of the Hall' at the entrance. This was done ceremoniously as it denoted the 'equality of personal being' with everyone in the hall.

When this was over, Jet extended his left arm around and to the right of the Queen, and introduced her to his wife, Susannah, who then in turn passed her on down the receiving line with her husband. After everyone had been introduced, Madam Chairman was then shown her seat at the head table on the immediate right side of the U.S. President's place. Jet then turned back toward the entranceway as the 'Guest of Honor' and the American First Lady prepared to enter the dining hall.

"To all our honored guests, it is my pleasure and honor to give you our Guest of Honor and America's birthday boy, the President of the United States and First Lady, George and Arlene Anderson." Just as Jet finished talking, the orchestra on the lawn struck up a stirring rendition of Hail to the Chief, quickly followed by 'Happy Birthday to You'. A short fireworks display erupted on the South lawn of the New Whitehouse.

As George passed Jet he quietly and smilingly said, "You guys are dead meat," and continued with his friendly greetings. George's Chief of Staff, a lip reader and sign language expert was having trouble containing himself and let a chuckle escape his lips. George's penchant for practical joking had come home to roost.

"You in on this, Bill?" the President asked while firmly squeezing his hand.

"Paybacks a bitch, ain't it," he chided quietly through a toothy smile.

Jet's wife whispered reassurance to Arlene, "Everything's set," which brought a broad conspiratorial smile of 'mischief' to her face. They continued toward their seats at the head table, where Jet and his wife, Susannah, took their place on the President's left. As Jet was the gala's emcee he sat down last, at which time the waiters and waitresses began serving. 'Jet' glanced over to the electronic marquee and verified tonight's agenda: -

1. Dinner

2. Welcome - introductory speech

3. Madame Chairman of COWA - acceptance and reply speech

4. The President's speech of gratitude

5. Ballroom dancing and entertainment

6. Closing ceremonies and fireworks display

7. Guests' departures

This was also the opportunity that Bud Davies needed to talk to the Marshalls who, luckily were sitting beside him. It was Angélique to whom Bud addressed and introduced himself with his lovely wife, Darlene.

Conversational topics progressed from introductions, through comments about the food, gala décor, who's who, and personal current events. Bud couldn't beat about the bush any longer, and introduced the topic of deep space travel.

As if to test his footing with Angélique he said, "You know, although there is one school of thought that Earth's destiny lies in space, there is also an opposing and equally aggressive school of thought, that mankind has no business going into space. And that he should concentrate his efforts here on Earth trying to improve our way of life by better understanding the planet we live on and its resources. And that means delving into its people and resolve social problems that exist today."

"Why Bud, I would have thought that you would have been more passionate about space, being SETIA's number two man. What's caused the development of the double loyalties?"

Upon hearing this question from Angélique, her husband Howard and Bud's wife Darlene stopped their conversation and gave attention to Bud. He had a hunch he could continue now, safely.

"It's a long story Angélique, and mostly one based on my naïveté, which unfortunately has progressed to a stage where it's beyond my control. Something I wish I could reverse quickly," he said, trailing his voice, hoping she would offer help toward a resolution.

"Bud, I was contacted by COWA today, before coming here, and was told that someone would contact me with some important information concerning SETIA. Would that be you?"

Leveling his gaze at her directly, he asked factually, "What level of clearance do you have, Angélique?"

Returning his gaze, she quietly said, "As an intelligence operative for SETIA level one; as far as COWA is concerned that's on a need to know basis. Why?"

Leaning closer toward her he told her about Ira Bushnel's conversation of planned sabotage and that he was afraid that "technical difficulties" wouldn't be sufficient this time.

It was Darlene Davies who reacted unexpectedly upon hearing this remark from her husband, "Oh, Bud. Don't you realize that John Marshall is Howard and Angélique's son. And that Janet and I worked together just two years ago, on an oceanographic problem. I'm so sick of Ira's clandestine BS I could kill him this time, myself."

"Ira Bushnel, the Director of Central Intelligence?" asked Angélique.

"Yes," replied Bud, looking apologetic.

"Do you know how and when?"

"Now. A dogfight in space somewhere. No evidence. No witnesses. Clean. Those are his words, not mine."

"Your conscience is clear now. Is that it, Bud?" Darlene pushed. "You bastard, I told you to drop him some time ago!"

"Darlene, I know you're upset, but you have to know that it's mild compared to how I, we," placing her hand consolingly on her husband Howard's hand, "feel right now. And if we get any more boisterous, Ira's going to come over here," Angélique said, arching her eyebrow toward the table on her right. They looked in the indicated direction and saw Ira returning their gaze. They raised their wineglasses in a silent toast of acknowledgement.

"Well, obviously, nothing has happened that we should know about because you haven't been contacted, yet, Bud. Hopefully, it stays that way. Thank you for telling us but now what are you going to do about your situation since Ira will find out sooner or later?"

"Between Sam and I, Angélique, we will come up with some sort of resignation excuse."

"Good, now let's enjoy the party!" Angélique knew she would have to kill him if he didn't do it soon. Looking back at Howard she also knew she need not look far for volunteers to do the job. Darlene and Howard would kill him now. Both Mr. and Mrs. Marshall knew that as of right now they were also targets, for other reasons, and by others not necessarily present at this function. Their conversation had caught the interest of the Central Intelligence Agency Director.

From his table, Ira raised his wineglass to them once more and put away his package of pocket size facial tissue into the inside pocket of his jacket, while clicking off the miniature directional mike. He smiled knowingly, that irritating way he had with his moustache slightly raised to one side.

Chapter 22

John's parents realized that if Janet and John were in a ship together, somehow they would work things out for their survival. Ellis also had to have been at John's parents' place during the farewell. Reliably, he was. Apparently, the Marshalls' suspicions of a sabotaged mission were coming true.

"Captain?' Ellis began, "if memory serves me correctly, isn't there some sort of diamond-ring effect toward the end of the eclipse?"

The tactics area was becoming quite noisy.

John had introduced himself to everyone in the 'Ferris' Wheel including the officer in charge, Lieutenant Muhammad Abdul Toor; 'Buzz', to his friends. Buzz could not suppress his feelings of happiness when he found out this was the same John Marshall who had saved his brother's life and ship three years earlier.

In his jovial best, baritone voice, Buzz gave him a bear-hug greeting saying, "Colonel Marshall! I am very pleased, no, honored to make your...oh, hell! John, I am so happy..." kissing him on the left cheek, "...in knowing you. You are like a brother to me."

The noisy expression of joy in meeting John was heard throughout the ship...right to the bridge.

"That's correct, Ellis. Good grief, what the hell is going on back there?" Turning towards the aft part of the ship he loudly asked, "Lieutenant? What is going on back there?"

"Oh Captain, please accept my apologies. But I am being so happy that the great Colonel John Marshall is a guest on our ship. He is the savior of my brother's life and now he is on 'this' ship! We must all feel honored."

"Colonel?" Captain Noor repeated, turning toward Ellis with a facial expression that was searching for clarification.

Ellis sort of shrugged his shoulders and said, "He's rather shy about it, Captain, as he doesn't fee..."

"He's not a Colonel with COWA?"

"Well, he is and he isn't."

The Captain glared at Ellis.

"Captain, he's a Colonel with SETIA, which is part of COWA and, under certain jurisdictional circumstances, he will exercise this authority. And yes, that means take command of this ship if the need arises!" said Ellis, almost in exasperation.

"SETIA? We are on a mission to Mars and we expect sabotage from Aliens?"

Ellis looked at Julie as if the Captain had 'flipped'.

Commander Lau looked at Captain Noor and said, "Sir, both Marshalls outrank us but I'm sure there was no malicious intent. In fact, as you said earlier, the Marshalls are our mission and we must get them to Mars. If we can use their skills while enroute, where's the harm?

And they're ours, not aliens. They've been doing their level best to support all aspects of the space program since its inception way back in the twentieth century."

"I was just told to pick up you, Julie, and two V.I.P.'s and ensure their safe arrival at New Washington. Reason was classified. Transmissions were not allowed unless authorized. Tell me, how can they be authorized unless I've received permission?"

"Finally makes sense, eh Dilpreet?" said Ben smiling.

"What makes sense, this mission?"

"No, military intelligence," laughed Ben.

"Yeah, right. And that book sits on bookshelves right next to what man knows about women!"

Turning back to Ellis, "As you were saying, there is a diamond ring effect around the moon as seen from Earth. It occurs near the end of a solar eclipse when the Sun starts to peek around the edge of the moon as the eclipse ends. But what does that have to do with anything, Ellis?" asked the ship's captain.

"Sir, looking at our view-screen, I see that we are approaching the penumbra of the moon's shadow and as we move through it..."

"You figure the intensity of light from the 'diamond' will temporarily blind us visually, but more importantly provide cover for the saboteurs. Correct, Ellis?"

"Correct, Sir, and if they have weapons on board which could disable our computers, it would present itself as a golden opportunity, so to speak."

"Sir?"

"Yes, helm."

"We're still on course for the moon as you ordered, sir, but for some peculiar reason there seems to be an aberration of the 'diamond ring' ... and it's ... it's ... moving!"

They looked at the main view-screen. Near the mid-point of the 'diamond', the jewel seemed to have a reflection, not of itself, but of areas around it.

"There's our target."

"Correction, sir. Targets. There are three of them," chimed Robert.

"Quickly, lock in their co-ordinates and feed them to tactical.

Lieutenant, are you getting these co-ordinates on your computers?"

At that very moment a klaxon horn alarm sounded and the screen displayed 'INTENSE RADIATION'. Internal lighting was dimmed and a flashing yellow, lighting condition began. The computer's voice announced, "Incoming solar flare radiation; E.T.A. 2 minutes, 56 seconds; estimated duration period of 1.4 hours; radiation type

- micro waves, gamma rays, x-rays, and various ions. Shield 2x2 is being deployed."

"Acknowledged, Captain. They're locked in."

"Good. The ship's yours."

"Acknowledged, Captain. John, do you want the honor of first kill, because we have just 3 seconds?"

"My pleasure. Thanks, Buzz."

With the co-ordinates, already in the weapons computer, three ATM-3L7 magnetic disc-emplacement rocket missiles were sent toward the targets.

"Not so fast 'my brother'; with our shields deployed, we are blind. We can't even get to the bridge and Janet is isolated aft."

"Buzz, look, I, ah, haven't been to a good turkey shoot since I was a kid; but, I have never traded places with the turkey. What's happening here?"

"John, just give us some time for the missiles to work. It shouldn't be too long."

"Missiles in space?"

"You weren't supposed to find out about these until later, so a quick briefing now couldn't hurt.

They're miniature SF rockets with a missile casing to get past ground ordinance crews … need to know basis.

John, see where it says 'BSU' on your computer console?"

Buzz was talking to John from his location at the wheel's hub where he could monitor all the bubbles' activities and shut each one down and isolate it if the need arose. The 'gunner' in each cell bubble expected it, which was the main reason why gunner training and procedures were so strictly followed - to prevent cell excision from becoming necessary.

"Yeah, I see it."

"Good. Press 'A', then 'Sel'."

Touching his glass covered console at 'A' and 'Sel', John said, "My screen's displaying all sorts of information but shows that I do not have control over it anymore. It's on automatic."

"That's what's wanted, John. I'm going to set up your console such that your pod will operate independently of the ship and the other five pods. You'll be fed all the statistical and tactical data. Your console will also display the best solution to any given enemy maneuver, but you'll have the final decision to implement it. And one other little item John, you must wear your Saunders belt while in the pod because when your pod is drawing fire you will be environmentally isolated from the rest of the ship."

"Tell me that's beneficial, Buzz."

"As a matter of fact, it is. NASA engineers working with COWA have determined that varying certain mixtures of gases inhaled during combat conditions heighten the senses, improves performance, and reduces the build up of toxins in the blood due to lack of physical movement thereby keeping your vital signs normal. In other words, ..."

"It should feel like a computerized simulation when it's all over."

"That's the theory, John."

"Theory?"

"Ahem, yeah, theory. We've never been in a situation whereby the opponent has been able to engage or avoid us at will. Tactical L.S.D., so to speak," John offered. Seeing Buzz's facial expression, John offered, "Little Slow in Doing," but fast selling.

"Should be easy for you, Marsh" chimed Benson, who was listening from John's opposing pod.

"Stewart? That you?"

"You got it, dead eye. Who else would go to a 'turkey shoot' in space with the man who single-handedly cleaned up on six U.S. Military Personnel in a bar known to be frequented by GB's and SEALS?"

"Hey come on, Stew, they were all well trained in the ancient martial arts as well as ACERT."

"ACERT? What's that?" asked Buzz, amused and distracted by this sparring banter.

"Alien Crisis Emergency Response Tactics," said Stew. "John can trick the minds of anyone within a thirty-foot radius into believing what he wants them to believe. It means that John, along with a few others I suspect, has the uncanny ability to make certain species of the Animal Kingdom believe excuse me, I should say, react to their immediate surroundings the way John makes their senses perceive it. So, when those six ladies felt that they had been insulted by the likes of a visiting 'Canuck flyboy' it was just too much to bear. After all, they were Green Beret and SEAL instructors in hand-to-hand combat. And they were there with a few of the course graduates, among whom was my sister, Marnie."

"Yeah, so what happened?" pried Buzz, interested in his hero's past antics.

"Well, Marnie told me that this 'northern nut' and his two buds, Saunders and Davidson, had been drinking that new drink, 'shooting star', when one of them said, "Geezus, John, life moves so damn slow in Fayetteville, there's mold growing on the military's heads." So, that caused Johnny and his other pals to burst out laughing.

Well, the drill Captain, Sabrina Greene, overheard this insult and looked at her other instructors who were also concerned about the affect it might have on some of the grads in the tavern. So, she took it upon herself to go over and introduce herself to her 'country's guests'.

Being an attractive, tall, assertive, self-confident woman, it drew a long, lecherous, low whistle out of Saunders as she stood with her back to him just inches from John's face. Apparently, Saunders foot slipped off the foot ring of his bar stool, accidentally kicking her left tendon area."

Benson paused, causing Buzz to say, "Go on! What happened next?" Buzz kept his eyes on his computer screens while listening. The gunners in the other four pods were all ears as well.

Marnie said, "Well, Captain Greene moved so fast with her hands that the three northern visitors were laid out on the floor before they could take their next breath." Marnie just gasped in awe at Sabrina's action.

Then the three visitors apparently started chuckling, while picking themselves from the floor. Then John said to his friends so everyone could hear, "Well, people, apparently, the mice want to play with the cats."

One of the other instructors sitting at Sabrina's table, stood up and accompanied her near the bar. She scoffed a reply, "Cats? What's a cat without claws and teeth, but rat fodder?" This brought laughter and caterwauling from the rest of the patrons, marines and civilians alike.

Both of John's friends had complete trust in him and followed his lead. He challenged the girls to step outside where they could demonstrate their skill on their terms. He was firm and convincing because in the next few seconds everybody in the tavern went out to the parking lot to watch the action.

"Come on, Benson, get to the point. Where does the 'virgin territory' reference come in? We've three minutes left until the radiation level has subsided to a point where we can take guarded action." Buzz was clearly showing his irritation with his gunner's treatment of his newly found friend.

"Well, I don't think even John knows the extent of his special skill and just how far reaching it is or how deeply it can affect some people."

"Yeah, that's true. Still exploring" John said, as Buzz looked back at him.

"When they spilled out into the parking lot, my sister Marnie, in anticipation of some pseudo-combat fun, removed her eyeglasses, which she uses as the result of an injury incurred during a cold survival course."

"Your point, Benson?" Buzz pressed.

"My point, sir, is that the Colonel here didn't take precautions during this... what 'he' later describes as just a friendly demonstration."

"Meaning...."

"Meaning, my sister's vision is reduced with her eyeglasses removed and she didn't succumb to the Colonel's antics. So, she started laughing at what was going on and stood beside the Colonel's two friends who apparently were doing a spinning ballet movement on their toes."

"Yeah, so..."

"He later told her in the hospital bed, that she was standing beside what appeared to everybody else as two men spinning with medieval spiked balls on chains and that the other grads were defending themselves as best as they could. She probably appeared vulnerable to them, so they took her out."

"And."

"And they practically crippled her for life," John interrupted, "destroying her ability, among other things, to have children. And, Stewart is still carrying a grudge." Looking at Benson but talking to Buzz, John continued, "What he has failed to tell us is that two years after I met Janet I made good a promise that I made to Marnie."

"And what was that?" asked Buzz.

"Yeah, big John, what was that? To experiment on her, and have her die on the table so my family could bury her. Some promise," jeered Benson.

Buzz was definitely showing visible signs of discomfort about his friend's character but before he could voice his concerns, John piped up and said, "Before this mission is over Stewart, I shall allow you to retrieve the honor which you believe you have lost. And no tricks this time."

This seemed to placate Benson's swirling, hot temper for the time being but, John now had to rescue himself from Benson's character assassination.

"Buzz, can I have a word with you in private?" John implored.

"Certainly, switch to frequency five." Switching to F5 John heard Buzz in his headset ask, "What's up, my friend?"

"Buzz, in case something happens to us here and you survive, I want you to introduce yourself to Captain Marta Bjorgennsen on Mars in the Extra-terrestrial Food Production and Research Center and relate to her this incident. And Buzz, you must work the phrase 'glacial striations' into your conversation so that it seems a natural part of it. Will you do that for me?"

"And what will happen?"

"She'll ask you how Stewart is, and then fill you in on what happened and how she got to where she is now. She won't recall anyone or anything prior to the tavern incident. She will recall Stewart because he visited her in hospital during the surgery to replace her reproductive system and complete eye transplant from her clone."

"Why didn't your wife give memory-recall back to her at the same time?"

"She did, or rather she didn't interfere with those parts of her brain. A post-operative complication developed and since her clone had already been prepared for burial it was impossible for Jan to retrieve the remains for a complete brain transplant under current laws and ethics. What we do in space now is whatever it takes to survive. So, laws and ethics are decided by Jan concurrently during procedures. In effect, she is the law and enforcement body while in space. Marnie was given the opportunity to join Jan in her work but was told she would lose her past identity - that's my specialty - and therefore, her death and burial were staged to protect herself and her family from the same element of society that frowns on space travel and all its spin-off discoveries and advances."

"What good will it serve awakening her to her past family life?"

"Because it will give them both meaningful purpose for the rest of their lives."

"Both?" queried Buzz.

"Yes," said John. "Do it while Stewart accompanies you but stays out of sight until the right moment - you'll know it when it happens," John said reassuringly.

"My friend, if I survive, I'll do it if it's the last thing that I do. And I'll do it even if Stewart doesn't survive; I'll do it for him and Marnie."

"No matter what the outcome of this little skirmish my friend, I can assure you it just might be the last thing you do as far as Earth or its beings are concerned. When we were summoned to Mars, I'm afraid there was no consideration given for our return," John said, trying to remain jovial for Buzz.

Chapter 23

"Any sign of them, helm?"

"Nothing yet, sir."

"Well let's stay on our toes because with the equipment we have there will only be a split second to perceive and react!" the Captain reminded everyone.

"1.33 seconds to be precise, Captain. And sir, I think I can cut that time down with an amendment to my idea.

Robert, do you have information on captured bodies in our solar system during the earlier part of this millennium, say around the year 2000?" asked Ellis.

"Just let me dig it out of history, ah, here it is, Ellis, but what ...? Wait a second, the orbit of this asteroid, Grozny, comes between us and... Sir, may I suggest we take immediate evasive maneuvers!" Robert requested urgently.

"Do it Robert."

Ellis had already plotted a course for Robert, so he just 'Entered' it. Although there was no 'visual' sighting of the three ships, as yet, Captain Noor sensed he had reacted in time. The Sun was now making itself completely visible. Their ship had aligned itself as if expecting its foe to suddenly emerge from the cloaking cover of the asteroid, yet keeping in mind the 'blind' spot produced by the diamond effect of the waning solar eclipse. Apparently just in time.

John's diametrically opposite gunner was chuckling at him and said, "Seems our 'super-shooter' here can't get his bearings. "Hey, John? Colonel Marshall, sir? The targets will be coming from that direction, sir," Corada said, pointing towards John's backside. Stewart chuckled in the one-upmanship.

"Listen pal, I have always trusted my instincts in the past and found that, if the solution reached, is based on a high probability of success, then I go with the opposite finding, particularly with events in which man is involved. By that I mean, if we were smart enough to solve a puzzle, then the 'puzzle' is smart enough to change the outcome, and that my friend is about to happen.

Look," John said pointing toward the Sun.

The young gunner barely had enough time to swing 180° when an energy bolt hit the side of the ship with a weak glancing blow. John had a lock on the targets, which automatically fed into the computers of the other gunners' stations of the 'wheel'. Simultaneously, a volley of return fire erupted from the wheel traversing the 256,387 miles of space in 1.37 seconds resulting in two gigantic fireballs and flying debris, lasting three and a half seconds.

A jubilant eruption of conquering joy could be heard throughout the ship...except from Ellis and John. John spoke directly to Ellis through his headset microphone. "Ellis, is that 100%?"

"Negative, John. We predicted three. We're searching."

John did a complete 180° turn and his 'Targeting Window' on his computer screen showed an anomaly of what appeared like a panoramic view of space moving toward him - when it should be moving away!

"Targeting" John said into his microphone.

Everyone fixed on John's targeting co-ordinates and waited.

Without hesitating, he targeted the center of it and fired a full burst from his high impulse energy canon. Space in front of him, three thousand miles away, exploded destroying the remaining ship, which was bent on a suicidal ramming run!

"There, probability of target destruction, 100%. Now, they can cheer!" said John through clenched teeth.

And cheer they did.

Chapter 24

Justice Davies was settling down for a relaxing evening of sipping 15-year-old Normandie Napoleon brandy, while being entertained by Schubert, Mozart, Beethoven, and Chopin. Bud knew that after his earlier H-link conversation his life would be on borrowed time. So, following that and a harrowing day of anxious waiting, he was feeling freed from his load of guilt. He thought that he would usher the 'musical greats' into his living room with a recording of Anderson Lee's Mass Martial Music Hour to stir up his blood. And so, it would have, if his H-link had not signaled an incoming communication.

"Damn! You do pick your times, Ira" Bud cursed, while preparing his entertainment program.

"Relaxing, were you, Bud?" Ira goaded.

Taking a sip of his brandy, Bud noticed that he had another incoming message on his H-link and replied, "Ira, I'm going to have to put you on pause. I have a high-priority incoming call."

"Okay, Bud. But, don't do anything foolish," Ira warned. Ira was suspicious, but then, Ira was always suspicious.

Bud closed him out only to see the H-link reveal a full size 3-D image of Samuel Davis. He was calling from Mars. The Link displayed only the information the receiver needed to know, like the caller's hologram and the communication time delay between Mars and Earth of 1.75 seconds. (c=2.557 x10^7 m/s if Mars was 45 million miles away)

Litecom, the communication company contracted to COWA since 2295 A.D., had the exclusive extra-terrestrial communication contract. They were the best company to manage the security of the transmission, and at hundreds of times the speed of light. Bud had the call unscrambled and greeted Sam Davis, chairman of SETIA.

"Good evening, Sam." Bud sensed the reason for the call but tried to appear nonchalant. Hopefully, interplanetary interference could assist with the convincing.

"Bud, good to see you finally. Bud, I'm sorry for not getting back to you earlier but I, excuse me, we have been extremely busy lately. If you recall our last conversation."

"Sam, I'm resigning. I want out."

"Bud, let me show you something to which I am certain you will raise an eyebrow."

A second image appeared beside Sam. It was that of Bud talking earlier with Colonel Harding, John and Janet Marshall, near the Dolphin display at the marina.

"But, there was no one else."

Sam cut him short. "Do you recall the mother on the bench, nursing her baby? She's about to request entry to your home. She's a soldier Bud, sent to protect you."

"Have you known all along that I was being forced to …"

A knock at Bud's entrance door interrupted the conversation. He walked to the door and waved his hand in a downward motion. A section of the door appeared to become transparent like a large window. The built-in scanner revealed a woman and more. It revealed that she had a hand 'Lazer' holstered under her left arm and a recharged power cell in her handbag. Also, she had a filling in her upper right second molar and a COWA implant pager in her right ear. His eyes, examining the rest of her body, noted a pen scanner in her body-hugging left, inside jacket pocket.

Bud couldn't help but glance down and notice that she was wearing a vaginal trap - a painful, barbaric device to rip off any male's penis. He winced but knew she meant business, even though she was rather attractive. Since she knocked on the door, he would have the skin cells, which she would leave behind, analyzed for genetic material, and any existing biological problems. The scanner quickly revealed a chemical imbalance consistent with bodybuilding, menstruating hormones with birth origins in arid environments. Bud depressed the PRINT/SAVE icons and would pick up the information in his den later.

He closed the scanner, watching the screen dissolve into the door almost invisibly and admitted her to his home.

Entering quickly and quietly, she pursed her lips and put her left index finger to her mouth indicating silence. The American CIA may have monitoring equipment in Bud's home and she made him read the scribbled note in her palm. She produced her pen scanner and adjusted the top of the pen by twisting it into three positions, scanning the room after each adjustment. Bud watched with growing amusement.

It was all for nothing. She shrugged her shoulders as if emphasizing the negative results.

Bud returned quickly to his call with Sam.

"Sam, have you known all along that I have been forced to cooperate with Ira and his cutthroat CIA henchmen?"

"Bud, let me put it this way. I want you to meet your bodyguard for the next few days, Anouke Ketabi. She will be at your side in whatever capacity is deemed expedient. And she is good, but, be warned, she is all business."

Sam, if memory serves me, she was nursing a baby on a nearby bench when I was at the Marina with the Marshalls and..."

Quickly seizing the moment Anouke interjected, "I was on a protection assignment, Bud, for Sam. It was authorized by COWA." She knew he would verify this information with COWA's Internal Affairs Bureau. Her GGEE contact in the IAB at COWA would ensure he would receive the 'correct' information.

Bud made a note of Anouke's claim and would contact SETIA's representative at Internal Affairs. "Let's just say I've had a few friends look out for you, Bud, but just the same I think it would be best for all concerned that you relinquish your position in SETIA. You must understand that Ira is not going to take this lightly because you know too much. So, I would also urge that you come up with a very plausible reason for resigning and discuss it with me before submitting it. And one more thing, Bud, you're not going to like this one, so you better sit down." Sam watched him as he sat down on the couch and Bud used this opportunity to interrupt the flow.

"Sam, I have Ira waiting on the holo-com. Should I get rid of him?"

"No. Tell him that you are talking with me and you'll get right back to him."

"Hang on, Sam."

"Ira, sorry to keep you waiting so long but I'm talking with Sam Davis, the Chairman of SETIA."

"I know who he is, Bud. But what is she doing there?" Ira asked, his head nodding in Anouke's direction.

"We can talk about that later, Ira. Right now, it is important that I conclude my business with him."

"I'll call you in ten minutes, Bud. But, just be careful what you say," Ira said, menacingly. Ira glared at Anouke as his hologram winked out.

Anouke and Bud watched Ira's image disappear to be replaced with Sam's.

"Sam, I terminated Ira's call, but he told me he was going to call back in ten minutes."

"Good, by that time we'll have a plausible explanation for your resignations."

"Resignations? Don't you mean resignation?"

"Bud, in your state of stress you are not thinking clearly. In fact, how much does Darlene know? How much of your clandestine life with Ira has affected your legal life? And chance meetings of people unrecalled? And little unexplained events or things? Are you a gambler, Bud? Remember, you and Darlene are at stake; not your best asset.

No, I think it's better that you resign from both posts, for both your sakes and we'll work out the future and what happens from here. I promise you, you won't regret it."

"Sam, resigning from SETIA as second chair is simpler than my position as center chair for the Supreme Court of Florida. I also head several committees."

"On the contrary, Bud, your resignation as Florida's Chief Justice will be much simpler. For example, declining health, accompanied by a deteriorating psychological profile all requiring a convalescence of, say, a few years which will bow you out of there quite nicely. People will see it as administrative burn out, quite common. Gracious to the public for that matter which could prove useful later.

On the other hand, the paperwork submission of your SETIA resignation will be its only simple step. Right now, you know too much, and I am damn sure there are others on Earth, besides your buddy Ira, who would dearly love to feed your body with nutrients, while they drain your brain of its memory protein. I figure they could prolong the agony for years after they obtained what they really want, so you could be one of their 'teaching' specimens. They might even make you watch some experimental procedures on Darlene, as an added feature for their students."

"You've made your point, Sam! I hadn't given it much thought. I never truly believed these factions would go to the extent that the news media has reported."

Sam's irritation with Bud's obvious 'clean' naïveté crept into his voice. "The bloody news media doesn't know the half of it for geezus sake, Bud. Some ... look, if Ira is mixed up in it, and he's head honcho for the CIA, you can bet your tonsils, there are a few supporters from within countries like Russia, Iran, Iraq, Afghanistan,

Pakistan, China, France, Germany, Canada and, especially, the United States. And those are the ones that have been caught lately. I'm damn certain he's calling in a few favors and repaying others."

Calming down a little, Sam continued, "But, Bud, you have to know COWA's secret police is on top of this."

"Is this the reason for Anouke's presence, to protect me?"

"You and Darlene," Bud.

Glancing nonchalantly about the room, Bud looked for his wife and Anouke. He saw neither mentally noting it, but pressed the intercom button just the same.

"Bud, I know you are going to receive some quizzical, suspicious queries about your resignation from your fellow Justices. I have had my people check for any potential backlash, both directly, and indirectly, and they say, you shouldn't have a problem."

"Yes, Bud?" Darlene was on the intercom.

Turning his head to his left, Bud directed his voice to the wall receiver, "Darlene, come on in here for a sec, will you?" He turned back to look and listen to Sam.

"Okay, Bud. I'll bring Anouke, too."

"Moreover, someone, whom you've trusted with your life, will visit you soon and she feels as I, that there is someone who bears watching. Don't reject what she says as she has very good instincts."

"Who is she, Sam?"

"You've already met her, Bud, so for security reasons, I won't mention her by name."

Anouke and Darlene were entering the room from the solarium area on Bud's right side. Both heard Sam's last remark resulting in two very different responses from the newly arriving audience members.

From Darlene, "Well, can we expect our additional guest for tomorrow, Sam?"

"I don't know. It's good to see you again, Darlene. You are looking well."

"Thank you, Sam. It's good to see you too. Your work seems to agree with you."

Anouke stood casually in the background, watching with interest the players in this deceptively warm conversation, maybe too much interest! It was Bud's way to be aligned, so that he could look directly at his wife, while observing persons of concern over his wife's shoulder. In this way he caught a glimpse of Anouke's facial expression of disappointment when Sam disclosed he would not name Bud's expected visitor. Another judicial mental note was made.

"Believe me, Darlene, when a doctor tells you to watch your weight, it's very tempting <u>not</u> to calibrate the bathroom scales properly. I thought I was almost 70% of my Earth weight at one point, but that bubble quickly popped with my next physical. But I am glad to see that you are still the same as the last time we had a barbecue. Right Bud?"

"She does change very slowly, Sam," giving her an affectionate squeeze. "But that's only one of the reasons I love her more each day."

"O-o-o-h, quite the diplomat," Darlene said, squeezing her husband's arm.

"Heh, heh," Sam chuckled. "Bud, I'll hear from you later, okay?"

"Talk to you, Sam, soon."

The hologram winked out just in time as Ira was calling in again.

The moment Bud's image disappeared from Sam's transceiver, his aide said, "We got her, Sam. But the bad news is she is a mole. She works for GGE, God's Garden of Eden, the saboteur faction."

"Angélique must know this already and is letting her run for some reason."

Sam and his aide looked at each other in quiet agreement.

"Prepare for John and Janet's arrival William, while I use this information when I speak with George at the site to plan a defence. I think we'll notify Shaneen as well William," said Sam.

"The COWA Chairman, Sir?"

"Yes."

"Of developments to date, Sam?"

"Yes, and where we expect to be with all of this in the future. And do it through my closed channel."

"Sir, I think NASA has some scheduled Lunar events this week, so our timing has to be accurate."

"Very well then, let me know if you experience any transmission difficulties and I'll punch in my private security line."

"Acknowledged, sir!"

Damn, Bud doesn't even know thought Sam.

Bud Davies' facial expression revealed subdued irritation with his hologram caller, yet he was cautious not to let it interfere with his analysis of any given situation.

"Ira, I'm glad you waited. Something has come up that I will let you know about as soon as I work out the details."

"I hope it doesn't involve any resignation scheme that you and Sam Davis may have worked out while you had me on hold. I just want to remind you Bud that both Darlene and you are willing partners in our combined efforts."

"Ira, answer me a question, will you?"

"About your safety?"

"No. About our so-called combined efforts and our goals."

"Oh, for Pete's sakes, Bud, you're a friggen adult. How many times do you need reassurance that what you're doing is right?"

"I just want to make sure that the page you're on is the same as mine."

"So, ask the question."

"The reason the corporation, GGE, exists is to prevent the exploitation of the Universe, its celestial bodies and any life forms Earth might encounter. And by contact, I also mean aliens landing on Earth. Correct?"

"Over simplified but that's the gist of it," Bud.

"Ira, I think there's more to it. I've had some people do an investigation for me and I don't like the conclusions we've reached."

"Such as?"

"Such as the financial gains seen on the Common Stock Market in astro-techs, solar-sys geos, bio-gens, nuc-fuels, lite-comms, and so on, but always noted after some development surrounding any space tragedy."

"Speculation and coincidence, Bud. You're reaching and I would be careful who you say this to publicly." Ira was showing his irritability with Bud's naïveté.

"I guess the increases alone would be insufficient proof, but not when they're paired with long term contracts between the suppliers to the main space development and exploration facilities and the companies I've mentioned. When that is coupled with the fact that the benefiting spin-off companies have as their major shareholder, our beloved corporation, God's Garden of Eden, it's a bit more than simple speculation and coincidence."

Ira continued, "So, it all comes down to nothing more than a few money-making schemes. Furthermore, when we reviewed the archival news records of events surrounding space accidents and tragedies we found that some key personnel were directly involved before or after the events related to GGE."

"Do you have any proof for any of these allegations, Bud? Because if you don't, and you go public with it, you shouldn't have any problem resigning as second chair for SETIA, and the center chair in Florida's Supreme Court."

"Ira, I think your ego has perforated your ear drums. One of the laundering schemes GGE is concerned with supplies military equipment for some covert operations that the CIA participates in and we have your signature and President Anderson's Chief of Staff, William Henry Rogers, as co-signer for a few of these contracts."

Anouke and Darlene were watching with alarming interest, but Anouke was watching Ira, while Darlene was watching Bud.

"Bud, I'm going to have some people come over to see you shortly and they're going to take you to my place as my friend. I must convince you, that your evidence is at best circumstantial but more importantly, Rogers and myself are completely innocent." Ira glanced in the room, and looked at Anouke. She understood his look.

"You do that, Ira. You do that." Bud closed the transmission while a bead of perspiration trickled down his right temple. His bluff worked and Ira revealed their guilt in a manner he didn't suspect. Now the problem was not Ira's people, but Rogers' legal thugs. Ira knew he couldn't recognize them and that Darlene would be vulnerable.

"Honey, why don't you go make us all some hot chocolate."

"Not for me, thanks," said Anouke.

"For us then, Dar, in my special mug, please."

"Darlene looked at him, and caught his meaning." She sensed that Bud didn't trust this soldier who was sent from SETIA to protect Bud. But, she also knew that Sam wouldn't be in on any execution attempt of Bud. So, when she pulled the special mug off the shelf, she read the inscription, "To Edmund (Bud) Daniel Davies, Big Brother of the Year, 3341A.D." The mug was presented to him from Angélique Marshall. She knew she had to contact her without Anouke knowing it. What she didn't know was that Angélique was enroute to Bud's place at that very moment.

Chapter 25

If Mars and Earth were in conjunction with all the planets, then the Sun God Apollo, could ride his steed from Pluto to the Sun, in a straight line to inspect his planets. Robert and Ellis were discussing these points when the Captain requested an intercepting, arcing trajectory to Mars to minimize fuel consumption and travel time.

"Ellis, Mars is approximately 48,732,000 miles from Earth, orbitally speaking. And from what the computer tells me our best window will cover 61 million miles. Can we cover that distance in eight weeks?"

"If by eight weeks, Robert, you mean 1,344 hours, then this ship has to travel at 45,386.9 miles per hour. I had thought these ships were designed to travel only at 35,000 mph as their upper limit."

"If we use these engines only, yes, but not if we sling shot around the Earth, thus producing another 11,000 mph. And that 'window' is 2.2 hours away if we are at these co-ordinates." Ellis showed Robert the co-ordinates as he spoke.

"Captain, we need to be there in 2.2 hours," Robert said, pointing to a point in space near Earth's orbit.

"Can we make it in time, Robert? I sense you are asking me for some reason."

"Sir, I'll need to do a special fuel burn."

"So, do it. Let's move. Ah, ha! I see what's troubling you two. Do it, Robert. The rest of us will watch to see if any hounds give chase."

The Captain knew the special burn would light up their trajectory like a comet, which could be seen by astronomers working for GGE.

"Bridge to John Marshall."

"Go ahead, Captain."

"John, come forward will you, please."

"On my way. Talk later, Buzz."

"Plenty of time, buddy." They gave each other high fives in passing.

"Yes, Captain," John said, entering the bridge compartment.

"John, we have to do an 80% burn for quite a few minutes to put us in an optimum position to slingshot around Earth, on our way to Mars, and get you there within the shortest time possible. Does that bode well with you?"

"What's the real reason you're telling me this, Captain? Is there some concern for our safety; wait a minute. You think there's a possibility of more attacks. In this part of space, the extra long and bright burn will appear like a flare to anyone watching? Like a well-lit target; damn!"

"Very astute, John. And what's more in doing it, we may end up short of fuel in case we have to 'limp' back to Earth."

"And by that you need a constant burn to prevent a gravitational grab by Mars? Or Jupiter?"

"Jupiter. It will be in a better position to affect us if we can't produce nominal thrust."

"Pulling us through the Asteroid Belt," John completed the Captain's claim of doom. "Death by stoning. How befitting for God's Garden of Eden - they chase us to the stoning site and make sure we can't leave. Watch us die and disappear. Biblically blameless, so to speak."

"Sounds perfect to me, John."

"Ellis, do you have any better ideas for us?" John asked of his friend.

"At risk of sounding like you John, it's bush pilot territory."

"You're right."

The Captain looked at them with that 'huh?' expression on his face.

Turning to the captain, John said, "Captain, let's do it and we'll improvise as we go."

"Excellent. Keep it off the log Robert, unless we get into deep shit."

"Shit, sir?"

"Never mind. If the hounds show up, put the ship's log on 'chronometer' only until they've been destroyed."

"Aye, Sir." Robert looked at Ellis and quietly said, "He is human after all. He swears and does things for expediency."

"I'm going back to the wheel Captain to brief Buzz and his crew. And I'll talk to Jan."

"Good." Turning back to Robert, he said, "As of right now this ship is on high alert - no white lighting. The light emitting diodes in the gauges and computer consoles will provide adequate lighting. Movement through corridors is to be illuminated by blue lighting, and kept at medium intensity. Intercom usage kept at a necessary level only; friendly banter can be done in person."

Arriving in the makeshift trauma center John closed the hatch. He couldn't readily see Jan so he did the next best thing. He called out.

"Jan?"

Recognizing the voice as that of her husband she replied, "Are you alone?"

"Yes." He looked in the direction of her voice and watched the curtain part slowly.

"The Captain's put the ship on full alert because we expect more attacks on the way." In the dim blue light John thought he was seeing things as his wife emerged from behind the curtain. She was almost naked and what was covered left little to the imagination and no room for why. From her head to her toes she moved with the grace of a spider on its sticky net of gossamer webbing.

Spider prey would struggle. John didn't, or wouldn't, and swallowed hard. His heartbeat increased and so did his blood pressure. His pupils enlarged. He felt a good reason for getting out of his pressure suit in a hurry.

She walked to the bed, turned invitingly and asked, "How soon can we expect the first attack?" She had extended her right arm out to him, giving him a very definite message.

In space, right now with his suit removed, it was apparent that John's ego and id were clearly in charge. Slow movement be damned!

Jan smiled, appreciating her effect on her husband and cooed, "Care for some mountain climbing time, darling?"

He grasped her around her waist gently but firmly, pushing unmistakingly against her. She chuckled gutturally, into his mouth as he bent to kiss her saying, "Is that a piton, darling, or just an anchoring device?"

He returned her kiss ardently, while laying her back on the bed. John noted its pressure sensors were turned on.

In silence, they made love as if they had not done so for a very long time. And they hadn't in over eight and a half months. Their passions intensified. The sensors didn't sound any warning; they had orgasms simultaneously.

They whispered about starting a family and made love again. Then they rested.

The klaxon horn preceded the intercom announcement, "Full alert! Full alert!"

Jan and John quickly kissed each other on the lips, got out of bed and suited up. They strapped on their Saunders belts.

"Take care, honey," Jan said affectionately, as if John was leaving home to go to work.

John replied mockingly, "I'll be back."

They laughed light-heartedly. Deep down the alternative caused them to cross their fingers mentally, their inner thoughts of safety being identical.

Chapter 26

There are two things on Earth mankind can rely on, that the Sun would rise in the East and that Ira Bushnell was lying whenever he expressed concern for the well-being of anyone, not named Ira Bushnell. How many times had Bud been reminded of this fact?

Bud pondered and mumbled while sipping the hot chocolate that his wife had brought to him. The scars on his body showed as permanent markers. Well, the son of a bitch wasn't going to get away with it this time.

What was it he said exactly? "I must convince you that your evidence is at best circumstantial but more importantly, that Rogers and myself are completely innocent. Damn him! He even said it the same way as always - putting the other person first!" Bud smiled inwardly. Now let's get the proof together for Angélique for when I see her. Oh, yeah. "(He) must convince me." Heh, heh. "We'll see who convinces whom. You snake in the grass!" Bud said aloud to himself. Hmmm, I wonder how much Rogers is involved?

Bud wanted to tell Darlene but something told him not to trust Anouke. He thought aloud again, "She was too casual, too…too… too quick with a comeback," he exclaimed to himself, and continued musing.

"That was it. Too quick in replying to Sam with her reasonable explanation of why she was present at the Marine Park when he was meeting with the Marshalls.

Then how did she know the 'where' and the 'when'; from the office? Was his secretary a suspect? No way! She was on SETIA's payroll as an agent. I trust her completely. She's not a mole either because COWA screened her. Then my office must be monitored. Must make a mental note for Angélique. Hell, I'm resigning so what's the difference? A-ah hell, tell her anyways.

Question now is, how to get away safely for Darlene and myself? Ira and his CIA thugs knowingly or unknowingly chasing Bud was one thing, but attacks from two fronts was another. How would Anderson's Chief of Staff come after him: - character assassination and public shaming as a State Supreme Court Justice? Humiliation was always a tried and true method historically for any public figure for that matter and safer, because it was hard to isolate the source."

Bud sank deeper into the soft, rich comfort of his leathered sofa chair and let his mind absorb this information. The warming influence of the hot chocolate seemed to bolster his confidence in the defence he was developing.

If only he knew Anouke was also planning their deaths. The knock at the door startled them from their thinking. Neither Anouke's, nor Bud's plan, would see fruition.

Angélique stood far out of sensor range while her aide stood in front of the door. The built-in door scanner would scan her aide only. She was completely stripped of any identifying connection to SETIA as well as all weaponry. That was hanging on the wall to the right of the door. Held there by a Velcro fastener in a holster - he or she could grab it easily upon entering Bud's home. Darlene answered the door. The light beside the door's electronic locking mechanism showed yellow indicating the aide was being scanned.

"Who is it?" She was looking at a non-intimidating male figure of 5'10", medium frame, about 155 lbs., clear, but swarthy complexion and firm, honest-looking facial features. She seemed to sense she could trust him. She checked the scanner's lateral screen and the information confirmed her feeling.

"I've been sent by Mr. Armstrong's office to obtain some signatures, Mrs. Davies. I was told to tell Mr. Davies these documents were being used in court tomorrow. Justice Armstrong has been trying to contact him."

Darlene quickly scanned him and concluded he was clear. "Bud, Fred Armstrong has been trying to contact you to sign some documents and there is a courier at the door with them. Should I let him in? He shows clear."

Bud stood up and came towards the door saying, "Sure. Shouldn't take too long. Seems like Fred might want my support on a decision again."

Darlene pressed 'admit' and the scanner made the door appear solid again. The electronic lock 'clicked' the door to 'unlock'. The courier grabbed his weapons, stood back and kicked the door open. He slammed Bud to the floor covering him with his body. Angélique followed right on his heels, shooting Anouke with a body-destroying energy bolt blowing her lower, central chest completely away. The surrounding cavity area immediately cauterized. No bleeding whatsoever! Her body, steaming around the cavity, went backwards like a falling domino.

Bud's jaw just dropped limp, wordless. She then pointed her weapon at Darlene, adjusted the setting on the energy chamber and shot her in the chest. She fell limp but unconscious into Angélique's arms. Bud threw his protector off him and got up.

Before he could speak or act, Angélique signaled silence. She scanned the house and shot at the walls where the heating vents were. Five wireless mikes each with 3-D hologram constructors were exposed.

Damn, Bud thought! They're no bigger than shirt buttons. Further scanning revealed all else was clear.

"What the hell is going on, Angélique? Why did you shoot Darlene? And what's with all this surveillance equipment?"

He shook off the restraining hand of her aide and brushed at his clothing. The stoneware mug of hot chocolate had spilled its contents onto an area rug but was a victim itself of a forceful impact.

"All in good time, Bud. We think she's a mole. Right now, you're extremely upset. We must get you to safety and Darlene into a holding cell. We want to question her under protective custody."

"You mean you don't know now? Well excuse me that I should be upset!" Bud demanded. "For crying out loud she's my wife! She's always been at my side. I've trusted her with my life. And by God Angélique, you'd better have a damn good reason for this treatment or myself aside, I'll make sure you are incarcerated for good."

Unperturbed by his political grandstanding she looked at him motherly and said, "She's a mole, Bud. A spy in a psychological seedpod waiting for the right conditions to germinate. We know how she was planted. We just want to find out who her target is and to what extent who else is involved. More to the point, we need her to confirm this information"

He was visibly upset as the recent events were having an emotional impact against the intimacy in their marital relationship of late.

Yet, even though he had been a doting pawn for the GGE, Angélique knew that he was loyal to the point of committing suicide if it was discovered that he was the cause of any fatal event in space.

Cuffing Darlene's hands behind her back with a restricting waist attachment Angélique roused her and helped her stand. Her left high-heeled shoe fell off revealing her stocking clad foot. The baby toe didn't look right causing Angélique to comment, "Your toe looks like it was broken, Darlene? Was it?"

"Yes. An accident as a teenager broke it in a fall."

At a casual glance from Angélique, her aide moved over by Darlene's right side to grasp her arm. Angélique looked up at Darlene examining her lower leg to her knee and saw no evidence of any scarring consistent with a fall. She reached into her pocket and brought out a pen-sized scanner.

"What type of fall? Off a bicycle?"

"Yes, as kids. My friend and I were riding our bikes in a school-yard when some boys started chasing after us on theirs. I didn't realize in time there was a ground-anchored bike stand when I rounded a corner of the building. My front wheel caught in one of the slots and I went ass-over-teakettle to the cinders on the other side. My toe broke when it caught in the strap on the pedal and the force of the fall freed my foot. My bike came down on me and the handle bar gouged my inner right thigh."

The aide grasped Darlene a little tighter knowing her right thigh was going to be checked. Angélique ran the pen over Darlene's toe and up her leg, under her skirt and down the other leg and foot. She looked at the scanner, stood up, and instructed her aide to put her in front of the door.

"Bud, have you ever scanned Darlene at the front door?"

"No. Why would I? For Pete's sake Angélique, is this really necessary?" Frustrated and angry Bud said, "I've made love to Darlene and know every inch of her. I know what she looks like!"

"Do you? Look."

Bud looked. After many years of fond memories an expression of utter disdain slowly formed. He saw artificial enhancements, surely, during those stolen moments. "Oh, shit!" He felt used. Cheap. A contorted look of disgust formed.

Angélique's aide touched the back of Darlene's head, just under her hairline, with some handheld device and she went limp. He stepped away.

"But I don't understand. She's given blood, real, red blood. She's type AB negative. She even menstruates!"

Bud was for the first time absorbing it. Maybe for him, it was better this way. Clean, no ties!

"Her right thigh contains her blood supply, Bud. She gives and receives blood from the right side of her body."

Suddenly recalling, "That's right. She's very strict about that. Now I can see why," he said in a hateful voice. He realized their marriage had been a tool. He felt used.

Darlene was a bione; a marital bione, expressly designed as an intimate lifetime partner with hidden enhancements he had known nothing about.

"Bud, we've traced her history and we know the background of 'whom'. We must now get her to a location to question her for 'when', 'how much', any others, etc. But we need to hear it from her. If we can get her to talk, then the code keeping her in check as a mole will be cracked. That should lead us to others who are involved. We know you are a pawn and so was President Anderson's sister-in-law."

"What about his wife?"

"Clear for now. Darlene is harmless. She's been shut down. When she's activated again we want to be in a 'safe' facility. So, we have to get you there in the car outside."

"Okay then, let's go, sooner there, sooner done."

"Bud, we're going to blindfold you in the car and give you a knockout drug, all right?"

"Why? I'm willing to help."

"As a precaution and so you can't form any sensory memories to reveal later to others in the future." They went to the car.

In the car, Bud asked Angélique if her son and daughter-in-law know. She nodded acquiescence. "And Sam?" She nodded again while injecting the needle.

Bud shuddered as he recalled some of their torrid love making sessions, in their car, Darlene's office, and sometimes in his chambers, then blackness.

Chapter 27

"Captain, could you send Julie back to me if you don't require her on the bridge?" Julie looked over her shoulder at the Captain who nodded yes. "Acknowledged, Janet. She's on her way. Is everything all right back there? View okay?"

"The view is, uh, pretty much the same as when I was up here last."

"How's that?"

"Seasonably black or bright depending on the angle of the Sun, with intermittent 'pot lighting' of starlight and unless one is looking at the moon or the Earth, there is no immediate sense of movement. Boring really, yet awesome at the same time.

Captain, I need her assistance in conducting some tests, so if you need her at anytime just give a holler."

"Thanks, Janet. We just might as we're going to slingshot around Earth and swoop out to Mars around 45g miles per hour in the hopes that we can elude some expected but unwanted company. I've informed John and he's in on this sling shot plan."

She's in good spirits, he thought. That's good.

"Thanks, Captain."

"Janet, don't worry. We're going to do our level best to avoid any confrontation and any reason to use the infirmary."

"Good, I wasn't looking forward to using it."

Julie arrived through the hatch as Jan was finishing her conversation and could read the concern on Jan's face.

"The Captain has the crew on high alert so there shouldn't be any surprises," she said, trying to calm Jan's concern.

Julie didn't know what Jan sensed. The gut feeling Jan had earlier seemed that much closer to reality. Julie would be her best bet to collate her records. Jan knew the information which she was going to install in Julie could be retrieved by COWA personnel at a 'later' date, like her termination date. At least, if it was installed in Julie, there was no way anyone could accidentally retrieve and restore it. That was protected by an access code, an access code only Julie's programmer could know.

"Julie, I would like to explain some highly confidential information to you which may have to be retrieved and restored by SETIA later."

"Oh, Mrs. Marshall…"

"Please, call me Jan or Janet."

"Janet, do you really think this is necessary? I mean, I know the Captain is preparing for the possibility of more attacks from the GGE factions, but don't you think we're capable of a successful outcome."

"Of course, I do Julie, but as you are aware accidents do happen. And with what experiences I've had over the past few years, I just didn't want it to go to waste because of a human memory problem. Do you see my point?"

Julie's attention had been carefully guided to the medical laboratory area now in front of her. This enabled Jan to smoothly reach under Julie's hair and switch her off. Catching her by the armpits, Jan gently placed her on a lowered operating table and then raised her to an optimum level. Time was of the essence.

She quickly removed some stem cell fluid from the bione's storage area in her thigh and mixed it with hers. Very carefully the 'Canasurgeassist' robot arm injected this fluid into Jan's cranium while siphoning off an equal volume to maintain fluid stasis. In a couple of weeks or so, Jan could harvest the 'neural fluid crop' and place it back into Julie, so she would unknowingly transport it back to COWA. Everyone could benefit but not Ben.

Rousing Julie, Jan showed concern for her. "Julie, Julie? Are you alright?"

"What hap…?"

"You just passed out for some reason. Here, let me look," Jan said, reaching for Julie's head. "Hmm, you seemed to have bumped it. Let's do a quick CAT-scan."

Julie acquiesced with a silent nod and lay down on the table.

Jan operated some buttons and a large oval ring passed over the table down to Julie's shoulders and then returned.

Examining the results against a lit panel Jan saw the 'expected' fluid build up. She explained the results to Julie and advised her to return to Jan in a couple of weeks for another CAT-scan to check its progress.

"In the meantime, Julie, I want you to tell me of any unusual changes. Okay?"

Jan made a mental note that the siphoned, neural genetic fluid, from her head into Julie's would incubate sufficiently in 336 hours (2 wks.), that it shouldn't be noticed by Julie or Ben, her superior, back at the orbiting station, should she have to pass through screening.

Julie agreed, "No problem, Jan," and returned to helping Jan, none the worse.

Chapter 28

Angélique emerged from the interview room to speak with Bud who had been watching through the one-way window. He had been looking at his wife Darlene with contempt and yet a lost fondness.

"Well, Bud, we can talk here or in a more comfortable room such as my office. Whatever you prefer."

"You're right. I need answers so let's go to your office and talk over some coffee."

"Good idea," Angélique agreed. After taking a long, last look at his wife with the remaining two investigators Bud left, walking quickly down the corridor to the elevator. Everyone they passed seemed engrossed with their thoughts, but never failed to display the customary smile of acknowledgement, which was returned in kind, or initiated by Angélique, depending upon the person approaching. Uniformed personnel snapped salutes upon seeing Angélique.

Puzzled, Bud had to ask, "Out of uniform how do they recognize you so quickly?"

Chuckling, Angélique replied, "They don't." She saw the quizzical look on his face and continued saying, "They see the red dot on my I.D. Badge which triggers a conditioned response."

"That being?" Bud pressed, inquisitively.

"Salute, then shoot." she replied. "All other colors, they shoot then salute."

Patting his arm reassuringly, she said, "Don't worry, you're with me."

"And if I have to go to the …?"

"…washroom?" Angélique said completing Bud's question.

"Yeah" Bud said, grunting an agreement.

"Oh, well, that's where their training and common sense kicks in. They look at the clock on the wall and give you ten minutes. Then they speak into their wrist mike notifying their control center of the situation and come after you."

She watched his face for reaction. Seeing none, she ever so slightly raised her brow.

Reaching the elevator, she said to the guard, "Room 7034," and returned to her conversation with Bud. "They reassess the situation, again reporting to the center with an update, positively or negatively. Believe me, positive is best. These guys don't get out much," she finished, retrieving her ID badge from the guard who turned to the elevator and used the only magnetic key to open the elevator door. He then withdrew it from the recessed depression located beside the door.

Inside the elevator car Bud asked, "Is there more than meets the eye to get into the elevator then? Or am I becoming neurotic?"

"You noticed?" she asked, almost surprised.

"Noticed what?" Bud replied

"The fact that the guard only has one half of the ID keying process to use the elevator," she said.

"Believe me, Mrs. Marshall, it hadn't crossed my mind at the time so I'm pressed to ask just how far does this ID process go to get into your office?" Bud asked. Quietly, he thought…it never stops. Bud was only now beginning to understand the depths: -

1. the GGE faction would have to go through to find out info inside the SETIA Secret Police Building;

2. the obvious counter measures the secret police required to protect the information from falling into the wrong hands, and most of all;

3. why an 'inside' contact would not be out of the question. Yet, he was the # 2 man in administration.

During the elevator ride to her office she briefed him on the ID process operatives must undergo during internal movements within the building. By the time she reached her office she concluded, "So you see Bud, SETIA's operatives are so tied up with checking and counter-checking identification, it consumes one-third of our day."

Holding her door open to admit him, Angélique caught his eye as he entered. In that moment, volumes about budget were said and understood, to which he addressed out of the side of his mouth, "I'll recommend and vigorously pursue it in Council at the next budget meeting."

A quiet gesticulation made behind his back said it all, 'Yesss!'

After settling down in her office they quickly came to the business at hand. Angélique darkened the room with a sweep of her hand over her desk, a push of a button and the room was soundproofed and a decibel monitor was turned on to keep in check the intensity of their voices. The metal collar she gave him ensured it.

"Bud, I am going to reveal the information to you on Synthopaper which self-destructs when your hands let go of it. So, put these gloves on if you need to re-read the information."

Bud declined the gloves.

"Bud, we needed to know when your wife would become an active agent for God's Garden of Eden. We have the answer and you're not going to like it."

"Tell me. I'm quite sure I won't be surprised," he replied, sounding cynical.

"Apparently, when you are both at home she always answers the H-Link service. One of those times will expose her to a GGE agent or 'contact' during which a pre-programmed sequence of events will be triggered. We have determined that H-link event has not yet occurred Bud," Angélique said, matter-of-factly. Swiveling her chair to the left, she reached for the ten-page document that was coming off her printer, stacked, packed, and powdered for incineration assurance.

Handing Bud the document in her glove-protected hand she said, "Enjoy. Coffee?"

"Thanks a lot. Arabian, medium roast, ½ tsp. of sugar, 5% cream, standard cup size, thank you."

Bud was deeply engrossed in his reading when she replied quietly with one eyebrow arched almost to her hairline, "Right! Brown slop, five days old, whitened, poured into a used mug, wiped with a napkin. Our guests get the best." She smiled turning back to him and handed him the coffee. Seating herself at her desk, she pulled open the bottom drawer on her right. The split-screen displayed everything about Bud from his current weight and internal bio-stats such as heart rate, blood pressure, metabolic rate, oxygen saturation, respiration rate, etc., to political loyalties, past and present, and a comparison projection chart, which utilized the Thompson, Fadar, Urqhart accuracy probability factors.

The chance of Angélique saying anything about Bud would be inaccurate once in one hundred million assumptions. Mindful of this and no flashing cursor, she looked up at Bud again and closed the drawer while waiting for him to finish. Her H-link indicated an internal call. She saw it indicated that the interview room was waiting, and pressed 'Accept'.

"Yes, captain?"

"Colonel, we have the remaining information with a TFU error of 0 - .00000001."

"Good, Sheldon. Do me the favor of uploading it to my desk monitor link."

"Right away, Sir!" His formalness alerted her.

She looked at him saluting her, and knew she was not going to like the results, as it held no surprises for her. Looking at her monitor more closely, she quickly asked Sheldon how he got the information, and for Darlene's condition. This distracted Bud from his reading. He looked at Angélique, towards her H-link and then at her again, upon realizing that she had her privacy option on. She shook her head and he finished his reading. Bud folded the document in half, top to bottom, and placed it in her wastebasket. It ignited the moment he dropped it.

Bud turned back to Angélique, sipped some coffee, grimaced, and asked, "What's going on?"

"Bud, from the information we have collected from Darlene she will get an H-link call from a GGE contact, known or unknown to her, and during this interactive communication the phrase, *yea, though I walk through the valley of the shadow of death I will fear no evil* shall be used."

"Yes, I've read that in your document how the GGE operates and about our counter measures. What I want to know is why you still trust me?"

"Bud, I think you can figure that out yourself."

He knew then that he had been a pawn of the GGE all along and Darlene was their instrument. He knew what must be done. He was most grateful that his emotional side would now find closure enabling him to go on. He shuddered like someone had just walked over his grave.

Continuing on, Angélique detailed how Darlene's role would play itself out. "Between Sheldon and his aide they managed to trigger the 'wake' response in Darlene."

Chapter 29

The chronometer indicated a mission elapsed time of 172.5 hrs. since departing the Moon's orbit. Sensors indicated all was proceeding normally and the gravitational slingshot effect of the Earth had the propelling success they predicted. The blackness of space provided the perfect panorama of starlight to John's musical backdrop currently being played through the ship. The latest edition of The International Philharmonic Orchestra's *Strings in Space* Concerts, interspersed with John's selections of 20th and 21st century classics such as Elvis Presley's, *Such a Night,* and Judy Collins's, *From A Distance* and Joan Osborne's *One of Us,* and others, soon had the entire ship enjoying the tedium of waiting out the passage of time until the predicted attack from the GGE's second onslaught of suicide ships.

John's view of space was breath-taking and addictively consuming at the same time. He thought of a poem.

For You

Whenever life gets me down
I stop what I'm doing and look around.
I see the colors of the flower,
The twinkling of the stars at night;
Urban life with sounds of power,
And feel becalmed by country sights!
Whenever duty gets me down

I stop thinking and erase my frown.
I see the terror in human eyes
And explain away bewildered 'whys?'
I know there is a better way,
'Cause, hope is in another day!
Whenever loneliness is gripping
I grit my teeth in believing;
The Universal God of us
Has made this life so wonderous
He sent to us such romance;
Your face reflects His countenance!
Now I'm 'prisoned in a place,
And all I want is "out" of Space;
The memories of my life so dear
Seem so far, yet very near;
Wars, romance, and foods exotic
Plague my mind as strong narcotic;
'Cause living on that Orb so blue
'T was out in Space, I went for you!

Any person who has had the good fortune to take a trip into space as a tourist or on a mission, military or scientific, has been stricken with the same dueling set of emotions. John's reason was the same as one of the astronaut's who expressed it best upon being interviewed fresh from a return journey from Mars. John recalled it in his mind.

Interviewer: "Colonel, how do you 'feel' about space travel and do you think 'we' can feel the same from Earth?"

Colonel Sheila Starks: "When a puny being such as I, who is using foolproof (gesturing quotation marks) space exploration equipment and know-how can get down on my knees in all humility to pray to a "Supreme Being" to spare my life from a 5 gm. pellet of iron ore hurtling through space at 35,000 miles per second, or be brought to those same knees in tears of joy upon discovering reproducing bacteria on Mars, only then can I let out the exhilaration that overwhelms me at being given the privilege to really see the power and the glory of the universe."

Pointing, she said, "You asked if 'we' can appreciate it on Earth as in space? If a soldier, because he is a soldier, can look his enemy straight in the eye while disemboweling him and then care for his enemy's little child with all the tenderness and love of a parent then there is hope for him. If the politician who sent him there to do this horrible thing can shed a tear to fall on the seeds of permanent peace, then there is hope for mankind. That will result in all of us glorifying this planet or, as you put it, appreciate it. No more questions, please!"

John was deeply engrossed in listening to his music while taking in the view of the solar system. Even the filters to remove or reduce the harmful rays from the Sun couldn't dampen his appreciation. His eyes closed for about five seconds as his mind took over producing his imaginary conductor's baton-waving movements.

As if he was drawing a crescendo from his orchestra he gradually lifted his left hand upwards, while simultaneously increasing tempo with his baton. He opened his eyes to bring in the kettledrums from the percussion section only to see something slip behind an asteroid. He immediately punched an icon on his computer which quickly switched the music to Wagner's classic *Ride of the Valkyries* and suddenly the ship went to high alert and battle stations!

John's ability to pinpoint accurately where he had seen this 'something' resulted in co-ordinates being fed into the tactical system. Every turret was now facing in that direction. The computer's large display screen on the bridge displayed an electronic visual and flashed the source of the alarm as being John's turret.

"Is it our expected company, John?" the Captain asked.

"I believe so, David," John replied. "I caught sight of a single flash of light like the sunlight reflecting off the scope of a sniper's rifle."

Ellis turned to Julie as she whispered to him, "Incredible! What are the chances?" she asked in almost mock admiration.

Ellis didn't help when he compounded with, "He must be one of Odin's favorites."

The ship was coming up on the 9million-km. (5,625,000mi.) mark into their journey to Mars. Success would be measured by the media's reports of 'gone missing for some unknown reason.' Passenger lists   might include Colonel John and Pioneer Professor Janet Marshall' - on one of COWA's best military ships and science expeditions to Mars.

"Captain?"

"Yes, Ellis."

"Sir, Julie and I speculate that it must be one of the GGE's longer ranging ships, and that it is going to play cat and mouse with us," Ellis offered.

"John, do your goggles tell you anything more?"

John's 'goggles' filtered out the darkness of space focusing on any ion signature emitted from a ship, within an imaginary sphere having a radius of a thousand kilometers. The sphere provided a background of a faint green light and a 'target' would show as a red dot accompanied by a series of numbers such as range, size of object, continued course probability, velocity, and the object's identity.

"Captain, if I lock onto our target their ship may have enough sensory devices to determine this thereby giving them a fix on our position. So, with your permission I'd like to volunteer as a decoy." Without waiting for a reply he began feeding the target's stats into the ship's computer just as Janet could be heard in his headset to say, "John, do you realize you'll be a sitting duck?"

"I hope so, honey, in every sense of the word."

Realizing what John had just said Ellis punched up a projected position for a hunter who had spotted his prey, *i.e.* John's turret capsule, located at a point in the middle of a lake relative to the 'target' ship.

"Granted," said the Captain, as John's capsule was separating from the main body of the ship. Turning to Ellis, he asked, "You and Robert know what to do?"

"Yes, Sir!" said Robert. "Maintain a steady-as-she-goes course Captain, while keeping a lock on the Colonel, Sir!"

"Lieutenant, how long will he last?" Captain Noor was watching John's maneuvering blasts carry his capsule away from the ship.

"Captain, his capsule was fully stocked and charged, I figure a week."

"Good, keep it steady Robert. I'm counting on their not having a lot of extra detection and monitoring equipment in their ship. John may not show on their screens as a threat but rather as an object that we passed."

John's capsule had shut down with no apparent external signs of life such as navigational beacons, lights, or internal lighting. His capsule would appear spent, ransacked and abandoned, space junk. The G.G.E. ship wouldn't have the internal-life-signs detectors; a luxury, suicide ships wouldn't need and a calculated risk most zealots were willing to take. Ellis checked with the turret's computer system's 'Disconnect Stores' and saw that John had indeed taken a Saunders Belt. He knew John wanted to get rid of the G.G.E. even at his expense if need be - this made Ellis more determined in his focus on John. Ellis also knew that no one could remove a Saunders Belt without triggering an elapsed time or status monitor and a location beacon signal -unique to each belt and charging holder.

Chapter 30

So, as not to arouse any suspicion the Captain requested that John's *Ride of the Valkyries* continue playing throughout the ship. After all, the ship could be monitored and why give the 'enemy' the advantage.

While Corada, one of the Ferris Wheels' best gunners, and Benson watched John's turret, The Main Tactical Turret, depart the body of the ship to become the sitting duck target for the G.G.E.'s suicide ship, the backdrop of Richard Wagner's music stirred their bodies rhythmically to what they both were hearing mentally: -

"Valkyries, ride over the battlefield
Ride your horses and come to me
I'm waiting for you to take my soul,
high in the sky to Valhalla of old
Valkyries, ride over the battlefield
I'm dying and glad to bleed
Because I know today I will take my place
With the heroes in Valhalla of old
For none but the brave, be he king or a slave
With a pounding heart in his chest
Will be worthy to ride and with the Valkyries fly
And ride to Valhalla of old."

Lyrics from the Internet – by Domine

John thought to himself that this bait idea of his better work before his turret's supplies run out.

Buzz, using his helmet's mic, quietly spoke to his two best gunners practically scaring them out into space. "The Captain is going to try and draw fire positioning the suicide ship somewhere between John and us. Stay on your toes and well, just don't miss!"

John looked at the bleak, eternal, darkness of space for anything that would reveal the approach of his enemy. His mind lapsed mentally into hearing the "Charge of the Light Brigade."

Leaving them with reassuring shoulder pats Buzz climbed into the empty turret – his! Both Corada and Benson found new confidence with Buzz in the wheel.

The patience people have in a hospital's trauma triage room is displayed best when you are next for treatment, can remain calm yet return to your seat while four children are wheeled in from a fire.

But that doesn't even compare to the patience John had to show while waiting for his foe to show. Patience he had to have for the mission was still ahead of him. John worked on tactics in his head and that helped pass the time. "♫♪...were one of us...♪♫"

It was while he was going through these tactical analyses musically that John reached a most apt solution, dismissed it, suddenly doing a 180° pitch and roll facing his attacker just 2000 kilometers directly in front of him.

John fired first, cutting the enemy ship in half.

Almost simultaneously, six energy bolts left the Transporter Ship like a gigantic Colt 44 firing, totaling rendering the enemy ship into dust. John's tactical computer ensured their aim was accurate.

Even Robert Shaw from the movie Jaws would be proud to see John's facial expression; steely eyes, jaw set tight and a satisfaction in finishing with a pest – no jubilance, no tears from sudden tension release, just the satisfaction from a "job" done successfully.

Leaving his locator beacon on, John awaited pick up. After the Canadarm had placed John's turret back in place, he came forward for a debriefing on the bridge. David and Buzz, along with an obviously jubilant crew, were eagerly waiting for him. Both Ellis and Julie shared their doting attention, along with their duties and John's welcoming. Only Jan was less sober in her welcome.

"Honey, I do wish you'd pick less dramatic music. One of these times your Valkyries could prove real, or do you want to make a widow of me?"

"Jan, just hold me for a sec or someone might think my knees are a couple of castanets."

"Tell me later." She bussed him on the cheek just as David and Buzz were approaching.

"So, Buzz, what's all this scuttlebutt I hear about a new gunslinger in town?" the Captain asked, while nodding his head toward John.

"Just gossip, Captain." Buzz continued, a little more seriously. "It seems our hero here needs some consoling a little later David, eh, John?" Buzz said with a little compassion in his sarcasm.

Addressing the Captain, John said, "Believe me, Dave, next time I volunteer to make myself the bait for the enemy, hit me will you."

"Out in space like that, I imagined some harrowing scenarios that I don't mind telling you scared myself plenty. That's when I felt I was on the boat waiting for the great white shark to show. It did and it broke through the side of the boat. I could hear John Williams' music in my head, and suddenly realized my enemy would come at me from below, like the shark. So, I pitched and rolled the turret, just to come face to face with the ship. I fired instinctively, breaking it in half. Lucky for me your turrets tactically received the co-ordinates and your shots finished it."

Ellis looked at Julie and under his breath whispered, "He's feeling his mortality, he may be more cautious on this mission." She winked in acknowledgement.

"Robert, set a course for the Martian insertion point and give me the time, please."

"Twelve minutes for the first window, Captain," Robert replied, double-checking his helms' instruments.

"We concur Captain, chimed Julie and Ellis.

"Good. Now then, just to make sure we're all on the same page, our mission this trip is to deliver John and Janet to Mars in one piece. Therefore, check all our systems to make our efforts successful. Any questions?"

Having none, the crew was anxious to get started. David looked at his "watch" and said, "We have just less than 10 minutes until insertion, let's pop a champagne tablet, then toast our latest success, and get to work. Cheers."

The crew, talking among themselves, replied in kind, and then dispersed throughout the ship to check their various systems of responsibilities.

Robert noted 8 minutes, 43 seconds, until insertion.

Julie verified life support and cryogenic systems were ready. Ellis and she, were to monitor the ship during the trip.

Ellis set his instruments for monitoring and tested the protection shields. His long-distance scanners revealed a weakness which he was quickly able to correct.

Jan informed David sick bay was ready including a trauma section.

Captain Dilpreet (David) Noor made an entry into the ship's log about preparations being underway for insertion noting Robert's calculations for their ETA. "Robert, your ETA to Mars includes decelerating time?"

"That's correct, Captain", Robert replied. "It should take us approximately 967.2 hrs. or 6.045 weeks."

"Ellis, you and Julie set the cryo-alarms for 960 hrs. to wake the crew, OK?"

"Acknowledged, Captain," Ellis replied.

David finished his entries and a klaxon alarm sounded for cryo-shutdown for the crew. The Captain was the last one into his tube and as it was closing Julie realized how lonely it was without the background clamour from the rest of the crew. Ellis and Julie set to work on the bridge to confirm all would be peaceful for the next 960 hours or so, and they would now have a well-earned break from being on "duty alert" to their human 'masters'.

Chapter 31

"Well, Mr. Ellis," Julie said, almost seductively as she stood close to him, "just exactly what do you want to do with your down time?"

"Since we are meant to mimic all human behaviour, and I do mean all behaviours," Ellis said huskily, moving closer to Julie, "why don't we take this opportunity to do what we have always wanted to do?"

Mistakenly, Julie tenderly moved very close to Ellis and kissed him on the lips in an unmistaken invitation. Gently he removed her arms from him and, already affected by her charms stammered.

"What I meant was…"

"Yes", she said, watching the effect but knowing that he equally possessed the emotional strength to overcome it.

"…was to write some poetry since our minds will be unfettered by all the background noise."

Looking at him for sincerity, she said, showing deep interest, "Okay. But something profound about Earth and we'll compare them. Sound good to you, Ellis?"

"You're on," he replied.

They separated into two corners of the bridge and after a few minutes they shouted, "Ready!" almost simultaneously.

Like little children, "You go first."

"No, you," countered Ellis. They finally agreed on alphabetically. So, Ellis began: -

For ambience while they were writing, Ellis played one of John's music selections: - *"What If God Were One of Us"* from Rico McFarland's Album <u>Tired of Being Alone</u>

**Earth - My Home,
My Heaven, My Hell**

Chorus:

*Through my viewer, I can see a sight so glorious;
As mortal men, we stop and ask, "Is that orb meant for us?"
That 'place' we see so blue and bold constricts our throats so tight
When we return from outer space, Earth's such a welcome sight!*

Gravity, as we've been told, in space is very rare,
And astronauts are people trained to fly away out there.
So, on a whim, and 'count from ten,' they point their ships away
From Earth, they sail to conquer space and then return some day!

It's black 'outside', with specs of light, if such a 'side' exists;
'Cause in your face, yet gone in space, are points of ref 'rences.
Up, down, all around; it's all the same to me;
So focus I on the hatch that shows me where to pee!

Here in the 'void' you must defend yourself against the 'waves'
And when 'they' come we're once again locked in special 'caves'.
The fragrant scents of Earth's rare plants invade my memory
And dance around inside my mind to cause insanity!

Repeat Chorus: -

*Through my viewer, I can see a sight so glorious;
As mortal men, we stop and ask, "Is that orb meant for us?"
That 'place' we see so blue and bold constricts our throats so tight
When we return from outer space, Earth's such a welcome sight!*

Upon its surface, we were raised, and flew through skies
bright blue,
We ate its foods and climbed its rocks and used resources too;
But races grew and lands had 'shrunk' so nations looked for pals
To stand by them in times of woe and fight their private hells!

Chorus

To you, I know this orb is nothing more than this,
You see my friend, this home of mine holds all my happiness.
So, I can wreck it, or I can check it, or put it up to sell;
Our planet Earth, in dirt or mirth, Is our Heaven, Home, and Hell!

Repeat Chorus: -
Written by Ellis

"Ellis, that was so beautiful!" Julie gave him a special hug.
"Okay, let's hear yours," Ellis challenged.

Julie began reading: -
While Julie read, she could almost hear Neil Diamond singing
"There's a Beautiful Noise" from his album <u>Hot August Night</u>

This Planet Earth
Our Beautiful Blue-Green Earth

(Our Birthplace)
Throughout this universe so vast there's matter everywhere,
And when it's coalesced en mass an orb might form right there.
Our Earth, oh beautiful blue-green Earth, was made so long ago.
The matter then formed our ten planets, so the story goes;
And some disaster we've surmised decreased them in stone throws.

Chorus:
Oh 'orb' so blue we give to you our lives and loyalty
You are for us our place of birth; our beautiful blue-green Earth!

David L. Pritchard

(Our Hopes)
Upon these lands, we have lived, through centuries long ago.
Through peace and wars, we have survived; a future to behold!
So, to the stars we have turned and focused all our energy;
That out in space we will learn of peace for all eternity.
As men look out to see the 'view' they'll see our planet blue!

Chorus:
Oh 'orb' so blue we give to you our lives and loyalty.
You are for us our place of birth our beautiful blue-green Earth!

(Our Memories Forever)
When spring had sprung and new growth was carried on the breeze
The Sun would melt the ice and snow; and we would lose
our wheeze.
If God once was, and God still is, and God there'll always be,
Then out in space or on this Earth, he's made a home for me.
We won't forget our place of birth, our beautiful blue-green Earth!

Chorus:
Oh 'orb' so blue we give to you our lives and loyalty.
You are for us our place of birth our beautiful blue-green Earth!
-Julie

"Oh, Julie, it's heart warming. Have you been thinking about it for some time?" Ellis asked. "I mean, it seemed to come to you so quickly."

"I have, Ellis. The last stanza I had trouble in putting it to paper because of the troublesome word 'God'. Then I realized out 'here' in space, being human, or bione like us should not become so restrictive for us sentient beings when we define "God." We're on a mission to deliver the Marshalls to Mr. Davis on Mars and who's to say what that could entail afterwards - for them in their duties or us on our return to the Space Station?

I would rather put no definition to 'his' name and that way there are no rules as to how "God" is defined - and maybe, worshipped or not, individually or collectively, but that there is absolute respect for <u>life</u> everywhere, *e.g.* beings from other worlds and their *"God"* definitions. Are we so arrogant that only Earth's definition is correct?

Out here, in space Ellis, that view of Earth," nodding towards the portal, "against the backdrop of the Universe made it so clear to me that I could finish the stanza. Looking at our planet in its context of the universe we should be warriors and wipe out all other planets that don't believe in our definition of GOD. Or, we explore in peace a most wonderful universe."

"You sounded upset at the end." In a softer voice, "All I can say Julie, is, the entire poem is beautiful. Just remember it is based on lore, beliefs, faith and handed-down traditions. What do you say we put the poems somewhere so John and Janet can see them later?"

Hugging each other, Julie and Ellis both agreed to enter the poems into their personal diaries as well.

Chapter 32

Julie and Ellis stood for the longest time together in the Cryo-Room just simply holding hands and looking at Janet and John. It was Julie who broke silence.

"Ellis, I do hope they live happy, long and healthy lives together. They are the epitome of the so-called 'happy couple'. What he doesn't think of she does and vice-versa."

"What makes you say that?" Ellis asked her.

"Janet was last into the cryo-chamber, right?"

"And so?"

"She played a little joke on John for when he revives."

Ellis looked carefully at John and said, "Oh, for the love of Pete!" He was wearing one of Jan's near-n-dears. Ellis started to chuckle appreciating the humour.

"Are you going to remove them Ellis?" asked Julie.

"No way. Jan's also testing our loyalty to them - to leave them alone regarding harmless private and obviously personal matters. But it is funny."

"Well, my love, would you like to remove some 'others' then before returning to full alert?" she asked, snaking her arms around Ellis' waist in an unmistakable and inviting gesture. Ellis bent for the kiss, picked her up and carried her to a nearby privacy chamber.

Privacy times for biones, like Ellis and Julie, only came when and while their status was 'Monitor Only'. Whenever status levels were on 'Full Alert', they were granted private time as their masters, those who requested their creation could mutually agree.

Ellis, an acronym for L. S., the initials for Lorne Saunders, was requisitioned jointly by Janet and John Marshall, on approval from C.O.W.A., the Council of World Affairs. They are his 'masters', the only persons who could, and would eventually, request his return for 'recycling'. Ellis also knew that if both Marshalls were killed, then he would automatically be recycled. He had good reason to keep both alive.

Julie came by her existence when David Noor lost his first officer in an Aircraft Carrier accident. Commander Judith Liethwood gave her life when assisting her men during her 'watch'. Having already demonstrated mutual loyalty, an uncontrolled 'Wolf Class' came straight for the Bridge and exploded on impact. Captain Noor has never been the same since. He made the requisition for her and gave the acronym 'Julie'.

Chapter 33

The cryo-chambers' clocks marked off the elapsed time and began the awakening procedures at exactly 960 hrs. Fifteen hours remained on the travel time chronometers to reach Mars for retro-braking procedures to take hold. Ellis roused Robert, the Captain and Buzz's staff. Julie assisted Janet and her nursing staff. She then went to food processing and water recovery to verify their efficiencies. They were working at peak.

The Captain hit a button on his chair and requested all sectors to report their preparedness.

"Engineering, can we go to full braking?" asked the Captain.

"On command, sir."

"Now, fire retros." They came on full power. The ship shook and vibrated like a ferry boat docking.

"Keep it steady", Robert. "

"Sir, I think a four-hour burn and a sequence of shorter, computer-controlled burns will put us into a perfect position for a parked orbit around Mars."

"I concur, Captain," said Ellis, looking up from his computers.

"Good, let's do it."

The Transporter's shuttlecraft off-loaded its special cargo in an area away from the hub bub of activity which always occurs at terminals. The security check point for receiving Lunar and Terran passengers had been placed on high alert. Terrorists, or otherwise, were always expected but the Agency's Chairman had put this request into the terminal's management.

"Would Captain Dilpreet Noor report to room B331 on level 3, please?" The P.A. message was very abrupt.

"Sounds like you're needed in one of the boardrooms, David," said John.

"So, later then, Dave?"

"Later, John. See you." Everyone shook hands and departed, David to Level 3 while the rest went with John and Janet.

Going to an information counter, John inquired about Mr. Sam Davis' office location. The girl behind the counter gave her most sincere smile and asked, "Are you the Marshall party he has been expecting, sir?"

"We are they, my dear," he replied, mimicking her heavy Martian accent. Eyeing her left breast area, he noted her name tag as 'Ramona'. He didn't know if she was French raised in an Irish setting; or Irish raised in a French setting. Terran Airlines sure knows how to hire he thought.

"Good," she continued, "an airline limo will take you to Mr. Davis' building in New Washington, Sir. Come this way please."

Grabbing his wife's arm at the elbow he whispered, "Is she one?"

"She's probably the instructor, darling," Janet cooed back in his ear.

Julie tightened her grip on Ellis as he moved towards Ramona. The glass protective shield over the terminal didn't provide such a cause for a temperature increase that people would perspire but Ramona was perspiring. Ellis placed himself between the Marshalls and Ramona.

As soon as she opened the door to the Limo area two men beset the Marshalls. Caught by surprise both Janet and John could do nothing. Ellis ended up holding the door open while Ramona quickly dispatched both thugs. Their faces were exposed from under their hooded masks and were identified as G.G.E. terrorists. It didn't take much more after this to impress John. Ramona was now an ally.

"His office elevator is at the end of the corridor on the right."

"Thanks, Ramona." They walked along the corridor and pressed the elevator call button. The door slid open, they boarded and Ellis surmised correctly that the only button of any significance was the one labeled 'S.E.T.I.A. Ellis pressed it and pulled back his finger thinking to himself, "What a good boy am I?"

A recording came on: - "If high pressures affect you please tell Ramona now and she will direct you to a waiting area. Otherwise, grasp the hand rails as this device takes less than twenty-three seconds to travel 2 miles underground. Place the face masks on if you feel nervous. At the sound of the tone the car will drop to Mr. Davis' office." They heard a middle 'C' tone and then…3…2…1.

The door quickly opened to a set of darkened, double-glass doors with gold lettering, 'Council of World Affairs' arched over reflective blue lettering, '*Search for Extra-Terrestrial Intelligence Agency*' cupped like a bowl below it. In between were the letters OPERATIONS in black on a reflective yellow background. Ellis and Julie held the doors open for Janet and John. No one needed the face masks. As the outer doors closed an air pressure gasket was heard to snap sealed. The lighting dimmed yellow and each in turn was asked to supply their fingerprints, an eye scan and a DNA swab of their mouths.

When these were found satisfactory the inner doors opened to reveal a world of flora and fauna usually granted by wishing for it.

They inhaled the fragrances and gloried in the spectacle of sights and sounds before them. As if playing host to this underground tease of the senses Sam Davis walked to them from the greenery, wearing a broad smile of pure white teeth encased in a handsome black frame. Janet recognized him first and greeted him, "Sam, you are such a salesman. Are you responsible for this setting? It looks like you're pimping for a second Garden of Eden!"

"Well, young lady I am." Holding his arms wide for a hug, "and I have you to thank for it!"

"It's absolutely gorgeous Sam, and the nurseries?"

"Fungus and infestation free," said Sam happily. "But I digress. You must introduce me, Janet." Sam expressed his best emotional 'hurt' in his full bass vocal tones. "Your husband?" he asked, with a questioning nod towards John.

"Sam, I am remiss." Grabbing her husband by the elbow she proudly stated, "This is the body behind the voice that you have been hearing on your audio."

"Glad to finally meet you, John."

Sam escorted his "Marshall" party along a path through the greenery, and came to a glade. Just then their limousine arrived to whisk them to Sam's private office. Once again security protocols had to be followed completely; Ellis and Julie went through one set of doors, while the Marshall's went through another.

John watched Ellis plug wiring into his right thigh area and aid Julie for the same thing.

Janet and John's retinas were scanned, finger prints taken, DNA typed and dermal S-readings taken. John looked at Sam inquisitively during his S-readings.

"Your wife's idea, John, not mine, but I do agree with it. Sometimes skin transplants can pass by security check points."

John chuckled to himself recalling Jan's story of Ellis' reproductive organs restoration surgery. Good thing Ellis only needs his circuitry checked. Ellis had already finished and was watching John during the taking of his S-readings. He sensed why John was chuckling to himself and for some reason just started laughing aloud which incited everyone to laugh except Sam and Julie.

Finally, Sam came through the gas-locked doors leaving whispered instructions with the sentries. Passing through the inner doors Sam turned to insert his card into a magnetic reader. As he did so the entrance disappeared, calming music could be heard and they all turned to witness six biones monitoring a wall of screens. Of note was the view of the Lunar Science Center where E-T's always seem to be reported. Ellis mentally noted the security enclosure of the six operators and their 'control' panels: - accidental accessibility was impossible.

Sam led everybody into his inner office which also doubled as his living quarters. Closing the doors behind him, he inserted the second card from around his neck and from the outside the office-living quarters seemed to disappear while looking from the inside, the outside appeared to become a tropical flora and fauna diorama.

Jan teased, "Seems like a lot of security trouble, Sam, to escape alimony back pay." She elbowed John and winked.

Sam harrumphed and chuckled, "Yeah, if my first wife only knew," he said, as he gestured to take a seat.

"I hope you are both comfortable right now because you must know you're not here for a visit so l shall get to the point. Jan, your uncle George contacted me a couple of days ago with a message of underlying urgency." Jan looked at John and seeing no reaction, looked back at Sam with an expression that said, "continue."

"You two are to go to him for a special mission which was sent encrypted under SETIA PROTOCOL # 1."

John and Jan looked at each other knowingly. Looking at Sam, John asked, "Anything hinted at?"

Ellis contributed, "Did General Lassiter hint at any expectations of the immensity of this project?"

Sam responded saying, "...only to the immediacy of the situation, Ellis, and the impact on Earth."

"I guess what I am really trying to find out is this: - do you both expect a time to use the DNA code that was sent to me?" Ellis pressed.

"Ellis, and nobody knows this better than Janet," looking at everyone in his office, "that, only you will know the when and why to use the code!" Sam stated emphatically. "You may find that Julie will be of great assistance to you when that time comes. I can see already that you two are forming a kinship," Sam continued while a broad grin formed on his face.

"Right now, I think it's time that I break open that bottle of expensive champagne and have a toast to your health, happiness and a successful journey. An ambassadorial journey at that if all goes well." Sam added. Pressing an icon on his desk sent for Ramona. He then selected five of his finest flutes and poured them each some champagne.

While Sam handed out the champagne John decided to speak on his wife and biones' behalf. "Sam, if this is the last you ever see of us I, we, hope not to let you or Earth down. I have a gut feeling the 'good luck' you wished for us will come in handy!" Having said that John threw his glass into the mock fireplace behind the bar followed by the other glasses and a hearty, "Here, here!" from everybody else.

Simultaneously, Ramona entered Sam's office. She stood between Ellis and Julie where he could see she was well prepared for escort duty, noting the taser slung low by her right femur. Ellis knew she would have no second thoughts if the need arose to use it.

"Ramona, escort our friends to the 'shuttlebus' to go to the Ganymede dry-dock and launching area," instructed Sam. "Yes, sir," she said. He shook hands with everyone as they left his office with Ramona. They stopped by the suit room to put on their G-Suits and were led to the shuttlebus waiting outside through a hatchway from a corridor with an airlock.

When the hatch opened, they saw their shuttlebus for the first time. There was no mistaking the bus was a product of COWA engineering. Their trip to the pad took all of fifteen minutes, causing Ramona to say secretly, "Try to do better next time." Ellis overheard the admonishment but said nothing.

After boarding the military transporter ship to Ganymede, they participated in departure preparations checking their suits, helmets, Saunders belts and generally following the public announcements inside the cabins. Pressurization could be heard and a ten-count-down to lift-off.

Lift-off was not like the old days of shooting rockets out the back end of huge three-staged boosters. Instead it launched straight ahead into a death-defying roller coaster climb. The effect was the same but far more comfortable. They could see Ramona had boarded the 'bus' back to New Washington Square and Sam's office.

One hour into their journey and their captain, Major Stephen Lau, entered their cabin area to answer any questions they might have. Each question regarding their ship would be answered best when they saw it in 'construction dock' and spoke to its chief engineer, Colonel Davidson, "Whom, I believe is an acquaintance of yours, John," said Lau, smiling.

Hearing this John asked one question. "How long to Ganymede?"

"Good, something tangible that I can answer. We are using our recently developed ion propulsion system and an arcing course to avoid asteroids, so that Ganymede will be in a perihelion orbit to Mars, or apogee to Jupiter, if you will. We should make it in fifty-one weeks, Earth time, all things being equal. However, as of now you all have the option of Cryogenics if you so choose," said Major Lau.

No one opted for it.

As they approached Ganymede on the 353rd day of travel, John looked out the window where he sat and elbowed Jan. They looked at each other in total disbelief. Their ship was huge and they still had five days of travel time left.

Just then Major Lau came through the hatchway and could see John had a question on his face as he pointed to the ship. Lau put his hand up as if stopping traffic and said, "I know, I know, it's huge but it is our first practical Galaxial Cruiser. It has been constructed following plans from an alien being from beyond our galaxy, not just our solar system."

"What?" asked John and Ellis, incredulously. "And we are to trust him?"

"John, just to give you a bit of comfort, 'matchbox' couldn't believe the specs either but as he got into it, it became like a magnet to him; to build and travel in the first real cruiser to the stars that Earth pioneered would be an honor. You remember our first one was built basically to explore the Milky Way. Having said that John I think it is too cumbersome to travel microgravity or not."

"Just how big is it?" John asked.

Clearing his throat, Lau said, "You might not believe this so hang on. The main deck, called the grav-deck, to exercise all the crew travelling with you, will have a gravitational environment that is akin to Earth's, to keep their bodies fit. The deck's surface area could house soccer, all the baseball, football, hockey games; all the religious conventions that take place in North America, and still have room left over for two military airfields."

John looked at Ellis and whispered, "I'd hate to get the power and energy bills," he quipped and turned back to Major Lau. "Built by matchbox and an alien engineer?" he whispered.

Just then a sudden retro-shudder was felt as their transporter was preparing for approach alignment. An announcement was heard which would bring Major Lau to the bridge in a hurry. "Please ensure you are all securely fastened in and your Saunders belts are working. We have approaching asteroids and will be using our Laser canons."

Major Lau said, "John, we still have a few more hours to travel before we arrive but now I have to go to the bridge."

"Sure, Stephen." John and Ellis returned to their seats. They looked at each other in disbelief.

Chapter 34

The military transporter had slowed to docking speed as it was a couple of miles out. The Marshalls, Ellis and Julie were looking agape out their portal windows as the immensity of the Cruiser was having its full impact on their viewing.

"John, just exactly what roles are you and Clinton going to play on this monstrosity?" Janet prodded.

John spoke into his helmet mic, "Stephen, we will get an introductory tour, won't we?".

"Without question, John. In fact, I think Clinton is waiting for you who is now at the ramp entrance," Stephen replied, pointing.

John looked towards the ramp entrance and saw three astronauts standing there; one in a white G-suit with orange sleeves, one in a very reflective orange suit, and one in a blue suit with a gold right arm sleeve; all were wearing clear, gold shield pressure helmets. John thought, blue for administration, got to be G. Lassiter himself. I'll bet Clinton is in orange and he's talking to one of his supervisors.

An announcement inside the transporter indicated docking procedures were now taking place. "Please secure yourselves in your seats for docking and remain there until indicated otherwise. Thank you. Stephan Lau, out."

Ellis and Julie were seated together facing John and Janet Marshal. Ellis asked, "John, "Do you think there will be time for us to have an introductory tour of the ship and its personnel?" like Major Lau said.

"Janet asked the same question," said John. I would imagine that if this mission is our responsibility, then it follows that we're going to have to know two things – 1) the what and where, and 2) how do we get there? In a word, yes. There will be a tour, so don't fret."

Thinking to himself, Ellis is beginning to show concern that he might not be able to support us in the time of greatest need. I'll tell Jan later.

"Then, Ellis and Julie, I suggest you two be extra vigilant for John and I," said Janet. They nodded in silent agreement.

They all felt their ship dock, waiting for the departure sign to illuminate before unfastening their belts. Major Lau appeared in the hatchway, "I want to wish you a happy, safe, and successful journey. He then said, "It appears the brass is waiting for you," smiling with a silly grin and shaking their hands as they were leaving.

Stephen watched until they reached the three waiting to greet them. Janet and Julie were first followed by Ellis and then John. Clinton Davidson, in the solid orange suit, made introductions to General George Lassiter.

"Nice to meet you Julie," he said smiling, grasping and shaking her hand. He by-passed Janet and extended his gilded right arm to Ellis standing behind Janet. "Ellis, glad to meet you. We've heard so much about you. We'll chat later, okay?".

"Uh, sure, General, sir," he said uncertainly.

"Aahh, finally; my sister's daughter. "With his arms opened wide, Janet stepped in for a 'Ganymede' hug and squeeze. John said, "Careful Uncle George. She hasn't done the mission, yet, ha, ha."

"How long has it been, love?".

"Too long, uncle. The last time you saw mom was for our wedding and that was to have some cake for your sweet tooth," Jan said gently but affectionately patting his belly.

"Ha, ha," George chuckled. "If I could only get you to give me a new pair of eyes, return my 20/20 vision for all light intensities, I would lose 60 lbs. in a month. But I guess that's the price one pays for working so far from the Sun. Anyway, my dear, I'm going to take you and this handsome fellow of yours on a tour with his friend Clinton. COWA would like this ship back if possible and in one piece so we better get started."

Having said that, they moved off to join John and Clinton, who were just a few feet ahead busy talking.

"And it doesn't matter where you are, on or near the ship, the audio monitor in the main computer can relay your message and react accordingly." They overheard Clinton talking to John.

"Ah, General, did you want to take over, Sir?" asked Clinton.

"I did want to say something of a quick introductory nature here, John, on behalf of COWA and COSSIOS, of which, Jan being secretary and chair, probably already knows. John, you have sole responsibility of this ship's mission. Colonel Clinton Davidson is your Captain, chief engineer, head of security. Jan is the ship's head of medicine, life sciences and the only authority on genetics during the mission. She is also second in command to you, John, for the mission. Now if there are no questions or comments, let's get this tour over with, Clinton."

"Yes, sir."

At that moment, a sergeant came up to the touring parties and said, "He wants us in the briefing area as soon as possible," General, sir.

"Very good, Hamilton. We're on our way," said George. Speaking to the entire party, George Lassiter said, "Clint, will you lead the way please?".

"Certainly, sir," said Clinton, motioning for everyone to follow him.

When they entered the auditorium, they were quickly ushered to the head table where the General stood at the dais to introduce the Marshalls, Ellis and Julie to their crew and their roles on the ship. The crew's complement of men and women, dressed in uniforms which designated their various jobs of expertise, was quickly scanned by the Marshalls. Some were recognized, others were introduced by the Operational Captain, Clinton Davidson.

John noted they were all wearing their Saunders Life belts; good, he thought. General Lassiter stood and introduced the personnel at the head table, explaining their roles on this mission. He closed by telling the Marshalls that only the personnel assembled, the ship's construction crew and the transporter crew, were privy to the general nature of this mission. At this point a public-address message was heard.

"We have an incoming communication."

There was a deafening silence throughout the auditorium. A holographic figure appeared between the head table and audience crew, about five feet above the floor. He scanned the room and turned to face the head table. Standing with hands together, clasped easily in front of him, he began to speak in English, which almost caught the Marshalls by surprise because his lips weren't moving. And he looked human.

"Greetings my friends from the blue planet you call Earth. I am called Gariff from a planet we call Ffraiteron. A planet hitherto unseen by your viewing devices and had I not convinced my people of further space exploration I would not have met you. So, I am pleased at your positive and peaceful response to meet with me. Although I am not an emissary, nor an ambassador from Ffraiteron, I believe I can benefit both planets by opening a dialogue between us."

John stood and replied, "We welcome you, Gariff, and I speak for myself, that when I heard you speak one of Earth's most common languages, I felt both surprised and in awe. My name is John Marshall and my wife is Janet," he said, putting his hand on Jan's left shoulder.

"It is my pleasure to meet you both," Gariff said, but looked at Julie and Ellis, who were now introduced with the remaining personnel at the table along with their significance on this mission. Ellis, Julie and Janet looked at John in astonishment at disclosing that information and just as quickly relaxed realizing Gariff's specs were used by Clinton to build the ship. There had to be mutual trust notwithstanding Earth's history of violence.

"John, I think it would be best if we could meet physically to have a diplomatic discussion," Gariff suggested.

"I agree," John replied, looking at General Lassiter for approval. Seeing a broad smile, John quickly inquired of Gariff if he included any rendezvous data in his specs to Clinton. He had, along with the special astral computers to get there safely. When John looked back at Gariff, he said, "Then it is settled my friend. We shall meet at the rendezvous point and get under way as soon as possible. I do have one request. Have you given our communications officer, Commander Chris Donaldson his necessary information to stay in touch in case any emergency devel…?"

"Most assuredly," Gariff gently interrupted before John could finish. Gariff turned to find Chris standing and responding with, "Gariff, they are working perfectly."

"Then, in that case, Gariff, we shall depart in two hours," said John.

"Until we meet, John," Gariff said, waving his right arm in departure.

John turned to Clinton to say, "We need the tour of the ship now – the fast version."

Janet grabbed John's right elbow, "You were very tactful my dear, a quality I am surprised at how adept you are. My uncle was very impressed and has asked Clinton to carry on with the tour." Jan was glowing with obvious admiration secure in the knowledge that John will be a fine representative for Earth.

"John, you will be happy to know two new LP's have been placed in orbits as navigational beacons for us, upon returning to our solar system," said Clinton, on behalf of communications.

"Excellent, but if my math is any good they may not be around by the time we will need them: - space collisions or target practice for the saboteurs," John said, shrugging his shoulders.

"The Listening Posts were Gariff's idea, John."

"I figured that Clint, but even he doesn't know what those bastards are capable of especially in the time frame of our expected return, centuries from now."

Patting his friend Clinton on his shoulder, "So, take Ellis and I on the tour Clint or do you still like your nickname from the academy, being 'matchbox', heh, heh?"

"I don't mind so much if you still like 'robot,'" replied Clinton, chuckling. Ellis was busy filing this comradery away and didn't notice Jan and Julie being whisked away by one of Jan's supervisors, Commander (doctor) Marion Wentworth, for a tour of all the life sciences' areas and medical facilities.

John was fulfilling his desires of checking the structural integrity of the ship, engineering sections, weaponry, the goose-neck escape extension and general overall operational parts for propulsion, crew quarters, communications and internal movement. "Clint, I am in absolute awe of the work that your engineering crew has done with the diametric grav-deck. I am sure had we known about its construction earlier there would not have been such a hesitation in space exploration."

"Knowing us and our potential for violence we probably would have wiped ourselves out," commented Clinton.

"You could be right," said John. "Anyway, let's get this ship underway, Clint?"

Chapter 35

Entering the bridge they heard the First Officer say, "Captains on the bridge." This brought everyone to attention with a snappy salute to show respect for their uniforms. It was returned with Captain Davidson's command, "As you were."

Captain Davidson began to address the bridge personnel, "Now, first and foremost, this ship has been assigned to go on this mission by our Council of World Affairs. It is top secret and therefore no one is permitted to contact Earth for any reason. Janet will have sole discretion and authority on that matter.

Secondly, John Marshall is the boss Captain of this mission and will occupy this chair whenever. Thirdly, Ellis will occupy the Science/First Officer's station when required by John Marshall. Fourth, this mission will be scrubbed without question if Mrs. Marshall deems it necessary.

Lastly, I am the Operational Captain and Chief Engineer. Your orders will come from myself or John. Are there any questions?"

Ellis stepped forward and suggested the space dock be entered in the navigational computer as the mission's point of origin.

Captain Davidson said, "Enter that as such, Spike."

"Yes sir," said Spike.

"On that note people, we have further information that John has to disclose. John, go ahead."

"Thank you, Clinton. First, I want to welcome all of you for this mission and since you and the entire crew are all volunteers we," looking at Clinton, "are going to exercise a little freedom. There is no regulation during this mission stating you must wear your uniforms, but we do insist wearing your I.D. name tags and your Saunders Life belts. Pick your tags up from 'stores' a.s.a.p. Next, your second freedom is romantic in nature, due to the ungodly time to reach the RV point with Gariff. Romance is encouraged as well as childbirth. Again, you must always wear your Saunders belts. Disputes will be dealt with swiftly, so act responsibly. Now, some facts we won't like. Ellis, how long will it take to reach the RV point?"

"John, if the input info is correct, I estimate 66. 647 lifespans to reach the suggested RV point, unless that is altered."

"Okay Ellis, unless Gariff contacts me otherwise I believe there was a cryogenics area on this ship which will be utilized," said John. "More on that later. Right now, let's get this ship under way. Clinton, the Sir Isaac Newton is yours, and from now on this ship will be referred to as the Newton."

John went to his private quarters where he contacted Janet to meet with him. Meanwhile the Newton was backing out of space dock, and when it reached a safe distance, John felt the build up of the propulsion systems and the heavy thrust indicating they were on their way.

"Weapons?"

"Jules here, sir."

"Jules, I want men to man the laser cannons until we have cleared our Solar System by 3AU's."

"Three astronomical units, sir?"

"Correct, Jules. And use your best men!"

"Acknowledged, sir. Jules out."

Clinton clicked off his communication switch and made appropriate entries in his log.

Jan appeared at John's doorway and asked, "Is everything alright, honey?"

"I don't know. Up on the bridge I may have encountered a problem, expected but far more reaching then we anticipated."

"How so, John?"

"Remember at the Colonel's office in Florida we asked Sam if we could leave our clones there and he said yes?"

"Uh, huh. I remember because there was a high probability that we wouldn't return and so?"

"Well, there is a crew complement on this ship of 1,000 people and not one was drafted. They're all volunteers which means they have not had the opportunity that we had regarding their clones, Jan. I just feel guilty about it."

"Darling, you needn't feel guilty. COWA had funds pre-allocated for just such an auspicious occasion. Each surviving family received money, a life-insurance policy pay-out if you will."

"You knew about it?"

"In a manner of speaking, yes. I put a motion on the floor at a COSSIOS general meeting, quite some time ago. It was passed and acted upon to present to COWA's General Assembly meeting. It made headlines in all the newspapers and infuriated taxpayers everywhere. However, it certainly increased public interest in space exploration at the same time. And I know what you're thinking, John. It's also become just another impetus for those people who are against spending funds on space exploration."

"It had to be one of those times when I was on a military field exercise and I should have caught up on it while on my way to Florida for our initial briefing. Honey, it's water under the bridge now. Do you know of anything else of which I should be aware?"

"Not now. Why John?"

"You're going to think I may be crazy, but here goes. While Clinton was giving Ellis and I the tour of the ship, Ellis came with, a sort of supposition, like time travel. But since you just informed me of this pay out process, like a death benefit to the surviving family members on behalf of their volunteering family member, I started to imagine some truth in it. Good grief Jan, the alien has a ship capable of travelling galaxy to galaxy. Clint said that if he had not been given the construction specs, we wouldn't be doing this mission, let alone bringing the personnel to Ganymede to build the ship."

"John, I think that modern day insurance people have come up with all sorts of clauses to prevent fraudulent claims. Identification procedures have vastly improved since the 21st century, what with retinal scans, DNA collections, blood analyses, photo-ids, dental impressions, etc. So, no I don't think you're crazy, it's good that we are now on the same page.

When I was given the tour of my areas of expertise, I too was stunned to see all the developments that hitherto I could only imagine but have now become a reality. I think this mission John, is going to be very much of an eye-opener for everybody on this ship or Earth for that matter, upon the ship's return."

"Now, that, I think we can take to the bank." John said, smiling, as he rose from the desk to give Janet a warm embrace. Just as he was hugging her, his desk holophone advised him of an incoming message on his private line. It was Gariff. John answered it quickly.

"Gariff, good to talk to you again my friend. What news do you …?"

"John, good news for you. You must quickly update your navigational computers to alter course to these coordinates."

"Let me put them into my personal computer so I can transfer them to the helm when I go back up to the bridge." After he put them into his personal computer John asked, "Why the change, Gariff?"

"So, we can rendezvous quicker and you won't be travelling so long. Also, could you advise Clinton that after 336 hours of travel at the ship's top speed there will be a further boost up to 500,000 km/hr. Don't worry, the ship can take it. Gariff out."

"Honey, I have to get to the bridge and give this new course information to Clinton," said John, quickly kissing his wife on the cheek.

"Wait for me I'm coming also." she exclaimed, grabbing his hand.

Entering the bridge, the Marshalls could hear some dialogue going on within Tactics. "…it's coming at us 2 degrees starboard, 0.9 degrees of pitch and…"

"I see it!" Rolling with that minor course change, Tommy fired his Laser cannon using full impact. Everyone on the ship watching their monitors saw the results and witnessed a 3km sized asteroid pulverized into dust.

An extrapolated potential course appeared on the screen thirty seconds later, like a game replay. Everyone's jaw dropped in awe as they saw the Newton blown apart. A loud cheer could be heard all over the ship.

John took this opportunity to talk quietly with Clinton about his recent discussion with Gariff. "He suggested that we quickly enter these co-ordinates into the astral computer."

"Did he say why?"

"No, but I feel timing was important." Clinton looked at John questioningly as it was almost 180° starboard from his initial course input.

"John, what do you bet that with Gariff's expertise and your good fortune, heh, heh, it could be a high-energy anomaly?"

"You mean a time tunnel?"

"Why not?"

"You're nuts matchbox."

Clinton thought to himself that he had better trust this information after all, they were travelling in the ship he and Gariff built.

Raising his left eyebrow Captain Davidson then called his helmsman to his chair to show him what John had just shown him. Clinton said quietly, "Spike, put these corrections into the navigational computer, okay?"

Spike said, "These indicate a point about half way between Dubhe of Ursa Major and Polaris of Ursa Minor's tail end. We're looking at a major travelling distance measured in parsecs, sir."

"And so?" questioned the Captain. "You have a union meeting or some place you would rather be?"

"Well, no sir! I just wanted to be sure this wouldn't come back to bite us," Spike replied, assuring the Captain of the helm's advisory capacity.

"Don't worry, Spike, I'm sure John has a few more tricks up his sleeve," and with that Spike returned to his position at the helm to enter the new data.

Turning to John he smiled and asked, "Well, do you?"

"Do I what?" challenged John.

"Have any more tricks up your sleeve?" The Captain countered.

John looked at his e-pad. "Oh yes, this little item here," said John pointing at an upcoming velocity change almost teasingly.

"I'll see you on the recreational deck where I'm going to knock the hell out of you in a game of squash, ha, ha!" Clint said between clenched teeth and a broad smile.

All this chatter on the bridge brought a smile to Janet as she watched the two friends going at it in all this formal ambience. She caught the raised eyebrows and smile on the face of Lt. Commander Rochelle Nicholson, the ship's third officer and communications officer on duty.

Getting up from his seat after making entries into the ship's log, including Spike's advisory, Clinton crossed the floor and quietly said to Spike, "Keep up the good work and, by the way, you can expect a gradual increase in velocity when we surpass 336 hrs. of travelling. Don't worry, it's pre-programmed."

"To what velocity, sir?"

"To at least 500,000 km/hr."

Spike gulped in absolute awe trying to visualize this giant goose travelling at that speed.

Chapter 36

The two Captains were talking in frivolous aggression as they entered the squash court when Janet confronted them with the news that she was going to be the referee and emphasized her neutrality looking straight at John. Clinton chuckled to himself thinking he could use the 'mizuki shot' he had practiced on since the last time they played. He had learnt it well after watching some old squash videos.

John's reach was much greater by two inches over Clinton's and seemed to be emphasized by their squash court whites. However, Clinton was very quick on his feet and extremely agile. Just so they wouldn't complain afterwards, Jan ensured they had identical racquets. She was tingling with anticipation of the entertainment and the game's outcome.

They both agreed there would be no quarter given and the match (3/5 games) would end at a score of 10, period, regardless of rules! After all, they had a ship to run.

They constantly changed in rallies and serves. Jan was absolutely mesmerized by their apparent equality on the court.

"Come on big guy, you said you could trounce me. I'm waiting," challenged Clinton. John served the ball as if he was trying to put it through the hull.

She knew medically their bodies were getting an excellent workout. If they could keep this up throughout the journey she needn't worry about their physical conditioning.

Thinking to herself, she could do the same with Julie or better yet Marion, the chief medical officer. She had to see Marion soon, anyway. After the game, they took showers and went about their respective areas of duty - Clinton to the bridge and John to his office and residence quarters.

Sitting on the side of his bed, he was reading some information on the ship's construction when Jan entered the room leaving no reason to misinterpret her marital intentions.

Quietly laying in John's arms after a torrid love-making session, she played with his chest hair and asked, "Honey, do you think it will be very long before we reach Gariff's point of rendezvous?"

"To be honest, yes, at least a few years. However, he is full of surprises! Why do you ask?"

"Well, we could start a family, couldn't ..."

John quickly sat up, supporting himself on one elbow, and asked, "Are you preggers, angel?"

"Marion and I are pretty sure and we'll know tomorrow or in a few hours when the results are in!" Jan replied, smiling at John's newly found happiness. "Well, we better make sure," John said suggestively, while making an obviously amorous move on her.

She groaned lovingly in his arms.

Chapter 37

When John entered the bridge, Clinton greeted him with a high five indicating tacitly that he lost to John, a move which didn't escape Ellis's watchful eyes as he smiled to himself. Ellis was manning the first officer's position. Bogdan (Red) Rozsinzski was the relief operator in the helm/navigation position and Commander Donaldson was back on Communications.

Seeing the opportunity John suggested that a general department heads' meeting take place next time at relief changeover. Captain Davidson advised John that would be in two hours in the briefing area of the diametric grav-deck.

"Excellent, Clinton. I'll grab a couple of general service personnel and prepare the area."

"Good I'll see you then, John," said Clint.

"Safe driving 'til then, pal," again accepting Clint's high five.

Up to now John wondered if Gariff was forthcoming with his rendezvous information, so he was determined to find out. While musing about this matter he heard, "All department heads are to assemble in the briefing area in one hour and bring your e-pads with you."

John knew Ellis and Julie would be there as his and Jan's support. After everybody had assembled in the hall, Clinton called for quiet, while John stood to speak.

"I'm sure everyone is wondering like me just how long this mission will probably take given the facts as we know them to date." Looking at the navigations/helmsman, John said, "Correct me if I'm wrong, but isn't the speed of light approximately 186,292 mi/sec..."

"Sir, permission to speak?"

"Go ahead, Commander."

"Sir, may I make a correction for you regarding that speed."

"Continue, Chris."

"Sir, Albert Einstein postulated that the speed of light in a vacuum was 186,292 mi/sec or 299,792.458 km/sec but he also added that there were no inertial forces involved adhering to Newton's second law of motion."

Clinton said, "I know where he's going with this, John, and he's right."

Chris continued "Sir, I believe that speed is slightly altered with the Newton travelling at its current speed of 500,000 km/hr or 138.888 km/sec which is insignificant in comparison with light's speed."

"Thank you, Chris. In other words, our encouragement to form romantic relationships holds true and unless Gariff comes up with a better and safer travelling speed, our grandchildren several times removed will be doing the rendezvous. Any questions?"

An audible groan permeated the area. Just then, "Captain to the bridge, please," was heard. Responding to the intercom message, Clinton nodded his head for John to come with him.

While they were in the turbo lift, Clinton prodded, "You're not saying everything, John. What's up?"

"Remember when Jan came to my office?"

"Of course, go on."

"Two things – 1) both Marion and Jan think Jan's pregnant," John said, smiling, and 2) Gariff indicated a further big surprise for us, meaning you, my friend," patting Clinton on his back between his shoulder blades.

Entering the bridge, Commander Donaldson said, "The Captains are on the bridge," giving recognition to John Marshall also. Looking towards the large screen in front of the Captain's chair, they both saw Gariff's hologram standing between the chair and the screen. It was Gariff who spoke first.

"My friends, John and Clinton. I hope I find you both well but I suspect a little bewilderment on your part, John. What is troubling you?"

"Gariff, my math may not be the best but I think the suggested rendezvous point is at least 10 of our lifespans away, based on a lifespan of 75 years. At the speed we are travelling," pointing at everybody, "we won't be alive. I don't believe that was your intention."

Raising his hand to signal for calm, Gariff said, "No it wasn't, John. During our communication, I indicated I had some more surprises for you but mostly Clinton. First, your navigational computer has you on course to a space/time anomaly which some of your fictional literature refers to as a 'worm hole'; 2nd) your ship is built to withstand the forces in there, and 3rd) your wife is pregnant with your son who will be approximately 18 years old by the time you exit the anomaly; and 4th) the anomaly will not affect your aging or that of your crew, however, your son, who will be a few hours old, will not have cells protecting him from the anomaly until adulthood, meaning he will age normally."

"Gariff, how do you know we'll have a son?"

"I was going to tell you during our office talk but now that you know your wife is showing an aura about her which indicates a male birth. My eyes can see that aura because of our genetic make up. John, we have so much to talk about at the rendezvous."

"How soon will we reach the anomaly?"

"John, your wife will have given birth, so a few hours after that. In case you are wondering your son's birth is just a coincidence and could not be foretold.

Clinton, could you have your engineering staff put this information in their computer programming and we'll all meet just outside the anomaly."

Taking a small plug-in memory stick from Gariff, Clinton said, "Thank you," and asked "What will it do?" He watched as it materialized in his hand.

"It should enhance the existing program to 1) work faster and 2) protect it from any possibility of faltering while in the anomaly."

"Thank you again, Gariff. We are indeed indebted to you."

Gariff responded, "You have a saying 'what are friends for' which I like. So, the next time we meet my friends, will be at the rendezvous," Gariff said, waving goodbye.

After Gariff left, John, Clinton, and Ellis put their thoughts together in John's office. Ellis spoke first saying, "I think we now have a better idea of our travelling future, John."

"I can't disagree with that Ellis, so any recommendations for the time between now and the point of rendezvous?"

Looking over at Clinton, John had a questioning expression on his face.

"Gentlemen, I think we'll do what has been done on ships for years – prepare for the unexpected and (pardon the pun, John) the expected. We'll get the crew to drill, maintain, check and recheck, exercise, etc., so by the time we get there we'll be sharp and prepared for anything."

John and Ellis said at the same time, "Excellent." Ellis started putting some data onto his e-pad, and enroute to the bridge, showed Clinton and John. Looking at each other in the turbo-lift, John said, "I think this is a terrific schedule Ellis."

Clinton agreed to a point. "John, I don't think you should participate in these extra-vehicular activities. You should let our maintenance personnel handle them. You're too important to this mission to risk an accidental injury of any sort."

"John, I concur with Captain Davidson. And as a reminder my name …"

"I see your point gents, but I will get in some exciting activities like squash, structural inspections, engineering checks, and a thorough check of our escape section, including some target practice against bullseye, who I would like to meet."

Ellis's squash schedule was designed by Julie for exercising reasons and paired the main players as such: -

1. John vs. Clinton

2. Janet vs. Marion

3. John vs. Ellis

4. Janet vs. Julie

and so on, so that each player played against others throughout the list. Because of the games' vigorousness, and Janet's pregnancy, care was taken to prevent any injuries.

Finally, there was an overall championship match between Ellis and Julie, which had Julie come out on top.

Jules thought his best gunner, Bullseye, could beat John in any targeting session they could design. It was this rivalrous comradery which kept the ship's personnel in the highest of spirits which could be to their advantage at the rendezvous.

During Jan's final days of her last trimester she could feel labor pains. She checked herself into Marion's infirmary.

At first the pains were ten minutes apart and worked up to two minutes apart, finally 25 seconds apart. As it turned out, the Marshall's good luck held out even in child birth. Soon Jan let out a few loud groans which seemed to make the situation happier and humorous at the same time.

John responded to Marion's call and was just entering the room to see his son being born and give his wife some much needed support. Taking the baby from Dr. Wentworth after she had cut the cord, the nurses cleaned him up, wrapped him in a receiving blanket and handed him to John where the baby seemed happier because he calmed right down.

Moving beside Janet's bed he held her hand, bent down and gave her a loving kiss. She asked him, "What are we going to name him, honey?"

John looked at her and suggested, "Why don't we name him Adam Matthew Marshall?"

Looking at John she asked, "Why?"

"Well he is our first born. He is the first child born in space beyond our solar system. He is the first child born on a first-ever cruiser to the galaxies for the planet Earth. I suggested Matthew because this, motioning with his arm, all herald's a new beginning in the era of space exploration."

She looked at him thoughtfully for a couple of seconds and very happily agreed. John handed her the baby and Marion said, "I'll just record this on his birth record but I also have to add one little item."

"What is that?" they asked simultaneously.

"His nationality, since he was born out here, I have to put him down as the first citizen of planetary extraction meaning he is a citizen of Earth not of any one country," said Marion. This news put a broad smile on the Marshall's faces and they both gave their son a loving kiss.

John returned to the bridge and told Ellis and Clinton and the personnel on the bridge this very happy news. Feeling John's elation Clinton said he was going to have a party for the crew on the main deck.

"This is the Captain speaking. At 13:00 hrs. today there will be a birthday party on the grav-deck in honor of John and Janet's baby boy. You are all excused to attend for a few minutes if on duty, and as long as you want, if off duty. Alcohol free. Captain out."

Everyone was caught up in the moment of the Marshalls' birth. There was music, dancing, an all-you-can-eat buffet table and the usual doting admiration of the baby. The members of the crew who had managed to form relationships by now, seemed to express tacitly their mutual wishes for similar happiness. The crew had silently adopted Adam as the Newton's son which made them all latent parents. It was a relationship they all enjoyed.

It was 37 hours after Adam's birth when helmsman Spike said to Captain Davidson, "Sir, there's something going on up ahead which seems to be distorting everything."

Looking in his scanners, Ellis said, "Clinton, I think it's the space/time warp that Gariff told us about."

Clinton looked and could see it was the anomaly. Turning to communications, Clinton said, "Give me an open address system, please, Rochelle."

"Yes, sir."

Clinton said, "This is the Captain speaking. All hands are to secure their stations and go on full alert. We are about to enter a space/time anomaly and may experience the unexpected. Be prepared until further notice, Captain out." The Captain gesticulated across his throat to cut off further transmission.

Immediately, every crew member snapped out of his recent emotional jubilance to give full attention to his work station. John had relieved Clinton and was now sitting in the Captain's chair when Ellis said, "Sir, we will enter the anomaly in one minute."

"Everybody fasten your seatbelts. It could be rocky in there!" John exclaimed.

Just as they entered the warp Ellis looked at his chronometer noting the exact time on his log.

When nothing seemed to change, Ellis looked at John as they exchanged puzzled expressions. This action was punctuated when the door to the bridge opened to admit Janet who was quickly followed by a tall, strappingly handsome lad of about eighteen years of age. The access security men each grabbed an arm until his admittance was approved. That job fell on Jan's shoulders when she held

John's right arm and said, "Adam, come meet your dad," while she beckoned their son to come. Seeing Jan call for him the security personnel immediately released him.

This action caused Ellis to check his chronometer and supervisory navigational gauges. John was perplexed, at first, and then recalled what Gariff had said to him. Coming out of his puzzled stupor, he stood up and hugged the boy saying, "Son, it seems like only yesterday I was holding you in my arms as a baby. Now look at you!" John exclaimed, beaming with pride while looking at his wife. "Gosh I am so proud of you, Adam. Has mom told you anything about what's going on with us that is, everybody?"

"Oh sure, dad. We are on a Galaxial Cruiser called the Sir Isaac Newton, named after a famous scientist from the old days on Earth, our home planet. Dad, I should brief you about my knowledge."

Janet cut in and said, "John, his current knowledge includes a Masters Degree in Astrophysics, a Masters in Earth History, a Bachelors in Aquatic Ecology, 3rd seed in squash and he is second to Bullseye in Tactics."

"Well, son, it seems you need a little more time with those laser cannons of ours," John said, proudly adding, "you have really outdone yourself."

"Gee dad, Bullseye said that you were the top man to beat."

"Thanks for the vote of confidence son, but if I didn't have horse-shoes up you-know-where I wouldn't have won."

Rochelle interrupted, "Ahem, Sir?"

"Yes, Rochelle, what is it?"

"Sir, we have an urgent message from Gariff."

"Put it up on the big screen, Spike."

"Yes, sir."

Janet gently pulled Adam away from John's chair to watch the proceedings.

"Who is Gariff, mom?" Adam asked.

"He's the person we have been sent by Earth to meet. He comes from another planet he calls Ffraiteron. He is a Ffraiterite."

Puzzled, Adam said, "But he looks just like us?"

"I know, son. However, your dad and I believe he is equipped with abilities a little more than we human beings and we also think that is one of the things he wants to talk about during our meeting. Let's listen."

"So, either we postpone our meeting or try to resolve their dispute so there will be peaceful co-existence."

"I agree, Gariff. Let's be their arbiters and show them a peaceful way. I'm going to inform the ship's personnel of our intentions."

Rochelle Donaldson opened the ship's address system again for the Captain.

"This is the Captain. We are a short distance from the rendezvous point. It seems there are two armadas bent on doing war with each other at the same point of our rendezvous which has been confirmed by Gariff's navigator and ours. Since we don't want to postpone our meeting unnecessarily we have agreed with Gariff to act as arbiters and settle their dispute peacefully. Therefore, as of now your full attention to your duty stations is demanded, from Tactics to General Service. You are all on a warning. We might have visitors. Captain Marshall out."

"John, let me introduce ourselves to the leaders of these armadas, if that meets with your approval?"

"It does, Gariff. Do I transfer to your ship or how do we do this?"

"I think we should meet on that gravity deck we built, John. There should be ample room for all concerned and I can have some of my crew transferred there as well to help out."

"Splendid, Gariff."

"Jules, could you get your men to put out the welcome mat for our visitors from Ffraiteron?"

"Any special considerations, captain?"

"Not that we have been made aware of, Jules. I'll have some general service sent to help, also.

Ellis, Clinton, you're with me. Commander Donaldson, you have the bridge."

"Yes, Sir."

"Spike, have you got those two armadas in view yet?"

"Yes, sir."

"Good, on screen please. How far away are they?"

"Sir, if they maintain their present course and speed they will both be here in six hours."

"Good," said Chris. "It should give us enough time to transfer the TGCTriang crew from Gariff's ship to ours safely. Let John know, Rochelle, okay?"

"Yes, Commander."

Chapter 38

John returned to the bridge. A change in the bridge personnel produced Lt. Commander Bogdan (Red) Rozsinzski at the helm, Ellis remained at the first officer's station, Commander Chris Donaldson at communications and Colonel John Marshall took the Captain's chair. John quickly caught up with the ship's log.

"Red, keep an eye on your dials please and let me know when there is an hour before the armadas get here."

"John?"

"Yes, Janet."

"John, everything is set and ready here and Clint and Gariff are on their way to the bridge.

"Good, we'll be able to address their leaders together.

Red, how much longer?"

Clinton and Gariff entered the bridge simultaneously each taking up a position to the left and right of John.

Chris said, "We have an incoming hailing message, sirs."

John had just finished shaking hands with Gariff in a welcoming gesture of greeting when a voice on the screen said, "To the leaders of both ships on our courses, take warning we have no quarrel with you but if you remain there we shall obliterate you. I am Natas, Admiral of the Srennis Ralos 12 and have spoken!"

"Chris open us up will you? Natas, I am John Marshall of Earth's galaxy cruiser, Sir Isaac Newton and this is my guest, Gariff Tterszin of Ffraiteron who is Admiral of the ship moored beside me, the TGCTriang. We wish you no harm and come in peace."

Another voice just as gruff in manner as Natas, spoke, "I am Wehttam, leader of the planet YI's Armada in the star cruiser HRI Closer and warn Natas we shall defend the two ships in our path and then completely destroy your armada, Natas."

"Why don't we just do battle ourselves, Wehttam and then claim these two ships as the spoils of battle for the victor?"

"I agree, Natas."

"Gentlemen, I wonder just exactly how brave and strong you are; enough to come on board this ship and confront Gariff and myself in talks? I don't think so," said John.

John had the screen blanked out. Turning to Ellis, John said, "We just might need some of your hidden talents, my friend."

For both leaders, John invited them to board the Newton via the gooseneck. He wanted them to take up his challenge to come on board the Newton. John was a believer in the adage... 'keep your friends close but keep your enemies closer'... He quickly made plans with Gariff for greeting the armada leaders. The greeting Newton crew members were all dressed in their G-suits and wore Saunders life belts.

The leader of the Srennis was first to arrive with his two escorts. Everyone was dressed in their versions of suits to do combat in microgravity conditions.

Next came Wehttam and his escorts wearing battle garb for war in space and helmets much like the ancient Vikings of Earth.

"We welcome you all aboard the Sir Isaac Newton. There are some refreshments laid out for you to help yourselves. Come and sit down and let's talk." After appropriate introductions were made they all accepted John's invitation to sit at a large round table to discuss their disputes.

"Gentlemen, in order that equal time is given to both sides regarding voicing your dispute we must stipulate that you follow our rules.

When discussions have ended, Ellis will make copies for you to sign stating only the facts of claim and the proposed desires of correction. As arbiters of this dispute John and I, Gariff, will sign as witnesses. Ellis will make copies and you will take back the proposals to your business people to obtain signatures of acceptability or a statement of rejection with the reasons. Your people will notify us in the future for the settlement date. Do you understand and accept this ruling?"

"We do," they said.

Natas from Ralos was first to speak in his deep gruff voice claiming, "Wehttam's people had cheated his fellow Ralosians on previous contracts."

John asked if Natas had brought copies of those contracts with him. He did.

Gariff asked Wehttam if he also brought his copies of the same contracts with him. His escort handed the copies to Gariff. Ellis was to take them to research.

"Gentlemen, we're going to take a few minutes to study these contracts," John and Gariff said, "and when we come back we'll give you our ruling. In the meantime, stay here and our crew can offer some refreshments."

John handed the contracts to Ellis instructing him to check them carefully in the forensics labs and let us know as soon as possible. While Ellis was doing that Gariff took the time to contact his ship to update his crew and give them some special instructions. John did the same with Clinton; instructions which also insured a peaceful departure by his armada visitors. What John did not know was that his son Adam was helping the crew members serve refreshments to the warring visitors.

After what seemed like forever, Ellis returned with the contracts in his left hand and the report (4 copies) in his right. He handed a report copy to Gariff and one to John.

When they reached the table, John said, "Well, gentlemen, it is not our job as arbiters to assign blame but to comment on our investigation. We have circled those parts of your contracts which show discrepancies. Your business representatives need to be advised on these alterations and make appropriate changes. When this is done return the contracts to us as arbiters and when approved a final decision amenable to both parties will be made."

"That is fair to the Srennis people," said Natas while getting up from the table.

As if not to be outdone Wehttam stood up and in just as gruff a voice as Natas, said, "We agree and say the same thing."

While enroute to the exits in the 'gooseneck' one of Wehttam's escorts stumbled causing him to fall forward. While recovering his footing his rifle-shaped laser weapon accidentally discharged. The bolt hit Adam right in his solar plexus area. The impact threw him backward causing him to hit a bulkhead. The injury he sustained broke his neck, severing his spinal column and trachea. It was fatal! John and Ellis were at his side immediately.

The Newton Tactics crew members already had their weapons trained on the visitors of the warring armadas. Ellis picked up Adam and looking at John shook his head 'no' answering a tacitly questioning look from John. Janet and Marion arrived breathlessly. Seeing Ellis carrying Adam caused Janet to collapse sobbingly into John's arms. Dr. Wentworth looked at Adam, looked at the Marshalls and shook her head 'no'. Their grief became the ship's grief. Rage started to rise and Gariff signaled for calm.

Gariff rose to calm everyone. "People, I witnessed everything and trust me, it was a complete accident." Walking to the soldier whose weapon fired Gariff asked to check the sighting scope.

Wehttam said, "Show him your weapon." There was no aiming record made confirming that it was accidental.

John was absolutely stunned by the event and grabbed Ellis by the arm loudly saying, "He was wearing his Saunders belt! Why was it fatal?" Ellis. "Why?"

John was quickly caving into his grief. His wife's tears were melting him quickly. Commander Jules Armstrong saw the armada parties safely off the Newton to their own ships. When Clinton was informed of what happened he had Gariff's ship, the TGCTriang, contacted to come to a full stop. Understanding, they extended their condolences and agreed.

A funeral was planned and Adam was laid in an open coffin for viewing. He would be interred in space. He was not embalmed. When his casket would be ejected, it would journey directly toward the nearest star. Until then he lay in state while the crew members of the TGCTriang, the Newton and the crews of the armada ships all strolled by Adam's coffin.

In the background the music of The Prayer could be heard. The 'wake' immediately followed whereby John, Janet, Gariff, Ellis, Julie, Clinton, Marion and Jules stood to greet all 6000.

Suddenly, an unannounced figure appeared through the hull of the ship and stood beside Adam's casket. The person, who looked human, was clad in a hooded cream-colored robe. The entire deck became silent as all eyes were on the 'visitor.' John started to make a move and was quickly restrained by Gariff.

"John, it's a SEEDER!"

"A what?"

"A SEEDER, John! Traditional lore has it, that this is a race of beings that travel through time and the universe performing the wishes of the Galaxy Ordering Director. If the Director wants stars and planets somewhere, they collect the matter and make it so, including the chemicals of life. They are also immortal!"

John just stammered, "Unbelievable!"

"Ssshhh, listen in." The SEEDER began to talk and John thought, oh, great. It's a ventriloquist. I can hear him but his lips aren't moving. Must be telepathic. Can all of us understand him?" he asked Gariff.

"Yes, sshh, listen."

"To all present, I extend greetings from your Galaxy Ordering Director. The stars, cosmos and celestial anomalies that you have all experienced or wish to explore have been designed and created by the Director. Everything that happens in this universe happens because of his plan. This young lad's life was taken to illustrate to you all that you can NOT take life without impunity! The 'Director' has spoken and instructs me now. Behold, HIS WORK!"

Having said that, the SEEDER held his arms and hands upright to the ceiling of the deck while a column of rainbow-colored light seemed to pass through the ship's hull to hit the SEEDER. He then brought his arms down and placed one on Adam's chest and the other pointed at the soldier who accidentally killed Adam. All who were present heard the SEEDER, "Sir, are you now sorry for this young lad's death by your weapon?"

"Yes, and I beg forgiveness."

"Then let it be so," and the soldier became cloaked in light and was forgiven. Adam awoke immediately startled by everyone staring at him. This action was witnessed in awe.

Speaking again the SEEDER said, "Let all who have witnessed this event know that the beings from the planet called Earth and their friends are the Director's chosen Peacekeepers of His Universe and as such will not be deterred!" The SEEDER then disappeared as mysteriously as he arrived walking through the hull of the ship.

Jan and John rushed to the casket to hug their son. They both shed tears of joy as everyone started to applaud in recognition of the happy life-giving event. Jules asked a crew member to find a copy of "The Hallelujah Chorus" and play it in the background.

John and Gariff wished the warring parties a peaceful return to their home planets and a successful renewal of their contracts. They were reminded that Gariff and John would meet them later to provide an affirmation decision when they were ready. The warring parties expressed their gratitude and departed.

John, Janet, Adam, Ellis, Julie and Gariff all met as previously arranged and discussed everything in science, space exploration, biology, genetics, environmental ecology, computer sciences, evolution, the SEEDERS, *etc.* Adam asked, "Why are so many aliens resembling this basic body form that we have. I thought some of them would look like some of those old space movies portrayed, you know, large black eyes, silvery skin, or gigantic acid-dripping lizards?"

Gariff answered him, "Yours isn't the only culture that portrayed aliens like that. Heck, we thought you Earthlings would resemble fish-like beings because of how your planet's blue color looked from deep in space. Adam, from a distance everything looks different like opinions of other beings."

John and Jan both agreed. John said, "In fact, we weren't sure what Gariff would look like, so you can imagine how we felt about our orders to rendezvous. We were even more amazed seeing the SEEDER who brought you back to life. All cultures to some degree, exercise fight or flight. This colors our opinions and views on many aspects of our lives on Earth. If man worked together like bees in a hive, or ants, for example, then space exploration would be accomplished sooner for all our benefits.

If we treated Earth like our home moving through space instead of using proprietary competitive means to get into space humans could be what the SEEDER said we were designed to be – the peacekeepers of the universe!" Way back in history, Marshall McLuhan was quoted as saying, "There are no passengers on spaceship Earth. We are all crew."

"Dad, in your opinion do you think we could work together to achieve that common goal, clean up our planet?"

"Ancient cultures on Earth, Adam, developed doctrines for the preservation of their people. The so-called wise ones, priests, sages, shamans, tribal elders, kings, *et al.*, all sought ways and means by which they could control their people for preservation reasons. Anarchy would soon wipe them out because people could see it was the power behind all of it. The expression 'might makes right' was the credo of the anarchists but they did not want to hear the rest of that expression – power corrupts but absolute power corrupts absolutely.

Gariff and I cooperated for a common good – to bring two warring races together to settle a festering dispute and it worked. They went away happy and we had our meeting. Gariff has learned, and we have learned, and that knowledge has strengthened our bonds of friendship. Isn't that what makes life worth living?"

"Thanks, dad. I'm proud of you too!" Adam said, hugging him and his mom. John glanced at Janet and could see she was proud of the father-son relationship in her family.

"Well, I think we might head for home, Gariff, so, until we meet again, peace, happiness, and success to you."

"The same for you, John. I hope those gifts prove useful to Earth. Farewell until next time."

"Farewell, Gariff."

After seeing Gariff off the Newton plans were made for their departure. Both Julie and Ellis would accompany the Marshalls to Earth. Julie was going to return to Dr. Wentworth's sick bay unit to help.

Clinton welcomed Ellis and the Marshalls, all three of them, to the bridge. The order was given to enter a course for Earth into the computer.

Acknowledging Clinton's order, Spike said, "Yes sir ... ahem ...Sir?"

"Yes, Spike. What's the problem?"

"We don't have to .... Gulp .... We're already there!"

"On the main screen, Spike .... On the screen! Oh, my god! John, are you seeing this? Spike how far ...?"

"Three million miles out, sir. And the chronometers indicate a mission elapsed time of t-t-two years!"

"I concur, sirs," said Ellis.

David L. Pritchard

John whispered to Janet, "and Gariff gave us those two new genes, neuraline and endurine."

"Janet added, "Don't forget the gravity drive, dear.""

"I know, but I wonder what other new developments have occurred?"

"Knowing Earth, darling, that's the least of our worries. How do we explain our eighteen-year old son when we have only been gone two years?" Jan asked, gripping John's arm a little tighter while hanging on to her son's shoulder.

Adam said quietly to his dad and mom, "Besides having a vacation you guys are going to have an interesting time ahead of you."

"How so, son?" asked John.

"Debriefing the Council!" he said and smiled.

"Crap, he's right!" Jan said, laughing. "It should be fun." They thrilled at the sight of Earth gradually coming closer. A rousing musical rendition of Land of Hope and Glory from E. Elgar's "Pomp and Circumstance #1", was being played on the bridge: -

Land of Hope and Glory,
Mother of the Free,
How shall we extol thee,
Who are born of thee?
Wider still and wider,
Shall thy bounds be set,
God, who made thee mighty,
Make thee mightier yet,
God, who made thee mighty,
Make thee mightier yet.

"Well, I'm going home to my BBQ before it leaves me for dead!" said John.

Jan squeezed him in agreement. "I'm with you on that, honey. Who knows, we could get called back under your new title and the never-ending gripe of the G.G.E. faction. So, let's enjoy a little rest, while Ellis and Julie are minding the Newton."

EXERCISING
BESTOWED ABILITIES

Chapter 39

Margret had returned from shopping with some Sunday food basics – chips, herbal dip, pop, ice cream and John's favorite Oreo cookies. She forgot the ginger ale. "Damn," she cursed under her breath. "I gotta go out again. I better tell Janet." She knew Sagitarrius had to be with Janet as there was no barking when she entered the house. Jan was on her patio lounge chair nursing her favorite mint julep. While she approached the door, she could see someone slowly picking his way towards the family. She quickly took John's colt 45 from the holster hanging in the laundry room. Checking that it was loaded, she aimed and fired four bullets into the would-be assassin; two in the head and two in his chest. They were all lethal!

He fell backwards over another patio chair which knocked the laser from his hand. Sagitarrius, the golden lab picked it up in her jaws growling her threatening best at him, all the while her tail was wagging! The commotion got the attention of everybody else in a big hurry. The next-door neighbors were away for the day. Janet rushed inside to Margret to console her. She was so upset that she broke the one sliding glass door to the patio when she shot the intruder. John removed the ski mask and quickly identified him as a GGE operative.

Police sirens responding to a telephone call could be heard approaching the front of the house. Two homicide detectives rolled up behind them and slammed their car doors when they got out.

"Marshall's place again, Ken. Three time this month, damn." Ken shrugged it off.

During the investigation, it was found that: -

1. the intruder was none other than the garage mechanic from the service station that the Marshall's frequented for fuel and auto repairs;

2. the intruder was human, satisfying Janet's weird request of the police; furthermore, he was a (mole) operative from God's Garden of Eden (GGE);

3. Margret, an expert marksman trained by the Marshalls always hit what she aimed at, was unhurt;

4. identifications were made and given; the event was kept from the public; the police wrote the investigation up as an act of self-defence taking appropriate photographs of the scene; the laser was taken in as evidence;

5. the gun shots were explained as target practice which the Marshalls often did;

6. Angélique Marshall arrived coincidentally and confirmed the intruder's identity and the reason for his visit to the Marshall's only.

"George, I've recorded everything."

"Good, should satisfy Emerson's council and the media. Keep the Americans back; they can get copy from the Canadian News or COWA."

"I'll get some coffees for us, okay?"

Angélique informed John and Janet that Colonel Harding had some news for them that they might not like; and, were told to report to him by 16:00 hours tomorrow afternoon.

John said, "Thanks, mom. See you later." Janet gave her mother-in-law a hug goodbye. But Adam was made a fuss over by his grandmother and seemed to relish it. His grandmother headed up the SETIA secret police.

The 'agency' (Search for Extra-terrestrial Intelligence Agency) was quite covert in their activities and nobody appreciated this fact more than the Marshalls. Genetic engineering could easily produce beings looking just like humans. These beings could mix with them, copulate with them, enjoy them in a variety of ways, without their knowledge and then suddenly destroy them when, the time arrived.

Mrs. A. Marshall knew this as lead operative of SETIA's secret police. John, Janet, and Adam knew this from their recent rendezvous visit in outer space with Gariff from Ffraiteron. Fear in mankind is strongly developed when confronted with the unknown. Alien beings that don't look like us put us on guard from the get-go. Alien beings that look like us, act and behave like us, break through our psycho-emotional defences easily, until too late to act.

Chapter 40

Since they time-shared in Florida's Fort Lauderdale area they wanted to leave at 11:00 hours to see Colonel Harding by 16:00 hours. Monday rush hour traffic was always hectic, especially for travelers to Patrick Air Force Base (45th Space Wing) or Canaveral's Air Force Station. John's air car handled it with ease. Some shopping enroute would be on the agenda as well.

"John, did you ever find out what your dad Howard might like for his birthday?" asked Jan.

"I think a nice little visit to an exotic Texas game farm outside of old Dallas would be a great surprise for him. Remember Bert Thompson telling me about it when I was last up in Canada's hunting parks?"

"It sounds great to me, John. Your mom could accompany him too."

They stopped at a shopping center for a few minutes and bought some pink lemonade and bacon-with-cheese tea biscuits for WJ. His favorite foods brought in by friends like the Marshalls, would bring a huge smile to his craggy, wind-carved face. They drove finally into P.A.F.B. and were quickly admitted by the gate house guards after Adam was confirmed as an invitee.

WJ met them at the doors to the administration building and took them to his private office where he could be 100% sure of complete security. Their debriefing and explanation of the mission that he was about to impart to them demanded it. "Come into my dungeon for some talk guys." Adam hesitated. "You too son," WJ said encouragingly.

"If this is going to be a long talk, WJ, then we brought some goodies for refreshments," said Janet, handing him a bag. "I see congrats are in order, WJ."

Taking the bag from Janet, WJ stuck his nose in it and smelled 'the heavenly aroma' of a bacon and cheese tea biscuit- his favorite. He was like a kid at the candy store looking at his favorite candy only this time it was a tea biscuit and lemonade. Between munching and drinking some lemonade he asked John to talk about his last mission.

Looking at Harding a little closer John noticed a Star on WJ's epaulets and said, "Lt. General of the 45th Space Wing. Yes Bill, congratulations. It's about time the DoD approved it."

John related the mission's story matter-of-factly as though it was an everyday occurrence. "We had 1) a trip to the CSS; 2) an unsuccessful assassination attempt and scuttling of a trip to Mars by the GGE saboteurs; 3) a rather elaborate greeting by Sam Davis on Mars and briefing on the mission; 4) an introduction and tour of the Sir Isaac Newton; 5) the meeting of, and with, Gariff of Ffraiteron both on the Newton, and at the end of a trip through a time anomaly of space; 6) the birth of Adam; 7) the meeting of two warring Admirals, and the subsequent interim arbitration of their dispute; 8) the accidental killing of Adam by one of the Armada soldiers; 9) the surprise visit of a COSMIC SEEDER and his restoring life to Adam, and; 10) everyone's departures including our return to Earth from a surprising short distance and in a minimal passage of time! Boring, really," John said, winking at Jan and Adam.

When John had finished his recounting of the mission, he looked at Janet. She tacitly shook her head 'no' meaning … try not to disclose the gifts, yet!

John silently agreed.

"So, any questions, WJ?" John asked, noticing he stopped feeding his face.

"Some, but I think the answers will be rather diplomatic *i.e.* truthful without full disclosure. I will ask for the whereabouts of Ellis and Julie, though," Harding said while glancing at Janet.

"WJ, let me answer that query," said Janet. "Ellis and Julie asked to remain on the COWA Space Station to assist the new Commander with the station's duties and Newton's recruits and research requirements. Further, Ellis is there to facilitate easy access for assistance on the Newton, our Galactic Cruiser, which is in a parked orbit 5,000 miles beyond the CSS."

"Good," said Lt. Gen. Harding. "In that case, if you have need of their services on another mission they will be easier to pick up."

"I take it you have another mission, WJ?" John asked.

"John, I would much rather have invited you two for a gab-fest but unfortunately the man from Mars has indicated otherwise."

"So, what is it this time WJ? Does SETIA want us to meet another alien race or have we been called back to arbitrate another dispute?" asked Janet.

"Well, I'll tell you. Sam has indicated that this mission be an open book for you and your crew. However, there is to be no radio contact between you and any Earth related base. Physical appearance only is acceptable."

John asked, "Does Sam Davis, SETIA and COWA, all believe there is an underlying reason for this mission and that any radio communication could subvert it?"

"John, in a word, yes. But with no proof available yet we can't act. All I can show you right now are these reports that COWA has received from the various space agencies and radio telemetry data. They have checked, rechecked, disbelieved and put it to research scientists around the world. All the results are the same."

Both and Adam and John looked at the data, read the conclusions and said simultaneously, "This is bull****, WJ!"

"We all said the same thing guys. But it doesn't change anything. We need confirmation from first-hand observers." Janet rose from her chair to see the data and looked just as perplexed at Adam and John.

"Bill, how is it possible to destroy matter of this magnitude, and still not see evidence of an energy fluctuation?"

"It isn't, Janet. That is your mission: to determine why the most fundamental law of physics – *energy can neither be created nor destroyed; only rearranged* – is not being obeyed. Now, I know you both met an alien representative from the Triangulum galaxy system, so we were hoping you could enlist his assistance in resolving this enigma."

John spoke up and said, "Bill, does Sam want to see us first or can we just pick up our crew from COWA's Space Station and be on our way?"

"Sam has authorized Adam's bione creation and instructed that he be known to your biones to live together as a family. Your biones first names are Jomar, Jamar and Admar and the instruction stands that you all remain incommunicado as far as they are concerned. Take precautions when you visit with your parents so that the biones don't run into each other. Janet, I know you understand the reasoning behind this instruction."

Still prodding Gen. Harding for more info, John asked, "And Alpha Centauri isn't trying to swallow up M33, the Triangulum galaxy?" Adam quietly giggled at this cosmic quip.

"The researchers were hoping that would be the case but alas there is absolutely no evidence to support or give rise to that possibility. Simply put, nobody knows or can explain it. Science fiction people think that area of the universe is undergoing a dimensional change which hitherto has no observable or detectable evidence, just belief," countered WJ smiling at his most level-emotional self.

Adam who recently received his PhD. in Celestial Physics, looked at his father and said, "Wouldn't it be great if we return to Earth with an explanation? We could get our Pioneer Status in that field of study, dad."

Looking at his wife, John knew if he said anything to this effect, WJ might suspect that the alien life form from Ffraiteron gave the Marshalls a gift of which WJ had no knowledge. WJ would prod them for this information, something the Marshalls wanted to keep to themselves for the time being. John kept silent but did give his son a little chuckle, which WJ passed off as Adam's immaturity. "Well, honey, I guess we're going for a little drive through the universe. Feel up to it?"

Adam looked at his father and choked out a response, "Dad, by comparison Alpha Centauri is a 'drive' away, to quote you; the Triangulum Galaxy is 2,723,000 light years away, never mind going to any black hole which might be in it. Mom, has dad gone bonkers? He's talking, by my calculations, 106,722,147,236,544,000 miles *i.e.* if light still travels at 186,292 mi/s."

"John, with Clinton's help and the anomaly, do we have any concern?"

John knew what Jan was alluding to and tacitly cautioned Adam for silence. "WJ, I think with Clinton as our chief engineer this mission may just be possible especially if we can enlist Gariff's help."

"Okay, John, but no matter what you encounter out there do not endanger yourselves, the crew, or the ship. The event horizon is out of bounds by at least 1,000 light years. And if you suspect a supernova then get the hell out of there! That's COWA's directive."

Glancing at his wife, Janet, and his son, Adam, John asked, "When does SETIA want us to get started?"

"As soon as possible, John."

"Good. Does anyone mind if we arrange a 'good-bye' meet with our parents first?"

"No. In fact, we have taken the liberty to have them meet all of you in the Base Convention Hall. Indeed, John, they are over there now. Do you want a ride there?"

"Thank you, WJ. That is very kind of you," said Janet. Thinking that her son might naïvely blurt out something which might lead WJ to ask further questions about their previous trek, Janet distracted Adam by asking him to help her up out of the beanbag seat she had plunked herself in. She said firmly, "WJ, keep some lemonade for us when we get back."

This caused Adam to choke out, "If we get back!" He escorted Janet to the waiting limo while she kept his attention away from any conversation that her husband John might have with WJ on their way out from his office.

"Well, Bill, I do hope we have more to tell when we return. I'm sure it might be more informative and who knows, more emotionally arresting, ha, ha" John said, shaking Harding's offered right hand.

"John, I am almost positive it will be very revealing," said WJ while handing John a file. The file was sealed and labeled **'TOP SECRET'**. Taking the file from WJ, John put it under his left armpit. He turned and walked toward his family who was standing beside the limo's rear door. Janet was smiling at him because she knew that they were both on the same page concerning the gifts bestowed upon them from Gariff when returning to Earth after their previous venture.

"Adam, now you are going to see why I fell in love with your mother when you meet her parents. I told you the story of how but now you'll know why, son." Janet squeezed her husband's hand just a little tighter feeling secure in her feelings for him after their meeting with WJ. For some unexplained reason she sensed this space venture would be more intensive then previously.

Chapter 41

Samantha and Henry Lassiter were standing near the Hall's main entrance talking to Howard and Angélique Marshall as John and Janet's limo arrived. As they got out of the limo Adam waved vigorously at his grandparents for the second time in his life. Using this moment of inattention to themselves Janet grabbed her husband and gave him the same kiss she gave him at their wedding. Breaking, John asked, "What did I do right?" almost surprised.

"Later," Janet quipped.

Watching their son Adam greet his grandparents they heard a long ogling whistle from him as he approached the Lassiters. John squeezed his wife around the waist a little more and quipped, "I knew he would see the reason why I married you, honey!"

"Face it, John, he loves professors," ha, ha.

"Bull, he loves legs just like me," John replied chuckling in her ear. They extended their arms to hug their respective parents and then hugged their in-laws with the same exuberance. Howard and Angélique Marshall, along with Henry and Samantha Lassiter, all entered the Hall for a farewell conversation with refreshments. They were greeted by Colonel Clinton Davidson, his date – Lt. Commander Kathy Richardson, along with Ellis and Julie the biones.

John asked Ellis, "I thought you two were going to stay on the CSS for easier access to the Newton and recruit training?"

"We decided to come to this farewell party in case you needed us for anything John."

"Well alright, but it might be your last time on Earth which you'll find out about later."

"Long and dangerous mission?"

"Later, Ellis, I'll tell you later okay?" John and Janet observed all entrances to the Hall were guarded by military police. The Entrance Door was closed behind them and they all sat at a table set with the best white linen table cloth, their favorite red wine and some of the finest mouth-watering foods and desserts.

John summoned the Captain-of-the-Guard to the table to ask for a case. "Sir, could you give me a lockable attaché case for his file?"

The Captain replied, "Give me a couple of minutes, sir and I'll see what I can do."

"Thank you, Captain."

"Moms, Dads, let's toast this meeting to our health, success, and mission resolution," said John, lifting his glass of wine to them.

"To your health, happiness, long lives and quick return," they replied simultaneously, while 'clinking' goblets. Sitting back down John turned to accept the attaché case.

"Thank you," said John. The Captain snapped a salute, then returned to his post. John placed the file in the case.

Until now Ellis and Julie were beside themselves with curiosity wanting to know the reason for this mission but it was Clinton who broke the silence in this regard. "John, what are we doing?"

"Later, my friend. Later. So, moms and dads, how are you; what's new, and so on?" John asked, loving their presence.

"Yes, moms and dads, I agree with John," Janet joined. "How are you; how's school coming along; anything new on the saboteur front?"

Angélique Marshall started talking between bites, "You both know they will stop at nothing to rid Earth from all space exploration but while we were waiting for you Henry and Samantha were making some startling statements to the effect that the GGE would be willing to wipe out the world of all non-believers, and their property, if that were the only resolution to their cause."

"Don't they realize that the world would end for them also?" queried Janet.

"Yes, but they don't care! For some zealots, mostly, it fulfils their deity's wishes."

"But, mom, nowhere does it say in their Holy Book or Directive, to kill others. For that matter it only says in their doctrines the same thing it says in all doctrines to bring others to know their deity. Only the zealots interpret this as capture infidels, imprison them and condition their minds to think like them or execute them. It's Nazism all over again," said John. "One religion says 'love one another as you would have them love you."

"Adam, because this world has human beings inhabiting it there will always be people who exemplify the adage – *power corrupts and absolute power corrupts absolutely* – so what I'm saying is, don't give up living your life or dreaming of the life that fulfils your idealism, son." Janet's hand covered her husband's in comfort as his father was talking to him. "More news, Adam. I don't think alien life forms like us would be any different; just a hunch."

Ellis said, "During our last trek, Colonel Marshall, we all came very, very close to not being here today. A fluke maneuver on John's part saved us all."

"He told me, Ellis," said Howard Marshall. "From what I have been told and what I surmise, this mission you are about to depart on is going to be fraught with dangers you can't even imagine."

Looking at John, Janet and Ellis, Angélique said, "We're using speculation, educated guessing, *etc.*, but no facts have been given to us, any of us. Right Sam, Henry?" Angélique prodded.

"That's right, John. We have all been told that this could be the last one for you all, Clinton, Ellis, Julie   and Rochelle and your crew," Henry Lassiter said. "So, while we're all sitting here enjoying ourselves, I say we join hands and recite the Lord's Prayer."

Joining hands, they prayed. When finished, they hugged and kissed, expressing their farewells and absentee aspirations for each other. Adam walked with Ellis and Julie, out to the waiting limo. Adam was expressing himself with just a little bravado, causing Ellis and Julie to think he was nervous about a successful resolution to this mission.

Julie took Adam's hand and said, "Your parents Adam, are two of the most level-headed people we know and if your mom is alive or not bed-ridden your dad's morale will be unconquerable. Ellis, me, and the rest of the Newton crew are all behind him 110%. I also think that Gariff sensed John's sincerity, determination and focus on space exploration during our last venture, which is why we all believe there will be a successful outcome to the mission."

"Adam, I couldn't have expressed it better. I agree with Julie" said Ellis. Adam seemed to settle down a bit in the limo while his dad was holding his mom's hand talking quietly with Clinton.

They stayed overnight in the astronaut's waiting area until the call for the departure window came up. Leaving a night-lite on for Janet while she finished in the shower John lay back in the bed and read some of the research information again. He suspected something but wasn't quite sure what. When she finally came out John knew to-night was 'Oscar' night. He gulped, and placed the papers on the table beside him. The clock's LED displayed 8:30 p.m.

"Honey, I have never loved you more than today," she said, shedding her robe and climbing on top of him. "You asked me what you did right, well, babe, everything. You could have disclosed the 'gifts' Gariff gave us and you stopped Adam from prying too much and said nothing. You did everything right. Now I'll show you how a lady does everything right and thanks her man."

The last thing he saw was the clock's LED showing 12:15 a.m. She felt warm, cuddlesome and secure in his arms. They slept.

When the departure window came they had a nutritious liquid breakfast and were whisked away to be suited up like the rest of the party namely Clinton, Rochelle, Ellis, Julie and Adam. "Looks like NASA's going to have another 7-UP launch," John said, chuckling to Jan.

Jan groaned upon hearing another one of John's puns. "Would you stop?" she demanded, but relaxed, knowing that this was his way of making light of a dangerous situation.

Twenty minutes later Clinton said in his microphone, "Well, John, back in the good old blue yonder, pal." They smiled and chuckled.

Later, "Sirs, we should be seeing the CSS shortly," Ellis said, apologizing for the interruption.

"Yeah, it sure feels good, Clint. I'd sure like to be in one of those new fighter jets and flying again pal. You never know what might happen on this mission, buddy. I can't wait to brief the crew, Clint. We have a mighty tough mission ahead of us so we just might see some action."

Chapter 42

"Sir, the CSS is ten minutes in front of us."

"Thank you, Ellis. We're slowing to docking speed."

Clinton received a radio message from the CSS regarding his approach advising that his craft is to use the designated 'homing' frequency for dock locking. Julie inquired if she could assist in anyway, due to her familiarity with CSS procedures. Clinton agreed. Ellis, like Clinton, was experienced in the piloting and guidance of their capsule and among the three of them the docking connection to the Space Station wasn't even felt. Adam, Janet and Kathy, weren't distracted by any of the docking action and had to be advised of the connection. John disturbed the quietude when he said, "Next stop, the Isaac Newton."

The Space Station notified NASA of the successful completion of the journey and docking procedure. Piling out of the capsule into the station, they each met and shook hands with the relief Commander, Michael Williams. While shaking his hand, Ellis had a *déjà vu* feeling, but kept his silence for the moment. John inquired about the waiting time at the Station for a shuttlecraft to the Newton. The Commander told him about 1.5 hours as they were already enroute.

"Good, I'll catch up on some research notes that I brought with me." Janet, John and Clinton disappeared into one of the station's wings for a quiet discussion. Janet said, "Don't talk aloud because I saw Ellis sort of wince when he met Williams."

John replied, "We were just going to discuss some navigational aspects of this mission; especially the distance and time involved."

Clinton added, "We were expecting Red or Spike, the Newton's navigators, to have plotted the anomaly we encountered last time, enroute to Triangulum, so that it could be archived for possible future use."

Ellis interjected with, "Sir, have you been informed the Newton has an additional navigator?"

"No. Who is it, Ellis?" Clinton asked.

"Lieutenant Commander Diedra Bianna; nick-named Goldie, sir?"

"Ellis, please ensure all personnel check with 'stores' and pick up their name tags and Saunders belts for this mission, okay?"

"Yes sir."

"Geezus John, all the nick-names on the Newton can be confusing – Rocky for Rochelle, Spike for Doug Thompson, Red for Alan Kosakowski, Goldie for Diedra Bianna. Should we call you 'The Boss', Doctor Wentworth 'Bones' and Janet, the mission's Genie for genome or Ms. DNA?"

Clint added, "I don't care about my nick-name, just don't say what that old-time actor once said, 'c'mon punk, make my day!' ha, ha."

"Well, at least it does boost low morale due to the long times of doing nothing or being event-free in a universe of vast distances. By the way Clint, remind me to ask Marion how her immunity system research is progressing. We should know before we reach the Triangulum system. Furthermore, WJ directed us to not go any closer to our objective than a thousand light years. We should have that put into our navigational computers."

"John, are we going to that system's bla…?"

John muffled Clint from finishing. "Later, buddy, later," John took his hand away. Clint's face expressed - what's up? - but trusted John's decision. John glanced sideways at Ellis and realized that Ellis had figured out the mission's destination but not the reason. Ellis asked John, "Are you going to call a department heads meeting when we're aboard the Newton?"

"Yes, and I want a full turn out. Also, Clint, you are going to have to select one of your supervisors to attend as well. During this mission, you can't afford to pursue a double portfolio."

"Okay, John. I'm going to ask Jules to head up ship-board security."

"I was hoping you would pick him," said John. "Ellis, make sure the board room is equipped with electronic head gear for every attendee and the room itself is sound proofed."

"But Sir, what about the ship's computerized audio system?"

"Find the receiving module for the room and remove it for later re-installation. Do not simply disconnect it."

John could see the quizzical look on Clint's face so he put his hands on both his and Ellis's shoulders and said, "In the board room for a complete explanation, as to why I have not gone bonkers. And 'guys', please keep Adam in the dark on this until the meeting, okay?"

Janet, Julie and Kathy were returning from the other end of the CSS, as the shuttlecraft to the Newton was docking. John took his wife's hand and brought her closer to whisper in her ear, "Honey, I'm calling a department head's board meeting when we arrive on the Newton. I want you beside me and Adam on the other side of you while Clint and Ellis sit on my other side, okay?"

Janet looked at John in depth and could see both his sincerity and seriousness in his face. "I'll make sure Marion sits across from us, John."

"Damn good idea honey, and Julie beside her. Everyone will be issued electronic head gear."

Janet placed her hand on John's chest and felt his heart pounding. She walked with him to the shuttlecraft tacitly letting him know that she seemed to know what he was suspecting. Departing the CSS an announcement from the pilot indicated the travel time to the Newton should be about 2.5 hours and seatbelts and Saunders

Lifebelts must always be used. We will be travelling at 2,720 mph to reach the Newton approximately 6,800 miles from us at our insertion point. He also pointed out that there's a World News documentary available to them for viewing, entitled Solar System Updates.

John, Janet, Clint and Chris, used the two and a half hours to get some rest. Adam, Julie, Ellis, and Kathy watched the News documentary. Ellis noted that John had placed his 'top secret' file in the case, so that it couldn't be removed for scrutiny. Ellis thought John must have some very damning information in it to account for his recent secretive behaviour. Ellis felt for him.

The two and half hours went by so quickly, and without incident so that when they arrived at the Newton, Julie cracked a joke about John and Clint's snoring; something about using a noisy, internal combustion engine, to run the shuttlecraft, which only Adam really appreciated.

Chapter 43

They exited the shuttlecraft in single file. Adam patted his father on the shoulder to soften Julie's teasing humour of John's snoring. After they all entered the Newton's Gooseneck loading entrance, closed the hatchway and donned their respective in-flight spacesuits. They departed for their regular areas of duty. John, Chris and Clint, headed for the bridge, Kathy for astronomy, while Janet and Julie went to the medical-research wing. Ellis headed for the boardroom to prepare for the meeting and Adam went to cosmic investigations and research. All of them prepped for the expected meeting by updating themselves with respective reports and related equipment readiness.

Since Adam had to cross the diametric grav-deck, he paused to reflect on the memories of the actions which brought him back to life, and the COSMIC SEEDER who did it. He mumbled to himself, "Not this time, please?" As if he could be heard he started to feel 'comfort' within himself and added, "Help my Dad, please?"

When John and Clint reached the bridge, Clint ordered the first officer to remain in the captain's chair while John spoke into the department's phone requesting Jules to the bridge.

"Jules I want you to attend the department heads meeting today with armed guards to be left at the doors for admission. Crew members entering must show I.D. and be wearing their Saunders life belts. I expect them to have some sort of recording device with them which is optional. Understand?"

Acknowledging John's orders, Jules said, "Yes, Sir!" with a salute. John dismissed him and glanced at Clint as he was talking quietly with Commander Donaldson. When Clint looked at John he nodded his head slightly and they both went to speak to Red and Spike who were manning the Helm and Navigation positions. Lt. Commander Diedra Bianna was in her office reviewing helm and navigation reports. When Clint and John had finished talking to Spike and Red they went to the center of the bridge and Clint picked up the P.A. mic. Whispering to John he confirmed 13:00 hrs.

Clint clicked the microphone on to 'all call' and the ship's computer channeled the call through all speakers. "This is the Captain speaking; all department heads are commanded to attend a meeting in the main board room at 13:00 hrs. today. Bring your updated department reports, and your e-pads with you. The meeting could be lengthy so govern yourselves accordingly. Captain Davidson out."

Dr. Marion Wentworth looked at Julie and Janet for any telltale signs of fore knowledge regarding this meeting. Janet shrugged and said, "John received some astronomical research reports from SETIA's #2 man containing some confirmed inconsistencies of a physical reality in them. He was told these reports were global in agreement regardless of methodology of observations."

"And that's the aim of this mission?" prodded Marion.

"Knowing my husband, I think not," Janet replied. "SETIA's #2 wasn't very instructive with John other than something to do with M33, the Triangulum Galaxy."

Julie interrupted to say, "S-s-s-h-h-h; someone's coming!" It was the infirmary's head nurse to tell Marion the trauma area was prepped. Marion expressed her gratitude to her and told her to look after things while she was at the meeting. She also said she should assist Dr. Usher if the need arose.

Looking at the clock on the wall they noted the time was 12:45p.m. Grabbing her updated reports and e-pad off her desk she handed them to Julie and they went to the meeting.

John and Clinton watched everybody entering the board room. Ellis said to John reassuringly, "The room is prepped, sir," he said in passing. When everyone was seated, Clinton told John that all were present. He then stood up and requested the doors be closed and locked.

Standing to the right of John and beside Ellis Clinton started to speak, "The point of this meeting is to brief you on a mission which must be treated with the utmost secrecy therefore, we want you to wear your head gear and plug in your e-pads to the ports in the table so all can share in your information. Marion, you can use the 'med port'." Clinton put on his headgear and then turned the meeting over to John. Seated, John began talking, "This mission is going to be done in steps but first, we are going to see if this ship's friend is available for assistance. Gariff's home galaxy is at the center of this mission and he has a right to know. Communications I want you to see if you can raise Gariff. I really believe he is nearby exploring our solar system. Chris, Clint or I will give you Gariff's narrow band to contact him.

So, those steps are: -

- Everything about this mission is on a need-to-know basis;

- There will be no communication beyond this ship;

- Sabotage will be shadowing us all the way; how, when, what, can't be addressed at this moment; when it occurs, the perpetrators will be imprisoned, tried, and punished;

- Adam, I want you, Kathy and the astronomical department to verify or refute the conclusions in these reports and report to Clint or me on your findings;

- Marion, everyone in this room at present is trustworthy; all others are to be treated suspiciously and therefore, there could be situations of using force when necessary; your trauma center may be needed;

- Jan, you and Julie will do your best to identify and codify everyone on board this ship, including me;

- Jules, you have exclusive security rights on this ship and will report to Clinton; maybe your best man, 'Bullseye', will get to defend his reputation after all;

- Goldie, make sure your manpower, and computers record, document and archive every move this ship makes; next, see if you can dig up the history specs on that time anomaly encountered enroute to rendezvous with Gariff."

Sighing, John continued, "Now then, the crux of this meeting. Adam, the reason I wanted you to confirm or refute the so-called conclusive information in this file is because it destroys with consistent supporting evidence the very principle of the most basic law of nature – *energy can neither be destroyed nor created,* by man or otherwise, - *only rearranged*! The research scientists on Earth sweated buckets before releasing this info to the Council of World Affairs. Their credibility was at stake. At present, it has not been released to the public; otherwise the public wouldn't believe the scientific community if something arose which would destroy life on the planet.

The Search for Extra-Terrestrial Intelligence (SETI) agency is covertly operating on Earth again for obvious public-info release reasons. We spoke with their #2 administrative head who requested Jan and I to resolve this dilemma. Therefore, I am letting you all know that both Ellis and Julie will act as our aides and are to be given the utmost co-operation.

So now, what has got us in such turmoil about this mission? Apparently, the black hole in the Triangulum Galaxy is 'eating' some of the closest orbiting stars. That alone is not amazing; what is amazing is the fact that the black hole is not, I repeat, not gaining in mass! Apparently, all the equipment that we have on Earth to observe astronomical activity in this universe is reporting the same thing." Looking at Kathy, John added, "Yes, including the Solar Telescopes."

Adam choked on this recent revelation and finally realized why his father has been acting so secretive lately. He blurted, "Dad, you know that info is absolutely impossible, never mind the basic law of nature being broken. The Chandra X-ray, infra-red filters and...." Jan covered her son's hand and whispered, "He knows, honey. Listen to him."

Addressing Ellis, John asked, "If money was no object, about how long would it take some corporation, company, whatever, to replace the solar telescopes' computer chips and the radio telescopes' chips, and X-Ray scopes and any other equipment, process, procedure, or problematic device or personnel in order to produce the result that M33's black hole is destroying star matter but not gaining in mass? How long, Ellis?"

Looking at Ellis and their own e-pads to watch him figure out the answer the boardroom's personnel waited expectantly.

Ellis gave John the answer. "A little over two years, John."

"Adam, how old were you upon our return from the last mission?"

Adam said, "18 Dad."

"And how old are you now, Adam?"

"I'll be 21 in three month's time, dad. Why?"

"I want all of you to enter your worst fear about encountering intelligent alien life-forms and we'll post the results on the main screen. Keep your answers anonymous."

The screen showed what John already knew about the human psyche. Humans were basically afraid of things or beings that did not resemble them in appearance. Acid dripping lizards, mechanical men with artificial intelligence, mobile plant life, intelligent insect life, *etc.* There were, however, some answers which agreed with John's entry – human beings that resembled them in every way.

John asked, "Why do unlike appearances frighten you rather than those beings that look like us?"

Marion answered, "John, I believe we as humans are frightened by that which we don't understand, or can't relate to based on experiences in our lives."

"Bingo! I too had a misconception about Gariff's appearance before I met him, but with what he did with Clinton in constructing this ship I relaxed and learnt very early to trust him. If he can convince my critical engineering friend here, that was good enough for me. Gariff's appearance didn't affect opinion. Of course, if he had been an acid-dripping lizard we would have asked him to do something about his drooling. Tactfully of course."

That brought a bit of a chuckle around the table. "But I digress. The point I am trying to make is this can we trust the info in this file folder or not? If we can't, then, why not? And if why not, why are we out here in space to explore or witness an event that was occurring approximately 2.723×10^6 years ago. If so we might have to reverse course and get back to Earth and find out what the hell is going on? That is why I need answers from Chris in Communications and Adam, regarding celestial activity focusing on the black hole in M33. Any questions?"

Jules had a question. "Sir, do you believe the information and that astronomical-studying equipment has been sabotaged by some group?"

"Jules, you weren't with us while we were enroute to Mars to see the SETIA chairman but those that were, can attest to the fact that the saboteurs will stop at nothing to accomplish their goal. That means Jules, they would rather destroy their world, the planet Earth, than co-exist with humans that don't subscribe to their way of life or believe in their religious culture."

"Sir, I understand you now and support your determination," said Jules.

"Good, now everybody get to your posts. Clint I'll join you on the bridge soon."

"Later John," said Clint.

John held Jan back until the room was empty. "Honey, until everyone has been identified and tagged don't let your guard down."

Kissing him on the cheek she said, "I won't. I'll be up shortly to I.D. and tag everyone on the bridge," she asked John.

"Oh, be still my foolish heart," blurted John, which resulted in a mutual chuckle.

Chapter 44

When John arrived on the bridge he went straight over to Commander Donaldson on communications to hand him the personal frequency Gariff had given him if the need arose for his immediate help. It was then that John noticed Chris' wedding band and couldn't help himself from finding out who was his bride. Chris looked at the frequency that John had given him, programmed his computer to transmit it and said to John, "You know how it is, boss. You eat together in the ship's cafeteria, strike up conversation and one thing leads to another." Looking at John, Chris could see he was looking for more. "Okay, my wife is Rochelle."

"Congrats, buddy; we've all noticed the chemistry between you two. I'm happy for you both," John said, gleefully patting Chris on his back.

"John, we also have a baby boy who's coming up for his 2nd birthday along with a few others."

Looking at Clint, John said, "We better make this mission successful and we'll all have something to celebrate, hey Clint?"

"You bet, John."

"Sir, I have a reply coming in from the TGCTriang" said Chris at communications.

John grabbed a helmet with earphones. "Is this you, Gariff?'

"Yes, my friend. What can we do for you?"

"Gariff, are you close enough to board our ship for a Top-Secret talk with me?"

"John, curiosity got the best of me after your departure from our last meeting so we have been studying your solar system. Presently, we are located 5 astronomical units (AU) beyond your Kuiper Belt studying Eris, Pluto and the Belt itself. My wife, Mariff, is heading up this research. Why?"

"We need you and Mariff to have a discussion on a highly puzzling problem we have been directed by COWA to resolve. So, we're just coming up on Jupiter's orbit but I don't want to meet on the Solar Plane. Can you meet us 4AU above the plane say somewhere above Saturn's orbit?"

"No problem John. It should take me about 16 of your days or 384 hours."

"See you then, Gariff. Commander Donaldson is sending you the rendezvous co-ordinates now." John turned to Clint and requested he contact Adam, Goldie, Marion, Jules, to have them meet me, Chris and yourself in the board room and set it up for Gariff, Mariff and another guest should they bring someone. We've got 384 hours to prepare so if any of them have any questions for this meeting tell them we need answers so their work better be up-to-date. I'm going to see Jules and Adam right now. Afterwards I'm going to the medical wing and speak to Jan, Julie and Marion. If anything crops up, Clint …"

"Don't worry, boss. You'll be the 2nd to know."

"Good, later, buddy." John left and took the tube to Jules in the gooseneck.

Chapter 45

Entering the gooseneck, John called out for Jules. One of his men was working on one of the Laser-pulse cannons from Astro Weaponry. They only employed military vets or reserves or retired police personnel. All employees had to be confirmed as Canadian citizens. They all lived in a gated community that was controlled by active Military Police. John expected the weaponry on the Newton to be 100% reliable constantly. John thought, another example of COWA's quality control, hh-mmm. "Where is everybody?" John asked aloud.

Popping his head up from a computer guidance console the armory-mechanical technician answered, "Sir, he's in his office talking to 'Bullseye'," indicating with his index finger up above them.

"Thanks, Niles," John said and took off up the stairs, two at-a-time. Knocking on Jules' office door and entering he said, "Jules, glad I caught you. In 384 hours, we are having a meeting in the boardroom again only this time I want you prepared to discuss weaponry solutions if and should, the need arise when we return to Earth."

"Sir?"

"It was discussed in the previous meeting that COWA and us have our suspicions about the results that the astronomical research scientists have collated and sent to COWA concerning the black hole in the Triangulum system. We expect to rendezvous with Gariff again to discuss this matter."

'Bullseye' spoke up asking, "Sir, are you insinuating that our armament may be used to take out targets on Earth?"

"It's a possibility, Mr. Armstrong. But Tommy, please understand it is only one possibility but if it does come to pass we'll need to be prepared for pinpoint accuracy from space when called upon." John looked at Jules and saw that he understood his tacit message and nodded. "Good, I'm off to astronomy. See you later then."

Jules said to "Bullseye" Armstrong, "We better get some practice in Tommy so you can hit a stone with pinpoint accuracy at say, 500 miles. Don't swallow so hard my lad. That's only orbital altitude for the Newton going around Earth at 15,000 km/h. And we now have 378 hours in which to perfect it."

Jules and Tommy rose out of their chairs and walked to the metal catwalk outside Jules' office. Leaning over the railing Jules put two fingers to his mouth and blew a long, loud whistle which probably could be heard on Ganymede, Jupiter's largest moon, if sound could travel in space. His cannon crew came running.

Chapter 46

Over in Astronomical Research John could see that his son Adam was working well with the scientists manning the facilities. The telemetry equipment was highly futuristic and made what Earth used seem like giant binoculars unless the Solar scopes' views were in use. Like those of the Newton they didn't have the atmosphere to look through first. Commander Kathy Richardson was the supervisor and John went to talk to her. He looked at his watch and saw that 374 hours remained before meeting Gariff again.

"Kathy, how's it going?"

"Sir! You startled me. We don't get VIP visitors here usually."

"Sorry, Commander, but I am here to tell you to prepare for a distinguished visitor from the Triangulum galaxy's planet, Ffraiteron. The TGCTriang is due here in, looking at his watch again, 373hrs. and 42minutes. I was hoping the observations reported by Earth's astronomical scientists could be supported or refuted by that time. Did my son Adam, mention to you my suspicions on this matter?"

"Well sir."

"Call me John."

"John, Earth has reported a collated observation to COWA yielding an agreeable conclusion which no one can actually believe in. Apparently your suspicion that M33's black hole not gaining in mass yet is 'gobbling up' some of that galaxy's stars has really turned out to be a celestial enigma. So, your son and some of his colleagues have really bitten into this puzzle. Are we going to have a preparatory meeting before your guests arrive?"

"Yes, that is the reason why I am here. I wanted your department to attend the meeting so we can approach our guests with an intelligent discussion and meet any necessary requests for assistance. I don't care about high percentages of confidence in your data; I would rather you give us your 'gut' feelings based on the results your team gives to you. Okay?"

"So, when is the boardroom meeting going to take place, John?"

"I'll have Captain Davidson announce it."

"If you have any questions Kathy, please ask myself, Ellis or the Captain, okay? Right now, I'm going to scoot over to the medical department and advise them. Oh, by the way, don't let anyone communicate electronically until my wife Janet has been in to tag everybody. I'll see you later."

John left the astronomy studies department and thought the women on this ship under normal circumstances, would be a major distraction to any red-blooded male; but these aren't normal. Tagging the ship's personnel like dogs must be done, damn!

Dreaming about women he thought, where's that set of legs I married. He punched a wall while walking to the medical department and noted the injury to his knuckles. He spat out a curse, "Shit!" Only later Clint, Kathy and Jan would have that foursome relationship without this wild goose interference. "Damn it, COWA!"

Chapter 47

John walked into the medical department's lab and was greeted by a young nurse.

"May I help you, sir?" she asked, wearing a very friendly smile.

John looked at her chest and read her name plate – 'Lily Wu'. "Nurse Wu, could you see if Dr. Wentworth is available or my wife, Janet Marshall?"

Hearing the Marshall name, she realized to whom she was talking and quickly said, "Right away Mr. Marshall, sir."

John had just missed them as they were busy tagging the ship's personnel. Julie responded to his call request by coming out from one of the recovery areas. "John, how are you?" looking at the injury to his hand. She took his other hand and led him into one of the triage rooms where she could provide some first-aid to him.

"Julie, if Marion or Janet returns here, could you please tell them I was here and that our friends from Ffraiteron will soon be visiting us in 371 hours and I would like you all to attend. Bring any assistive devices you need. We'll announce a meeting to the ship's personnel before then, okay?"

"Yes sir, I'll tell them."

"By the way Julie, what else do you do on the ship besides assist in meds?"

"I thought you knew, John. I'm education director for all the ship's children up to the completion of the secondary school's curriculum. I supervise all teaching assignments. It's quite a portfolio but I do enjoy it."

"Well, now I am impressed."

"Thank you, John."

Chapter 48

Police officers and military everywhere should take target practice to hone their shooting skills but not with the work that Tommy 'Bullseye' Armstrong had to put into his practice. He had to shoot and destroy a stone no bigger than a baseball from 500 miles away, and not miss!

Not missing yet hitting the target under any condition including blinding sunlight while moving was within Niles Anderson's purview. He was responsible for the laser cannon's computer controls, all six cannons. If "Bullseye" was good he had Niles to thank for it; *ergo* "Bullseye" ensured Niles received a full printout on his target practice. 100% was the only result that John Marshall was interested in. Furthermore, a consistency of this percentage was demanded if push came to shove upon their return to Earth. "Earth, COWA and every human being may have to depend on it," said Niles and Jules.

'Bullseye' was getting results of 96% and it was his Commander, Jules Armstrong's job to determine why and upgrade it. "Tommy, I know we have the best laser man in that seat and I staked my reputation on it with John. When we get back to Earth I just know some event is going to demand ace marksmanship. Whatever you need, ask."

His first step to this end was to provide his gunners with an impetus which would yield immediate rewards. He contacted the sport department's physical supervisor and requested some tennis balls. Julie's responsibilities included the management of all phys-ed equipment and sent Jules a case of tennis balls as part of Jules' start up target practice.

Next, Jules brought Niles into his office showed him a tennis ball and asked if he thought he could hit it at 1000 feet. Niles said, "No way, Sir!" Jules looked at him and asked, "If you altered the ball somehow, internally or externally, could you do it then?" Niles picked up the ball again and turned every which way in his hands and then squeezed it. Looking up at Jules again, Niles smiled slightly and said, "Sir, if you want 'Bullseye', or anyone to hit this ball at the 500-mile mark while we are moving and with sunlight shining through an atmosphere in our vista, then I would have to put a tracking device inside it. But to hit a target on Earth is a huge problem unless…unless the target was painted somehow. I remember some old videos in which targets were painted so they could be detected and destroyed. But that was on the Earth's surface."

"Niles, we are meeting Gariff soon and John has given us a no-limit requisition for equipment or procedures except 'get the job done, now! Do you think you and engineering can come up with a solution so we can use it, if required?"

"Yes, sir," Commander Armstrong.

"Good, we now have 366 hours to demonstrate to the ship's administration our defensive capability including to our guests from Ffraiteron. So, let's get to work."

Chapter 49

Returning to the bridge John spied a beautiful sight up ahead and hastened his step to put his arm around her. His wife Janet had her back to him but felt a familiar set of arms embracing her. Cocking her head to one side she turned her head as John moved in for a long-awaited kiss. Breaking he said, "Geezus I've missed you, honey."

Seeing Dr. Wentworth over John's shoulder Janet moved in tighter to John very suggestively and asked, "Why, John! Missed me? Me or this?"

John had to hold her tighter and suddenly felt a needle enter his neck. He knew they were tagging him as ordered but asked, "Am I last or do you have more to do?"

"Two more honey; Marion and I."

"Good, do you want to meet me in our residence quarters, say, in an hour?" John looked at his watch and said, "We have 363 hours before Gariff arrives but we all need to meet in the main auditorium before then. Right now, I have to talk with Clint and the rest of the bridge personnel."

"I'll see you in our residence in about an hour then," said Jan. "I can see you need some bed rest, darling. Did Marion hurt you?"

"No; I was totally distracted," John said, with a telltale smile on his face.

"Maybe you better examine the full package then when you come to our quarters," Janet teased, and walked away knowing John was watching her.

He hurried to the bridge to brief Clint. After entering the bridge Clint asked him, "So, how did your departmental visits go, buddy? Kathy called from astronomy to update me."

Smiling at his best friend, John said, "Everyone is aware of our expectations concerning Gariff's arrival so all we must do is plan what we're going to say when he does arrive, and hold a meeting with the ship's personnel in the auditorium before then.

Right now, where are we with regards to the rendezvous point (R)?"

Clint said to navigation to put it on the screen, a large 3-D, 120-inch screen for all bridge personnel to see where the Newton was in relation to their surroundings. It included the course required for the Newton to take to reach the R-point and whether they were successful in travelling to it on the North side of the Solar System's equatorial plane. Pluto, like everything else in the solar system was 'pockmarked' with meteors colliding with it. The orbital arcs showing eccentricities were displayed as yellow lines.

"Clint, if we could only predict which way the pieces would go our gunnery personnel could have a field day with the asteroids in the Kuiper belt."

"John, I left Jules with a suggestion to keep up with his practice sessions but if he sees the opportunity to safely target the smallest asteroids to go ahead and do so, but advise the bridge first. Maybe we can help with some unexpected maneuvering on our part," said Clint with a raised eyebrow.

"Good thinking buddy; we just may need the 'Ride 'em cowboy' shooting-technique later! Chris, has Gariff made any further contact yet?"

He didn't answer John. Instead he just looked up and pointed at the big screen. Gariff's ship had closed the gap between them to 125 hrs. Gariff appeared on screen and used sign language to communicate.

"Ellis, are you getting this?" Ellis kept quiet as well. Clint said quietly to John, "I think Ellis is focusing on Gariff's communication John. We should wait."

Two minutes later Ellis turned to both Clinton and John, "Sirs, I think Gariff is thinking ahead of us and wants no more communication until he arrives in 5.2 days."

John and Clint put their heads together agreeing in not holding a personnel meeting on the grav-deck until Gariff arrived. Everyone would receive the same information at the same time. "Good idea, John. And just to bring you up to date all personnel have been 'tagged' and they are wearing their color-coded I.D. badges."

"Excellent," John said, grabbing the nape of his neck remembering Marion's sneak attack while Jan distracted him. "Clint, I'm going to my residence for a little R. & R. I'll be back in 36 hrs. We can plan a briefing meeting for Gariff at that time. Okay, my friend?"

"I'll see you then, guy. Chris, you have the chair, buddy."

"Yes sir, Clinton. We'll call you if anything crops up."

"Good, I too will be in my quarters."

Chapter 50

Hearing someone at their residence doorway, Janet called out, "John? Is that you?"

Damn, John thought. All that beauty and elephant ears too. "It's just me, dear," he replied. Entering the bedroom, he saw a stocking-encased leg ending with a stiletto-heeled shoe sticking out from behind a drape. John thought, "Oh, you have done well my friend."

Thirty minutes later John was fast asleep. Janet watched his chest rise and fall with each breath and knew the stress he was going to be under once the results of the mission's findings came to him. Calming him she wrapped him in her body, no snoring, just sound sleep; something he really needed. She pressed the 'Do Not Disturb' button beside their bed.

All the time Clint and John had been friends Clint always was the bachelor type. These missions and the time spent in space, however, had finally taken a meaningful toll on his psyche. He felt the need for companionship; a relationship of steady, gratifying intimacy. Commander Kathy Richardson volunteered to join the Newton while at one time 'parked' in orbit about the Earth. Only after her boarding, did the recognition of their secondary school history hit them. She had taken the same courses like Clint and they became science lab buddies. Graduation from high school separated them in their early adult lives. Clint buried in the finest engineering schools like U. of T. in Toronto, Can. and Cornel in the N.Y.C. He joined the U.S. Marines putting his knowledge to work in design and construction of military ships.

Kathy enjoyed astronomy as a hobby and followed this interest through to become an Astro-physics and cosmos-exploring professor at some of the elite space academies with COWA. When the advertisement was posted for this type of position in space she was interviewed and surpassed the 75 other applicants. She never knew what awaited her. Clint never knew what awaited him now in his quarters.

Both women, Janet with John and Kathy with Clinton, knew their husbands needed stress relief because their future activity unbeknownst to anyone could be like sitting on death row awaiting their doom. Kathy did her best to relax him and he felt well-relaxed when awakening 9 hours later. This time she demanded Clint tell John about their marriage.

When she looked at John's eyes when he visited in the Astronomy department she could only see a set of 'male' eyes looking back at her. Still, she reveled in it and she wanted to tell him then but he might feel like he had just betrayed Janet. She wanted to become friends like a foursome, a trusting foursome the way it should be and not be suspicious of each other.

Out here in space there would be no time for suspicions of each other when they already had a problem as the focus of this mission. The first thing Clinton did upon waking was contact Jules' defence department to check on their targeting progress. Upon finding out there were at least 8 of his 'gunners' who were obtaining 100% target scores at least 98.9% of the time he had to ask about "Bullseye's scores.

"Sir, Tommy is one for one 100% of the time but," said Jules, "he doesn't have enough times to say with 100% probability he will hit the target."

Oh shit, thought Clinton and then sarcastically he said, "Has he tried taking on the Kuiper Belt's smallest asteroids, Jules?"

"No, sir, but we will if you want us to do it."

"Take out no more than 100 then make your calculation but do it on the solar plane facing the Sun as background."

Clint started to get out of bed but his wife had a better idea. Pushing him back on the bed he groaned happily about the perks of marriage. She drained him of all his energy and then bid him a good day on the bridge. This time he was going to tell John about their marriage.

John was preparing to head for the bridge but his marital spiders' web trapped him and its main occupant let him go only after he groaned in complete submission as his energy was sucked from him causing a healthy, throbbing, heartbeat.

Both Clinton and John arrived at the entrance to the bridge simultaneously each offered to hold the door for the other. Chuckling, Clint said, "John, I haven't told you everything."

"Huh?" queried John. "What haven't you told me?"

"John, I haven't told you because I was waiting for the right moment. Last mission you left instructions that all personnel had full rights to form relationships with whomever, if there was full consent by each person involved. Right?"

"Right, and so?"

"John, the last replacements brought Kathy Richardson to the Newton and we fell in love all over again and got married."

"What, married? You, son of a bitch and you never invited us to the wedding?"

"Kathy and I wanted a formal wedding back on Earth and have the reception at your place if that's all right with you two?"

"You're on buddy!" John blurted. "I gotta tell Janet about this news." John patted his friend on the back and embraced him warmly. "Clint, the eternal bachelor caught in the marriage web, heh, heh. All the best, pal."

"John, I suspect you might be a little late. Jan's been out with Marion to tag all personnel and I think they may have had a little 'tête-à-tête' about this and that and whatever."

"Buddy, I felt there was something strange about Kathy when I briefed her in the astronomy department. It was like her eyes were trying to tell me something like hug me, we're friends now."

Clint said, "That's exactly how she put it to me, heh, heh."

"Attention all personnel, we are about to receive some special guests from Ffraiteron. Please man your stations. Acting Captain Donaldson out."

"Let's get in there, John."

"Right behind you."

Chapter 51

Entering the bridge Chris Donaldson stood and said, "I stand relieved Captain Davidson."

Returning his salute Clint assumed the chair and asked Chris to report. "Sir, all is quiet and I requested the crew be ready to greet Gariff and his party."

"John and I will take care of it. You have some R. & R. coming to you and Rochelle. We'll see you in 8 hours on the diametric grav-deck. Okay with you?"

Smiling Chris said, "Yes, Sir. 8 hours, sir." He left the bridge in a big hurry.

Looking at John, a mutual smile was shared. "Ellis, how much time before Gariff is actually here to transfer to our ship?"

"He should be here in 37 minutes, John."

John pressed his intercom button and contacted the astronomy department. "Kathy, how are we doing with that puzzle we gave you, love?"

Love? She thought to herself, he knows, good. "John, either our equipment is from the stone age or we're out here on a wild goose chase. Adam, any further developments?" Kathy asked.

"No, Commander. Ursula and I have tried everything at least twice. We have no evidence to support Earth's findings." Hearing this, Clint high-fived John, saying "We'll see what our alien buddy says when we tell him the story."

They smiled at each other again and the rest of the bridge crew seemed a bit more relaxed. Jules greeted the Newton's guests and was introduced to Mariff Tterzin, Gariff's wife. "Gariff would you like to come to the bridge with me?"

Gariff said, "Be happy to do so, Commander." The rest of Jules' staff welcomed Gariff's entourage. Tommy's focus was so completely distracted by the four women that came on board that he got down from his turret seat to greet them.

"One moment please, Jules. I want you to meet my daughter, Hertiff and my ship's captain, Merziff Gregzitt."

"Thank you all for coming to the Newton and welcome," said Jules. Please, follow me to the bridge. So, how are you all doing with your space exploration?"

"We are so pleased to discover similar life forms in your galaxy," replied Captain Gregzitt.

"Yes," added Hertiff. "I will definitely be doing a study for my work back on Ffraiteron."

Gariff added, "Jules, Hertiff like John Marshall, is well-acquainted in the same field of interest with the added benefit of being a cosmic enviro-psychologist."

"Well, here we are at the bridge," Jules said, relieved that he wasn't involved in any more matters of diplomatic discussion. The two guards at the doorway opened the entrance and closed it after they had all entered. Jules returned to the ship's gooseneck to check on his gunners and their progress.

Both John and Clinton, upon hearing the bridge entrance open and close, turned to greet their special guests.

"Gariff, glad to see you again my friend," said John extending his hand in greeting. Clinton, standing beside John did the same greeting action.

Gariff introduced his accompanying party members, "John, Clinton, I'd like you to meet my wife Mariff, our daughter Hertiff and my ship's Captain, Merziff Gregzitt."

"Ah, John Marshall," said Merziff. "I finally get to shake the hand of my admiral's friend and colleague. And, Colonel Davidson, so, you are the engineer who reliably followed instructions in this ship's construction. We would have understood any mistrusting that you might have had in doing so. Congratulations! You must take me on a tour."

"Sir, I shall do that at the first opportunity we have but I think we have some important business to get out of the way beforehand."

"Of course, Colonel."

"Gariff, John and I wish to hold a meeting of both ship's personnel, based on the information our astronomy department comes up with concerning the black hole in your galaxy. Apparently, our astronomical scientists on Earth have requested an objective study of the black hole to confirm or refute the results."

"And what did those results reveal that is so perplexing?" Gariff asked.

"The black hole is eating star matter and not gaining mass," said John.

"Gentlemen, if I may interrupt? That alone is preposterous. Eating star matter I understand but our planet's scientists proved that energy can neither be created nor destroyed without some effect on stellar matter, which has mass," said Hertiff.

"Hertiff, like you John, has made her life's work and focus on Astro-physics and its significance. She also studies in cosmic-psychology for interplanetary colonization. But, she has yet to age to the point of cynicism like us.

John, Clint and you too, Chris I think my captain will back me up in this regard. If your researchers and ours too, all come up refuting Earth's conclusions about the gain in star matter but not in mass then we had better hold that meeting as suggested."

"100% Admiral. I'll contact our ship and get it started," said Captain Gregzitt.

"Can I get all of you to come with me to my office and Ellis, could you escort Hertiff to our astronomy department?" asked John. "Chris, you have the chair, unless you can get Sam Sherwood here; we'll brief you shortly," said John.

Entering John's office, he asked if anyone desired a little refreshment. It was turned down politely by all present. John closed the door and locked it. Sitting in his chair, John looked at everyone and asked, "Gut feelings?"

Captain Gregzitt started with, "Admiral, it's how you said on the ship, that the Newton has been sent on a wild bird chase."

Gariff corrected him, "A wild goose chase," he said, smiling at his young captain. Turning his attention back to Clint and John, "Tell me what you want us to do to help you."

"To be honest Gariff, I don't know. What I will do however, is tell you some speculative points that we have come up with and show them on my viewing screen. Recorders 'on'. Clint, Chris and I, and when Kathy, Marion and Janet arrive we might have some more points. Okay? Here goes: -

- Have your scientists seen any unusual activity with your galaxy's black hole?

- Next, would your daughter like to speak to this matter when she attends?

- Do you have a defence system which can pick off a target as large as a baseball at, say 600 miles while orbiting at a speed of 8,178.561 km/h or 5,081.92 mph for example?

- Should we need back-up when we return to Earth, would you be able to support us?

"Recorders 'off'."

Chris, Kathy, Marion, Janet, Julie, Adam and Hertiff, were at the office door knocking. Clinton opened the door, admitted them, closed and locked it afterwards. When they were all seated, John said, "Whatever we discuss in this meeting will be condensed into information which most likely will be imparted to our guest crew members, as well as those of the Newton. In that meeting the head table will consist of Gariff, Hertiff, Mariff, Janet, Marion, Kathy, Clint and myself. So, don't hold back comments or questions because I'm sure some personnel will ask some tough ones in the general meeting – looking at his watch – say in one hour. Clint, could you check with Jules and find out about his gunners' accuracy consistencies for me, please?"

"Sure, John. I'll give you his printouts before the meeting and suggest he talk to you personally."

"Thanks, Clint."

"John, correct me if I'm wrong, but are we assuming if some unpleasant results emerge from all this investigation you are going to return to Earth double quick because you suspect something like sabotage has sent you out here?"

"You are bang on target Gariff!"

"Then we are with you shoulder-to-shoulder," my friend.

"Thank you, Gariff. Well, Kathy, have you been able to refute or support the black hole enigma?"

"John, the enigma has been resolved negatively. Out here in space beyond the orbiting bodies of our solar system and having 100% clarity of vision, we have discovered that there is no evidence supporting Earth's conclusion that the black hole in the Triangulum system is consuming stellar matter without gaining mass."

"Adam, do you agree?"

"Yes, Sir."

Turning to Gariff, John asked, "Did your astronomy department run a double check for us?"

Turning to her husband, Mariff said, "Honey, you know Hertiff and I always watch our home galaxy whenever we explore deep space. There is no supporting evidence from our department's astronomy scientists. We must support John's next plans to return with our results to his Council of World Affairs."

"John, my wife has given voice to my thoughts exactly. So, what are we going to say to our ships' personnel?"

"Well my friends, the time has come for us to take action as the submission of these results to COWA will dictate. I think it goes without saying: -

- The research done on Earth was concluded under false assumptions

- The assumptions were based on collated false information

- The false information was well coordinated

- The hardware and/or the computer software required to perpetrate this scam had to be done on a very timely basis

- The financial costs were exorbitant

- This had to be done by the saboteurs - the GGE

- They could be holding the Earth hostage even as we speak

- We may have to exert a well-planned enforcement to resolve this situation to bring the perpetrators to justice.

That is what we must inform the personnel of both ships to accomplish that goal. If you are all with me, then let's prepare ourselves for some difficult questions they might have by asking them here and now. Anyone?"

"John, what if any of the crew members find out someone in their family tree is involved?"

"Clint, you asked the very question I would have asked."

"John, may I offer an intergalactic solution?"

"Go right ahead, Captain Gregzitt. By the way, my friends, there is no formality to be observed in here."

"I suggest that once you achieve an orbit around Earth, we should form some planetary investigative teams with weaponry back up 1) on our persons, and 2) from the ships. As I see it right now, we have absolutely no idea who we are fighting and who might be our allies. Are you with me so far?"

John, Janet, Clinton and Marion looked at Gariff and his administration and almost shamefully Janet said, "Gariff, when we returned to Earth after our last mission, we never informed anyone of you, your crew, your trustworthiness, and your capabilities. The reception for that information was just not there. Sam Davis, the head of COWA's SETI agency was on Mars and he would have been the only person we would completely debrief. The greed existing in us humans could result in absolute chaos and, if our suspicions of sabotage prove to be true, there is no telling how deep our investigations have to go to uproot the perpetrators."

"I see what you are up against, John. Those extra genes we sent back with you and the new Gravity drive, pulsating-engineering for your ship would be worth having a war to obtain. Furthermore, this whole process is complicated by the fact that our race and your race look alike. Your adage, 'it is hard to tell the wolves from the sheep, if they all look like sheep' is very apropos."

"Dad?"

"Yes, Hertiff."

"What if the Newton's medical department and ours work together and come up with some method of infallible identification procedure for our investigative teams, moreover an infallible interrogation procedure as the need arises?" She held Adam's hand for support as she was suggesting to her father an idea which could sound improbable.

"That is a terrific idea," Marion said to Hertiff. "John, I can contact the engineers and medical staff of both ships and together, we should have results before we arrive near Earth's orbit."

"John, I can assure you right now there should be no problem in that regard," said Mariff.

"Good, that problem is settled then. Next to discuss - weaponry. Clint, can you talk with Jules on this matter?"

"Done. John, I just have to give you the printout results."

"John, my defence department will also assist in this matter," said Captain Gregzitt.

"Good, does anyone have any ideas about Clinton's theory of family member(s) involvement? No? All right then, if my suspicions are true this mission will demand absolute objectiveness on everybody's part. Steel hearts and impassionate treatment of any perpetrator brought in for questioning. Your kinship is not threatened in this effort. Our home planet is and I for one do not intend to give new meaning to the term 'homeless.' If any crew member does not agree, then they stay on the Newton for however long this investigation takes. Okay?"

Indicating to his crew at the table, John said, "None of us have any clue as to how deep this investigation is going to take us, or how deep a person may be involved. However, there will be some people who are being coerced in their involvement who could be asking for our help. We must be prepared for cases such as that. Furthermore, there could be those involved who may seem untouchable such as politicians, or governing bodies. This is all going to be talked about at the general meeting for all our crew members in three-quarters of an hour on the grav-deck. So, let's get our stuff together and get up there. Gariff, are you going back to your ship first or coming with me?"

"John, I'm beside you all the way. My Captain can go back to the ship and send my people over here."

"Good." Mariff and Hertiff accompanied John's entourage. Janet noticed Hertiff and Adam holding hands and smiled to herself. "Gariff, both Janet and I looked a bit puzzled when WJ Harding was briefing us on this mission as if he was doing it because he had to leaving no room for a discussion which might have led to a mission-abort conclusion."

"That's right, Gariff. He was acting rather peculiar; friendly as usual, but odd. I couldn't put a finger on the reason."

"Then, my friends, we are going to run up against some mighty tough situations with this investigation. Situations which might tear us all apart; so, we better compel our crews to stand together – you know, united we stand; divided we fall – as you have said in the past. So, whatever is discussed during the general meeting for our crews, we will all agree on, in order that a focused approach by all of us, will better handle this investigation."

"Absolutely, Gariff," said John.

They entered the main auditorium on the diametric-grav deck and saw that Clinton had done an excellent job in assembling both crews. The head table consisted of Gariff, Mariff, John, Janet, both ships' captains and their defence commanders. Department heads of each ship sat in the front row in view of the head table. John stood to speak.

After ascertaining that all present could hear him, John began, "We welcome our friends from Ffraiteron and to all gathered here today, Admiral Gariff Tterzin and myself, with the input information from our respective science departments have come to the grim conclusion that the Sir Isaac Newton galactic cruiser was sent out on false information. We strongly suspect that all of Earth's equipment which was used to collect this false information and provide COWA with the basis for this mission was sabotaged." John paused to allow the audience to calm down. "Furthermore, Gariff and his advisory staff have sided with our advisory staff that as of now none of us can say with 100% certainty just exactly how deeply this sabotage has gone. Gariff, would you like to say something?"

"Yes, John, I would. To all my fellow Ffraiterites, we met these people from Earth under some extraordinary circumstances. It is not too long ago that we believed the Earth people would look like fish because of the watery world where they lived." This brought a snicker from some of the Newton's crew members which was quickly hushed. Continuing, Gariff said, "Both of our races have since determined that with some exceptions to our genetic structure both Ffraiterites and Earthlings are the same. Janet, Marion, my wife Mariff, Julie and Ellis, and all our respective medical personnel have good reason to be friends; yes, even intimately. For this reason of friendship, I have proposed to John, his Captain, Clinton Davidson and our Captain Gregzitt that we accompany the Newton back to Earth. While enroute we should like to prepare a strategy for resolving the enigma behind this mission and determine just how involved some people of Earth might be. John, I am going to turn this part over to you."

"Thank you, Gariff. Now then, has anyone been in contact with Earth to date? How, is unimportant; anyone? Then from this point on, there will be absolutely no contact with Earth or our solar systems. Until we have determined the who, what, when, why and how this sabotage was carried out we will maintain absolute radio silence and converse in Morse code between our two ships. Chris and Diedra, the supervision of that order is your responsibility."

They nodded in acquiescence.

"Captain Gregzitt, you will assign someone to that task as well."

"Now then, it is presumed that no one from Ffraiteron has any blood relatives living on Earth" (scanning the room for correction and seeing none, John continued) "therefore, when we get back to Earth and start our investigation in depth each crew member from the Newton will be accompanied by a crew member from the TGCTriang. You shall both have Laser side arms with one additional condition. Your Ffraiterite partner has orders to shoot to kill you, if the need arises. A report will be expected with as much conclusive evidence supporting this action at the earliest time possible. That report will be adjudicated by Gariff and myself. Severe disciplinary action will result if the evidence is weak or inconclusive.

Next, you will all be issued with a pocket-sized communication device in order that you stay in touch with our ships. The ships shall be in orbit around Earth and our defence systems have orders to back you up as the need arises. Gariff, I guess this is where our crews will learn the true meaning of an allied approach.

"Ladies and gentlemen, our defence commanders have developed a program which provides a consistent accuracy of 100% destroyed targets at the velocities of both ships and at the altitudes of each orbit. Overly simplified, this means each of our laser gun crews can destroy any object, the size of a tennis ball, from our orbital altitudes and respective velocities.

For clarification on this matter your sidearm weapons will contain a device to pinpoint a target for the defence crews. If that means you must surrender your weapons to your abductors, then do so. But help us by handing them the weapon and don't throw it on the ground or away. Avoid capture by surrendering. Any questions?"

"Yes? The person in the back row; you have a question. Stand up and identify yourself, please."

"Arthur Beckerson, computer programmer, sir. Our ship's navigator, John, has calculated an equatorial orbit of Earth wherein both ships simultaneously circumnavigate your planet every 5.6343 hrs. Sir, I feel this is ineffective as a support for the ground team investigators. I think it would be better if that time was cut down so that there would be a ship every 84 min. 31 sec. and at the same altitudes, but diametrically opposite each other while circling the globe."

"So, you're saying at the 500-mile altitude there would be 4 ships equally spaced to provide orbital coverage every 84 minutes and 31 seconds."

Looking at Gariff, John smiled. Gariff said, "Mind reading 101, John." He shrugged his shoulders ever so slightly.

"Arthur, you voiced our thoughts exactly; thank you. You will all be issued, or at least checked that you have time pieces that are very accurate. Any more comments, questions or additions?"

"Both of our engineering and communication's staff will be working on a means by which our ground teams will be covertly outfitted with devices to keep each of you in constant contact with our ships. Our personnel and medical departments will also be in constant contact with each of you. Our Captains will be responsible for launching the shuttlecrafts to the planet. Our defence teams will design protocol for weaponry, its use and its failure, should it happen.

All these assignments shall be accomplished enroute back to Earth. Further, you will need to travel; sleep; and blend in with the people you will be among in order that you can carry out your investigations. So, everyone will be issued five very important items: -

1. a <u>passport</u> from the Council of World Affairs so you can have freedom of passage into any country; and,

2. any necessary <u>licensing requirement</u> to operate any equipment; and,

3. a COWA I.D. <u>card</u> for medical needs/services; and,

4. a <u>credit card</u> acceptable for any business, service, medical attention, equipment rental, housing/lodging, emergency transportation via land/sea/air, and local cash advances; and,

5. an <u>ear implant</u> for communication to each other, or to the ships; these ear pieces will provide you with two-way communication ability from anywhere, without any static or transmission interference or otherwise.

"John?"

"Yes, Gariff."

"I think we could give our ground investigators more support and boost their confidence, if we provide that proposed extraction availability time of 84 min. and 31 seconds."

Nodding in agreement, John called, "Ellis?"

"Yes, John."

"I should like to meet with you, the two ships' captains, and me in my office after everybody is dismissed."

"I'll see you in your office John."

"Are there any more questions or comments?" John asked the audience. Seeing none, John said, "Okay, everyone. Let's get to work; we have a little over six months to get back as far as Mars and two weeks after departing from there, unless we can come up with a travelling miracle again," John added, with a grin, looking at Gariff. He smiled back at John.

John started for his office and was trailed by his captain, Ellis, and Marion. Catching up to John, Janet put her hand on his shoulder and asked, "Are you okay, honey?"

"Actually, no; I'm not okay. What if we're wrong; like, dead wrong?"

"John, don't forget your mother is the top agent for SETIA. Surely, you trust her, don't you?"

John's grip around Jan's waist tightened ever so slightly as he started to talk to her. "Honey, I trust both sets of our parents. Still, we must keep in mind that we have been sent into space on a fact-finding mission. A mission that COWA knew and we now know, was a wild goose chase based on information that was put in place by the GGE, God's Garden of Eden. What I am saying, Jan, is I have reached the point of not trusting anyone who is on Earth at this moment or for that matter, in the COWA Space Station. If the Solar telescope can be breached to send back phony messages to Earth's monitoring people and all the other Earth-bound monitoring devices can support Solar's data with their own data to lead us on a wild goose chase, then I can not help but believe these saboteurs will stop at nothing to accomplish their goal. That is why I have called the senior administration of both ships to meet with me in my office."

Arriving at his office doorway, John pressed a button on the 'Access Lock' mechanism and issued some instructions after his identity had been established. He did not want to be disturbed but 'Access' was to admit who he had sent for, also, the following personnel: - Jan, Ellis, Gariff Tterzin, both ships' captains, Dr. Wentworth, the CMO of the TGCTriang, Commanders Donaldson, and Armstrong, and finally the chief engineers of both ships.

After everyone was seated, John sent for the Personnel Resources department heads of both ships. John began his meeting after their arrival.

"Okay, everyone, Gariff, up till now we have had a pretty easy go of things but as of now, I want you all to look around this table and think how difficult would it be to look at a person and be able to determine if they are a saboteur, or a spy, or a mole; or someone you definitely can not trust. Both Jan and I have heard the story of such an event when Angélique Marshall, my mother, had to reveal the identity of our #2 SETIA Rep.'s wife as a mole from the GGE faction. She was a woman whom he trusted with his life; a woman whom he loved deeply.

Before coming on this mission our garage service man had worked on our vehicles for years. We trusted him. Thank heavens our maid saw him creeping around our home and killed him before he assassinated us. I reiterate, we can no longer simply trust people. Before we arrive within reach of Earth we are going to need a protocol, a means, something in place to ensure trust and assure ourselves individually that trust is deserved. Otherwise the outcome of our attempts to salvage a peaceful life on Earth could be very devastating.

Anyone have ideas, comments, or questions?"

"John, just so we can get a little perspective on the matter, I have a comment to make."

"Go ahead, Ellis."

"Well, sir, Gariff you must know by now that these people John is talking about have the means to chase us through our solar system. For example, if they sabotaged the Solar telescope it means they could catch, match and install pseudo cosmic info and leave, all the while the Solar Telescope orbited the Earth: -

1. every 97 minutes,

2. at an altitude of 559 kms.; or 307 nautical miles; or 353 miles,

3. at a speed of 17,500 mph or 28,000 km/h

It was just as surprising to us to find three suicidal ships chasing us while we were enroute to Mars. Luckily, we were able to destroy them."

Turning to John, "So John, I think we better tighten up security because when we are on Earth we will be in their ball park, so to speak."

"Thank you, Ellis. Now, if memory serves me correctly we established that we would be orbiting the Earth at an altitude of 500 miles or 434.85 KN. and by we, I mean the two ships and the two shuttlecrafts. Furthermore, we will all have capable laser-cannon operators on board with their respective armament mechanics. Our navigational computers will keep us all on course for accuracy and so Earth's Solar Telescope will not accidentally intersect with us if we must use our weaponry.

The Newton will act as base, the TGCTriang will be Eagle-Eye-1, and the shuttlecrafts' call signs will be Pet One and Pet Two. All of us will be equipped to provide back-up weaponry needs and quick extractions as the need arises. Detention cells will be available on the Newton, but all the other ships will have a holding-cell capability.

Now the main reason I wanted to hold this meeting; Ellis, you mentioned tightening security." Looking at Gariff and both ships' chief medical officers, John said, "No one is going to like what I am about to say, but I have to say it. Identification protocols must be put in place which are foolproof upon returning to the ships. All data on all ground crews must be channeled through security, medical, personnel resource departments and then, networked through all computer memories before allowing entry to our ships. Just one of our ground crews needs to be captured, tortured, imprisoned and dissected, yes dissected, to cause the GGE to put out a warning message to all their members, voluntary or otherwise."

"John, it sounds like you are preparing for a war here," Gariff said.

"You better believe it. I would have preferred any other type of approach but if they can do what they have done in the past then there is no telling what they can do nowadays. Modern medicine, worldwide availability of information, the modern progression of science, the sociological-overtly-dispassionate government actions of some nations, the environmental raping of the planet and acts of terrorism have given me cause to leave it all behind and emigrate to your planet Gariff.

However, notwithstanding my feelings my wife Janet and I swore an oath that when we became agents of SETIA we would do our best to protect Earth from all harm originating from extra-terrestrial causes. The GGE crossed that boundary twice first when they tried to assassinate us enroute to Mars and secondly, when they supplied pseudo-cosmic information to Earth's scientists regarding the Triangulum Galaxy's black hole."

"So, John, as of right now my personnel joining yours as the ground investigation force will be in extreme danger if we are determined during a captivity situation to be alien life forms, (ALF)?"

"Gariff, as usual you are on my wavelength. If your personnel are discovered their genetic makeup will be more than enough to cause utter chaos all over the planet and the Martian community settlement combined."

"My God, John! That would drive the entire GGE underground or open it right up. We have no way of knowing where this could end."

"Janet, you just gave voice to my thoughts exactly. If they ever did determine that COWA has supported the introduction, the maintenance, and the fulfillment of an intergalactic friendship they will turn on this friendship in such a manner that it could end in an intergalactic war. Don't forget everybody that when our son Adam died it was a Cosmic Seeder who mediated the Galactic Ordering Director's wish that Adam be restored to life and that the people from Earth were not to be deterred from their existence as Universal Peacekeepers.

Remember, we still have a grievance to settle between the two worlds of YI and Ralos, when Wehttam and Natas call us back to the arbitration table again. The GGE's anger could spill into space with a vehemence the likes of which could take centuries to settle or even eradicate. I don't want our efforts of friendship to shatter because of a Terran religious fanaticism. Let them keep it on Earth and not involve the cosmos.

Gariff, you said yourself that Ffraiteron had not sent you into space as the Ffraiteron Ambassador to establish peaceful ties with the Terrans from Earth. You were only out on a mission to explore and serendipitously, met us. Correct?"

"John is right, my friends."

"And furthermore, we have been shown a time anomaly; genetic improvements and a new propulsion system which we had only dreamt about."

"John, I think I speak for everyone at this table when I say we are all behind you 100% with whatever you want us to do."

"Thank you, Captain Gregzitt." The personnel at the table agreed unanimously and in unison.

"Good, then we can expect protocols from all departments on how to handle each of the concerns in this situation which should include expecting the worst." John's heart was pounding as he relaxed back in his chair. Quietly he thought, it was one thing to fight an enemy but it was clearly another thing to fight an enemy having a culture-based ideal. How was that adage worded again? John thought, 'you can take the weapon from the man but you can't take the spirit of his ideal – or kill the man; give life to his martyr.'

John thought, if every planet nurtured the idea of killing beings because others don't believe in their deities or live by their governing laws then co-existence in this universe would be one continuous, catastrophic, inter-galactic war based on the fact being 'our planet' and its people, are more important than yours. John shuddered at this image.

Chapter 52

Both ships were travelling side by side enroute to Earth all the while developing the means, the protocols and skills needed to investigate, collect evidence, develop the presentations and reports for the Council of World Affairs upon their return to Earth.

John's need for perfection and consistency in efforts was infecting everybody including Gariff's personnel. "There will be a practice covert operation to obtain information on the grav-deck at 11:00 hrs. You will not be told what you are to look for but that goal will be at 17:00 hrs. on the grav-deck. You will disclose your findings at that time and you will be issued stun ray guns for defence. Partner up with a crew member from the other ship and not the one you are a member on. You have twenty minutes to begin."

"Diedra, can't this velocity problem be reduced?"

"John, if Clinton's engineering and Gariff's engineering personnel can put their heads together and make this goose travel faster than 310,685 mph under its current construction then I say yes. Our navigational computers can handle up to ten times that speed, Sir."

"5,000,000 km/h?" inquired John.

"Yes, Sir, and the computers could even handle a further factor of ten."

"I think this ship would be better served at your first factor of ten, Diedra." Arithmetically Diedra that works out to be about 53 ¾ days. Are you certain of this?"

Checking her figures again, Diedra said, "Yes, Sir."

John thought, incredible. "Good, I'm calling Gariff and Clinton to my office. Thank you."

John thought, it's only 0.5 AU to Earth from Mars so at that potential speed we could make it in 14.9 hours. Clinton arrived followed by Gariff by two minutes. "My apologies Gariff for appearing like I'm playing yo-yo with you."

"John, you wouldn't have sent for me if it wasn't important. What's up?"

"We could be back at Earth in about two months with a short stop at Mars, my navigational supervisor advises me."

Looking at Clinton and then at John's desk Gariff said, "We could increase your new gravity drive by a factor of 10 subsequently boosting your speed by a factor of ten but we would have to consult with our engineering staff regarding structural integrity."

Clinton agreed. "John, Gariff's engineers and mine will have a meeting and get back to you say in an hour and a half with a probability for the transition of this occurring." Looking at Gariff while standing up and walking to the doorway Clinton raised his eyebrow with that 'what-now?' expression.

"Clinton, the Newton's maximum speed for now is safest and fastest that my staff and I could come up with at the time of original construction. However, we must admit that unless our speeds can reach the millions, it will always be slow going for us. Even at thousands of miles per hour it would be dangerous because of space debris. After all, we don't want our ships to end up like Lorne Saunders helmet."

"Well, Gariff, we're going to have to design some sort of shield to protect our ships to repel most things that could intersect with us."

"Clint, I think the design which we constructed the Newton with left us room for that future possibility. I know our space program included the possibility to explore the radio frequency sources which we were receiving from the Milky Way galaxy specifically your solar system. When my ship's astronomers finally isolated the source, we almost collided with a strange looking probe whose orbital path was traced back to your planet."

"Wow, Gariff, if I'm not mistaken your astronomers saw one of our space probes, Voyagers 1 or 2, that were launched during the last quarter of the twentieth century. They're at least a few hundred years old by now."

"That, my friend is going to be one of the main topics during our meeting. The other will be the structural integrity of the ships. I don't think there will be much of a change other than minor ones, to the gravity drives.

"Let's get some drinks in the Newton cafeteria and mull these problems over before the engineering teams return." Enroute to the cafeteria their wives, Janet and Mariff, were walking in the same direction. Gariff said, "Ladies would you like some company?"

"Don't mind at all," Mariff said. The men fetched some drinks from the counter and sat down with the women. Janet started talking, saying "Was I the only one who noticed that there might be some romantic relationship existing between Adam and Hertiff?"

"Do tell," said John.

"They were holding hands a little while back at the meeting and I suspect that Kathy knows a little more than us."

Gariff said, "Hush, here comes Clinton and Kathy now."

Spotting her friends, Kathy joined them at their table. Retrieving some things from the counter Clinton turned and walked towards them. "Well, honey looks like we can have a real talk now, ha, ha. Since Chris is minding the 'store' we can relax."

John spoke saying, "Kathy, have you noticed you have two love birds working for you?"

"You mean Adam and Hertiff, John?" Kathy replied.

"Yes."

"Janet, Mariff, I think we are all going to have a dual ship-wide wedding event on our hands before we get back to Earth. Those two seem glued to each other yet their research work isn't suffering. In fact, they're moving the entire department and its morale further ahead than I could've anticipated. I think it's wonderful."

Gariff patted John on the back and Mariff hugged Janet. Clinton, reaching for his wife's hand gently squeezed it.

"Ladies, John and I were musing a short time ago about a few changes which might have to be made to our ships so they could travel a little faster than what they're doing now. Furthermore, it will definitely involve some E.V.A.'s (extra-vehicular activities) on our ships' personnel parts."

"Should we be inferring Gariff, that the medical departments should prepare for some traumatic triaging and care?" asked Janet.

"I think that you both should know that our engineering teams are putting together a plan by which we will install some sort of repulsing shielding to the ships. Since most of the rock matter, meteors and asteroids, contain metallic elements it might be possible to repel them from collision courses with the ships or even give our gunnery crews some target practice as well. It's never been done before so there could be some injuries," said John.

"Girls, in addition to what John and Gariff have told you they're also working on some improvements to the propulsive systems which can boost our speeds by a factor of ten. Goldie has told John that the navigational computer systems can handle up to a factor of 100 but we only need a factor of 10," said Clinton.

Looking at John and Gariff, both wives asked, "And still avoid being hit by dark space matter?" Kathy looked at her husband Clint in wonderment. As if their ears could hear their table talk the two senior engineers walked into the cafeteria and sat at the table beside them.

"That's why we need a trauma center ready-to-go so to speak," said Gariff's senior engineer. Looking at John and Gariff, "We overheard your conversations and thought you might like to know that 1) the gunnery crews of both ships are ready; 2) the equipment for the repulsion shields are ready for installation; and 3) the propulsion engines have been upgraded to produce the speeds wanted, Captains."

"Well, Commanders, we should all report to our assigned posts after a toast to our successful return and help where we can."

"Good idea, John," Gariff said, raising his glass. "To all, good health, safe and swift return, no investigative obstructions and have a successful outcome."

While clinking their glasses, they turned to look at the entrance wondering about the cause of the cheerful, boisterous noise. Apparently, on Ffraiteron, it's acceptable for the girl who has been kissed passionately during intimacy to propose marriage to her lover. Mariff quickly explained the reasoning behind this was because most males being timid would enlist in some occupation that would take them off world and into space. Janet looked at John. "The crews are all occupied with a practice covert mission until 17:00 hrs."

"Well, Gariff, it looks like we might have a wedding to go to when we get to Mars. Should give something for Sam Davis to do and his wife Linda to plan for us, heh, heh."

Janet said, "Don't jump the gun, guys, their jubilance could be due to them becoming engaged."

Mariff said, "If I know my daughter she will have Adam wrapped around her little finger already."

"To that I will agree," said Kathy, chief astronomer of the Newton. Seeing their parents in the cafeteria they ran towards them; Hertiff to show her parents her engagement ring and Adam to explain to his parents how it came about. Another toast, this time for parental approval, was given all around to health, happiness and many babies.

Chapter 53

After all the proposed changes, had been done to the ships and bruises, cuts and abrasions had been attended to, John notified Gariff about his state of readiness. Gariff agreed that his ship was also prepared. They both agreed to break away 1000 miles and test the repulsion fields; their gunnery crews had loaded some of the smaller rock matter from the Kuiper Belt into two reassembled cannons to fire at each ship. The subsequent projectiles would travel at 100 miles per second. There should be no damage to either ship if the shields worked.

And they did work; however, they hadn't taken into consideration the trajectories of the rebound. Both ships were hit three times which caused laughter on both bridges because now they knew their ships could withstand a pummeling by a meteor shower.

"Gariff, have you read the analyses of our covert spies?" asked John.

"Yes, my friend. Apparently, morale is up all over and your ship is of the same energy level."

"Agreed. Let's get to Mars."

"Shoulder-to-shoulder my friend."

"Jules, good work to you and the boys. One day, 'Bullseye' and I are going to have a shootout," said John. Tommy's smile almost pushed his ears off his face.

Gariff did likewise with his crew. The ships sailed in formation heading towards Mars. Captain Davidson requested a communiqué be sent to Sam Davis on Mars via his private, secret frequency to prepare for the Newton's arrival and plan a wedding ceremony.

"Sir, won't that be heard by others?" asked Commander Donaldson.

"Let me know when you have composed the message Chris, and then route it through the Captain's Log to Source Origin Frequency whereby it will be automatically scrambled."

"Do you want any additional info in that message, Sir?"

Looking at John, Clinton answered, "No."

"Okay, people, let's get a move on. Blondie, are your computers ready for the jump?"

"Yes, Sir," she said. Diedra's hand was poised to engage the ship's engines to produce ten times the current propulsion rate. The first officer alerted all personnel, via the P.A. System, to the ship's expected increase in speed and get strapped in for safety. Spike Thompson set the computers for the expected jump and placed Mars as the terminus. The ship would slow to an orbital speed ½ AU away from Mars while Mars was travelling in orbit ahead of the Newton.

Again, looking first at John and then the big 'heading screen' on the bridge, Clinton said, "Diedra, punch it." The G-force to the ship was expected but it felt like the highest roller coaster in the world without the pressures to the face. This sensation lasted for 47 seconds. When it was at its point of equivalence in pressures and force everyone seemed to relax. John picked up his P.A. Systems' handset to contact Julie. "Julie, how are the children?"

"John, they were all secured to take a nap at the time of the speed increase. They're all okay, including the two eldest." Julie looked over all the children, more to satisfy herself than anyone else and noticed two things: - a page of paper on one of the older one's desk and an envelope addressed to mom and dad; no surname, just mom and dad. She read them and thought she would let Janet and Marion know about this.

Looking at John, Clinton saw the relief on his face and asked, "What's up, pal?"

"Thank you, Julie. Clint, I was just thinking about some of the things we seem to be complacent about on this ship because of the dia-grav deck's construction. Back in the 'old days' such a deck if mentioned to your colleagues would have been cause to wonder where you left your strait jacket. It still mystifies me even now and out here in space that feeling is compounded by having babies, raising them, schooling them and then introducing them back into an environment that a planet like Earth can provide. Reading some old history books, medical doctors examined returning astronauts and discovered silly things by today's standards, like perspiration fluid pooling at the lumbar area of their backs. Flatulence permeated their space environment interior over 40 feet away in seconds because of lower air pressures. I was just concerned Clinton, nothing special."

"Good, because you had me worried there for a minute, John. The things I am very grateful for is our ability to produce, store and have both potable and sewage water and recycle all waste matter, ours and all materials on the ship. We must mine for ores and refine them for our needs. There's a lot of things we should be grateful for John, but Janet, your wife put that in a nutshell, when the world's nations got together and voted for the formation of our Council of World Affairs, COWA."

"Well, buddy, we're going to thank them by resolving this astronomical enigma and from what Blondie has told us and our engineers confirmed, we should be back on Earth in about two months. Of course, there's a little side issue of a wedding on Mars, ha, ha."

For the next 1200 hours, personnel on both ships, developed, tested and where necessary, improved on their skills and procedures to resolve the enigma issue and present a resolution to COWA.

Relationships already in existence became closer and new ones developed. Space travel truly brought people together. Adam and Hertiff were not interested in the formality of a wedding as much as the ceremony itself. The friends they made on both ships truly displayed an intergalactic bonding. Theirs would be the first of such enormity as far as Earth and Ffraiteron were concerned. Linda Davis knew it when she was contacted to prepare for their arrival.

Ellis was doing research at his science station and realized something that hadn't yet been expressed. He questioned John. "Sirs, we've been sent to confirm, or refute, what Triangulum's Black Hole is said to be doing as observed by Earth's astronomical societies. Correct?"

"Right," said John, "and so?"

"I don't want to be argumentative but I don't recall reading anywhere that maintenance crews were sent out to the Solar telescope to check its electronic transmission systems so that the appropriate receiving stations on Earth could get real time images. Like Gariff said, he would have noticed something like that as his wife and daughter are scientists of the astronomical field. Furthermore, our scientists should have mentioned the big obstacle in the scope's info since it hasn't been orbiting Earth for more than 2,780 years. The scope itself was launched way back in 1990 and is occupying a near circular low Earth orbit of about 347 miles in altitude and orbits Earth about every 97 minutes. Maybe that was a factor to be considered for a maintenance team, which doesn't logically connect since the NASA space program sent Solar up in a shuttlecraft called Discovery I believe. If the GGE people can afford to send people up to scuttle the scope's information systems and get around security teams located at the Earthbound sites surely the authoritative people can get maintenance teams to the Solar scope regardless of its orbit."

"Don't confuse the old Hubble with the new Solar scope. Your argument works well for Hubble." Ellis checked his work on his devices.

"John, I mistook some data, sorry." "Good; keep this information in mind, Ellis, because I'm sure that Sam Davis has some insight into this matter. However, Ellis, the distance of 2,780 x 10^6 light years doesn't figure in your argument, since it may have taken that long for us to see what was happening. Remember back on Earth we were told in science class, that light from our Sun takes 8 minutes 20 seconds to reach the Earth and the fun we had with that knowledge?"

"Clint, John, Ellis, just a little update for you, we are approaching Jupiter's moon orbit which is in perihelion to Mars."

"Which moon is that, Diedra?"

"Ganymede, sir."

"Home, sweet home, Newton, old boy," said Clinton, chuckling to John.

"Listen, my friend, I know you are kidding, but you and your engineering teams along with Gariff's men have made our travels in space that much more relaxing. Gone are the so-called good old days during which our astronauts used to travel under when they could easily die from minor things like a cold or blood disorders, *etc.* Thank goodness for pioneers and the space programs they travelled under. I expect one of these days Earth will develop a system whereby we could have a fleet of ships in space and establish settlements or stations like we did when North America was the land of discovery almost a thousand years past."

"John, you are truly aggravated by this sabotaging enigma," said Clinton, as if to calm John down. All the bridge personnel were riveted to the conversation from the Captain's chair when Diedra interrupted once again.

"Captain, sir?"

"Yes, Diedra" said Clinton.

"Spike concurs with me that there are two alien space crafts following the Newton and the TGCTriang."

"Put them on-screen, Blondie, please."

When they were up on the screen a communication came in from Gariff's ship. "They're back, John. I believe they wish to finish the arbitration procedure," said Gariff.

Transmitting back John said, "Who knows, we just might have a big shin-dig after all, Gariff."

Chris said, "Captain, incoming messages, sir."

"Let's hear them, Chris."

"I am Wehttam from YIs and I am here with Natas from Ralos. We wish to have our grievance settled by our arbitrators, John Marshall and Gariff Tterzin."

"Wehttam, can you and Natas pull alongside the Newton and match our speed or would you prefer that we come to a full stop?"

"John Marshall, I Natas, would like you to come to a full stop."

"Wehttam, be advised we are coming to a full stop."

'Good, gentlemen let's all meet in the neck of our Galaxy Cruiser EGC -3349, the Sir Isaac Newton." John waited for their arrival with Jules in the cruiser's neck. "Jules, when everyone is aboard I want you and Chris to separate the neck and move off about one mile straight ahead, okay?"

"Yes, sir."

"Good, contact Chris and let him know double quick, but discreetly."

"Captain?"

"Here they come; go!" Jules excused himself and went forward to the head of the goose. He contacted Chris who came down to the neck and sealed the hatch. Natas, Wehttam and Gariff, all entered the receiving portal and went with John to the main dia-grav deck toward an area to discuss contract settlement. Meanwhile, Jules and Chris had separated the neck from the body of the Newton and parked exactly one mile in front of the main body. If one viewed this scene from a distance it would be totally humorous as if someone chopped off the neck to a gigantic, polygonal, spherical goose.

"Jules, did John say why we are doing this?"

"No."

Chris thought there might be some trouble and had a hunch Gariff's crew Captain was already primed in this respect. "Jules, just to be prepared strap yourself into a cannon seat don't turn it on but be ready."

"I'm going to pre-program the nav-com with an escape course just in case. I know Gariff's ship will defend the Newton, itself and protect our escape if need be."

Chapter 54

"Gariff, you can sit beside me and gentlemen, please take a seat across from us." Sitting down John then asked, "Who would like to start?"

They both started to speak at once and then stopped, looked at each other and then repeated the same action. Gariff and John looked at each other, turned to their guest complainants and requested they show the contracts their home planet's extra-terrestrial, contractual businesses had written up with any corrections that John and Gariff sent them back to have done.

They handed over the documents. One was done on what appeared to be like old papyrus, while the other was done on a white cloth material. Gariff and John asked each of their guests to please sit at the table for a few minutes. They complied with the request. Gariff and John went to another table to discuss the contracts they had been handed.

"Gariff, these are mining contracts for ores found within some planetoid bodies. Do you recognize the locations of these orbs?"

"John, if I am not mistaken they are both poaching from orbs located in other star systems."

"I think we had better go back to the table and carefully question them on this matter."

"I agree, John," said Gariff.

"Well, gentlemen, you have both impressed us with your speedy returns to arbitrate these contracts. Gariff and I have a question that we would like resolved."

"Anything we can help with, Mr. Marshall," said Natas. "I agree with, Natas," said Wehttam.

"Can we ask you both for honest answers?" prodded Gariff.

"We agree to be honest." John then stated questioning, "These contracts over which you are disputing with the full backing of your home planets' businesses, are they privy to the whereabouts of the ore locations?"

"If you are wondering if we stole the ores that are listed in the contracts," said Natas, "we did not! The ores were discovered in a star system you call Cygnus, but is well known as Rathern -101. The star Rathern-101 has a planetary system, Rathern-101A. As far as we can tell, it is the only habitable planet without any life forms on it."

"I concur, Gariff and John," said Wehttam. "Are you suggesting that if the planet had been inhabited, all ores in that planetary system would belong to them, regardless if they were incapable of space travel?"

"Exactly. If either one of you, during your first trips into space, discovered the other persons had built edifices on what you believed to be uninhabited moons in your planetary systems wouldn't you feel they had no business squatting there?"

"Squatting; what do you mean squatting?"

"Shouldn't everything that is originally part of the confines of your planetary systems belong to you as the intelligent race of people living and evolving within the system; unless there is more than one inhabited planet within the system? Wouldn't you take great offence if we came and inhabited one of your moons, or planets, and removed some of the ores, or resources, found there? Let's face it, gentlemen, wars have been fought between countries and, quite possibly, planets for no other reason than economics.

What could be mined, processed for consumption, bought and sold, will always be a reason to go to war. So, we are asking again, were the places that you obtained the ores, mentioned in these contracts, inhabited, or have planets within their planetary systems, with evolving inhabitants who could lay claim to the ores?"

"No, John. No!" said Natas and Wehttam together, sounding exasperated.

"Good. We do not want to be involved in granting permission to any alien race to commit theft, or fraud of resources from any occupied solar systems' hitherto vacant planet or moon. And, further, to have your business people sue us for any losses incurred."

"I believe what John, and I, are getting at gentlemen is this, we want you to put in writing on these contracts that the ores mentioned therein were obtained from all uninhabited sources, neighboring or otherwise, within a stated planetary system. And the products manufactured for trade, or business, have come from those freely obtained ores and resources," stated Gariff.

"May we retire to our ships and have our business people scribe this information on these contracts, your honors?" asked Natas.

"You may; but you must return in 2 hours" replied John, and with that request John signaled for a security officer to take them to one of the Newton's spherical exit areas as the gooseneck was stationed a mile out in front of the sphere.

"John, what made you think of planetary poaching?" asked Gariff.

"You know I have been watching some old historical, film footage of early-entrance- into-space-exploration by our planet, right? Well, did I ever mention anything about the UFO sightings and reports, from various air force pilots, airline pilots, astronauts, ground observers, *etc.*?"

"No, not that I can recall," said Gariff.

"Did I ever mention anything about cities, life signs, *etc.* found on our moon and our closest planet, Mars?"

"No, why?"

"I am suggesting by the time Earth actually reached the point in the 21st century of putting people on the planet Mars, all that it would have to offer would be somewhere to rest for a bit. The dwellings, Luna City, on the moon were dated, during that time, as being 1½ billion years old and were vacant. The UFO sightings were probably just checking us out to see if we would, or could take any serious action against them. Therefore, they must have thought we hadn't yet evolved that far. The 'poaching' of ores and resources would be a piece of cake to them."

"John, I didn't think you were a conspiracy theorist."

"Cynic, would be better in line with my personality, Gariff. I've always believed in 'show me first then talk' and Janet can vouch for that. I never believed for a second this ship could move through space or that I could trust an alien to construct it with my best friend, Clinton. Now, Gariff, I see you as the brother I never had and will defend with my life." John's arm went over Gariff's shoulder in a show of comradery. "And now, you have shown us a new type of propulsion drive and Janet has two new amino acids to research. Which reminds me, we must set some time aside to teach you my self-defence technique of ACERT, alien crisis emergency response tactics."

"Well, just to make you feel better my friend, I know why you separated the gooseneck from the ship's body so I left instructions for my captain to back any moves the 'neck' would have to make."

"Thank you, Gariff, I thought you might."

"John, it's Clinton speaking. I have a couple of things to tell you; 1) your complainants are returning and 2) I have something from Julie that we married folk might like to know about after this settlement is reached."

"Thanks, Clinton. After entering the arbiters' court room again, the two complainants assumed their seats.

They pulled their contracts out of their carrying cases, put them on the table and said, "Sirs, we believe we have reached and scribed a proper settlement." They handed Gariff and John the newly struck contracts. After examining them both arbitrators agreed to affix their seals of approval to them with the proviso that should these contracts prove faulty or insufficient under 'working conditions' to their businesses, upon the return to their home planets, then they would return with a list of comments at a future time for appropriate alterations. Furthermore, no changes were to be made or acted on without the prior, expressed approval of this court.

After agreeing to this proviso signatures were placed on the contracts and the two alien admirals happily stood up and prepared to leave.

Wehttam turned and said, "We heard some conversation about the boy who was brought back to life by the COSMIC SEEDER that he was going to get married to your daughter, Admiral Tterzin."

"That's correct, Wehttam, why do you want to know?"

"We were wondering if we could attend and help give them a real party to show our gratitude for this most thoughtful settlement," said Natas, of the Srennis' planet.

"Gentlemen, your generosity and consideration in this matter are very much appreciated. Both the bride and groom have requested of us that they do not want a big party, only the marriage ceremony. However, since you mentioned this and you were present for Adam's premature funeral I think we could have a reception party later."

"Moreover, we were on our way back to Earth regarding an urgent planetary problem," said John. "So, can we invite you then?" John asked.

"We'll be there, John. "We agree with Natas, John," said Wehttam.

"Good, have a speedy and safe journey back to your home planets, gentlemen," said Gariff, wishing them good bye.

After watching them depart John contacted the bridge and told Clinton to contact the gooseneck to return to station when the visitors had reached the 10,000-mile mark but in the interim to proceed to the opposite side of the sphere.

"Suspect trouble, John?" asked Gariff.

"Quite frankly, Gariff, I suspect trouble always but this time I honestly believe that Natas of the Srennis really poured his heart and soul into this settlement whereas Wehttam was rather glib. That meant settle for any reason and deal later. I believe his accompanying reputation of being conniving."

"You may have a point, John. Tell you what, if this was recorded then let's invite Mariff, and Ellis, to watch the proceedings and see what they think."

"How did you know I had this recorded?"

"John, one doesn't become cynical for no reason, ha, ha."

They summoned Ellis and Mariff to watch the proceedings and express their opinions about the grievers' trustworthiness. John contacted Rochelle at communications and ordered a closed communication be sent to the gooseneck to carefully watch the departure of the two alien spaceships. Upon receiving this transmission, Jules swung his cannon to face the crafts and set it to 'destruct' rather than 'disable'. As luck, would have it Wehttam's ship was in Jules target finder when he noticed the ship hesitate in its course. Jules had the range and the energy preparation; he only needed to 'squeeze the trigger'.

At that very moment Ellis advised John and Gariff, that Wehttam's behaviour during the arbitration was not consistent with a sincere attempt in settling their grievance dispute. Jules' sensors picked up an energy increase in the YIs' ship and Jules fired. The resulting energy pulse reached the YI's ship before their weapon could discharge, destroying the ship. The Ralosians seeing this action on their scanners came to a dead stop and contacted the Newton requesting an explanation. John invited them to return to the Newton.

When the Ralosians arrived to board the Newton, they were greeted by John, Ellis and Gariff. As they entered Gariff bent down to pick up an attaché case then opened it to find Wehttam's scrunched up copy of the grievance settlement. Showing this to both John and Natas, he said, "Wehttam" had no intention of returning to his home planet with a contract settlement. He did not wish to appear weak before his people who dealt with extra-planetary affairs."

"This means John, Gariff, that as far as my people are concerned they will know that I tried on their behalf to settle but now, our planets are still going to be at war," said Natas.

Looking at Gariff, John asked, "Just exactly where is your home world located Natas?"

"Do you have any star charts of the cosmos, John?" Natas asked.

"John, may I help?" asked Mariff.

"Certainly, Mariff."

Mariff took Natas to the bridge to look through the navigational computer files. If Natas' home planet could be displayed, then, so could a course be entered into the Newton's computer. Enroute to the bridge John and Gariff discussed possibilities regarding any detour actions without any commitment. Mariff asked, "Blondie, have some charts displayed on the screen showing what Natas had discussed while I'm enroute to the bridge, please."

"They'll be ready for you, Mariff."

Natas suddenly blurted, "There; that is where we Ralosians have been exploring and mining," he said, pointing to an area near Sirius, in Canis Major. "And that is where Wehttam's people come from," he said pointing to Betelgeuse.

Mariff said to John and Gariff, "You're looking at a distance of nearly 9 light years away, Gariff."

Diedra, the Newton's chief navigator concurred. Given that information, they asked Natas how his ship could travel that distance, and return inside of almost 3 years.

"Sirs, if you let me show you on your navigational computer, I can locate a space warping anomaly, which will cut down that distance to several AU."

"John, that distance at our current maximum velocity capability would take us 2.572222 years to complete, space anomaly included," said Diedra.

"She's right, John. If you are planning on returning to Natas' home planet to support him in his explanation of this grievance, then I would suggest doing it after our return to Earth," said Ellis. John looked beaten, because he felt he was between a rock and a hard place; postpone the wedding and look after Earth's problem hoping Gariff will come with me and maybe Natas. Should I honour my peacekeeping proclamation, given by the COSMIC SEEDER, on behalf of the Galaxial Ordering Director?

"Natas, John and I were on our way back to Earth to resolve an extremely important planetary matter; a matter, which, if left to fester, could result in the destruction of his world. Could you postpone your return and accompany us first or do you fear the war between your two planets will escalate?" Gariff asked Natas.

"No. When I left they were agreeable to a temporary peace treaty pending my return."

"Good," said John, "so you'll accompany us, then?"

"Yes."

"In that case, Natas, how would you like to do a little stop over with us and witness a wedding ceremony?" asked Gariff.

"Thank you for your kind invitation. We will accompany you."

"Natas, Gariff, could you both come with me to my office so we can discuss a few things?" John requested to which they did.

Chapter 55

"Diedra, could you check your calculations again for the time it will take us to reach Natas' home world?" asked Ellis. "I didn't say anything at the time because I had a hunch that trip might be shelved until this problem on Earth was cleared up first."

"Why? What have you noticed, Ellis?" asked Diedra.

"I think you based your calculations on miles per hour, like 5 million mph instead of km/h."

"Oh, sh#@$. Ellis, he's going to shoot me, for sure now."

"No, he won't. After this thing on Earth John won't even remember. I know him. But let's get it right, this time."

"Okay, she calculated it to be 1,511.982 days or 4.14 years to reach Natas' home planet. How's that, Ellis?"

"That's more accurate. Now, John may think the difference is because we're starting from Earth but if you don't say anything he won't figure it out because we are measuring from Earth, ha heh."

"Gentlemen, we are going to plan a coup. A coup, which, I hope, will scoop every zealot of the GGE faction including those members who have never been identified. Natas, how many of your crew can you spare, rather, how many of your crew would like to play 'spy'?"

Gariff looked at John with a questioning expression. As if reading his mind John said, "Natas, I would like your crew, Gariff's crew and my members to work together forming teams, so that when you place yourselves among the GGE people you will be able to blend in completely."

"Ah, you mean mannerism, language and territorial knowledge, *etc.*, John."

John said, "Yes, and that is going to entail some very deep training, some of which I can accelerate with my ACERT training. The training must be done safely for all crew members and innocent people of Earth alike. So, if you can transfer as many of your crew as possible to the Newton we can all get started with the training."

"They will enjoy the exercise, John, and won't fail you."

"John, I'll bring over more Ffraiterites for these training sessions."

"Good, we want as many teams as possible, in case a raid is necessary to prevent warning information of getting out. That should keep the element of surprise at a peak," replied John. Overall supervision of the training fell to Ellis who could speak all the languages on Earth and knew the mannerisms of every nation, because of his programming.

A knock at John's office door revealed Julie and Janet standing there, so Gariff and Natas left together and met Ellis walking towards them. Ellis already knew what had happened and led them to an area on the grav-deck to show them where the training was to take place.

Meanwhile, "This is Captain Davidson requesting the gooseneck reconnect to the main body."

Jan and Julie knocked on John's office door again. After letting in Janet and Julie, he asked, "What's up?"

"This, John," said Janet, showing him the two pieces of paper Julie had found in one of her classrooms.

John started to read: -

I Love You
"When we die!" we would hear,
That, "babies, children, shouldn't fear,
'Cause, angels sent from God above
Carry young souls on clouds of love."

"So, Mommy, Daddy, don't shed a tear;
I died on Christmas just last year;
But with my angels, up above
I celebrate this time of love!"

"Now lift your spirits to the sky
And God will show the reason why
The moon and stars keep shining bright;
To show my love for you at night!"

By Sariah Matma, 9years old
Ms. Julie's class, EGC 3349-Newton Public School

"And this has been untouched by anyone else?" John asked of Julie.

"That's right, John. She's the little girl who stayed on the Newton with her parents, Jake and Parvaneh Matma, while Parvaneh did some plant DNA research between the CSS and the Newton. Apparently, she was the victim of some accidental radiation exposure at the age of seven, developed cancer and died. Janet tells me that the cancer she developed can be cured nowadays."

John looked at Janet and his face expressed the frustration welling up in him.

"John, honey, I know this must be awkward for you but I want you to read this poem written by one of your crew members concerning his young son. The crew member is one of our top gunners and it's not Tommy."

"Why?" John asked Janet.

"Because when the investigation starts to route out the GGE zealots and the members of all three ships are down there on Earth they might realize that their training is of the utmost importance, more than their lives are at stake there."

"Let me see it; John read: -

David L. Pritchard

Are These the Drums of War?

Me and my boy were sitting in the door
Watching Ol' Sol fall to the floor.
Son turns to me and asks what to expect
Of life, yet to live and events not met?

I looked at his eyes and thought to myself,
("Son, I don't know! Just wish for good health!")
Returning my look, he pressed for the truth;
I knew it was time to act like a sleuth!

"What's troubling you, boy? What's worrying you so?"
"Daddy, I'm scared! Which way shall I go?"
Honesty and decency are taking a back seat
To lying and racism and crimes in the street!

There's fighting in Europe, the Middle and Far East;
The rest of the world is chanting for peace!
A recession is gripping this country so wide;
Which politician will stand on our side?

Technology and science are making great strides;
Yet children all over are suffering inside!
"Are these the drums of war?" he asked with a tear!
I looked in his eyes and saw hidden fear.

"Yes, my son!" and hugged him right close,
"These are the drums that beat out for most
A rhythm of race, hatred, and lies;"
(That sure comes to us as no great surprise!)

"This war is far greater than any we've seen,
For man is the enemy that threatens his being!
Look at your neighbour discarding his garbage
In rivers and parks; his head's full of cabbage!

The sun is so hot, and the air made hotter
From factories and chemicals cries Little Otter!
Canada, your country, so rich and so vast,
With five fourths century of events in the past.

It's blessed with fresh water and land so green,
And even today has areas unseen!
The people living there are unique and diverse,
Eliciting jealousy, and emotions much worse.

Your country united, is threatened to divide,
Spawned by the seed of overseas pride.
Yet even those people refuse to shed blood
For a nation so renown, as "Canada, the good!"

It's a war just as violent with much devastation
Which is why you need a good education
To fight the effects of an inner turmoil
And stop your country from going to spoil."

- By Anonymous Newton Gunnery Crewman, April 3349

"Janet, Julie, do either of you recognize the handwriting? Have you shown this to Marion for her opinion, because I am concerned about morale on this ship especially since we're going to be doing an investigation back on Earth among humans. The alien Ralosians and Ffraiterites have agreed to accompany our people during the investigation and we don't want that compromised."

"John, why do you think this poem makes you believe the poet might have a cause to compromise the investigation?" Janet pressed.

"Nostalgia, honey. He's explaining to his son about what and how, things on Earth, appear to him; but he is expressing it because of his experiencing the effects all of us have when viewing Earth from space. For instance, its serenity enhanced by the colors of the globe and the recalled, realistic, sensations upon being on the surface. Acclimatizing ourselves to the surface's environmental effects on our bodies, has been minimized by our ancestral astronaut visits into space and their debriefing/medical sessions, as well as the environmental improvements to our enclosures while travelling in space. If we could go back in time and tell NASA, ESA, the Japanese space program, *etc.*, that in the future you can have children while in space, run around on gravity-varying decks, survive time warping anomalies, use gravity-varying propulsion systems and so on, they'd laugh in our faces. Yet, here we are and I'm still mystified at this ship's abilities.

Travelling at 5 million km/hr., shielded by a magnetic force field for protection and able to use laser cannons to hit targets the size of baseballs with 100% accuracy and consistency, impresses me to no end. Target-engineering technicians like Niles Anderson working with cannon gunner "Bullseye" Armstrong, are people we need on this ship for everyone's protection. When "Bullseye" sits at the cannon one can almost hear him quoting a famous line from an old movie, "do ya feel lucky punk, well, do ya?" just before he fires the cannon at an unsuspecting meteor."

"So, you don't want him to lose his nerve or hesitate at the moment of a split-second decision which could affect his aim," said Janet.

"That's right. Our ground teams will need him. And others like him. I know the Srennis crews have some equally good gunners and so does Gariff's Ffraiterite crew. We must co-ordinate them with ours which is why Marion should get together with her counter parts on those ships and check those involved for psychological purposes. Maybe Mariff could be a big help as well. I'll leave all that up to both of you," John said looking at Julie and Janet.

"We'll do our best, John."

"Honey, ever since I married you, your best has never ceased to amaze me," John said, rising from his side of the desk to come around and hug her.

Talking into his mouth she said, "You better find out how much time we have before we hit Mars' orbit."

"Damn, none," he groaned. "Training is much more important!"

"Success, honey," Janet wished him.

"You, too, Jan." John turned and went to the bridge. Clinton had ordered the 'Gooseneck' to reconnect with the main body some time ago, and was already prepping Commanders Donaldson and Sherwood regarding expectations concerning their impending return to Earth. Upon entering the bridge, they updated John including the crunch in time for training, being 21 hours.

"John, I don't think we have enough time unless we slow down a bit."

"Clinton, I don't think we should worry about that. I'm sure Sam Davis will have some information that will add to the time we spend on Mars for the wedding. Speaking of which where is Gariff?"

As if prompted Gariff chose to enter the bridge at that moment accompanied by Natas. "Am I ever glad to see you two. Since we are not too far away from Mars do either of you have any comments about Hertiff and Adam's wedding? Why I'm asking is because the news about the wedding is probably going to reach our planets before we do. They have both agreed and requested the ceremony be a traditional one like those done on Earth."

"John, I have no comment at all," said Natas, "other than I thank you for inviting me and those of mine who can spare the time to come."

"Just make sure my wife has plenty of tissues, John, because she tends to cry at happy occasions like these," said Gariff.

"Ellis."

"Yes, Diedra, what is it?"

"Could you verify an object about 5 astronomical units off the starboard stern?"

Right away this alerted the rest of the bridge crew to look at the big screen. Gariff and Natas looked intently as well. "Captain, the ship, or whatever it is has no identifying features."

"Magnify it, Spike," said Clinton. Magnifying it produced no better results. Spike compounded the problem by saying there was a similar one off the port bow about 8 AU in distance. "Navigation, put their courses and speeds on screen."

"Aye, Captain."

"Chris, any word from our guests' ships yet?"

"Aye, Captain. Just coming in now, sir. Natas' ship detects no life signs on the ship on our starboard side and Gariff's ship has detected no life signs on the port side object."

"Gentlemen, I think we can safely assume these are some sort of space projectiles armed with some explosive device in them. Somehow, they can follow us as we travel so without further adieu do you mind if we sent a message to your ships to target these objects from a safe distance in case of any harmful shrapnel debris. We will continue to be their bait, so to speak."

"Captain Davidson, this will give our crews some practical experience and target practice," said Gariff and Natas, "so, go ahead and do it."

"John, any comment?" asked Clinton.

"Just the one, Clinton. Have Gariff's ship fire on the port target from 1000 miles North of the solar plane and have Natas' ship do the opposite with the starboard ship, i.e. 1000 miles south of the solar plane. And notify Jules to get ready to pick off any debris coming our way."

Clinton was chuckling, because John was reproducing an old aerial combat dog fight he had seen in an old film from Earth. He said to John, "Well, do you feel lucky punk?" laughing and patting his friend at the same time.

Both Gariff's ship and Natas' ship hit their targets, destroying them completely. Ellis kept watching for pieces of debris. "Chris, contact our friends to maintain vigilance enroute to Mars because I don't think this is the end of this targeting."

"Yes sir. Ellis, contact Marion and Janet; I want them in my office now. Gariff and Natas please come with me."

"John, is something wrong?" Gariff asked.

"I'll explain in my office. Diedra, have this incident recorded and send a copy to my office."

"Yes, sir," Diedra replied.

Chapter 56

Knocking on John's door, Marion entered with Janet. "Honey, I got here as quick as possible. What's up?"

"Okay, I'll show all of you and I want to warn you two especially that if you want to break away and return to your home planets, please do so, but the rest of us are in a real quagmire." Depressing his power button on his computer John showed the sudden appearance of both unidentifiable objects approaching the Newton from astern and the bow.

Natas broke the talk with, "I know where you are going with this, John," and continued, "both of those objects could have broken off and pursued our ships, but didn't. They stayed on course with the Newton. Have they been sent by your saboteurs, John?" Natas asked.

"In a word, Natas, yes."

Gariff, interjected and asked John, "Did the Newton come in contact when it was awaiting your arrival, John?"

"The Newton stayed in an orbit high above the COWA Space Station and transported us via shuttlecraft from the CSS to the Newton."

Janet started to understand what John was thinking first looked at Marion when she was about to speak. "John, honey, this means you, rather, we have to have everyone who was with us on Earth including any recent crew arrivals to the Newton gather together for some blood testing to see if there has been a tracking chemical in our blood streams."

"John, that is going to take some time," said Marion.

"About how much, Marion?"

"It depends, John. The systems have to be analyzed and compared with previous records and, if a tracer is found, then we have to determine if it can be neutralized or destroyed without damage to the human host."

Looking at Natas and Gariff as if begging, John asked, "Can your medical departments assist our people?"

"Of course, John. It would be an honor," they said.

"Okay, in that case Marion do you have a ballpark figure for the time involved?"

"Barring any investigative obstacles John, I would guess at two, maybe three weeks."

"Damn it Marion, can't it be sooner?"

"John, your CMO knows that when you deal with the human body, people react differently. This can't be hurried," said Gariff.

"My friends, I know that. It's just bothering me to no end that once again we're sitting ducks out here in the meantime and we can't go near Mars lest whoever finds out our location and retaliates."

"John, don't worry. Our ships will stand sentry duty and we know you suspect that those two objects we destroyed are not going to be the last of them," reassured Natas.

"Our scanners, like yours John, have ranges of at least 10 AU. We also have a 2 AU scanner for life signs, and targeting at 0.75 AU; so, don't worry. We can also back up your Newton's gooseneck personnel."

Looking at both of his friends John extended his gratitude for their understanding and support. Gariff quipped, "After all, we all want some of that Martian hospitality and wedding cake, ha, ha."

Chapter 57

Marion, Janet, Julie, the Ffraiterite CMO (Jjerzit Smathsir), and the Ralosian CMO (Gremelsin Nitasin), along with 4 medical technicians each all pitched in to help with the research for any trace chemicals in the blood streams of the Newton's crew including John. After some very trying issues involved with the lab results they found nothing that could even be a carrier for a tracing chemical. Marion was stumped and said to Janet, "Something is missing." Calling Julie to her office she asked her, "Do you recall the events that took place when you were last on Earth with Janet and John?"

"I remember us all sitting in the convention hall while we toasted to a happy and successful mission the wonderful desserts and wines and comradery-type conversations. Then we all walked out to a waiting limousine to take us to an astronaut waiting area for an overnight stay. We all rose the next morning and went to the launch pad where we boarded a ship to take us to the CSS to await a shuttlecraft to take us to the Newton cruiser. I can't recall anything special happening. It was all very simple to me, Dr. Wentworth."

Marion looked at Janet who said, "That's pretty much it."

Marion pushed for more because she knew there was something else. There had to be! Calling the bridge, she asked that Ellis, John, Chris, Clinton and Kathy come to her office. She called through to Kathy, Clinton's wife to attend her office again. Once more their interviews revealed nothing because Marion was looking for something that could be placed in a human body.

It was Ellis that serendipitously gave Marion the information she sought. As if John read Ellis' mind he excused himself from the room and said, "I'll be back in a couple of minutes, Marion. In the meantime, notify your lab that they're going to have to inspect an inanimate object."

Marion looked quizzically at Ellis. He said, "John's gone to get the attaché case and file," he said smiling at Marion. When John returned, he told Ellis to go with Marion's people and if they found anything put it in a vacuum sealed container so we can inspect it for appropriate handling and counter-measures. Ellis had the case maybe five minutes when he called John to the lab. John brought Natas, Gariff and Clinton with him.

"John, do remember the 'black box and transponders' used back in the late twentieth century and onwards?"

"That's what I thought you'd find, Ellis."

"I didn't, John. I wish I had because it would be a simple case of find inspect how it works and then put something like a virus in its transmission signals."

"So, what have you found?"

"Sirs, I swear I have never seen this type of device. But if I had to give it a name, I would call it a 'Domino Bomb'."

"What, a domino bomb? What do you mean Ellis?"

"He means John, that if this case stops transmitting for any reason it will explode at the same time setting off other bombs. If you disposed of it in space all those objects you saw coming towards us would also explode. That might be okay but what if there are others and where are they located not just in space but how about back on Earth or even Mars or your moon. And how strong would the explosions be and type, incendiary, chemical or nuclear?"

Natas said. "We've heard of this type of terrorism in our Galaxies, John and quite frankly even I tremble that some of your fellow Earthlings have 'evolved' to this type of warfare!"

"Gentlemen, what are we to do?"

"John, you brought this case into space from Earth's surface after receiving it from a captain-of-the-guard at PAFB, in Florida. Correct?" prodded Gariff.

"Yes, why?"

"So, like Natas said, if this is a 'domino bomb' we can set it off now or it will go off later no matter what is done to dispose of it. The case doesn't matter. It's the domino explosions that do. So, we must find out the who, how many, where and a 'stop' procedure and pray to your deities that your suspicions of sabotage concerning the Earth are not as deep as you believe."

"John, let me just add to Gariff's comment. Our investigative teams had better be briefed concerning all explosive devices if they come across them. Do not, set them off. We have no way of knowing if they are connected in with this domino theory," said Natas.

"Gentlemen, you have been very helpful; so why do I feel we are already too late?"

"John, Gariff and I are going to stand beside you and your people, even at the expense of our lives. The only good news that I can see right now, is we can at least destroy their cosmic mine ships. We've already proved that," said Natas.

John commented that they had been very lucky in discovering the trigger for the domino explosions, that being the attaché case.

Chapter 58

Upon returning to his ship Gariff was greeted by his wife Mariff, to whom he explained the predicament that John had found himself in. After listening to her husband's explanation Mariff said, "So, I don't see a problem here."

"Oh, pray tell me, quick."

"Personally Gariff, I am surprised John or Ellis didn't think of it. You told me that the attaché case is the triggering device in the domino bomb theory, correct?"

"That's right; keep going."

"Well, doesn't that mean it is sending out transmissions to be received by other bombs in the domino theory?"

"Yes, of course it does," and suddenly Gariff grabbed her by the arms and kissed her. "I know where you are going with this. If we send the attaché case in a container to some distant star system millions of light years away it's going to take that long, times two, before its radio signals get back to Earth. Brilliant!"

"In the meantime, everyone can keep up with their target practice on those black objects that keep coming towards the Newton," said Mariff.

"Honey, this was your solution so please explain it to John and then we can put our heads together to construct a container to send it away. Hertiff and Adam can decide what the destination is to be. Sound good to you?"

"Sir?"

"Yes Chris."

"John, we have a message for you from the TGCTriang, sir."

"Mariff has told me something that we should have thought of ourselves."

"Go on, Gariff."

"I'll let her explain."

"John, Gariff told me that if you sent the case into space it might become compromised and set off the domino explosions."

"Go on, Mariff."

"Then why don't you and Natas and Gariff get together and design a container for the case and send it off to a galaxy or star system millions of light years away from Earth. You already know you can destroy the ships that come at you. What you want to do is stop the case from sending transmissions or at the very least, increase the time it takes for the transmissions to reach Earth. You know the speed of light so, those transmissions can't travel any faster."

John paused, pondering – now, or in the future – deciding, he said, "Thank you, Mariff. We'll design a container. But I have an addition to that plan. Let's match the frequency or frequencies and time the entry of transmitting so we can keep an eye on the source forever or someday stop it.

Now, are you coming back, Gariff?"

"He's already on his way, John."

"Chris, Natas has already been told, John."

Meeting in John's office again, they picked up the vacuum container with the case and went to engineering. In the meantime, Adam was advised to get together with the astronomy departments and determine to which star system or galaxy they were going to send it. They knew a million years or more would be a good start.

"Some place 500 million years away would be better," Ursula suggested.

Kathy, Hertiff and Adam took Ursula's suggestion but then changed their minds when Natas' astronomy department came up with a system that was not only 6 billion light years away but right near the edge of the expanding universe. That meant it would be that long in making transmissions while enroute there and at least that long when it arrived and was destroyed upon landing. John hoped that in that time the other bombs would be eroded beyond usefulness or destroyed, rather than unleash this terrorism on other unsuspecting planetary beings. With any luck the dark matter in the universe could also contribute to their destruction.

Chapter 59

The three leaders, Gariff, John and Natas left orders on their ships to stand guard for any future encounters with these black projectiles of death to completely ensure their destruction. "Before the idea was thought of by anyone, the answer was an emphatic, no!"

"John, don't tell us you can read minds too," said Gariff.

"But, John, it might be to our benefit if we capture one of these projectiles and take it apart for analysis," added Natas.

"Okay, do it, but under the following conditions – 1) you know in advance that handling the projectile will not send off any tampering signal, 2) your volunteers are at least 10,000 light years away before they start tampering, and 3) it's my planet that is going to be on the business end of any errors."

Looking at each other, Gariff and Natas apologized and said, "John, we were looking at it from a scientific, investigative point of view, sorry."

"Gentlemen, when I first saw them, I, too, wanted to see what made them tick. Luckily for me my conscience reminded me about the conniving nature of the GGE saboteurs and stopped me.

So, the container for the case and files, that are being safely stored inside is going on a journey of 6 billion light years?" John asked.

"We hope so. You know yourself John that we can do our best, yet the trajectory we select could still be compromised by colliding dark matter which could demolish it, or send it off course. It's a 'crap shoot' at best that it doesn't happen," said Natas.

"You're right. I am just a little anxious to return to Earth to see just how far these zealots have gone and if Sam Davis on Mars can contribute any helpful information. Right now, I'm going to find out our proximity to Mars." Pressing an intercom button to the bridge John asked, "How long before reaching Mars?"

Chris came on the intercom and said, "It should take about two and a half hours, John." Gentlemen, if you'll excuse or accompany me, it doesn't matter, I have to go to the medical wing."

"John, we'll meet you on Mars."

"Fair enough. Safe journey then," replied John.

Entering the Med-wing, John stood and watched Julie as she taught the children of the ship their education curriculum. He was impressed. Julie caught him in a sideways glance and smiled. He waved back and was about to leave when two people came up behind him and asked, "Not enough work on the bridge, John?"

Julie was chuckling as she saw Marion and Janet come up behind John. "I thought that was a familiar voice," as he turned to face it. A wifely kiss and hug served as the physical greeting and John asked, "How are things going with research into the extra amino acids for the human DNA systems?"

John's 'gut feelings' on any subject matter never failed him in the past so, he had no reason to believe different now. "Honey, didn't you mention to me when we started out on this venture that Ellis looked kind of peculiar after shaking the hand of the new commander of the CSS?"

"Yes, his look resembled someone who was experiencing déjà vu, John. What's going on?"

"John, something is troubling you but you can't put your finger on it, right?" prodded Marion.

"Look, both Gariff and Natas acted like they knew something, but didn't want to tell me; at least, not yet. And honey, you know

I don't like surprises; at least, not when it comes to extra-terrestrials and their related problems like the recent attacks on us in space. Both Gariff and Natas are too easygoing in agreeing with me, like they were guiding my thinking.

Come with me Jan. I want to speak with Kathy in Astronomy. Thanks, Marion; you've given me an idea. We'll see you later."

"John, what are you thinking about?"

"Jan, you know I love looking at old space exploration tapes or whatever media is available. Well I seem to recall where there was evidence on our moon and the planets Mars and Mercury to the effect that some alien life forms left some edifices, buildings, crashed space ships, *etc.* behind them when they left for whatever reasons. And don't forget the UFO sightings that were cast aside as collateral foolishness upon the dissuading of the so-called authoritative voices of NASA, or the Air Forces and the various government bodies from around the world who contributed to the space programs. Something about "national economies flopping" was the excuse-of-the-day to give to the public."

Arriving at the astronomy department Janet spotted Kathy and Ursula at one of the telescopes. Taking John by the hand they walked over to them.

"Well, John and Janet to what do we owe the honor for this visit?"

"Kathy, I was wondering if you could pull some of your archived information on early discoveries found on our moon and the planets Mercury and Mars?" asked John.

"Did you have anything in mind or do you want to just look for yourself?" prodded Kathy.

"Okay, I'll level with both of you but it stays here with us. Those involved will show their hands sooner or later. We already know Sam Davis has been honest with us and that 'New Washington Square' is built on top of a previous small, alien, encampment. We know the history of people on Earth sighting UFO's and how fast they could travel. We've questioned the building of pyramids in the middle East nations, South, and Central America and Great Britain's 'Stonehenge", China's Great Wall, *etc*. They've tried to explain the strange disappearances of planes and people and the lack of trace evidence. They couldn't explain the discovery in the 22nd century of the alien space craft found in Antarctica. On a need-to-know basis was the excuse given for a place like the U.S. Air Force's Area 51 in Arizona's Sedona desert."

"And so, John, what is all this leading to?" Janet asked.

"It occurs to me that what we have found as far as aliens are concerned is that they may not be so different from us after all. I'm not talking about physical appearance different, rather enhanced, genetic make up due to an environmental habitat. I'm talking about law and order, exploration in space for environmental needs back at home worlds and so on. Those explosive devices sent after us could have been the brainchild of an alien life form already established on Earth, maybe under the guise of a different cultural upbringing.

The GGE views us as a threat to their people, their culture and their religion; why? We suspect with good reason that they will stop at nothing to rid the planet Earth of non-believers. Their youth is encouraged to expose and or exterminate infidels. Why? Is it because we don't subscribe to their culture? Historically that has never worked in the long run. Sooner or later, even the spilling of human blood becomes too much for a person to bear and they no longer feel that it's right.

It's my feeling that some of those UFO sightings were 'cops and robbers' situations or aliens looking for answers to problems back on their home worlds just like we might have to do."

"Cops and robbers, John?" asked Janet, chuckling.

"You know what I mean, love. If Wehttam hadn't turned and fired on us my order to prepare for him or Natas for that matter would have looked mighty ridiculous. It was just a confirmed gut reaction on my part after Ellis watched the recordings of the arbitration proceedings."

"Here's the information you wanted, John and you can use that room over there."

"Thank you, Kathy. Do you have any Edusorb meds?"

"John, you know they are illegal and subject to 3-month jail terms if caught."

"I only need it for this time only. I don't want to cram for an exam or some education reason. And we don't have much time left in case we need to take some action. I know your department must keep some on hand in order that you can perform some lengthy, continuous observations on cosmic phenomena."

"Okay, but you can't use or ask for them if you or Clint just want to stay in the "chair" for prolonged periods of time. They might cause you to react to something that really isn't there. And one more thing John, I am not releasing them for language absorption learning during the training of our personnel for the sabotage investigative procedure."

Kathy unlocked a steel cabinet and pulled a bottle of blue pills out. She gave one to John who saw a stamped impression of 'EDU 10' mg., the pharmaceutical company on one side of the tablet. John went to the room Kathy specified and watched the recordings. When he was finished, he returned them to Kathy and he and Janet left for the bridge. Upon entering the bridge Clinton turned in his chair to greet John.

"John, why do you have a smile on your face like a Cheshire cat?"

"I'll tell you and Clint, after we all talk to Ellis. I want to run something by him first."

"Hey, guy, are you o.k.? You look kind of worried. It's not the wedding, is it?"

"No Clint, I want you and every one else to hear this speculation of mine after I find out something from Ellis." John asked Chris to ensure no one else comes on the bridge.

"Sure, John," Chris replied.

"Now remember, I only have circumstantial evidence information at best. Okay, Ellis, can you recall what happened when you shook hands with the new CSS Commander?"

"Yes, sir. I felt or rather I sensed that I had prior knowledge of him, like déjà vu. Why do you ask?"

"Because you and Julie are human reconstructs Ellis, and out of everybody on board this ship your makeup is from a genetic pool within which your parts could very well have had contact with those parts which are running into the mixes which might contain information from the past.

For example, suppose aliens had landed on Earth millions of years ago for no other reason than to refuel or go shopping for the resources they needed for their ships or their home worlds. The Earth, having come into its own was showing proto-plant life forms and early one-celled lives. Water was pure and the environment was lush. They loved it but duty called and they took off for their home worlds. Meanwhile others who were not so kind left stop over places like Luna City on the moon or the encampment discovered on Mars and head to the Earth. Chance meetings resulted in skirmishes, here or there, that resulted in being left without transport to leave Earth. They lived awhile in various parts of the globe but eventually died out.

Some of the more forward-thinking persons of their races develop a process of reproduction and through evolution humans develop the intelligence to explore space to the extent it's at today. But, wait for it, the prior knowledge and grudges or racial hatred is also passed on down through genetic coding waiting for the right time to make itself known sort of like a mole, or spy, waiting for the right moment."

"John, what did Kathy give you?" Janet asked, mockingly.

"Hang on a moment, Jan," said Ellis. "John, are you trying to get us to infer that life on Earth is the result of alien races who somehow left genetic material behind to evolve into what it is today."

"Exactly."

"But how do you explain the Yetis the so-called abominable snowman?"

"If I was to bury you and Julie somewhere on Earth how would future scientists explain finding you in the same strata as us? They would see that you are a "construct", but they wouldn't know the reason. Best estimates would be as slaves or test beings for diseases or for human perilous duties. In any case you would have the genetic material in you that if the race that left your material returned then they could reap the evolutionary benefits and leave for their various destinations. That is a damn good motive for starting wars, terrorism, or stopping space exploration and therefore any opportunity of chance discovery of past events."

"So, you're saying that if this idea ever got out to the public it would be received as the best entertainment of the century or millennium," said Clinton.

"Straight up my friend. I wanted to run this by you first because I am going to talk to Sam Davis about it when we get to Mars."

"John, after the wedding, please," begged Janet.

Chapter 60

"Well, Natas, do you think John knows?"

"Gariff, you know John better than I do, but from what I've seen of him lately, I don't think there is a computer that could match him. If it wasn't for our emotional makeup, there are some ideas that are scoffed at but shouldn't be. Didn't you tell me about the history of the computer on Earth that the idea of everyone owning one in the future was denounced during a meeting of one of the bigger computer companies?"

"Yes, Natas. So, you think that John might discover that both of our planets have been to his in the past and he might find this out through their DNA research, or Janet might."

"Damn good possibility, I think, Gariff."

"Interplanetary cousins, oh boy." expostulated Gariff and Natas. "And their kids may have children later in their lives. We'll make sure they have a good wedding."

"Sir, Mars is just ahead," Red warned the Captain.

"Put us in a close orbit, Red. Chris, inform the ship we are orbiting Mars and prepare for disembarking for those attending the wedding."

"Yes, Sir," both men said simultaneously. A Martian air-grav vehicle came out to meet them. It had room to board 400 personnel and would return for more. John and Janet got on the vehicle with

Adam and Hertiff and met the Amazonian-statured body guard of Sam Davis. "Good to see you again John, Janet."

"Ramona, meet my son Adam and his fiancée, Hertiff Tterzin."

"Oh, you are Admiral Tterzin's daughter. He was just here with Natas and they left for Sam Davis' office."

"Good," said John. "We'll meet them there as well." The rumbling sound they heard behind them was another Martian air-grav vehicle departing to pick up more passengers to bring to the administration building to attend the wedding.

Entering the building, John and Janet took the familiar route down to Sam Davis' office. He could see their approach as he kept talking to Gariff and Natas. As John and Janet entered they were closely followed by Adam and Hertiff. Sam was introduced by the proud mothers, Mariff and Janet.

"Well, it seems I am going to do one of my more pleasant tasks in marrying your off-springs. This calls for a toast, but first, let me get my wife, Linda, here first. I'm sure your women have a lot to talk about," Sam said, with a knowing wink at John who was sitting beside Gariff.

Suddenly Sam's office door opened and his wife entered in her usual grand flurry. "Sam, why didn't you call me sooner, honey? These ladies want to see what I've done for them preparing for this wedding."

"I'm sorry, darlin', but I was under the impression they" pointing at Adam and Hertiff, "wanted this to be low profile."

"Sam, how could you…?" Linda blustered. "A wedding of this magnitude – interplanetary, let alone intergalactic and two of the most wonderful people going. This shouldn't be treated so trivially. Ladies don't you worry; Sam's been so cynical lately checking on extra-terrestrials … ahem, I didn't mean it that way," said Linda, apologetically.

The men in the room looked down at their footwear as if something had scuffed them and John and Gariff hid a smile while facing each other with a downwards glance.

"Suppose I showed you ladies what I've done regarding the invitations."

"Sounds good to us, Linda," the two mothers said.

Hertiff added, "That's what I want to see as well, Mrs. Davis."

"Call me Linda, Hertiff. I consider you part of my circle of very close friends, like Janet, and your mom, Mariff." Linda showed them the invitation.

Mr. and Mrs. John Marshall of the planet Earth

And

Gariff and Mariff Tterzin of the planet Ffraiteron

Take pleasure in inviting you

To witness the interplanetary marriage ceremony of

Adam Marshall of Earth, to Hertiff Tterzin of Ffraiteron

Given under the ceremomial guidance of

Samuel Davis, Chairman of SETIA,

And Reverend of First Baptist Church of New

Washington Square

On the Planet Mars

At 601 Ontario Street, 11:30 in the morning,

In New Washington,

Mars.

R.S.V.P. -

to Linda Davis, New Washington Square, Mars
by radio telemetry.

"Linda, it's absolutely beautiful; everything I wanted on it. Mom, look at it." Mariff looked at it and was very happy with it. John and Gariff looked at it with Adam; Adam choked ever so slightly.

"Getting cold feet, son?" asked John.

"No, dad. I just want to live up to everyone's expectations."

"Just be yourself, Adam, that's who your lady fell in love with."

"Your dad is right, honey. After all, you've seen how your mom always supports your dad; so, I'll be there for you." Hertiff planted a kiss on Adam for reassurance.

"Well, I think you people all better get some rest tonight as you have a wedding tomorrow at 11:30 a.m.," said Sam.

"Before I go, Sam I want to pick your brain about something."

"Is this private?" John.

"No, but it is confidential. I want Gariff and Natas to hear it as well. Adam can stay if he wants but I suspect he would rather be with Hertiff," John added. The four men remained in Sam's office and listened to John's speculative idea regarding visits by ancient alien life forms. As he talked, Gariff and Natas watched Sam's face as he absorbed John's information.

When John finished, Sam said, "We're glad you have finally come out with this, John, but I think it best if you hear these two gigglers explain."

"John, both Natas and I have been wondering if you could stumble on this information yourself or whether one or both of us would have to nudge you a little. But Sam was contacted by Ffraiteron prior to our meeting and was sworn to secrecy. Your previous mission was hyped as dangerous but the only danger you faced were the three suicide ships while you were enroute to Mars from the COWA Space Station.

John, both the Ralosians and the Ffraiterites had ancient exploration treks of Mars, your moon and Earth. We have also been studying Sagittarius in your Milky Way Galaxy as you call it. What you couldn't put your finger on was who were the bad guys that landed on your planet and through their little skirmishes, marooned themselves on your planet," explained Gariff.

"That's right," agreed Natas.

"So, who do you suspect, John?" asked Sam.

"I don't think it was either of these two, Sam. I think it could have been some beings from Wehttam's planet, 'YI' and some other planetary beings who his conniving ancients pissed off somehow."

"John, let me show you something. Ramona, could you bring us that 'wedding gift' that we set aside for John?"

"Right away, Mr. Davis," replied Ramona. She wheeled in a large, heavy wooden crate sitting on a tilt-type dolly. Setting it down in the middle of the office she then removed the seal on the top edges and pried open the cover to reveal the skeletal remains of beings from the Betelgeuse and Sirius star systems.

"John, it's quite possible that someday your archeologists are going to encounter such bones but unless they have the ability and the technology to dig for the DNA information that is available to us they won't be able to make the connection. Furthermore, if the public keeps fighting the way they are they'll never be in possession of a peaceful future for space exploration. They're close-minded. Religion should never dictate how a nation lives. It causes racism, jealousy and suppressed boiling hatred.

Ergo, sects like the GGE will survive, rule and some of the people will succumb to its beliefs and infidel killing requirements. You and Janet are unique," said Sam.

"Sam, it's more urgent now that we return to Earth and inform COWA of our results."

"John, the Sir Isaac Newton was required to go on this wild goose chase mission, which everyone here already knew the outcome. That is why it is most important that your results get into the hands of COWA. I take it that you have disposed of the case in a timely and safe manner."

"We have, Sam."

"Good, in that case I suggest you gentlemen scurry along and meet up with the women."

"Thanks, Sam," said John.

"Just leave your glasses there on the table and I'll have someone clean up. Even I must get along to bed because I, too, have a busy day tomorrow," said Sam.

Leaving Sam's office, Gariff put his arm around John's shoulder and said, "Seems we could already be related, my friend."

"That's not so bad after all, my friends," chuckled John, which brought a cheer from all three of them.

Turning the corner of the hallway ahead of them was Clinton and Gariff said, "Speaking of the fourth musketeer, look who showed up," said John. "How you doin', cuz?" John asked while laughing. "Come join us."

Chapter 61

The two female parents Mariff and Janet had complimented Linda on what a beautiful job she had done preparing for the wedding including the invitation. After a good night's sleep the bride's mother Mariff, sat with Gariff. Adam's mother Janet, sat with John, while the marriage vows took place. Linda Davis was seated at the church organ's key board playing wedding processional music from Verdi's – "The Grand March" from <u>Aida</u>. Upon reaching the altar area, the music stopped.

The Wedding Vows

<u>Rev. Davis</u>: - **To all those gathered here today, in New Washington Square on the planet Mars, in the Milky Way Galaxy, we are here to witness the joining of these two people from different planets, in spiritual matrimony and take this time to request that if anyone knows of any reason why this ceremony should not take place let that person speak, or indicate by sign now, or forever hold their peace. Having seen none, you may proceed Adam with your promise to Hertiff.**

<u>Adam</u>: - **I, Adam Marshall of the planet Earth, within the Milky Way Galaxy, make this promise to you, Hertiff Tterzin of the planet Ffraiteron, of the Triangulum Galaxy that in sickness, health, planetary conflict, for rich or for poor, right or wrong,**

I shall love, respect, trust, and defend you, honorably, loyally, always, as long as I shall live.

<u>Hertiff</u>: - I, Hertiff Tterzin of the planet Ffraiteron, in the Triangulum Galaxy, known by us as Spiral Galaxy 111, make this promise to you, Adam Marshall, of the planet Earth in the Galaxy you call the Milky Way, that I shall always love, honor, hold, and adore you, in sickness, or in health, for richer or poorer, notwithstanding planetary conflict, honorably, and loyally, as long as I shall live.

(The wedding couple leave to sign the marriage registry; then return to stand again before Rev. Sam Davis.)

<u>Rev. Davis</u>: - Do you Adam Marshall take this woman Hertiff Tterzin to be your lawfully, wedded wife, to have and to hold, to cleave unto you, respect, and forsake all others, to love only her as long as you both shall live? (Puts his marriage ring on the third finger of her left hand.)

<u>Adam</u>: - I do.

<u>Rev. Davis</u>: - Do you Hertiff Tterzin take this man, Adam Marshall to be your lawfully wedded husband, to have and to hold, to cleave only unto him, forsaking all others, to love only him as long as you both shall live?

<u>Hertiff</u>: - I do. (Puts her marriage ring on the third finger of his left hand.)

<u>Rev. Davis</u>: - Then by the power vested in me, and by the exchanging of these rings, I now pronounce you husband and wife. You may kiss your bride.

The Marshalls kiss, turn to face their witnesses, while Reverend Davis announces, "Ladies and Gentlemen, it is indeed a great honor to present to you, Mr. and Mrs. Adam Marshall!" A huge round of applause was heard while Linda Davis played organ music. Janet and Mariff wipe away tears of joy.

Linda, like John Marshall loved history, especially musical history. Linda loved country pop music by female vocalists like Shania Twain, who was born in Windsor, Ontario, Canada, in 1965. Adam and Hertiff had Linda play Shania's rendition of "*Forever and For Always*" while they signed the marriage registry, in front of their parents and two witnesses, Kathy and Clinton Davidson; and again, as they turned to the audience of witnesses, during the recessional, she played Shania Twain's "*From This Moment On*".

"John, do you have any tissues?" Janet asked him. Kathy Davidson, overhearing the request tapped Jan on the shoulder and handed her a tissue. Both female parents were occasionally wiping a tear of joy from their eyes as they followed with their husbands in behind the newly married couple.

Mariff quietly said to her husband, "You realize this is going to make the 'personals columns' on both planets?"

"Hell, yes, honey. Interplanetary gossip rags, and maybe intergalactic news as well," added Gariff. Gariff had no idea how prophetic his reply was going to be a reality.

The news of the wedding hit the 'Personals Section' of the newspapers and other media back on Earth and Ffraiteron and Ralos. Unfortunately, the media loved to sell newspapers so the headlines on some papers read: -

- **Interplanetary Marriage Takes Place on Mars**
- **Ffraiterite Marries Earthling by Earthling Reverend**
- **Wedding on Mars Witnessed by Aliens**
- **Earthling Performs Wedding Ceremony of Human to Ffraiterite**
- **Does Interplanetary Marriage Have Intergalactic Implications?**

The last headline appeared on Ralos, Ffraiteron and newspapers on Earth. All three leaders John, Gariff, and Natas were steaming angry over that last one. This headline included the news that the

Ffraiterite girl who married the Earthling was also related to the leader who was complicit in the destruction of a third ship from another planet that was involved in a planetary trade disagreement. The groom was the son of the other arbiter. This news alone was enough to spark the anger between the two planets involved, the YI's and the Ralosians.

The planetary council on YI decided that it was quite evident that since their fleet admiral's ship had been destroyed the Ralosians were no longer going to be trusted and that two new enemies had betrayed Wehttam after the arbitration procedure. Those enemies were the Ffraiterite Admiral Gariff Tterzin and the Earthling leader John Marshall. The advertisement for a new Admiral to lead the YI armada on an inter-galactic space hunt for the two new enemies evoked a frenzy of sweaty, macho applicants for this very enviable position. Their old enemy Natas of Ralos seemed to fade to a subsequent enemy status compared to the others.

John, Gariff and Natas now had good reason to constantly look over their shoulders, yet they showed no concern despite the effect of the headlines appearing on the planet's medias. Of course, the fact that Wehttam's ship fired first was omitted. That fact wouldn't help the sale of newspapers or any other news media.

"Gentlemen, allowing for acceleration, travel time and deceleration I think we best be on our way to Earth," said John to his two comrades.

"John, we'll see you in a 500-mile high Earth orbit and we'll keep up the training enroute," they replied.

"Good; I'm going to talk to Clinton and Ellis. Later, guys," John said, bidding them farewell.

Entering the Newton's bridge, John said, "Clint, if everyone's on board we might as well head for home. The other two ships are going to orbit the Earth at an altitude of 500 miles, so that means three of us will be in that trajectory. Ellis if we want to maximize availability to our ground investigators how far apart and at what velocity should we be travelling.

"Sir, may I suggest the three ships launch shuttlecrafts, fore and aft, to their Galaxial cruisers to maximize availability."

"Good idea," said John, knowing Ellis was already calculating some numbers mentally.

"Sir, my calculations suggest a velocity of 754 km/min. to maintain spacing and altitude."

"Thank you, Ellis. Chris notify the other two ships of this and Spike input this information for use on our arrival." Keeping his finger near his intercom button John contacted Jules in the arsenal. "Jules, when we arrive at Earth we will be orbiting at an altitude of 500 miles and travelling at a velocity or 754 km/min. Could you advise Niles of these figures to input the data into his target-range-finding computers?"

"Will do," John.

"Clint, ask Commander Sam Sherwood to sit in the chair for me. Janet, Gariff, Mariff, Natas and I, will be on the first landing crafts so we can go to the Council and advise them of our observations of the Triangulum Galaxy's black hole. Please ensure that the newly weds are on standby in case we need them. Other than that, Clint, the ship is yours, and Sam's."

"John, I would appreciate your approval of this list of investigators I would like to present to the two ship captains."

John read the list and noted Julie and Ellis were at the top.

"Are you going to advise those two, pointing out their names, to be team leaders?" John asked Clinton.

"Team-West and Team-East," Clinton said, indicating with his right index finger.

"That's excellent, Clinton. They're completely at home with languages and customs in both areas of the Atlantic. See if Gariff and Natas can be of further assistance in that regard."

"Chris, see if you can contact their ships' Captains again regarding John's suggestion to have some team leaders having Ellis and Julie's abilities."

"Anything else, Clint?" asked Chris. Clint looked at John who just shook his head 'no'.

"Not now, Chris," replied Clint. "How long now, helm?" asked Clint.

"Sir, we can be in a geo-orbital trajectory in 45 minutes," Spike answered.

"And we're going to be well above the altitudes of the Solar Telescope and COWA's space station?" Clinton asked to be sure.

"Yes, sir," Spike said, "by at least 125 miles at the closest."

"Good, because we will need the maneuverability for all of our shuttlecraft transfers and those travelling between the ships."

"Sir?"

"Yes, Chris."

"Are you okay with the call signs as: -

- EarthGCNewton -100 for the Newton

- EGC – 101A for shuttlecraft one outbound to Earth

- EGC – 101B for shuttlecraft one inbound to the Newton

- EGC – 201A for shuttlecraft two outbound to Earth

- EGC – 201B for shuttlecraft two inbound for the Newton

"Make it so Chris, but the Newton stands steady on the orbital arc for everything. Furthermore, Chris, drop the letter designations while they are occupying their positions on their orbital trajectories."

"Aye, Captain; I'll inform the pilots of those crafts. Also, they should all be prepped by now."

"Good, because I think navigation is about ready to announce entry into the Geo-orbital trajectory. Spike?"

"Two minutes, sir for point of insertion," Spike said.

"Navigation, how are the other two ships doing?"

"Captain, the TGCTriang is following our lead and Natas' ship is right behind it."

"Thank you, Diedra," said Clinton. Continuing, Clinton asked Chris to co-ordinate with the other two ships and their shuttlecrafts regarding call sign designations. He further suggested that all targeting computers be networked for further ground crew defensive support. Chris received confirmation on both items and was given all their call sign numbers.

TGCTriang designations were noted and carried with them.

Natas' ship from Ralos would be known as Srennis' GC 100.

"Clint, I'm going to scoot over to the launch area and meet the others who are accompanying me to the surface. Enroute I'm going to get to the bottom of what was causing Ellis' déjà vu feeling with the new CSS commander."

"Use tact there, buddy; it sounds ominous to me."

"Don't worry, I'll stay in touch and remember, if I use Morse code I will be in the presence of someone, or something, that we don't want overhearing."

"Okay, John and God speed."

"Thanks."

Chapter 62

When John arrived at the Newton's launch deck, the two shuttle-crafts were prepped and already had Janet, Ellis, two of Gariff's best linguists and two of Natas' best linguists, and the pilot on-board. John requested two security personnel as well. Already clad in his transfer suit and Saunders life belt, John sat next to Janet. The shuttles were to be launched from the gooseneck hanger areas located just forward of the main transfer deck door where all personnel embarked, prisoners, visitors alike. The defence area where the laser cannons were located was forward of the exits for the shuttle crafts. The prow or head of the gooseneck was at the very front and was the Newton's escape ship, detachable from the main geodesic-shaped body of the galactic cruiser. It had a capability of travelling 100 light years, a distance no one volunteered to check out.

"Honey, I feel like I'm leaving our second home." Laughter was heard.

"John, we were all just thinking and saying that very thing." John continued, "Honey, I had Julie board the other shuttle so she could get started with her ground team but I want us to start with the Space Station's new commander. I want Ellis to see if he has that feeling when we came aboard last time. I know you have an uncanny ability of being able to read people, so we can watch while Ellis talks with him. Sound good to you?" John asked.

"John, you know I have always supported you, but if you're right with this idea. We could be in a real bind."

"How so, Jan?"

"Because the station will be without a commander for a time and Earth will know about it right away. That could be the trigger for a global warning for the GGE sabotage group."

"I've already counted on that possibility, honey. Ellis can be dropped there and with his capability of mimicry, he can duplicate the commander's voice and the COWA ground crew won't know the difference. We can stop at Harding's airfield and pick up a replacement on our return," said John.

"He's another one John. Don't you remember, he sounded ..."

"... kind of funny when we visited him last," John said, finishing her thought. Yes, but I would rather handle a criminal investigation over attempting to exorcise an ideal any day. I feel that General Harding has been coerced lately for some hitherto unknown reason - family, space program, position in SETIA, *etc.*"

"We could introduce him to Gariff or Natas and watch his reaction John, because I don't think he quite believes the extent to which alien life forms exist. He also doesn't know about the gifts Gariff imparted to us from our return trip in meeting the COSMIC SEEDER."

"John, I have a surprise for you." This caused John to turn his head and quickly glance at her abdomen. Seeing his look, Jan said, "No, I'm not pregnant, but I do have some important research news for you."

"Do tell me, hon," he said with his anticipation well suppressed.

"Those two genes, mentalline and endurine, that Gariff gave us have been researched in the lab and so far, have proved invaluable to the point where we're ready to start clinical trials. The twentieth generation of animal species tested has out-lived their natural life spans by 4 times as much and, more importantly, have shown a learning of some procedure, movement, or sensory perception that the original species went through. The genetic research staff can't wait to start clinical testing."

"Jan, you may disagree with me on this but I think genetic testing ought to be done on humans that are cosmos bound for the rest of their lives. With the resources and diversity of life styles available to our race I'm afraid we could start another idealistic "perfect race" problem, like history recorded in the twentieth century and, in a way, has been reborn into a religion with the GGE people."

"I see what you mean John, since we can't control their lives the mere fact of being human is fraught with our own weaknesses like greed, envy, pursuit of wealth, and power, *etc.*"

"Exactly; we can only hope to cope with those problems living in an environment so open like Earth's, and resources that seem forever renewable. In an enclosed environment, such as a galactic cruiser, there is a greater possibility of success in survival of life on board the ship. But if it can be demonstrated that mankind could live with each other and the environment in an ecologically successful manner, then those new genes could be tried on Earth."

"John, that's like asking everyone to treat Earth like a gigantic ship travelling through space. There are people living on Earth that can't conceive of their next meal's whereabouts, never mind living the next day."

"Like I said the last time, dear, *them who have, have forgotten them that don't.* You know, out of sight, out of mind, speaking of which, we've arrived at the space station. Ellis, when we greet the new commander, don't get taken in by his civility and gentleness of manner."

"Sir? I don't understand why. I see it now. Okay, John, but I want you to know that if I say anything that has to do with sport fishing I'm signaling you to know that my déjà vu needs reconciling."

"No problem, Ellis. We'll join in at that time."

Since the hatch to the space station was opening, John, Janet, Ellis and two security guards made their way through it. The commander was waiting for them in the central 'control module'. Greeting each by shaking hands the commander said, "Welcome aboard. To what do we owe the honor of such a distinguished visit?" Ellis shook his hand last and Lt. Commander Makeen Karzai hesitated before letting go. He asked, "Ellis, have we met before? Something seems to remind me. Ellis, have you ever been to Lashkar Gah by the Halmand River?"

"Yes, sir, to watch a soccer game in the stadium with some people I know. Why?"

"Because when someone was trying to get past me to his seat he was thrown off balance when an explosion occurred. I think that someone was you," replied Makeen.

Ellis took a good hard look at Makeen and said, "You were wearing a cap which supported Italy's soccer team and went to hit me because when I fell I accidentally crashed into your sisters in the row ahead of us. Also, if I recall correctly you stayed at the Marriott Hotel in room 411."

"That's right. Ellis, how did you know?"

"I knew because I was in room 413 and heard you talking all night. John, this man is a CIA operative who is working for SETIA."

Hearing this information, John asked for the communication code for greeting and Makeen gave the right answer. Ellis asked Makeen if he had met Lt. General WJ Harding at the Florida Air Force Base, 45th Space Wing.

"Oh, sure, Bill meets and greets everyone who's going to spend time on COWA's Space Station. I believe he must be plying us with some sort of sedative preparation he calls lemonade, ha, ha, ha."

"Yeah, we can relate with that," Ellis responded, "but has he ever talked about his fishing exploits?" Ellis prodded.

"He was telling me about his recent vacation in one of Canada's Recdome areas where he went marlin fishing," said Makeen, "but I said I had to depart for an early trip to the station and needed to prepare so I excused myself and left. Why?"

John looked at Ellis intensely as if trying to read his mind. Using his left hand Ellis reached behind his waist and pulled out a nylon zip-tie while John standing to one side of Makeen grabbed his closer wrist and twisted it to meet the other wrist. Ellis slipped the zip tie over Makeen's wrists and told him he was under arrest.

Makeen countered with, "What for?"

John answered and said, "Terrorism, Makeen, terrorism, and for that we can hold you indefinitely because of your present location. Furthermore, I believe you already know your rights, correct?"

"Yeah, yeah."

"Makeen, you should've done better research on Lt. General Harding because he can't stand angling. He prefers a simple wooden row boat floating in a quiet lake where he can bait or fly cast with his fishing rods," said Ellis. John called the station's crew members to inform them of their commander's arrest and requested they inform 1) their mission control and, 2) contact the Newton for a prisoner pick up.

Lieutenant Allie McGarver complied with John's request. John and Ellis remained on board until the pick up was made. "Ellis, I was going to have you stay behind to command the station but I need you with me. Allie, will you be alright until a replacement arrives for Commander Karzai?"

"Sure, Mr. Marshall; if I get into a bad situation, I can always let the Newton know and they'll help me."

"My dear, on that you can definitely rely and thank you for your co-operation."

After expressing his gratitude John turned and said to Ellis in confidence, "We're staying because until Makeen is picked up I don't want to leave the crew exposed to him, cuffed or otherwise. I would guess he already has had a substantial educational background in being able to persuade anyone into helping him."

"I'm with you on that matter, John," said Ellis.

"Mr. Marshall, the 'pickup' ship will be here in 10 minutes, sir," said Allie.

Ellis looked out a viewing window and saw the ship pulling into a docking position. The COWA flag and Newton Logo and call numbers were easily seen. The two security guards accompanying John and Ellis admitted the prison guards to the station and explained to them to handle the commander with care. He could quite easily overpower them and escape. When they arrived at the Newton they were to strip-search him again, put him into isolation in prison garb and restrict movement.

The guards followed John's orders. John confirmed his wishes by contacting Clinton. Having done this, he turned to Ellis and said, "Let's get back to Janet and scoot down to see General Harding."

Chuckling, Ellis said, "On your three, John." Heh, heh.

"I'm glad you see something humorous pal, because quite frankly, that s.o.b. scares the shit out of me."

"I know John, but you've got him tied up like a pit bull with rabies."

"If he gets free while he's on the Newton, old friend, we're all going to wish there was no space travel or ships to do it in. Using some info that Clinton and I just talked about that man is a danger to mankind. I hope Marion and human resources have broken him by the time we get back.

Pilot, could you put us down right on the base landing strip, close to the admin bldg.?"

"No problem Mr. Marshall, sir," replied pilot Henry Sykes.

"Ellis, both Jan and I noticed something peculiar about Harding during our conversational briefing with him. If you can pick up on it also, don't hesitate to let us know as tactfully as you can."

"No problem, John." They walked to the Admin building and talked, "Honey, what do you suspect?" asked Jan.

"I don't really know for sure dear, but I wouldn't discount some sort of coercion. That last briefing left me quite cold, with a matter-of-fact type of sensation; like he was just going through the motions."

"I agree, John, that's my feeling as well."

"Well we're about to find out love, because we have arrived." Alighting from the shuttlecraft, they met Bill at the bottom of the stairway. Shaking hands with WJ again John noticed a cut just above his right eyebrow leading towards his right temple. John jokingly asked, "So, Bill, what does the door look like after you banged into it?"

Following John's gaze, Lt. General Harding went to put his left hand up by the cut and chuckled, "Splinters, old friend, splinters. I left one of the cupboards open behind the bar and forgot about it when I turned to watch the telecast of your son's wedding. Hertiff is gorgeous. If my wife ever divorces me I'm going to get me one of those women from the Triangulum Galaxy," he said, laughing.

Hearing this both Ellis and John moved to each side of their SETIA friend, WJ Harding and John put their hands on Bill's back guiding him towards the step ramp of the shuttlecraft. Unperturbed by the movement WJ kept on talking about all the current events since the Marshalls left on their investigative exploration of the black hole in the Triangulum Galaxy. When they were inside the craft, Ellis took over holding WJ while John moved to stand in front of him and put a finger to his lips to gesticulate "quiet, but keep talking" to which Harding obliged. John quickly retrieved some old clothes for Bill and indicated to him to put them on.

Ellis retrieved an electronic wand from the nearby entranceway and ran down WJ's uniform. The beacon light started flashing, indicating WJ's uniform had been bugged. After donning his casual duds and going outside with John and Ellis, WJ practically broke down from the release of pressure he had just been relieved from. Grabbing John and Ellis, he asked, "I'm so glad you noticed. Now, can you send some people to my place to ensure my family is safe?"

The seriousness of this situation hit John in his gut because this was now the number two man in SETIA and one of his best friends. John was concerned about how long it had been going on. WJ was also wondering what initiated John and Ellis into thinking that he had been "bugged."

John said, "Oh, Bill, you're our friend and when you pointed with your left hand to a wound on your face and said you banged into a cupboard door that you left open, we knew right away that you were misleading us for some reason because your cupboards are sliding doors, not hinged."

"Well guys, I am ever so grateful. Now if something can be done about my family's safety I will be in your debt forever."

"WJ, have you ever discussed with your wife the possibility of aliens befriending us and their willingness to help us with our problems such as stopping these saboteurs?"

"No, but I have discussed 'work' with her. Why do you ask?"

Ellis looked at his watch and up in the sky and said to WJ, "Well, she's about to meet a Newton crew member and a person from Ffraiteron."

"From where?" WJ queried, looking at John.

"From Ffraiteron, WJ," chimed John, sporting a big grin on his face.

"He, or it won't frighten her, will he?"

"Don't worry WJ. I too was bewildered by not knowing the first time we were to meet. But then again, they were stunned with us the first time because they thought we looked like fish because of the vast expanses of water on Earth. Trust among our three races has developed into a real interplanetary friendship. All Newton crew members would be proud to refer to the Ffraiterites and Srennis from Ralos as our siblings in the Universe."

"John, the teams from SGC 100 and TGCS 100 have discovered one of the GGE launch pad areas along with an armory plant and storage area in, ("say again Sam," said Ellis, while holding his right ear) the desert about 200 km North-northeast of the triple border point of Saudi Arabia, Yemen and Oman."

"Ask him if the armory and pad are dug into the land and hidden from over head."

"Yes, sir, they are."

"Newton, did you get a read on what Ellis found out?"

Clint answered, "Loud and clear John, "and Jules has a direct bead on their co-ordinates John."

"Good, tell Jules to take it out and the surrounding 5 km area."

John, Ellis and WJ watched as the Newton, and her two shuttle-crafts, all fired simultaneously from their 500-mile altitude perch, lighting up the Eastern sky like a huge lightening bolt. The curvature of the Earth prevented any further view. John knew this would cause ripples everywhere.

Clint told John the targeted area had been destroyed. The other ground teams nearby had moved in closer to provide back up as needed. Their credit cards were good no matter where they went and could obtain the latest air cars available, with all the travelling luxuries any driver would want. *Ergo*, paved roadways were not a problem, nor traffic jams an obstacle. They preferred overland travel anyways. Particularly the teams who received the assignments to cover the remote areas like Antarctica and the arid desert areas Earth had to offer. Ellis was checking in on those teams to monitor their progress. John called the Newton to get a connection to his mother's work or wherever she happened to be at this moment. Anyone observing them driving, would be thinking to themselves damn speeders and just ignore them to the teams' benefits.

"John?"

"Yes, Clint."

"I have Angélique on the line for you."

"Mom, what's the sixth decimal place number of pi?" If she doesn't hesitate I'll know she's alright John thought.

She said, "6 or 2," depending. What's up? Are you OK?"

"Yes, mom. Could you do me a favor and pick up WJ's family and take them to a safe house now like right now? Hold them there until we contact you."

"Sure; I'm on my way." As a top member of SETIA's secret police discussion over a phone would never take place, if ensuing a coded intro like John gave his mom. John turned back to WJ.

"Thanks, John. No more lemonade for you, being that I owe you a favor, ha, ha," said WJ Harding, very gratefully.

"No problem, Bill. You must come up with a replacement commander for COWA's space station. Turns out the last one you sent, was a CIA-trained double operative of the United States."

"John, it's not just the United States if I'm hearing this right," said Ellis, "but we better let Jan in on this as well."

"What are you hearing Ellis?" John asked.

"WJ, about how far is it to the nearest COWA location?" asked Ellis.

"About 2700 miles, Ellis, why?"

"John, I've just learnt that the world's water supply has been contaminated and all the ground teams have reported seeing dead or dying plant and animal life everywhere and the ocean currents are soon going to be carrying the contaminant along the American eastern seashores."

"Okay Ellis, let's locate Janet and boot it to Callao, Peru, John," chimed WJ.

"Callao, Ellis. Tell her we have to go to Callao, A.S. A. P.!"

"She's coming now, John," Ellis said, as they looked up toward administration and saw her running towards them. They boarded the waiting shuttlecraft and told the pilot to take them to Callao, Peru immediately.

"Yes, sir!" he said picking up on John's urgency.

Chapter 63

After getting in touch with the Newton, John instructed Clinton, "Tell them not to drink any water. It is toxic and extremely lethal. Send water to them."

Looking at Jan he read her quizzical expression and explained, "Honey, we don't know how nor what but plant and animal life is dying in the oceans and it's going global because of the currents. We need the Council's approval to begin research on developing a counter measure."

"John, it's become worse than we thought. The oceans when they evaporate are recycling the water vapor as rain but not, I repeat, not chemically detaching from the contaminant molecules. Some of our teams have noticed dead or dying animal and plant life in areas far from ocean waters!" Ellis said, confirming John's urgent concern. John asked the pilot if he could fly any faster and whether he could give him a secure line to COWA in Callao, Peru.

"Sir, we'll be there in ten minutes," he replied.

"Good, then could you let them know we need a 'hearing' for a global emergency problem?" John pressed.

"John, we have to obtain approval from COWA for the counter measures but they will not give it to us if we can't give them a built-in date of obsolescence," urged Jan.

"Let me handle the persuasion love. Just assure me there will be an end-date, because if we wait for lab and clinical test results the

Earth's surface is going to be covered with decomposing plant and animal remains. Plus, include toxic water and the slow destruction of our atmosphere due to carbon dioxide and other chemical build-ups in the air."

"John, we are going to need help beyond what we humans can accomplish. I need you to talk to Gariff and Natas about this latest development and see if we can recruit some scientists who wouldn't mind staying on Earth to do some research with us. You know it is going to take some time."

"How much time, Jan?"

"It all depends on what we find that has polluted the world's watery ecosystems, and the death projections based on the data found. It could be weeks; it could be years; but it must be accurate for us to introduce into the global ecosystem."

"Janet, I guess I was looking at a quick fix, but that's what happened with DDT back in the 20th century. Long-term analyses revealed how it affected the ecosystems back then. I'll talk to Gariff and Natas for us and get some research teams set up. Right now, let's go before the Council and present some reasonable solutions for them. You feel up to it because they don't respond well to blame-oriented causes as far as nations are concerned?"

"Let's get in there and talk to the America's members and see if we can get a hearing," said Janet. "I'll look for an opening for you so you can explain the urgency but I know you won't mention anything about our investigative teams and the GGE."

"Don't worry honey I won't. I'll get Ellis to carry on with our plans while we're before the Council, okay?" Walking towards the door of the Council's building, they were stopped by two armed guards who were on access control duty. After a quick check of their identities they were admitted and told the location of the representatives' offices for which they expressed their gratitude and entered the building. Ellis departed and contacted Gariff and Natas to carry out the Marshalls' wishes regarding some research teams.

Looking at the office doors in the hallway corridor they located Arsenio Chavez's office and entered. They were greeted by his secretary and explained the reason for their visit as well as its urgency. She invited them to have a seat while she located Señor Chavez by page. He appeared 1½ minutes later and immediately rushed them into his office and said, "No calls, Wanita, please."

"This is obviously a matter of the utmost urgency to have the 'Chair of COSSIOS' in my office with her husband. What can I do for you?"

"Sir, John and I have returned from space after performing a mission for the Council and have discovered some disturbing ecosystem results that have global significance of extreme urgency!"

Interrupting Janet, Señor Chavez said, "Let me get my partner from South America in here to hear this as well. Wanita, could you ask Antonio to come into the office on a matter of global urgency?"

"Yes, sir," said Wanita.

"So, how was your space trek?" asked Señor Chavez.

"Unrevealing, sir," said John, "as speculated by all the astronomical scientists despite what their instruments indicated," said John.

"Good, because I was one who voted against the journey," said Chavez, looking at the doorway that had just opened to admit Antonio Melo. The Marshalls looked at him.

"But I was one who voted for the trek Mr. Marshall, more to turn the tide of cosmic thought regarding the insinuation that a fundamental law of physics was being broken. What's up Arsenio?" Antonio asked. "John and Janet, it's open to you," said Arsenio.

Both reps sat back while John and Janet explained. "Sirs, itemizing the problems we list them as: -

- The black hole in the Triangulum Galaxy was not doing what astronomical evidence was indicating;

- Two alien races resembling humans had befriended the Marshalls' while on this trek;

- The marriage event of a daughter of one of the aliens to Adam Marshall, their son;

- The betrayal of COWA's space station commander to Earth;

- The constant attempts of the GGE's destruction of their space station;

- The constant attempts of this very same GGE faction to destroy any country's efforts regarding space exploration;

- The GGE's ability to launch ships and/or weaponry to destroy the Lunar educational facilities as well as the Recreational/ Cosmic Viewing areas in the Sea of Tranquility;

- The frequent attempts on New Washington Square on the planet Mars;

- And finally, their current attack on Earth's Global ecosystem;

- And the Marshall's explanation towards a global solution which would involve enlisting the help of their alien friends currently orbiting the Earth as they spoke, along with the Newton."

The last bit of information really perked up their hearing.

"John, I take it they have weaponry on their ships," inquired Tony and Arsenio simultaneously. Reading their facial expressions of concern. Jan jumped into the talks.

"Gentlemen, please they will not use the weaponry, unless directed by a crew member from the Newton. They have pinpoint

David L. Pritchard

accuracy, and if you would feel better we can demonstrate outside. I just want to echo my mandate's requirement regarding the use of any alien weaponry within the confines of our solar system," expostulated Janet, in support of her husband's explanation.

"Good, let's go to the roof for the demo, so we can talk convincingly to the rest of the council," Tony said. Arsenio agreed with him. Arriving at the entrance to the roof, they explained their purpose to the armed guard, instructing him that they wanted no further admittance for a few minutes. He agreed, opened the door and instructed them to fasten their safety belts to a roof connection.

They complied and exited to the roof. John commented on the wind coming in from the Pacific Ocean noticing the gulls didn't even have to flap their wings. He thought, 'oh, to be free' and placed his hand over the com-link in his right ear to better hear Clint.

"Newton, if you are tracking me, ask your gunners how many fingers am I showing?"

"Three fingers, sir, of your right hand." John recognized the voice of "Bullseye" and observed that Jan was allowing the two Council reps to overhear.

"Now how many, Tommy?"

"Sir, three fingers, a thumb, and a tennis ball, speared by a pen," Tommy answered sounding kind of nervous, speculating what John was going to ask him to do.

John smiled while looking at the reps and then asked, "Tommy what is your altitude and location relative to mine?"

"Sir, please don't ask me to do what I think you're going to say," Tommy pleaded.

"Stay calm, 'Bullseye', I have complete faith in you, and Niles' targeting-computer system but I need you to do this, okay? So, where are you?" pressed John.

"Sir, I'm 675 miles from you and moving away at many miles per second!" said Tommy nervously. Jules, his commander was standing beside him.

336

"Tommy shoot the tennis ball only, just the tennis ball."

Jules comforted Tommy with his hand on Tommy's left shoulder and nodded to go ahead and do it. Jan and the two reps stayed still and watched John holding the tennis ball; when down from above they saw a bolt of energy vaporize the tennis ball without touching the pen that John was holding it with. Breathing a huge sigh of relief Janet walked to her husband and wrapped her arms around his arm which was just holding the pen with the tennis ball. Chuckling to himself John eyeballed Antonio and Arsenio examining the roof top area where the tennis ball might have been and could see no evidence of a sudden blast of high energy.

"Well, Mr. Marshall, the dictionary now has another meaning for the word impressive! And we are impressed."

"Sirs, sideshow aside I had this done because of what we might have to do to impress the GGE people, to support any military threat, or confrontation, in trying to arrest these people. As we talk right now they have somehow polluted the world's water supply such that life, plant and animal, of all eco-systems is dying. Sick and infirmed humans haven't got a chance in hell of survival. We need you to have the confidence to address the Council's General Assembly to authorize a method of research and implement a resolution," said John. They returned to the door to go back inside.

Jan added, "Until you get approval Sirs, nothing will be said about this matter or demonstration."

"We just want to understand one thing; this is not contrived to retaliate for their misguided reasons for killing off planetary life or an attempt to dissuade them from their ideology, is it," pressed Antonio Melo, the representative from South America.

"No sirs. It is an attempt to get the nations of the world to realize their cultures, beliefs and ideology is theirs and theirs alone. Enforcement of those beliefs, cultures and ideology onto people of another nation should not and will not be tolerated," replied John.

"Furthermore, it would do the Council well to understand there are extra-terrestrial implications here which, we already know will be beneficial to mankind as far as Earth is concerned. They have already proven to us the advantage of their friendship," John added.

Both reps wanted to hear more about this latter aspect of their demonstration during the Marshall's visit. Enroute to Arsenio Chavez's office Janet used her com-link to contact the Newton and request the chief medical officers of both ships along with Marion to meet them in Callao as soon as possible. She then requested Julie, Adam and Ellis to join them as well.

Back in Señor Chavez's office they were invited to have a seat while John and Janet related the advantages of this extra-terrestrial friendship. Meanwhile, Arsenio said to his secretary, "Wanita, could you get the Council's Secretary General on the phone for me and stress the urgency of this matter?"

"Yes sir, right away," she replied.

Sitting at his desk Arsenio said, "So, Jan, John, tell us about Earth's new friends from the cosmos." Just at that moment Wanita buzzed through to advise Arsenio the Council's Secretary General was on the holophone. "Thank you Wanita," said Arsenio, "give me a secure holophone line dear, please."

Seated around Arsenio's desk everyone had a clear, unobstructed view of the caller. "So, Arsenio, and Antonio, what's this urgent pressing matter that you two have come up with?" asked Ronaldo Bessborough.

"Ron, Mr. and Mrs. Marshall have discovered an active worldwide catastrophe."

"Go on, Arsenio, I'm listening."

"The world's water supply has been made toxic and is killing off all life from all four kingdoms – animal, plant, bacterial and fungi." At that moment, Marion was admitted into the office with her two counter C.M.O.'s from Ffraiteron and Ralos. They were quickly introduced to Arsenio, Antonio and Ronaldo. Arsenio continued his story to the Secretary General and invited John and Janet to join in. John and Janet explained how they came to meet three alien races from their previous trek into space and how it is continuing with the two friendlier races from Ffraiteron and Ralos. He was updated by Janet who spoke about the destruction of the global environment which was underlined by the Ffraiterite chief medical officer, Dr. Jjerzit Smathsir, who underlined Janet's assertions by giving the secretary a timeline of an irreversible beginning date for research.

Fortunately, the Ralosian CMO, Gremelsin Nitasin added, "Sirs, with your cooperative research approval we should be able to come up with a resolution within six of your months and begin clinical testing. Based on that success we can develop counter measures for the world. That should stop the destruction of your global ecosystem."

"Antonio and Arsenio, I am calling for an emergency meeting of the general assembly for Tuesday of next week. Bring your motions to the floor at that time." Ronaldo turned his head slightly to the right and said, "Shirley, put out an emergency member all-call to convene next Tuesday."

"Yes sir. Do you want acknowledgement to the E-letter?"

"Yes, Shirley. Okay, John, Janet, glad to see you both returned safel but right now I want to know a little more about this problem."

"Which one, Ronaldo; the ecosystem, or the people that caused it?" asked John.

"The people that caused it," said Ronaldo.

"Sir, our previous mission," Jan touched John's arm to take over explaining, "involved our going into space to meet an alien race who had summoned us. While enroute we were accosted by three suicide ships and luckily for us, and some good shooting on my husband's part, we made it out alive met the alien race and have been friends ever since.

Our son Adam married the daughter of their leader. We have managed to receive gifts from them which we could never develop on our own at least for another few centuries. Moreover, we have since befriended another race known as the Srennis from the planet Ralos. Combined, we have a scientific research team who could very well come up with a resolution to our problem in a very short time."

"You paint a picture of forgiveness Janet, but don't you want to seek revenge against these GGE people?"

"Sir, truthfully, if this was done in a school playground setting I would get a gang together and wipe them out; but I am now an adult who chooses where to live and under what conditions of social engineering exists there. Ideology can not be wiped out by force; people die, but their culture lives on. It's easy to disarm people but you must dissuade their thinking if you are ever to change them from their cultural upbringing."

John's hand squeezed Jan's just a little tighter. "Sir, I would like to explain to the members of the General Assembly, our thoughts on this matter and give hope for a quick resolution."

"Good; in that case, during our meeting you can press your recognition button and I shall recognize you right away."

"Thank you, Ronaldo, but I will bring some guests along with my husband."

"Those being whom?" he asked.

"Your Excellency, we wish to present to the Assembly Earth's new found Alien friends, Admiral Gariff Tterzin from the planet Ffraiteron in the Triangulum Galaxy, and Admiral Natas LeDeve from the planet Ralos, near Sirius, in the constellation Canis Major."

"Then let me introduce you as the Chair of COSSIOS returning from recent treks into space and your latest findings upon your return to Earth. Sound good to you both, Jan, John?"

"Thank you, your Excellency," they said, smiling while they said farewell to his hologram.

"Well," said Arsenio, "looks like you are going to have the ears of the world. We hope they give 100% cooperation because this is, indeed, a global emergency at any stage of its affect."

Chapter 64

After leaving Arsenio's office, the Marshalls were on the way to the assembly hall when they saw Ellis running towards them. Arsenio and Antonio kept on walking, each accompanied by their aides. Going up to Janet and John, Ellis spoke in a low voice saying, "It's worse than we thought. The investigative teams have reported and confirmed the following: -

- There are some yachts tying up in some ports in the Seychelles and dumping some chemicals overboard when coming into dock;

- These yachts, say the residents, have been doing this for two weeks;

- The currents in the area are taking these chemicals out to the open seas where they are spread in both directions, East and West;

- And, although it's only been two weeks, the equatorial weather has cooperated with their dumping such that rains have brought down poisonous water as far West and South where it has already affected food chains in the tropics.

"By how much, so far, Ellis?"

"John, Janet, apparently the African and Amazonian rain-forested areas have had their food chain cycles interrupted so badly, that the

top predators are now feeding on human lives in villages, towns and cities."

"Ellis, I want you to take a man with you to the military attaché in the North American Embassy for COWA. Tell him to go on military 'Alert' and await orders from COWA. Now, go. Jan, whoever these members are within the GGE, it's not enough to simply wipe out life on this planet, but they want to start a war as well and stand by, while some countries receive the blame possibly to make them seem to be the devil we know, rather than the devil we don't know."

"We better get into the hall, John, immediately."

"John, Janet, we're here with you," said Marion, running with Gariff, and Natas." Adding, almost breathlessly, "Their CMO's are behind us."

"Good, we'll advise the guards at the doorways," John said. They entered the hall, and noticed how hushed it was, while the Secretary General was addressing the membership: - "...and the importance and necessity for immediate action on our part must be moved, and accepted during this meeting. For that reason, this chair recognizes and calls upon our two guests, Mr. John Marshall, and Madame Secretary Chair of COSSIOS, Mrs. Janet Marshall."

"Your Excellency, Honorable Members of the Assembly, my husband and I have returned from a recent COWA authorized space trek to the Triangulum Galaxy, better known as M33 on the Messier chart of star systems. Our purpose was to confirm or deny the astronomy's Global research data that the Black Hole in that galaxy was consuming stellar matter, yet not increasing in mass." The audience started mumbling.

Raising her voice, Janet continued, "Because of our observations, and those provided by two alien friends, we must report that your newly constructed Galaxial Cruiser, the Sir Isaac Newton, the astronomy teams on the TGCTriang from Ffraiteron, and the Srennis' Galaxial ship from the planet Ralos, in the Canis Major constellation, spent a great deal of effort in observations, none of which corroborated Earth's global research stating a lack of gain in mass. We speculated that our mission was a wild goose chase, in the simplest of terms. My husband John would like to say a few words at this point."

"Thank you, Madame COSSIOS Chair. Your Excellency of COWA, and honorable members, first, I should like to tell all of you, that Janet and myself, are open for questions after this meeting, at the pleasure of his Excellency, the Secretary General. Secondly, it's long been a belief on our part, that aliens would not resemble us physically, but rather look scary in appearance. On what that premise was based, I have no idea, and that is why I would like to introduce you to Earth's two Alien friends, Gariff Tterzin from the planet Ffraiteron in the Triangulum Galaxy and Natas LeDeve, a Srennis from the planet Ralos, in the stellar constellation, Canis Majoris. I must add a little anecdote here; they both thought our race would look like fish since our planet has so much water on it. Now, thirdly, and this is the reason for this emergency session. We, the three of us, had a meeting in space and we concluded that since we were sent out on a wild goose chase we wanted to know why.

Upon our return to Earth, we have observed and acted upon the following: -

1. our international space station was being commanded by a saboteur; to what end, he is being held in custody and inter-rogated for determination;

2. your, pardon me, everybody's global water supply has been contaminated to the point, that as of right now, no one knows where it is safe to drink;

3. evaporation of our oceanic water does not remove the con-taminants; it still comes down with the rain;

4. recent observations have shown, listen carefully please, food chains have been corrupted, whereby the top predators are

feeding on humans in villages, towns, and cities along coastal areas, so far within the tropics of Cancer and Capricorn.

Further, the contaminants, as reported from the residents, are being dumped from yachts in the Seychelles. Whoever is behind all of this, we think, are terrorists who do not respect the lives of people from other cultures, and would rather kill the entire life on this planet, than coexist.

We need a motion for research, implementing successful test results, cooperation with superior, scientific knowledge from our extra-terrestrial friends and to leave you with the strongest suggestion for military action at the soonest possible moment. We would also suggest that extreme caution be used because we think these terrorists are trying to panic Earth into a global war. Thank you for listening to us." John took his seat.

"Thank you, Mr. and Mrs. Marshall for your inputs," said his Excellency. "The chair recognizes the honorable member from South America, Antonio Melo."

"Mr. Secretary, I would like to move that COWA set up a research program, provide laboratories wherever required and equip for research and carry out any and all successful recommendations from this research, effective at the earliest possible moment."

"Any seconders?" asked the Secretary General.

"I second the motion," said Arsenio Chavez.

"All those in favor?" The entire assembly voted for the motion with their electronic buttons.

"Any other motions?" Ronaldo asked his members.

"The chair recognizes Arsenio Chavez, the Honorable Member of North America."

"Mr. Chairman, I move that military action be put in place to enforce COWA Laws in all concerned countries for the purposes of reacting favorably to this global ecosystem emergency and to carry out, on an assistance basis, the recommendations made from this research."

"Any seconders to this motion?"

"I second it," said Army General Henry Hamilton, the Honorable Member from Great Britain.

"All those in favor?" asked the Chairman. Again, the membership voted 100%.

The recording secretary was requested to notify the military secretary of COWA's Department of Enforcement of the assembly's authorized motion and tell it that it was in effect as of now.

Ellis met with John, Janet and the rest of the investigative administration, to see if he and Julie could be of further assistance. John said, "Wait around for a moment, Ellis, "we want to talk with some people." The Council of World Affairs building in the Southam Center in Callao, a suburb of Lima, Peru, had a panoramic view of the Pacific Ocean.

Gariff and Natas, along with their respective entourages were now enjoying that view and deep breathing the oceanic shore-bound breezes. A constant soothing, lapping of the waves, slapping the shoreline, provided any hardened personality with nature's watery lullaby. It was hypnotizing in sound and beauty and it was in this environment where John and Janet waited to meet in person with his Excellency, the Secretary General, Señor Ronaldo Bessborough.

"Ah, Mr. and Mrs. John Marshall, and guests," said Ronaldo, looking at the Marshalls, cluing them for an introduction.

"Your Excellency …."

"Please, Ronaldo John, will suffice," said Señor Bessborough.

"Admiral Gariff Tterzin from Ffraiteron, Ronaldo," while shaking hands in greeting, "and this is Admiral Natas LeDeve, a Srennis from Ralos in the constellation of stars in Canis Major, your Excellency."

"Gentlemen, it is an honor and my extreme pleasure to meet you both. Whatever boyhood thoughts I might have held to date, I can honestly put them aside. From John's speech in the assembly auditorium, I saw that you both had similar childhood visions about other life forms in the universe. This meeting has been so enriching to our mutual knowledge despite the circumstances that made it possible."

Gariff had started to open his mouth when loud, blood-curdling noises could be heard from the sea port terminal area. Their attention was riveted on a pod of at least 30 Orcas which were turning over ships in port that were loading or unloading food based cargo. The Orcas were quickly devouring the crew members and some long-shore men.

Ronaldo witnessed the event in its entirety. It sickened him. Sharks, behaving like Hyenas, swam in a perimeter around the Orcas, quickly darting in and out, attacking the Orcas as they concentrated on their feeding frenzy. The water off shore quickly reddened and floated with dead bodies, human, whales and sharks. Ronaldo prompted John and Janet, "God speed on your research. You have COWA's full co-operation. Go, and good luck."

Gariff and Natas had already requested a shuttlecraft to pick them up and take them up to their respective ships. Jan asked that Gariff's research teams include engineers as well as medical sciences personnel. Turning to John, Jan said, "We may find a better or more immediate use of those genes Gariff presented us with at the end of our last trek in space."

"Oh God, honey, more bad news is running towards us," John said, nodding his head in the direction of Ellis. "Ellis, we were just on our way to the Newton, what's up?"

"John, all peoples having ocean-dependent economies have broken down to nothing and are under attack by sea life and land-bound life, predatory to insects and bodies are piling up all over."

"John, go down to the naval base and get a plane to take you to the Mediterranean area and coordinate military action. I'll notify the General to prepare," said Ronaldo.

Chapter 65

John said, "Goodbye love," and left with Ellis for the naval base at Callao. Both he and Ellis boarded one of the 33rd century's hypersonic, radar cloaking, military fortresses. John smiled to himself for a quick second, piloting this baby and just as quickly snapped back to reality.

Ellis asked, "Pilot, how long it would take to get to Qashio in the Gulf of Aden on the island of Socotra?"

The pilot said, "Depends. We would have to land in a near by base camp first. From there, take a helicopter ride, all of which, would take about 10 hours in flight time, landing delays notwithstanding."

Ellis made sure he would get top priority clearance. John came back to reality as their pilot was receiving top priority clearance. "Looks like that trip has been cut back to six hours, sirs," said the pilot after receiving a tower message of clearance. Just then they saw four fighter jets scream in along side of them for escort duty. The pilots waved their acknowledgements.

"John, you know that where we are going is a covert, secretive hideout headquarters of the GGE, don't you?" Ellis said, prompting him to say why they were going there. The planes were outfitted to do at least Mach 5.8 at 20,000 feet. They screamed across the Atlantic and up the Indian Oceans and arrived to see that their helicopter was waiting for them, complete with pontoons. Going to the helicopter, John requested a beacon to be put on him so the tracking satellites could pinpoint him. His personal ear piece tracking device for the Newton was also being used. He thought to himself that if he didn't come out of this alive at least everyone could locate his last position.

John contacted the Newton. "Clinton, instruct the interrogation team to confirm from their prisoner, Commander Karzai, the location of the head of the terrorists' organization, GGE, as that being on the island of Socotra. Carefully watch his face and get back to me." John, now turned to Ellis and said, "El, we are going to have a real problem on our hands if this meeting goes sour on us."

"Oh, how so, John?" asked Ellis.

"Well, first, they're going to frisk us for weapons, listening devices, or anything else they deem we can spy, or escape with. Secondly, they probably want to find out, how we know about this place on the island. And the worst part, they will probably want to tear you apart, as a bione, to see what you're made of and, then, execute me. So, keep your monitoring-locator working as long as you can so, at least, a rescue team, or 'Bullseye', can help us."

"Well, where is this place, John?"

"I heard that it is hidden underground, like Sam Davis' place on Mars. When we get on the island and go exploring, I expect to be surprised or at least confronted by GGE sentries."

"If that is true John, they will have already spotted us approaching the island."

"I'm counting on it, Ellis, so we can come up with a cover story as to why we're here.

"How about some highly poisonous insect life or spiders?" Ellis suggested.

"Good. It should offer us a good segue into a discussion of poisoning the water of the world and the entire ecosystem. Going undercover, like we are Ellis, we must act convincingly that we are like them or worse, without exposing ourselves. You know, to catch a thief, you have to become a thief."

Their little whisperings were interrupted by Clinton's speaking into their earpieces to tell them that commander Karzai claims he knew nothing about the location, but the psychiatric observer who was watching his facial expressions, said otherwise. Inserting a drug into him revealed that he knew the location. Clinton reassured John and Ellis, that the Newton was constantly monitoring them, and that a rescue craft was prepped and ready. "John, you know that if you find the place, they will take you both as prisoners, and it's a crapshoot after that, as to what happens."

"I know, buddy, I know. Do me a favor and comfort Janet; we hope to survive it," John said, sounding very unsure. The pilot let them know they were two minutes away from landing on a rocky beach area. When they alit from the copter they thanked the pilot and left for their destination.

Socotra Island off the Northeast coast of Somalia is hot and dry most of the time; but today was different. A heavy fog had covered the island and the ocean waters surrounding it. Visual captivation of their presence had to be done by radar, or some means of infra-red devices. If the GGE was watching the shorelines, then that's how they would be spotted. And landing by helicopter with the COWA insignia on it, would be a definite clue to cause a reaction on the part of the GGE. It did.

Going directly to where he suspected the location would be, John ignored the sign on the fence, which said, **No Trespassing** - ال التعدي على ممتلكات الغير in English and Arabic; severe punishment if disobeyed would be meted out – **Trespassers will be shot** وسيتم اطالق النار المتعدين and it's signed by them حديقة الله من عدن **God's Garden of Eden.**

Ellis thought to himself, we biones were created for this very purpose where the male brain is concerned; 'foolhardiness surpasses bravery' every time, especially with men. Ellis was on full alert, but was unprepared for the confrontation with anyone on sentry duty. They came up out of the ground, parting the sand covering the opening to an underground bunker, and laboratory. Stopped at gun point, they were searched, hands tied behind them and white hoods put over their heads.

Overhead 'Bullseye' begged his commander to let him shoot and was denied permission. Clinton called Janet to the bridge where she could view what was taking place with John.

When John and Ellis were placed before the GGE leader, they were hit from behind with rifle butts and fell to the ground. The leader requested they be put in chairs and tied securely. They were never asked why they were here as that had only one outcome – death. Concerns were - who they were; their backers; how many; their aspirations of their task; and why no weapons. Their captors removed their hoods.

Just at that moment a western medical person entered the room wearing an explosive, ankle-monitoring device and examined the prisoners. After his examination, he said, "This one," pointing to Ellis, "is a bione; the other is a human and probably the leader." Sitting in a comfortable, upholstered chair and stroking a Manx cat, the GGE leader thanked the doctor and told him to wait outside for further requirements.

The GGE leader introduced himself as General Abdullah El-Hashem of a city in Iraq; the exact whereabouts wasn't necessary. "What does concern you, are the answers to our questions."

John bit the bullet again and brashly asked, "Why are you poisoning the world's water supply? You are killing life all over; ecosystems are breaking down and food chains have totally been disrupted. Why?"

One of the guards went over and whispered in the leader's ear. "Oh, my, we have been very disrespectful of our guests, gentlemen. Apparently, we have a great astronaut in our midst, who has journeyed into space to help other beings of the Triangulum Galaxy and returned to Earth with an alien daughter-in-law. Could you ask the doctor to return please and bring our friend from Brazil, I think one wanderer of the universe should meet another wanderer."

The doctor entered carrying a large pickling jar housing a species of arachnid, the Brazilian Wandering Spider. The doctor cautioned all in the room, "Be very careful with my friend because with one bite it can kill a human in minutes, faster than Australia's Funnel Web, and North America's Black Widow. It uses a neural toxin which causes abdominal cramps, vomiting, failed breathing and cardiac arrest. This one is not to be fooled with, Abdullah."

"Don't worry doctor, we'll play nicely with it, won't we, my friends?"

As the guards were moving behind Ellis to prevent any evasive movement, John said, "Look, we came here on our own, to try and ask you to stop poisoning the world's water supply. No one knows we're here, and I only guessed this was where you were located, based on a conversation I heard in a tavern in Somalia some time ago, in March of last year." John hoped that would rouse his curiosity. It didn't!

The guard placed the jar on Ellis' right shoulder by his ear and opened the jar. The spider, affectionately called 'Pn', by using the initials of his biological nomenclature, *Phoneutria nigriventer*, did not take much coaxing to come out of the jar.

The Manx cat in the general's arms hissed and was quickly stroked reassuringly calming him down. The spider bit Ellis on the right jugular area killing him in 2½ minutes.

The General asked again, "Now, who sent you and how many are behind you?" showing determination for an answer.

"Sir, I work for COWA, and I have the entire world's military behind me. We simply wanted to resolve the issue of water poisoning and I came to talk to you directly."

The general nodded at a guard and John was knocked unconscious to the ground. The spider was quickly and gently put back in the jar.

"Get me a car ready on the mainland and my helicopter prepared. I'm going to Baghdad to appear on INN for world-wide broadcast. Send a message to our journalists in New York and London to print a headline like **Astronauts Return to Earth with Alien Daughter-in-Law.** And then punch up the story with our cause and that we won't back down unless COWA surrenders. When I get to Baghdad I'm going to execute this man for international media attention.

The guard looked at his leader and glanced at Ellis' body. Seeing his glance, Abdullah said further, "Put him in a bag and I'll have him carried in front of the media and torn apart for all to see." A large sadistic smile crossed the guard's face.

Chapter 66

"Oh, Clinton what can we do to help them?" Janet moaned. Adding angrily, she said, "Clint, if it was up to me, Tommy would get his wish and target that s.o.b. and his entire property after a rescue squad brought John and Ellis back up to the Newton."

"Jan, I don't know why but John and I have lately been on the same wavelength, even now, I feel something unexplainable is going to happen and my intuition tells me to wait and see. That's all I can tell you; I know it sounds lame, but it's killing me too; that's all I can say, hon. I'm sorry."

Clinton held her by the shoulders in a vain effort at comforting her. Marion, the Newton's CMO walked in on the bridge and saw her best friend in tears. She quickly walked to behind Janet to help console her, asking Clinton how bad it looks. Looking back at the main screen and turning the volume up they could fully monitor all the activity surrounding John and Ellis.

"Clinton, I'm taking her back to her residence for some rest; she's going to need it." Going out, she told her medical aide to up-date Clinton.

Entering the bridge the aide went to the captain's chair and told him what the research team had discovered so far. Horrified at the news, Clinton opened a link to John's ear piece to reveal this latest news.

"John, even though it's a synthetic reproduction of a mixture of all plant toxins, they added Australian Funnel Web spider and Brazilian Wandering Spider poison for some icing on the cake. Furthermore, we don't know what happened when they were making this toxic concoction but it is also radioactive with a half life of 150 years. When John heard this, his state of being unconscious had already cleared, he tried to sit up. His head was still in a hood but his stubborn save-humanity-and the-planet impelled him to talk to his captors. He had to at least try to convince them to reverse what they had done. Their deaths to themselves did not matter; it would serve them well in the afterlife, a reward they craved.

John quietly thought give me strength to convince them. "General, please hear me." Looking at his guards, John's hood was removed and the site of Ellis almost made him sick. "Your poisoning of the world's water has worked probably better than you anticipated. The oceans contain sea life which supports ecosystems everywhere. Therefore, it is my belief that you, or your doctor, have also synthesized a remedy to stop the toxicity of the water. How am I doing so far?"

The general's moment of very loud silence irked John but he suppressed his reaction and said, "Did you also know it has become radioactive with a half-life of 150 years?" At this point the guards became agitated that this information was revealed. The general looked at them and asked, "What happened?"

They said, "The doctor spilt some radioactive liquid isotope in with the solution, by accident, and told us not to worry because everyone was going to die anyways."

"You fool! You should have told me before we released the solution. I'll deal with this matter later, after we execute this man and pull his friend apart." They had landed at the airport and he told their driver to take them to the Federal Building where the media likes to hang out. Abdullah was told there was a message for him from New York. It indicated that the headlines in the next issue of World Today would read: - **Returning Astronauts Welcome Alien Daughter-in-Law**!

"Driver, take us to where the Federal Courthouse of Karkh was and thank you for the message."

Gariff had arrived at the Newton and was standing beside Clinton to give him reassurance. "You know they are going to be executed, Clinton," Gariff stated.

At that moment Natas entered the bridge as well. Natas reiterated everyone's sentiments by wishing aloud that there was something they could do to rescue John and Ellis immediately. Once again, Clinton spoke from the heart, that he seriously felt they should not interfere. Why not and similar questions, Clinton could not answer. He ached inside for his best friend.

Arriving in Karkh at the site of the old federal building, Abdullah and his two guards got out with their prize catches from COWA. The crowd that had gathered was chanting for their deaths and quartering. General Abdullah El-Hashem said to his guards, "Well, gentlemen, it appears this warm weather has made this crowd thirsty for some infidels' blood. H-m-m-m-m, 92°F and 68% humidity, good; it should drive them wild for the media. Put them up on the ledge there." John was led to the ledge and Ellis' lifeless body thrown beside him and the body bag removed.

Everyone watching the big screen on the Newton watched in horror and could do nothing. The General began his political grandstanding.

"I, General Abdullah El-Hashem shall now live up to my name, the 'Crusher', and execute this man here," pointing to John, "and quarter this man here." Arabian horses were backed up against the ledge and ropes were tied to Ellis' arms, legs and head.

"Does the Council of World Affairs wish to stop these proceedings?" the General asked tauntingly. "Are there no brave agents in this gathering to rescue these men? Then surely there is someone here who wishes to claim their bodies; still, no one to step forward?

David L. Pritchard

Then release the horses and rest in peace my friend." With that last remark, Abdullah drew his Arabian short sword and handed it to a guard who took it and swiftly sliced John through his throat, severing his head from his body between the fourth and fifth cervical vertebrae. He never felt a thing.

His wife, Janet, on the orbiting Newton, watching the event, vomited and sobbed uncontrollably. Then suddenly, while the eyes of the world watched the public broadcasting of this horrifying spectacle of glorifying the GGE and its power, a man clad in white, with a long white beard, and carrying a wooden knotted cane about six feet long, stepped forward. The spectators parted a path for him, to climb to the ledge that the General occupied with his guards. They tried to block him, but the General commanded, "Stand aside, let him through." They did.

A deafening hush came over all eyes in the crowd and, similarly, throughout the world. Marion, on the Newton cradled Jan while they watched in silence. All the orbiting ships' crews went deathly silent. The Lunar academies and vacationing areas had their monitoring holo-screens automatically switch to a simulcast of the event; ditto on Mars in New Washington's Square. The CSS watched when NASA was silenced during the broadcast. Every one on Earth, or of any concern of Earth, could see the event. Everywhere, people witnessed as the old man walked toward the General and asked, "Did you have this done to these men?"

The General raising himself intimidatingly, said arrogantly, "Yes, and would you like a bag to take them with you?" His guards chuckled. Unperturbed, the old man pressed.

"Can you put them back together too?" The elderly man's mouth never moved yet every body could clearly hear and understand him.

"Do I look like humpty dumpty's rescuers?" The gathered crowd chuckled at the old man's question, and the General's reply.

Still unperturbed, "Have you also had the water of this world poisoned?"

356

"Yes, and what do you think you are going to do about that?" the General asked, even more arrogantly. His guards moved closer to the old man in a vain attempt to overpower him if the need arose.

"I can do nothing that the Galaxial Ordering Director has not told me to do. I merely do as I am commanded. Like your guards, I am but a servant."

The guards raised their rifles at the old man to shoot him. The old man pointed and said, "All weapons pointed at me do not work." They pulled the triggers, but to no avail. The crowd pressed inwards to full attention. They listened and heard the old man speak. They understood him, yet his lips did not move. "Behold the wonders of the Galaxial Ordering Director!" and with that, the old man held his left arm to the sky and his right hand first touched Ellis' body parts and then John. Both men stood and looked at the crowd as it pressed even closer. The guards leveled their weapons at both and fired. The guns did not work. Pointing the barrels at themselves to check for any blockage the guns discharged killing each other. The crowd laughed.

The old man continued looking straight at the General, "Sir, if you can not bring a man back to life, then you must obey what you were commanded to do many years past. Thou shall not kill! And if you do, then you are considered evil, and the Galaxial Ordering Director shall avenge the lives you take – behold, he pointed again, even now the shadows of death approach," the old man said, pointing to the South. The shadows encircled the General and took him, screaming - "Someone help me!" - towards the East and into the Tigris River.

Looking at the crowd the old man saw a young boy with a large water jug on his head and bid him come forward. He looked at his friends but came forward as asked. The old man asked, "Do you have water in that jug, son?"

"Yes, sir," he replied.

"From where did you draw this water?"

"From the river, Sir," the boy answered nervously. Spying another lad in the crowd with his dog, a beautiful Golden Lab, he asked that he too come forward. The old man patted the dog on the head and stroked him gently. He then asked the first boy, "Pour a little water in my hand," and he let the dog lap it up. The dog yipped, whined and died.

The old man stood and said, "The water all over the world has been poisoned, so that you can neither bathe, nor drink with it. Again, behold the wonder of the Galaxial Ordering Director's mercy. Boy, pour the water from your jug onto your dog." The boy did so, and the dog got up and shook himself off and kissed his boy-master's face, who hugged him fiercely. "To all those who have witnessed this event, let it be known that your people, your children, now and forever more, are the Galaxial Ordering Director's choice to keep the peace throughout his house, you call the universe, and must set the example of abiding by his laws. His wonders shall accompany you anywhere you go and he shall bless and protect you. Do not fail him!"

The old man simply turned, walked and disappeared. John turned to Ellis and gave him a big manly hug. They went to the Tigris River and found the water was pure again and jumped in like two school chums. When they came out of the water John received a message that the COWA military was having trouble in keeping up with all the GGE's members surrendering and revealing their secret armories and strongholds. The research teams had discovered a resolution to the poisoned water and its radioactivity but they shelved it for the future if need be. Janet couldn't wait to hold her husband again, so Clinton had her transported to the surface. John chuckled, "Clint, where can I meet her?"

"At the European Economic and Environmental Centre in Manchester, England, John," Clint said smiling, now that his belief that something good was to happen.

"Come on, Ellis, let's get to Manchester and meet Janet."

Gariff, Natas and Clinton were high fiving on the bridge and Kathy came over to Clinton and gave him the longest loving kiss he had to date. Sam Davis on Mars was also overjoyed in his wife's arms.

Lt. General William Harding and his family relaxed and showing their gratitude gave John Marshall's mother, Angélique Marshall a huge hug in gratitude for keeping them safe. Bill was so relieved he drank a rye and cola and threw out all his lemonade, forever.

Through all the jubilance, an incoming message to the Martian SETIA monitoring system could be heard on the emergency help frequency.

Additional Notes

Note #1 – This book (and any sequels) is fictional and any appearance of, or representation to, characters, persons (past or present, alive or dead), governmental administration or procedures, events and or materials, is coincidental and not meant to be taken as factual.

Note #2 – Mathematical calculations, astronomical distances, and Solar Telescope orbital information is based on data from the Internet's Wikipedia notations. Course selections in space and references are done to support the realism of exploration in space.

Note #3 – All references to velocities in space, human existence on Mars, or orbiting space stations, are fictional, and as such, meant for reading entertainment and enjoyment.

1. - Astronomical Unit (AU) – is defined as 92,955,807 miles
2. - Speed of Light – is defined as 186,292 miles per second (m/s)
3. - Billion – when worded, is from the American system, defined as 1,000,000,000 or 10^9 distance
4 - units in the book are parsec (pc) and light year (Ly) and kilometers (km)

The author regrets any inconvenience this story, or parts thereof, insinuated or otherwise, may have caused.

About the Author

David Pritchard is a retired thirty-three-year transit employee from the City of Mississauga, Ontario. The observations of people coming and going during their busy lives, has had the most profound impact on his opinion of who he is, what he is, and where will he go from here, after death.

An illness-created situation, which hospitalized him for over a year, gave opportunity to research, write, and understand himself, and the impetus for his storyline: - that human beings are not alone in this Universe!

"It was absolutely amazing, and wonderful, to go to that bright, white light and be told to go back and finish your life!"

What is happening on this planet, is not unique. Law and order exists throughout the entire Universe. We will see that when we explore space, together, in peace, with faith in ourselves. The life energy that makes us who WE are, also makes them who THEY are. Maybe this is the true meaning of being created in his image. That sounds like an excellent premise to explore space, and write about the adventure, in my opinion.

David resides in Newmarket, Ontario with his wife, Paula.

CPSIA information can be obtained
at www.ICGtesting.com
Printed in the USA
LVOW11s0600150317
527283LV00001B/1/P

9 781525 504877